PRAISE FOR
THE FRISCO KID

"A picaresque, brawling hymn to beatdom . . . A
story worth listening to and chronicling."
—*San Francisco Bay Guardian*

"The beats are back! Here, out of Jack Kerouac
and Neal Cassady, with overtones of Nelson Algren, comes *The Frisco Kid* . . . Mr. Kamstra's
multitudinous characters are colorful as hell."
—*Saturday Review*

"Marvelous . . . cascading . . . he tells of the Kid
dealing in grass, seducing girls, being a 'voyeur
of the streets' . . . A gallery of colorful characters."
—*Publishers Weekly*

"A picaresque, Saroyanesque celebration of life
in the North Beach netherworld . . . with garlic on
its stoned breath . . . Intensely readable."
—*San Francisco Chronicle*

THE FRISCO KID: a story of real people, the Beats.

NORTH BEACH, SAN FRANCISCO: a real place.

THE LATE 1950s, THE EARLY 1960s: a real time.

JERRY KAMSTRA: a real person, the author.

"When I arrived in San Francisco in 1957, I discovered a community existing on the edge of the city unlike any other in America. Reckless, creative, frenetic, insane, it was too insane for a lot of people, for not many survived. I did, however, and in surviving came of age in the cheap pads and artists' lofts in North Beach. In the process I lost my innocence and my youth, but gained an indelible memory of a bunch of crazy people who lived, fought, struggled, loved and even died together with a sense of élan and community that I had never experienced before nor have found since . . ."

So, out of the time and memories of more than a decade and a half ago comes a marvelous hymn to the glories of Beatdom, *The Frisco Kid*.

The
Frisco Kid

Jerry Kamstra

BANTAM BOOKS · TORONTO · NEW YORK · LONDON

I would like to especially thank my editor, Virginia Hilu, for valor above and beyond the call of duty in her work with me, and for the consideration, insight, and general good fellowship she has constantly provided throughout the gestation period of this book.

Jerry Kamstra

This low-priced Bantam Book has been completely reset in a type face designed for easy reading, and was printed from new plates. It contains the complete text of the original hard-cover edition.
NOT ONE WORD HAS BEEN OMITTED.

THE FRISCO KID
A Bantam Book / published by arrangement with Harper & Row, Publishers, Inc.

PRINTING HISTORY
Harper & Row edition published April 1975
Bantam edition / December 1976

Portions of this novel have appeared in slightly different form in the following publications: *San Francisco Bay Guardian; City Lights Anthology—1974; 185 Anthology; Unfold.*

Cover photos:
Photograph of crowd by *Walter Chappell*
Photograph of author by *Ken Collins*

Someday when you are rich and famous (and even more notorious), you will look back upon the New Riviera Hotel days and think that it wasn't so bad—then you were only running away from the law. Someday when your wife no longer worships you and lives for you alone and your children have discovered that you are human after all, you will look back upon the New Riviera Hotel days and think it wasn't so bad—the most you faced was a few years in a man-made prison, not a lifetime in a self-made one. Someday when money is not an all-consuming problem and you have realized you aren't a fool after all, you will look back on the New Riviera Hotel days and think that it wasn't so bad. In fact, you will probably think it was good.*

This book is dedicated to Judy, my wife

*Note to the author from his wife

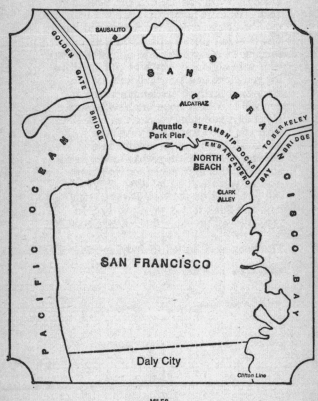

SAUSALITO

GOLDEN GATE BRIDGE

S A N

ALCATRAZ

F R A

Aquatic
Park Pier

STEAMSHIP DOCKS

EMBARCADERO

NORTH
BEACH

TO BERKELEY

BAY BRIDGE

CIBCO BAY

CLARK
ALLEY

PACIFIC OCEAN

SAN FRANCISCO

Daly City

Clifton Line

MILES

0   2   4

N

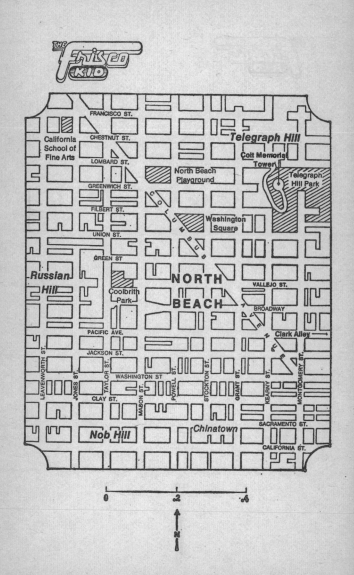

Tell 'em what I was,
Tell 'em what I did.
Somebody might care sometime.
Don't you hear me, Kid?
                    —KELL ROBERTSON

I see the boys of summer in their ruin . . .
                    —DYLAN THOMAS

Not me, by God, not me!
                    —JACK KEROUAC

1 I'm living in a loft on Roach Alley in San Francisco. San Francisco is the end of America and Roach Alley is the end of San Francisco. A roach is also the butt-end of a marijuana cigarette, which is nice. San Francisco and Roach Alley and America are littered a mile deep with the butt-ends of marijuana cigarettes. I contribute my share, puffing gleefully away at midnight, in the dawn, at noontime, puffing like an antediluvian steam engine and tossing the roaches out the window with a flick of my finger. People go by and stare and I don't care. I'm high on my roaches and Roach Alley and San Francisco. I'm especially high on San Francisco, a crazy mixed-up roach-tossing Frisco Kid.

To know America you've got to stand in the middle of the Golden Gate Bridge. You haven't experienced America, the sheer obscene power of her, until you've stood in the middle of the Golden Gate Bridge and listened to its roar. The Brooklyn Bridge won't do, nor will any of those other Hart Crane bridges back on the worn-out Eastern shore; they're part of another time, another epoch, really, and the songs they sing are not the songs I sing. That America is another country, a country gone like the water that flows through the Golden Gate in San Francisco. The Golden Gate Bridge is the new America! It is the new America risen out of the ashes of the old, an America tottering on the edge of the apocalypse, so wild, so insane, so intense, frenetic, schizophrenic, perverted, fucked-up, and Free! that all the angels—San Francisco angels—open their wings in delight and deliver themselves, *are themselves,* when they discover that magical flight! The Golden Gate Bridge is the new America in all its tensile strength, two hundred million people hacking and scraping and swabbing at the flecks of rust showing through, spreading paint over the cracks and creaks and hidden flaws, wrapping their own lives around the stresses and strains that are invisible to the ordinary tourist. The Golden Gate Bridge is the shivering wind-whipped wand connecting two worlds: the old one of pastoral peace and old men in back-country shoes, and the new one of highstepping young sons who march off their time in dreams and songs and endless vistas.

Frankie jumped off the Golden Gate Bridge yesterday. We bury her tomorrow.

I wonder what a person thinks about on that trip down? Suspended animation. That delicious edge of life. The crack between two worlds, as the Yaquis say, plunging toward the water at one hundred and twenty miles an hour—but in reality suspended, the body still, inanimate. Everything else is whirring past: the bridge cables, the traffic, the old fort, the waves, the world. Even under water the voyage continues, fishes pass, seaweeds swirl; another dimension is entered, the body returns to the *real* world, the world of *extrasense,* to where it belongs, really, to where it began: the end and beginning of all our West Coast San Francisco dreams.

Another kid took Frankie's leap. Yelling "Goodbye, loves" to passing strangers, he dropped like an arrow over the bridge railing. He didn't enter that other dimension, however. He fell like a pellet into the crystalline sea and bobbed up beside a small fishing boat waving his hands. Not a scratch. God's children. They smoke their dope and drop their acid, fling themselves off bridges, ride steaming locomotives into dark tunnels, and fly through the air in Golden Gate Park.

We're going to bury Frankie tomorrow. It will be informal, a pauper's funeral like all the rest. Frankie's body is still in the morgue. We don't need her to have the funeral. All we need is the memory of Frankie and the memory of that leap. That leap is etched in my mind like a protracted incision across my brain. I saw that leap in Frankie's eyes long before she walked out on that bridge. Frankie was jumping when I first laid

eyes on her in Milton's loft. She was a going, gone
chick with insanity in her eyes and an inconsolable fire
on her face. When I think of Frankie, I am reminded
of the distance between bridge and water I felt the first
day I saw her. I didn't tell anyone what I saw, not even
myself. It's something you see, and when your vision
becomes reality you look back and understand what
you saw. Maybe Milton saw it too. He acted like he
did. When he spread his hands around the nape of
Frankie's neck and pulled her face down to his, maybe
he saw. Maybe Frankie's leap was reflected back out of
Milton's eyes, a leap all the way across the pupil, down
into the iris, a leap splashing under the cornea and getting swept away in the tide of filaments and nerves. If
Milton saw it, he never let on. Now that I think about
it, I know he saw it. He saw it the same as I did, a distance between bridge and water that held everything
apart.

Frankie's funeral will be held in Golden Gate Park
among the bushes and shrubs and grass. Milton and
me and Little Joe and a few others will stand around in
a circle and pass a joint. I'll bring a jug of sweet wine
and that'll go around too. The memory of Frankie will
disappear with the sweet wine and marijuana smoke.
The roaches will join the millions of roaches outside on
the sidewalk underneath my window on Roach Alley.
Years later, when archeologists explore the ruins,
they'll discover the history of North Beach San Francisco written on bits and pieces of Zig Zag paper, strat-
ified on Wheatstraw like ancient geological sediment.
It'll be the history of America and San Francisco and
Roach Alley and North Beach and Frankie and her
leap off the Golden Gate Bridge. It'll also be the history of the Frisco Kid. Let me tell you.

The Frisco Kid is a guy who hangs around, who
drinks wine in the park with the rest of the guys, who
leans and dreams on streetcorners, who walks the
streets at all hours of the day and night, who listens to
the Bay bells and buoys, who prowls Market Street and
the Embarcadero and the Tenderloin, who wanders in
and out of all the small alleys of San Francisco, who

senses every heartbeat and solace, who sips coffee from cups that sit napkin-padded in saucers in Foster's Cafeteria, who knows the Hotel Wentley and the San Gottardo Hotel and Bouncer's Bar on Townsend Street and Harwood Alley and Coit Tower and the top of Russian Hill and Nob Hill and Telegraph Hill, who can name all the buildings on Jessie Street, who knows the park and all the secret little glens and glades in the park, who can call out the names of obscure Chinamen in Chinatown, who knows Edsel at Sam Wo's and Kelly and Mr. Hum, who knows which bakery on Grant Avenue gives free bread, which salami factory to go to for free rolls of salami, which market to hit on for throwaways, which produce dealers can be counted on not to complain when a few bunches of grapes are missing from their early morning boxes; The Frisco Kid knows which hotels will give a free flop when it rains, or, barring that, which buildings are deserted and will offer solitude, a place to sleep, and a place to score. The Frisco Kid is part of San Francisco. He loves it like the gulls that wheel and turn above the bay. He's part of it like the fog that comes sweeping in under the bridge in the late afternoon. He's there like the city itself, mute, white, inviolable. One day I was showing Zeke around San Francisco. I was describing the city to him. "You sound like the Frisco Kid," Zeke said. "You talk just like the Frisco Kid."

The history of the Frisco Kid is a history of days spent sitting in Washington Square drinking wine, of talking with friends, of walking the streets, of listening, breathing, being. It is a history of following gulls as they wing and sway, midnights and mornings and drifting days, of quiet afternoons on the Beach with Frankie, and when not with Frankie, thinking of Frankie. If this doesn't interest you, turn away from these pages. This book is not for you.

To get to Roach Alley you walk down Columbus Avenue to Pacific Street, and then left to Davis Street near the Embarcadero. I searched all over America before I found Roach Alley. I lived in a thousand different pads before I discovered my home among the warehouses and lofts and abandoned storefronts on the waterfront of North Beach San Francisco. Frankie knew where Roach Alley was all along. When I asked her about it, she said I had to find it for myself. When she said that, I grabbed her arm. She laughed and ran down Pacific Street and ducked into Roach Alley. I ran after her and found Roach Alley and I've been living here ever since. I'm not going to leave. When I die, my bones will join those of the rest of the tribe out there in the alley, buried deep in roaches, the sediment and strata of hard times.

My loft has giant windows that look out over the street. When I stand at the windows, I can see the world going by. On the side of my loft opposite the windows there's a white brick wall. Stability resides in those painted bricks. At night I lay my head on my pillow and watch the lights of the city flashing on the white brick wall and it soothes me. The far dark end of my loft is an indescribable array of abandoned equipment and junk and old machinery. I intend to revitalize the discarded equipment, reconstruct it into a system of giant dynamos and generators that will pulse the secret electric Roach Alley energy out into the rest of the city, harness the latent power lurking in the husks and remnants of the disemboweled rotors and engines and burnt-out generators.

Roach Alley is quiet until midnight; then lurching, still sleepy lumpers stagger in from all parts of the city in their frisco jeans and hickory shirts to join the coiled winos unwinding from that afternoon's drunk, limping among the brick buildings and wrought-iron warehouses with their scabby chins and torn ears in search of work, hanging around to help unload a truck, hoist and haul the crates of vegetables and fruit, eating their first solid meal of the day between loads, slipping portions and handfuls and half-crates of grapes and peaches and oranges into alleys behind the sheds for later, stocking up a fresh fruit breakfast for tomorrow.

All evening I stand at my windows watching the trucks, monsters with names like MACK and PETERBILT and INTERNATIONAL HARVESTER, rumbling in from the San Joaquin Valley with loads of tomatoes and potatoes and fruit. PETERBILT. I like that name. It sounds like a personal creation. I can see Peter standing beside his truck, greasy overalls on and a welding torch in his hand; it's a work of art. PETERBILT is a good name for a truck.

Before the rigs arrive, the lumpers and winos and out-of-work kids stand around the oil-drum fires in the middle of the streets swapping lies, wander into the tiny all-night cafes for coffee, stagger out again when the Jimmy from Modesto carrying twenty tons of peaches thunders down the street, the driver casual and serious at the same time, slouched over the wheel of his rig with a damn-it-all-if-I-ain't-here-in-San-Francisco-again expression, each chromewheeled, pinstriped, buffed, and polished rig a manifestation of the individual teamster sitting therein, the $40,000 truck an extension of the driver himself as he double-clutches up the narrow street and swings wide, kicking the brownie down a gear as he does so, positioning himself for backing up; the assistant driver leaping out to help guide if necessary; the driver looking first in the right- and then the left-hand mirror, easing the clutch out while a hundred pairs of supercritical wino eyes watch; the forty-five-foot trailer slipping in among the other tight-packed rigs with a sigh and touching the lip of the loading dock with a soft thump! the co-driver already up on the dock unlocking the rear doors and pulling the loading ramp out in one swift touch ... the winos and lumpers and kids standing around looking foolish until the first crates start rolling down the ramp, then two or three of them chosen by the driver start hustling boxes onto the docks in five-high stacks, ripping open a few samples, tearing into the load, and working feverishly as the crates grow up around them like nocturnal plants that thrive on the split wood and cracked beams of the old produce sheds and warehouses. Between shifts a wino slips down to Spadelee's grocery store with a borrowed dollar and buys a fifth of Valley of the Moon sherry, nipping it during lulls and passing it around to the others so the next guy will pass his around too. While the lumpers and extras hustle the loads out of the trucks, the drivers stand around looking bosslike and unconcerned, talking among themselves and laughing as they zip matches under their thighs to light butts, tossing the burnt-out matches into the street.

Roach Alley is in the heart of San Francisco's produce market. When the rest of the city is going to sleep, Roach Alley is just waking up. In the early dawn after all the trucks are unloaded and gone and the oil-drum fires are cold, the lumpers and out-of-work kids drift away and the winos stand around in front of Spadelee's grocery store with their bottles of tokay. When the sun comes up from behind the East Bay hills, the loading docks are quiet, the tiny all-night cafes closed, the streets empty. At this time a peculiar lilting music fills Roach Alley. After the cacophony and madness of the produce market softens, the sound of Pippen's piano echoes through the streets.

Pippen is a classical pianist who lives in the loft next to mine, the entire top floor of a potato and onion warehouse. When he plays at night and I'm lying in bed, it's as if I'm sleeping on symphonic mattresses, oceanlike beds with huge baroque combers that stretch out over incredible distances. In the early morning when the produce market is quiet, my loft is transformed into a giant music box. The smell of potatoes and onions blends with the music, and I ride the tum-de-tum-dum waves which curl and scud into the corners of my loft, eddy and fade on the windows, then disappear in the fog and darkness. The music sounds like the accompaniment to a famous but seldom seen silent film classic like *Birth of a Nation*. Whenever I hear Pippen play his piano, it always strikes me that the smell of onions and potatoes is just right for *Birth of a Nation*.

Living next door to Pippen is like living next door to Bartok, Beethoven, and Johann Sebastian Bach all together, three North Beach drinking buddies who sit down after dark and execute crazy cadenzas on the keys, each vying with the others like performers in a musical circus. When the music thunders through my loft, the abandoned generators whir to life for a few brief seconds, the rotors spin feebly a few times, the rust flakes falling away. Outside for an instant the lights of the city grow brighter, then everything is quiet.

Friday and Saturday nights are Pippen's favorite times. On those days the produce market is deserted, everyone has gone for the weekend. Pippen sits down at the huge Steinway piano hidden behind the inno-cent-looking bricks and wallboard above the potato and onion warehouse and puts his fingers to the key-board. His hands move across the keys, and suddenly Roach Alley is filled with classical timber, Black Forests and Alps and Grand Canyon deeps of sound. I sometimes imagine whole concertos lilting through the dark canyons of the produce market where there are no ears to listen. It's like the sound creates its own val-leys and canyons, whole mountains whose backs are covered with musical aspens. Late at night when I'm walking back home to my loft after an evening of drinking, I sometimes stand outside in the alley under Pippen's windows listening. When Pippen beats his ridges and gullies and rocky mesas up out of Roach Alley's stillness, I understand something of the essence of living alone with art.

2   Frankie's a vixen, a devil chick with angel written behind the deepness of her eyes. Like all angel eyes, when you look into them deep enough you can hear the distant sound of hyenas barking.

When I first kissed Frankie, I imagined Milton's big black lips on hers and I rammed my tongue down her throat, plunging for the bottom. Frankie sucked my tongue down and then bit. The bitch! We tasted my blood and I had to lift my knee into her crotch to make her let go. I was luckier than Larry. Larry kissed a fourteen-year-old virgin in Mill Valley who was stoned on grass and she bit off the tip of his tongue. Larry tried to make her let go, but what could he do? The girl was stoned and Larry was kissing her. Chomp! Larry talks like an orangutan now.

Frankie's body is like one of the cables on the Golden Gate Bridge—taut. Latex skin spread over plasticene bones. When I watch Frankie pull off her long black tights, I can see her skin crease under the cloth. Every crack is perfect, each hair exquisite, every little mole a mound to God's perfection. It's hard to analyze a body like Frankie's. A machine, that's what it is! A machine with so much horsepower designed to life up so many pounds at will. Frankie's body is one of those machines that scoop dirt out of the ground, a giant shovel capable of lifting tons, trucks, everything!

Frankie can do anything she wants with her body. Roll Frankie up into a little ball and bounce her around the room on the end of your dick and she's happy. When Frankie makes love, it's like Durrell says, "turning the lights out and slashing at each other with razors."

9

The first time I met Frankie was at Milton's loft. I'd gone over there for—I don't even remember why I went over. When I knocked on the door, though, Milton swung it open. "Kid!" he said. "C'mon in. I want you to meet someone."

Frankie was standing in the middle of Milton's pad, a pool of light enveloping her, smiling. She was beautiful. Like an angel standing in a mud puddle.

"Frankie's new on the set." Milton laughed joyfully. "Met her last night at Mike's Place. Ain't she a gas?"

I was stunned by her beauty. Frankie was tall and had long black hair hanging over her shoulders. Her eyes were shaped like almonds, deep and dark and turned slightly up on the outside corners. She looked foreign and mysterious and had a quizzical smile on her lips. "Hello, Kid," she said, offering me her hand.

"How are you?" I said.

"I was just telling Frankie about the Beach, about bo-hee-mee-aans, haa haa." Milton stretched the word out in a scornful, humorous way. "How 'bout some tea, Frankie? Would you like some, Kid?"

"Let me make it," Frankie said.

I sat down while Frankie brewed the tea. Milton was excited, dancing around his loft in quick steps, pointing out things to Frankie, where the tea was, how to light the stove, hurrying over to the windows and looking out, dancing back to the stove to make sure the water was boiling, touching Frankie on the shoulder, lightly, like he knew she wasn't his yet, but the newfound possibilities of the casual meeting the night before were definitely there. He had to be careful, though, because he knew a rare hummingbird had flown in through his open window and he had to rush to close it before she flew out again.

I'd rush to close the window too. Frankie looked ethereal standing in front of the stove, like she didn't belong there and absolutely had to have no talent for kitchen things (not true; it turned out later that Frankie had tremendous kitchen talents) and was only doing it to please Milton, who was also a rare bird, a butterfly really, a big black butterfly who'd opened his wings to her so she could snuggle under.

Actually Milton wasn't a butterfly at all but a black cat who loved to score white birds on the street. His latest find was a real beauty, though, and I immediately felt envious. I couldn't take my eyes off Frankie.

"Frankie's a college girl, Kid. Stanford. She got bored, though, so came up here. How you gonna keep 'em down on the farm after they've seen North Beach? Haww haww haww."

Milton's laughter was infectious. Frankie smiled as she filled the tea cups. I spooned sugar into mine and watched her. She held my gaze steadily when our eyes met. Her eyes were pools a man could drown in. When she talked, her voice was throaty, filling empty rooms.

"Kid, we got to take Frankie on one of your famous walks, show her the Beach. The Kid's a walker, Frankie; he knows every inch of this territory. Frankie wants to stay here, Kid. C'mon, we can both show her around."

The first few days with Frankie were hectic. She wanted to see everything, meet everyone. Milton and I walked with her down to Aquatic Park, sat with her on the grass in Washington Square, ate breakfast in the U.S. Restaurant, shot pool in Mike's Place, walked up and down the streets like two stud bulls escorting the newest, brightest star around the pasture. I felt good walking with Frankie, so did Milton. One evening we bought a jug of red wine and climbed to the top of Telegraph Hill. I pointed out the Golden Gate Bridge. When Frankie stood beside me, I could feel her breath on my neck. "It's such a wonderful city," she said, "so beautiful."

At night we went to Vesuvio's. Crowds of people gathered at our table, goggle-eyed, speechless when Frankie spoke. Mostly, though, Frankie was quiet, gazing with that eerie way she had into the eyes of everyone she met. Milton's boom-boom laughter drowned out the conversation, and we drank beer and rushed into the street to Chinatown to Sam Wo's, where Edsel Ford Wong, the incredible maniac waiter, pushed and shoved diners into chairs, spilled tea into their laps, cackled and shrieked with laughter when they complained. Nobody complained, though; Edsel Ford was the reason we went to Sam Wo's.

Late at night we walked through the produce market, along the Embarcadero, stopping at the U.S.S. Eagle Cafe for breakfast. The place was packed with longshoremen, and we gobbled coffee and doughnuts with them. As the sun came up, we walked back up to Washington Square. Milton passed a joint and we smoked it. Frankie laughed and ran under the poplar trees. I chased after her, lifting her up on my shoulders. Milton ran after us and tugged at Frankie's hair. We tumbled on the grass and then Milton and Frankie lay still. I got up and walked over to the statue of Benjamin Franklin. Milton has big hands. When he puts his hands on Frankie, they go all over her body.

Tomorrow I'm going to take Frankie to Golden Gate Park alone. Frankie loves to get high and ride the painted horses that buck and whirl as the merry-go-round turns. The organ plays "It's a Long Way to Tipperary," and when I'm whirling around in circles with Frankie on a bucking pink horse and the children are laughing and the trees and mirrors flashing, I know it is a long, long way to Tipperary.

Whenever I go to the park, I stop by and see Shoeshine Devine. Shoeshine Devine lives in the San Gottardo Hotel in North Beach, but during the day he likes to hang out around the children's playground in Golden Gate Park. He goes up to old Italian grandfathers who are babysitting on the benches and thrusts his shoeshine box under their noses and says, "D'you want a shine?" Sometimes one of the old men nods and Shoeshine Devine squats down in front of him—he doesn't use a stool—he squats on his haunches and bounces up and down as he spits and polishes the old man's fifty-year-old shoes, carefully cleaning and polishing around each hook and eye. More often than not, though, the old men say no, and Shoeshine Devine strides through the playground with his box clutched under his arm, moving among the swings and slides and benches like a spectral ghost, his gaunt jaw thrust

forward, pausing occasionally to give a swing a push or
lift a kid out of the sand. Sometimes he stands still
among the children's playthings with a look in his eye
that seems to pierce the metal of the swings. The kids
like Shoeshine Devine, but occasionally an old Sicilian
grandmother snatches her charge out of his line of
vision, hustling across to the other side of the playground, where they stay until he leaves.

The box Shoeshine Devine carries under his arm was
custom built for him by Mr. Hum who owns a restaurant on Washington Street in Chinatown. This was
when Shoeshine Devine was just emerging from his
hallucinatory period and was still called Johnny
Woodrose. What happened was, when Johnny was
coming out of his hallucinatory period he started hanging around Mr. Hum's restaurant. The restaurant is famous among the drifters and wine-drinkers of North
Beach because of its cheap food. Mr. Hum and all the
Hum relatives work in the back of the restaurant making pork rolls and steamed rice. Johnny could buy a
pork roll and a bowl of steamed rice for twenty cents.
That's a pretty cheap feed in anybody's restaurant.
Then, maybe because of Johnny's fading halluci-
nations, Mr. Hum started giving him his pork roll and
bowl of steamed rice for free. One day while Johnny
was eating his free food, Mr. Hum said, "You rant
crean table?" Johnny said, "Sure," and started to clean
Mr. Hum's tables. After a few months Mr. Hum approached Johnny again and said, "You rant eat black
loom?" Johnny started eating in the back room with
Mr. Hum and all the other Hums. When Johnny told
me about Mr. Hum, he said, "I have never seen such
translucent hands."

"What do you mean?"

"Looking at Mr. Hum's hands is like looking
through the transparent membrane of a fish."

I was interested in what Johnny said, so I went to
the restaurant one evening and looked at Mr. Hum's
hands. Johnny was right.

After working in the restaurant for six months, Mr.
Hum called Johnny into the back room. "You rant to
rearn tlade?" he asked.

Johnny shrugged. At the time, he was following the path of least resistance and he looked upon Mr. Hum as sort of a Buddhahead. "There are things the Chinese know that we haven't even started to think about, Kid. I think that all those guys who are standing on their heads and trying to Zen it through should go see Mr. Hum. He's already there. He's standing on his head."

Mr. Hum made Johnny a shoeshine box. Johnny looked upon the shoeshine box as a mystical talisman, a sign that he should go among the multitudes and shine their shoes, always giving a good shine for fifteen cents. "This shoeshine box is bigger than the Bank of America, Kid. I don't want any more or any less than fifteen cents per shine."

One day in Union Square a customer took a felt-tipped pen and wrote "Shoeshine Devine" on the side of his box. Johnny took this as further proof of his calling, so he changed his name to Shoeshine Devine and started keeping a journal. He called it *The Journal of Shoeshine Devine: The Will and Testament of an American Shoeshine Boy*. He kept it in a lined notebook on whose cover was an elaborate illustration of his shoeshine box. Inside, on the first page, was the title, and on the dedication page it said, "This is to testify that Shoeshine Devine is a good shoeshine boy." Underneath that dedication were the names of one hundred and fifteen satisfied customers.

Shoeshine Devine's intense intergalactic stare tends to frighten a lot of people. He is the only person I've ever known whose deep flint-brown eyes actually glitter. When he strides across the street, it's like watching a machete walk. "Hey, Kid," he yells, rushing across Vallejo Street toward me. If there's any traffic, too bad. Shoeshine Devine gives the impression that he'll walk right through a semi truck if it gets in his way. He leans into my face, his eyes an inch from mine, glittering, and says, "That's a bunch of shit about Jesus, Kid, that story they're laying down about him. He really wanted to have kids, you know that? He wanted to have kids and those bastards wouldn't let him." Shoe-

shine Devine licks his lips and grabs my shoulder.
"Jesus laid his set down in Jerusalem and decided it
wasn't the right place, you know, bad vibes and all.
When he was pinned up on that cross with his hands
stretched out, that wasn't where it was at! I know, I
was there when that action went down. I wasn't doing
much, just casting dice with the rest of the soldiers. It's
our own fault that all we got left of that cat is that pitiful image of him up there on the cross with his hands
stretched out wanting to have a few kids. It's all right,
though. Don't worry about it. Jesus is making it. He's
doing a few riffs out beyond Galilee, looking for a
place to work so he can raise a family."

I liked listening to Shoeshine Devine's Jesus Theory,
especially in front of the Caffe Trieste. The Caffe
Trieste is full of sailors off the *San Cristobal,* an Italian
freighter unloading down at Pier 45.

The first time Shoeshine Devine met Frankie, he
looked at her until she turned her eyes away. I'd never
seen Frankie do that before. Later he said to me,
"She's an evil bitch who'll die by violence."

"Bullshit!" I said. "Frankie's not going to die by violence."

"Hey, Kid, have you looked into that chick's eyes?"

I laughed. "Shit, the way you look into a chick's
eyes you're bound to see madness."

"You'll see when she turns against you," he said.
"Remember, you can't paint a sparrow to look like a
canary."

When I got back to my loft, I went to a mirror and
looked into my own eyes. "Shit!" I said. "Frankie has
no more violence in her eyes than I have in mine."

When Shoeshine Devine mentioned dying by violence, I thought of Wheeler Tippet. Wheeler was seventy years old and had a habit of talking about death.
The older Wheeler got, the more he talked about
death. I guess it was because of the obituary columns
he liked to read. When you're young, you read about
friends who are getting married and promoted and
drafted and busted and that sort of thing. When you're

old, you read about friends who are dying and getting buried and you spend a lot of time visiting cemeteries. Wheeler always talked about how a man should die at the age of eighty surrounded by teenage girls—preferably his own daughters. When Wheeler drove his Vespa motorscooter around North Beach, he always wore a Brooks Brothers suit, which he bought at the Society of Saint Vincent de Paul for seventy-five cents and had tailored on Polk Street for a few dollars. He always looked regal. I liked Wheeler. I enjoyed talking with him. He had great erudition. Erudition. I've always liked that word. One day Wheeler told me to read *Heaven's My Destination* by Thornton Wilder. I read it. I always try to keep up with what friends tell me to read. When Wheeler got a little tipsy on the Greek retsina wine he loved to drink, he'd ask me to drive him home on his motorscooter. When we got on, he would hold on tight with his hands over my balls. I thought he was holding on that way for safety. Maybe he *was*. My Levi's were too thick for Wheeler to feel anything but his imagination anyway, so I didn't mind. One night after I drove him home, he grabbed me in a gentlemanly Old World manner and tried to kiss me. I felt—what did I feel? Surprise at first, then disgust, anguish, rage, sadness, pity. When I looked at him, Wheeler blushed. "A pathetic old liplicker," Crow called Wheeler when I told him about it later.

"I feel sorry for him because he's an old man with problems," I said.

"He's had time to adjust," Crow said.

After Wheeler tried to kiss me, our relationship changed. I quit driving him home on his motorscooter. He still visited me, though, and he'd sit at the table with his hands folded in a prayerful attitude under his chin and nod with what can only be described as *majestic grandeur*. Wheeler's hands were incredibly long. His fingers tapered to infinite tips. Thinking of Wheeler's hands reminds me of hands in general. I can remember when I was a little boy lying on the floor drawing pictures of hands. I tore pictures of all kinds of hands out of magazines and pinned them on my bedroom wall. Sometimes when my father came home from work early, I ran up to him and grabbed his hands. What incredible hands! My father's hands, exactly the opposite of Wheeler's, were like mallets— huge, thick, callused monsters that curled around my head. Sometimes my father closed a nickel in his hand. He'd hold his fingers tight and I'd pull each finger apart separately. The rule was once I got a finger loose he had to let it stay loose. I liked the fingers better than the nickel. There's something about hands. In a museum once I saw a plaster cast of Abraham Lincoln's right hand. It was curled into a big fist. It was the biggest fist I ever saw, bigger even than my father's. I remember curling my hand into a fist beside the plaster cast and comparing hands. There was no comparison. Abraham Lincoln had big hands.

The night Wheeler died he came to my loft on Roach Alley and was talking as usual about death and cemeteries and then he said, "You know, the reason a person dies is because his spirit leaves him. His spirit leaves him because he doesn't surround himself with youth. A man dies spiritually if he doesn't stay around young people."

"I agree with you, Wheeler."

"Have lots of children, Kid," Wheeler said. "You don't have to get married, just go with lots of women and have kids by the best of them. Space your children out so when you're eighty years old you'll have a few teenage daughters around the house. Then you can die with dignity."

Later that evening Wheeler asked me to drive him home on his Vespa motorscooter. I said no. I was too busy. Frankie was coming. This was a lie because Frankie wasn't coming. I just didn't want Wheeler holding my balls. Wheeler drove himself home that night and got hit by a taxicab on Stockton Street and died the next day. I'll never forget Wheeler Tippet's fingers.

Frankie is sad. When she's sad, she holds her head low on her shoulder and tears well up behind her eyes. Frankie and Milton and I are walking across Washing-

ton Square. It's been raining and the grass is wet.
Frankie is holding Milton's hand. Milton is chipping
smack and Frankie knows it. Milton started chipping
smack because he scored three ounces for some heavies
in the Fillmore and he wanted to try out the stuff before he sold it. It was good stuff. Milton only chips
now and then, but when he does he walks with a peculiar short-jump shuffle. I call it Milton's heroin hop.
Frankie bawled me out when I first said, "Hey, Milton,
that's some heroin hop you got going."

"Don't ever say that again, Kid," Frankie said.

I laughed. "What do you want me to call it, Frankie,
the Fillmore shuffle?"

Frankie glowered at me and grabbed Milton's hand.
Milton snuffed deep in his throat and danced across the
grass in front of Frankie. "Ahh c'mon, baaaby," he
said. "Ole Milt can take care hisseff."

Frankie cracked a smile when Milton went into his
"Negro" routine. She looked up into his face. "Ahm
gonna give you a taste purty soon, Frankie, you gonna
see it's okay." Milton ruffled her hair and laughed,
then darted off at an incredibly fast clip around the
park, mimicking a character in an old-time movie.

Frankie touched my arm. "I'm going to move in
with Milton, Kid," she said. "I'm tired of yo-yoing
back and forth between your pad and his."

"Did he ask you?"

"It was a mutual agreement."

"I hope you don't forget where Roach Alley is."

"Oh, I'll come see you. It's just that Milton and I
have something special going. You know that."

Milton returned from his circuit of the square and
shuffled beside Frankie. I trailed behind them, watching the children playing in the square.

"Hey, Keed," Milton said. "Ahm gonna score a few
keys mañana. You wanna come?"

"Sure, give me a call."

I left Milton and Frankie and walked down Union
Street. Chinese children in bright rain slickers flocked
on the corner like large yellow birds, waiting for the
light to change. I stood among them, their slickers
brushing against my hand. From across Washington

Square I heard Milton's booming laugh. I turned around to look, but no one was there.

I bought a jug of sweet wine and climbed the Filbert Street steps to the top of Telegraph Hill. I walked around Coit Tower and then crawled under the bushes growing around its base. It was nice there, not damp, the rain having been kept out by the thick canopy of branches over my head. I stretched out comfortably and pooped the top of the jug. The sweet wine was comforting. I felt good as it ran down my throat. After a few minutes my eyes adjusted to the darkness. Someone was sitting not far from me. It was Laury. I smiled and held up my jug. Laury stared for a long time and then he smiled. Laury was on one of his "sense trips," as he called them. Each day of the week was set aside for one of the five senses: Monday for hearing, Tuesday for seeing, Wednesday for feeling, and so on all through the week and the senses. Laury seemed to be intent on seeing now; he sat very still and stared intently ahead of him into the gloomy green bushes.

I crawled over beside him. "Hey, Laury, want some wine?"

"No, thanks, man," he said. "I don't want to fuck up my head." I nodded and proceeded to fuck up my head.

The first time I saw Laury on one of his sense trips under the bushes, he was listening. He told me that if I listened carefully I could hear the trees growing. "You have to block out all the other senses, just concentrate on what your ears tell you."

I sat beside Laury and listened. What I heard was my own blood pulsing through my veins. My blood sounded like a diesel truck going through its gears in the Stockton Street tunnel. I listened for a long time and the wind blew among the bushes below Coit Tower and the trees grew and I sipped from my jug. When I swallowed, the diesel truck speeded up. It was carrying a heavy load.

I finished the bottle of port and walked down off Telegraph Hill, leaving Laury sitting under the bushes staring into the deep green gloom. I walked down the steps to Greenwich Street, and dropped my empty jug in a trashcan that said "trash" in Chinese. On Grant Avenue I turned left and headed down the hill toward Roach Alley. It was a magic San Francisco evening with the fog hanging just off the Gate, sending little probing fingers in under the bridge. As I walked, I concentrated on listening as Laury said, blocking out all the other senses. I tried to hear the fog as it slipped in. I heard only the sound my empty wine bottle made when it hit the bottom of the trashcan.

When I got back to my loft, Little Joe was there. Little Joe is a seaman friend of mine who used to be little. Now he's actually medium-sized Joe, but everybody still calls him Little Joe for old times' sake.

When Little Joe first came onto the Beach, he was an angel-faced little choir-type kid and he lived in Chinatown with two artists named Liam and Bob. They let him stay in their apartment because he was new on the set and they wanted to protect him. Little Joe painted miniature paintings that were very good and he slowly grew up into medium-sized Joe and then he didn't need to be protected any more. When he didn't need to be protected any more, he went down to the seamen's union hall and joined the Sailors Union of the Pacific. "I was going to join the National Maritime Union," he said, "but when I got down to Harrison Street and saw that statue of Andrew Fureseth and read the inscription on it I couldn't resist: *You can put me in jail but you cannot give me narrower quarters than as a seaman I have always had. You cannot give me coarser food than I have always eaten. You cannot make me lonelier than I have always been.* It has a nice ring to it, don't you think, Kid?"

Little Joe's an ablebodied seaman now, shipping out on freighters going to the Far East. When I first showed up on the Beach in my frisco jeans and hickory shirt, Little Joe said, "What are you doing in those waterfront clothes?" He always wore the same type of outfit. I didn't know when I bought the clothes at Ben's Surplus on Grant Avenue that I was buying the traditional longshoreman's outfit. To me they were just good workingman's clothes that didn't wear out in the first wash. Frisco jeans are black trousers with slightly flared legs, and a hickory shirt is a pillow-ticking type workshirt with a zipper going halfway down the front. Longshoremen top the outfit off with a white cap, but seamen usually wear black knitted watchcaps. I wore a watchcap and that's why Little Joe accosted me. He thought I was a seaman, which I wasn't. I told him I was a landsman in disguise, and that started our friendship.

Little Joe had just signed off a ship that had returned from Hong Kong and when I walked into my loft he held out a little bronze pipe full of hashish. I lit the pipe and sucked deeply on it. While we were getting high, Little Joe told me about his experiences in Singapore and Hong Kong.

"Kid, I'm in love with a Chinese whore."

"Every seaman falls in love with a Chinese whore," I said.

"I'm serious, Kid," Little Joe said.

When Little Joe and I were finished with the hashish, we were both floating up around the ceiling. I grabbed one of the beams that held the roof up. Little Joe was turning slow cartwheels in the dim light. He always did have a flair. I tried turning cartwheels too but I didn't feel right. Whenever I get stoned, I become conscious of every muscle in my body. A hundred little aches and pains I'm usually not aware of announce themselves, demons of the weed, released through the smoke and charm of the little bronze pipe. While I was hanging from the rafter, I started counting the muscles in my body. I was up to the adductor longus when I got tired of counting. I looked about for Little Joe. He was down on the floor heading for the door. He gave me a block of hashish as he left. "Take care, Kid," he said.

3 Milton's going to score. He wants me to go with him. "If you help me deal, I can cop a couple of extra keys," he said. "That way it's more money in the bank for ever'body."

Milton's been dealing for six months. He's North Beach's local connection now, and branching out. He's been trying to get me to deal for him for weeks. I like the weed but I don't like to deal it.

"It's a hangup, man, going around hitting on your friends for dimes and nickels to pay for weed."

"Hey, man, somebody's gotta do it. Besides, you handle it right and they come to you. Like, right now I got half a dozen keys spoken for, and no sweat on the avenues, baby. You could have the same thing going in a few months. Keep you in funds and keep your friends high."

I was tempted. Scuffling a living on the Beach was a hassle, part-time jobs in bookstores, helping friends move, picking up leftovers in the produce market. I had a whole string of businesses I made the rounds to, places that didn't mind boxing their throwaways and setting them aside for me. Every morning after making the rounds of the produce market I usually hit the Italian-French Bakery on Grant Avenue and picked up a few loaves of day-old French bread. Often as not one of the bakers would toss in a couple of fresh loaves, still warm from the ovens. On Broadway I'd occasionally visit Molinari's Salami Factory where butt-ends of salami could be copped for nothing. Every Monday evening after the Brighton Express Restaurant on Pacific Street closed, I'd hustle in and John Droeger, the owner, would lay all the leftover pastries, bread, meat, and vegetables on me. JoJo, his Japanese wife, would always add something fresh to the pile. That way I eased my financial burden on the Beach, but it was still hard. The idea of dealing dope for Milton had entered my mind more than once.

"Shit, you play it cool and pretty soon you'll have a couple of guys doing your work for you," Milton said. "You just take care of the big business and let the other dudes handle the shit on the street."

"Just like I'd be handling your shit on the streets, huh?" I said.

Milton laughed. "A boy's got to start somewhere. Just because you got your string of handout joints don't mean you're any different than anyone else on the set, Kid."

Milton was right. At his continued insistence I decided to accompany him on a dope-buying run. "If you're gonna deal, you might as well meet my man," he said.

"Is it smart turning potential dealers on to your man?"

"I ain't turnin' potential dealers on to my man. I'm turnin' you on because I trust you."

I went along with Milton because of Frankie. I didn't personally care about dealing dope one way or another, but Frankie hadn't been by since she'd moved in with Milton, and I wanted to see her. After Milton copped his dope, he'd have to take it back to his pad and I'd go with him.

Milton drove down Mission Street to Twenty-second and turned in to a small alley. "Wait here. I want to see Sam before I take you in."

Milton walked across the alley to a door and knocked twice. After a few moments the door opened a crack. Milton talked to someone and then stepped inside. I waited for ten minutes before the door opened again. Milton motioned me over.

Inside, the pad was dark. I followed Milton up a steep stairway. The walls on both sides of the stairway were covered with paintings, big and small, all of them ornately framed. At the head of the stairs stood a four-foot-high nude, female, carved from wood and embossed with gold leaf. Milton walked past the statue, through a small kitchen area, into the main living room. The floor of the living room was covered with Persian rugs, beautifully colored, and the room itself was packed full of overstuffed furniture, most of it old: Victorian couches, commodes, tables, and elaborately carved chairs. In one corner stood an upright piano, painted white, with a white marble statue of another nude lying on top of it.

The walls of the room were covered with more paintings, exquisite miniatures and huge baroque-framed canvases of voluptuous nudes and dancing nymphs. One wall was nothing but shelves and filing cabinets, every cabinet stippled with taped-on drawings and messages, antique postcards and miniature engravings. On the shelves stood dozens of ceramic and wooden clocks, stained-glass windows, old postcards, and more drawings. The ceiling of the room was high, covered with gold leaf, with an opening in the center revealing a huge stained-glass skylight. On the wall opposite the shelves was an open window which led to the roof outside. On the roof was an incredible array of potted plants and small trees, ferns and flowers, hanging vines and shocks of living bamboo. From atop the roof garden one could look across the bay to the East Bay hills.

"Sam, this is the Kid," Milton said to a fat man sitting at an ornately carved table in the middle of the room.

Sam was immense. His bulbous head seemed to be perched atop small mountains instead of shoulders. Thick rolls of fat girdled his neck, partly covered by the open collar of a tentlike white shirt. A small gold pre-Columbian figurine of two couples in an erotic embrace hung from a leather thong around his neck, looking slightly obscene amongst all the fat. Sam's hands were like hams, the wienerlike fingers protruding out, stroking softly a large yellow cat perched on his lap. "What's happenin', Kid?" Sam said.

"Nothing much," I said.

"Milton says you peddle dope real good."

"I've got lots of friends."

"That's all it takes, lots of friends. You want to roll one, Milton?"

While Milton rolled a joint, Sam eased up out of his

chair and waddled over to the piano. Kneeling down, he opened a small compartment in the back and pulled out kilos of marijuana. "Ever see a kilo before, Kid?"

"Sure."

"A very nice herb. Been used medicinally for centuries."

Milton finished rolling the joint and handed it to Sam. Sam inspected it and handed it to me. "Here, Kid, light up."

I lit the joint and took a deep toke. It was sweet, slightly sugary around the edges.

"It's been sugared," I said.

"It's still top shit, ain't it, Milton?" Sam said.

"Sam deals in nothing but the best." Milton looked at me.

I took another toke off the joint and handed it to Milton. I felt a little buzz from the grass. It felt good.

"How many can you take, Milt?" Sam asked.

"I want ten. The Kid's gonna sell a couple."

"Crazy. You bring the bread?"

Milton nodded and handed the joint back to me. "Where's your scales, Sam?"

Sam reached under the table and brought up a pair of market scales. While Sam and I watched, Milton carefully weighed each kilo. They averaged thirty ounces apiece.

"Top quality and good weight." Sam looked at me and smiled.

Sam placed the keys in a shopping bag. Milton pulled a wad of bills from his pocket and counted out one thousand dollars. He handed the money to Sam. Sam recounted the money and put it in his pocket.

"It's good grass, ain't it, Kid?" he said to me.

"It's pretty good."

"World's sweetest weed. A man can coast along a long time curing people's troubles with this medicine."

After scoring we drove back to Milton's pad. On the way I asked him about Sam. "Where does he come from?"

"Haa haa. Crazy dude, ain't he? He comes from all over. That motherfucker's been in every country in the world—and some not in it, if you ask me. He's an ex-seaman, chief purser or something. That's how he got all that shit in his pad."

"How long you been copping from him?"

"A few months. A friend of mine in the Fillmore turned me on to him. Sam deals a little of everything—grass, H, even pre-Columbian artifacts. You want it, Sam's got it. All you need is cash on the counter."

"Man, he ought to deal in some diet pills. That dude is fat."

Milton laughed. "Don't let the fat fool you. One dude I know tried to cop a little clay pipe off Sam's piano. Sam reached out and broke the dude's hand, snap! just like that. Four knuckles popped, baby, just like he was squeezing a snail."

When we reached the pad, Frankie was there, sewing buttons on one of Milton's shirts. "Let me have the table, baby. I want to break these kilos down." Frankie moved her sewing and Milton spread the kilos out on the table.

"You want some coffee, Kid?" Frankie said.

"Yeah, baby," Milton answered, "get us some coffee."

While Frankie fixed the coffee, Milton broke the plastic wrappers off the kilo. "I'm gonna break down four of these into pounds and four of 'em into ounces. You can break the other two down into ounces when you get 'em home."

Milton spread the kilos out on sheets of newspaper and got his scales from the closet. He picked up a knife and cut through the middle of four kilos, shaking the loose seeds and debris onto the newspaper. After weighing each kilo half, he wrapped them in cellophane bags. The other four kilos he broke down completely and made into ounces. I watched as he stuffed each ounce into its individual little bag.

"It's good to give your customers a little more than an ounce, then they know they ain't being burned."

"How much are you going to get for your ounces?" I asked.

"I figure fifteen. This is good shit. I wouldn't let any of it go for less than fifteen cents if I were you."

"How much do you want for those kilos you're laying on me?"

"What the hell, man, they cost me a yard. I figure you can have 'em for a yard and a half."

"That's cool," I said.

"It's a good deal. If you hustle you can make five, six hundred dollars."

"Crazy. I haven't seen that much bread in years."

While Milton was making up his ounces, Frankie brought the coffee. She filled the cups and then walked into the front room with her sewing. I followed her. I wanted to talk to her but I didn't know what to say. When I spoke, it was as if my voice came out muted, like speaking through a filter. Frankie was intent on her sewing while I sipped my coffee. Milton was humming in the kitchen. He was happy about his grass. He was going to make a lot of money. When I looked at Frankie, I imagined Milton's big dick sticking in her cunt. I felt depressed. I felt my dick should be there. Sometimes I wondered if I was prejudiced. My dick is better than Milton's. Not long after Frankie moved in with Milton, I'd asked her if black dicks were better than white dicks. Frankie smiled. "It all depends on the black dick and the white dick," she said. I pondered that. Whenever I look at Frankie, I get a hard-on. When I hear Milton laughing, I lose it. Up and down, up and down. It's depressing. I don't know if it's dangerous or not, getting a hard-on and not using it. Sometimes I worry that maybe we're only allowed so many hard-ons during our career: 5600 hard-ons for the Frisco Kid; use 'em or lose 'em.

Frankie looked up from her sewing. "How come you decided to start dealing?"

"I just thought I'd get into it, everyone else is."

Milton walked into the room and ruffled Frankie's hair. "How long you think it'll take you to peddle those two keys, Kid?"

"Couple of weeks, I guess."

"Crazy. Be careful when you take 'em home."

I stuffed the two kilos in a bag under my coat and walked down the stairs. By the time I reached Roach Alley, I'd worked myself into a paranoid sweat. I remembered the story Jere told me once, Jere being an ex-bigtime dope-dealing friend who'd fallen a few months before and was now back on the street hustling bread for his lawyer. There are two things about dealers: they never seem to have any bread when they fall, and after a fall they can't refrain from getting back on the street. Dealers carry a bigger monkey around on their backs than users, a dealer's monkey being status, his street rep, his need to be known and recognized by all the smalltime heads and hustlers. In the hierarchy of the streets, a dealer's status is just as important as a cabinet minister's is in his. Because of his fall, Jere lived in a miasma of paranoia, operating behind elaborate cover-ups, alternate escape routes, unlisted phone numbers, answering services, etc. One day, after an aborted delivery in the city, he was driving down the Bayshore Freeway heading back to Santa Cruz with his undelivered stash. By the time he reached Burlingame, he'd convinced himself that every car on the freeway was the *Man,* so he pulled over to the side of the road and dumped his stash in the ice plant. The next day he had second thoughts about all that good weed going to waste, so he hurried back to Burlingame to retrieve it. He searched five miles of freeway between Burlingame and Belmont but couldn't find his weed. It was gone, vanished forever into some horticultural union with the ice plant.

Tiptoeing upstairs, I realized that I was acting unnecessarily suspicious, peering over my shoulder like a second-rate second-story man. Inside my loft I inspected every corner, including the tons of equipment crammed in back, before removing the two kilos from under my coat. I unwrapped both bricks and laid them on my bed. They looked like turds left behind by a dinosaur with a square asshole. I didn't have any scales, so I divided each kilo into thirty equal-looking piles. I didn't have any little bags either, so I wrapped each ounce in newspaper, folding the edges over into neat little pirate-hat envelopes. I stashed the weed in a large paper bag on top of one of the beams that ran the length of my loft and then grabbed my coat. I wanted to get out. Illegality's weird. Nobody else is thinking about it, and you're thinking of nothing else. My loft wasn't my loft any more, it was my stash. Suddenly it wasn't a place to invite people to, but a place to keep people away from. I felt depressed. My whole life was changed in half a day simply because of a little weed. I buttoned my coat on the run and hurried up Pacific Street toward the Coffee Gallery. Maybe when my friends saw me, I could tell by their eyes whether I was the same person.

On the corner of Grant and Green I ran into Crazy Alex. Seeing him made me feel better. I automatically reached into my pocket for some change as I approached him. By day Crazy Alex sits at a corner table in the Bagel Shop and at night he stands under the awning of Ken's Grocery Store, black, thin, adept with words, passing sentence on passers-by with his prosonomasia. A hundred folk tales had blossomed around Crazy Alex. One was that he was a talented painter and sculptor, living in Ajijic, Mexico, with his white wife and baby daughter when one day his wife walked into Lake Chapala and never came out. The Mexican authorities took his daughter away and Alex cracked up.

Another tale was that he had an advanced case of syphilis of the brain, that it caused the accelerated pace of his flights of verbal imagination that astounded anyone who stopped long enough to listen. Crazy Alex never stopped talking. I mean, literally, in any twenty-four-hour period you would never, not ever, hear Crazy Alex silent. Occasionally a verbal wiseacre like the world debating champion from Stanford or Cal who'd heard of Crazy Alex's ability would come over to the Beach to test his wit, you know, catch one of Crazy Alex's jibes and toss it back at him, sort of a duel of words, as it were. Catching Crazy Alex verbally was like standing under Niagara Falls and trying to stop the flow with your tongue. At first I got no sense out of Crazy Alex; his talk was too fast, too bizarre, too unrelated. Crazy Alex speaks in magnified puns and symbols.

Then one day in the middle of a twenty-four-hour

monologue I suddenly realized that Crazy Alex was talking about me! I was speeding myself, having dropped half a dozen bennies the night before, and I suddenly saw that Crazy Alex was describing my life, my face, and my problems as he sat at the table. I was sitting in the Bagel Shop feeding him beers. He didn't look at me as he talked, just gazed out the window and spoke, incredibly fast, his moustache flecked with beer, his hands moving from mouth to glass to collar to table like a flight of skittery birds, and all the time his voice spewing out words in a sort of discordant rhyme that after a while assumed the rhythm of a litany, like "Yeah the light's all right if you're lookin' for light but you gotta see the night all right the sunshine's fine if you gotta dime buy the other side of the road if the road's for rent coffee ain't gonna help you if you ain't got beans know what I mean no beans no means no sunshine no funtime and keep uptight if your bread's all spent and turn on the radio no news is news all you gotta do is listen to the chime keep the soles on your shoes and watch out for screws hey baby times right for a dime c'mon it's mine if it's yours and you gottem all the time fine fine and don't pay unless you get a receipt good forever get you in all the doors even under the floors right so if you're afraid to get laid get on top and don't let it drop you can't walk the streets without being beat all reet and watch out for the heat cause if you ain't neat it's not the streetmeat you want to repeat all right it's all right baby so long's you come along and sing the proper song right or wrong ding dong hurry hurry now it's time give me a dime ..."

I often imagine that if Crazy Alex were taped and the recording played backwards or at a different speed, everything would add up. Sometimes when I hear Crazy Alex talking, I feel his cracked brain holds all the answers, the ones Einstein missed, Fermi never knew, Newton and Heidegger and all those other cats just streetcorner sitters without a Bagel Shop; Crazy Alex is the one, sitting at his table or standing underneath the awning of Ken's Grocery Store burdened with his gift of tongues, waiting for humanity to catch up with its gift of ears.

Crazy Alex spends half of his time in Agnew State Hospital and the other half on the Beach. When I asked him about Agnew, he said it was okay, only they played the radio all the time. "I know," I said. "It's terrible when they play the radio twenty-four hours a day."

"Hey, baby, that ain't the way. Where I come from, they play it twenty-five hours a day," he said.

Inside the Coffee Gallery I sat down at the bar near the chess table. The Coffee Gallery is a long dark two-roomed cocoon of piss smell and disinfectant owned by a crafty Austrian young-girlfucker named Leo, a genius with the dice cups, generous with his friends but cold as a glacier with those he doesn't like. For some reason the Coffee Gallery has always been one of the most popular places on the Beach, I suppose because of a hoving backwards toward elemental yearnings, pre-time and pre-morality; a prehistoric cave of graffiti and grime which can't be condemned because it can't possibly descend to the levels of meaning leaning at the bar. It takes a certain masochistic personality to enjoy the Coffee Gallery, and that's why it's always full of people. When you're suicidal, it's nice to know a place where there are people worse off than you.

I ordered a beer and scanned the room. In the back I saw Linda Lovely sitting at a table. Actually, two Linda Lovelys looming twice beautiful, mirror-reflected, mascara-eyed, voluptuously soft with pale milkbottle-blue skin in the dabbled bar light. Her long black hair formed a halo over her, and her fingers held a cigarette holder, its ebony slimness matching the etched loveliness of her limbs. Whenever I see Linda Lovely, I'm reminded of the time Crow, the writer, and I were walking down Market Street one amber evening. "That girl there," Crow said, pointing to a piano-legged lovely with four chins and sad eyes, "deserves as much happiness as Linda Lovely." Linda Lovely is our standard. "I agree," I said. "Somebody else will have to bring her happiness, though," Crow said.

Linda Lovely went off and on with a guy named

Steve. It was off now, so I slipped off my stool and walked over to her table. "Hello, Kid." She smiled.

"Hello, Linda, how you doing?"

"Fine. How you doing?"

"I'm doing okay."

Linda Lovely smiled. When Linda Lovely smiles, the world smiles. As I sat down, Linda Lovely's breasts brushed against my arm. Umm. Linda Lovely's breasts are like two zeppelins coming out of Lakehurst in formation. I wanted to lay my head on them. I did. When the *Hindenburg* exploded, I died. Linda Lovely took little sips from her glass of wine and nipped on her cigarette holder. Her lips curled over the end of her holder like pornographic rose petals. She breathed out the cigarette smoke and told me about Steve. Why do girls always talk about other men? "Fuck Steve!" I said.

"What have you been doing, Kid?"

"I'm selling dope."

"Great! Can I buy some?"

"Sure."

"I don't have any money right now. Can I pay you later?"

"You can pay me later."

"How's Roach Alley?"

"Fine. It's a good place. Would you like to come home with me?"

Linda Lovely smiled. "Sure, why not?"

I walked Linda Lovely to Roach Alley. When I opened the door to my loft, she turned around and showered my face with kisses. Linda Lovely has very moist lips. My face had never been showered with kisses before. Now I know what it's like. It's like standing under a carnal Niagara Falls. I showed Linda Lovely around my loft and then I took her to my bed. My bed is a mattress raised up a foot or so off the floor on two wooden pallets I copped from the potato and onion warehouse downstairs. Artsycraftsy Bohemian Flop. We stood beside my bed and undressed one another. I removed Linda Lovely's clothes with my teeth. It's called Kama Sutra haberdashery. You stand on your head and nibble at the foundation garments.

Linda Lovely doesn't wear a brassiere, just two soft zeppelins under her sweater with little dark conning-towerlike headlights. I ran my tongue over her headlights and they lit up, showing the way.

Linda Lovely makes love like a Bengal tiger, lots of clawing and growling and snapping teeth. Linda Lovely chewed furrows in my skin and then she licked the wounds. I licked her wound too, but it will never heal. When both of us were riding high with our mouths full of acrobats and elephants, as Walter says, I came and it was like the charge came all the way up from the bottom of my feet, blasting out of my body like soft sperm dum-dum bullets.

Linda Lovely screamed and beat her head into the pillow and plowed my back with her fingernails.

"Oh, God, that's nice," she said.

While we were making love, the telephone rang. It was Crow. When I answered, he was singing Italian opera into the line—Figaro Figaro *Fiiigggaaaa-aarrroooooow!*—which he learned off the jukebox at Caffe Trieste. Crow sang the whole aria complete with fortissimos and then he confessed that there were two girls in his bed.

"What are they doing?"

"They're fucking each other."

"What are you doing?"

"I'm hiding under it."

"Under what, the girls?"

"The bed, the bed, Kid! You've got to come over here and rescue me."

"I can't come, Crow. I'm being outflanked in a battle of my own."

"Oh, jaysus, Kid," Crow cried. "What would me dear God-bless-her-Catholic-soul mither in New Jersey say if she could see her boyo now? Oh, jaysus, it's wonderful!"

Crow. How describe him? Big. Funny. Actor. Raconteur. Writer. Ex-football player for Auburn. All these and more. Crow says that more than two is perversion. I was telling him about an orgy McCracken and I went to and he was piqued that he hadn't been invited. Crow never invites me to his highclass orgies. Crow goes to orgies with people who get their pictures in the society columns of the newspaper. Lovely, chic Miss Dinkenspiel was seen rubbing crotches with the young and handsome and very eligible Mr. Percy Longcock at yesterday's opening. It is rumored that Mr. Percy Longcock actually has one and is going to use it one of these days. Actually, I was going to tell Crow about the orgy so he could take notes for his novel. Crow is writing a book about his childhood and I think it needs some hairy scenes. A couple of highclass orgies and one or two lowclass ones would add just the flavor Crow's novel needs. Crow was pissed, though.

"Whenever more than two people make it together, Kid, it's not love, it's perversion."

"There's nothing wrong with a little healthy perversion," I said.

Early the next morning after taking Linda Lovely down to the U.S. Restaurant for breakfast and seeing her off to work, I walked over to Crow's place on Green Street. Crow must have been watching from the window, because the minute my finger hit the buzzer his door opened. I climbed the two floors to his apartment and Crow opened the door and bearhugged me. He was wearing an old rat-eared terrycloth bathrobe and when he was through bearhugging me he pirouetted across the floor in a tap dance and did his Pisser Burke imitation. Every time Crow pirouetted around in a circle, his ratty bathrobe fell open and his dick hung out. Crow stopped dancing and held his dick between his fingers, waving it in the air. "Oh, jaysus, Kid, me dork. The poor thing's exhausted."

I leaned against the doorjamb laughing. Crow hopped around the room and then ran over to the open window. He waved his dick out the window crying, "America, my America!"

"Crow, be serious."

"Oh, bejaysus, Kid, I am serious. Me dork performed above and beyond the call of duty last night. Here, I'm going to pin a medal on it."

He ran to his dresser and whipped open a drawer, fumbled for a moment, and whirled around, arm cocked in a salute. Embedded in his public beard was a medal, a Purple Heart, white on blue.

I doubled up on the floor while Crow strutted around the room with his medal. He goosestepped on the rug and the medal fell off. He tossed it back in the dresser drawer and pulled out an oblong plastic object. Crow held the object in front of my face. "It's happened, Kid. The Japs have finally done it."

"What have they done?"

"You know those bastards are always copying everything? Now they've copied the ultimate thing—and they've improved it!" Crow bounced the plastic dildo off the wall.

I picked it up. When I twisted it, a battery fell out. It smelled like come. Twist the other way and it vibrates. Crow grabbed the dildo and flipped it back in his dresser drawer. "It's those dirty foreigners, Kid. It's the Great Japanese Plastic Conspiracy. They're gonna put us good Christians out of business."

In the kitchen Crow made coffee. He plopped down in a chair and grinned. "Kid," he said, "things are getting out of hand. Last night I ground two American Beauty roses to dust in me own bed. There's come on every sheet. It's on the walls, under the dresser."

He jumped up and danced across the kitchen to the stove and turned the fire off under the coffee. "I had 'em steaming at the crotch. If it wasn't for the sanctity of a boyo's own castle, I'd be down on Bryant Street right now trying to contact a bailbondsman."

"I thought you said that more than two was perversion," I said.

"Oh, bejaysus! Perversion, the man says. A Protestant conspiracy if ever there was one! I kissed 'em on the twat, Kid, and they kissed me own little half-dead dork here and made it stand up for one more salute! Before the night was halfway over, they had each other up there on the chenille spread doing things a good Catholic boy has no right to see!"

I laughed as Crow swooped two cups of coffee off

the counter and set them on the table. "I broke their backs last night, Kid. I cleaned the old pipes out."

He looked at me and winked. "You know, I've rubbed genitals with every tribe in the world and there's nothing like it. You can pound that old girl's backbone down, you can jump on it, blast it and crunch it and it always bounces back. It's like the earth, it always comes back."

Crow sipped his coffee and mused. "It's all in the legs, Kid," he said. "I always have the knowledge of the strength of my legs. I may be getting old and a pot and all that, but I know that if I had to I could get out on that road right now and walk from New York to San Francisco."

That evening Crow and I walked over to Vesuvio's. The place was full of art school students and rioters deep in the middle of their usual Saturday night bash. Henri, the owner, rushed around behind the bar keeping order and making drinks. When Crow stepped through the door, he bellowed out in his glass-shattering voice, "Maaarreee, me little Irish prostitute!" A little waif of a girl threw herself into Crow's arms and hugged him. Crow was once an understudy of Marlon Brando on Broadway, and when he bellows out with his backstage voice everyone in the place is quiet. When Crow visits Vesuvio's, his table is the center of attention. I like to sit back and enjoy the show. I close my eyes and imagine Marlon Brando on Broadway. The houselights dim, the curtain rises. The stage is set and here comes Marlon Brando Crow in a dirty T-shirt bellowing, "Stella! Stella, sweetheart! I want my baby down here. Stell-laaaahh!"

Crow and I drank until two A.M. and then we walked home through the deserted streets. Maree walked with us. Crow was quiet. I told him about Frankie and Milton and Little Joe and the other friends I had on the Beach. He nodded as we walked, analyzing each friend as I described them. Crow didn't hang around the Beach much, preferring to stabilize his scene on the periphery so he could get some work done, as he said. When I mentioned Frankie, Crow shook his head. "Why the fuck don't your friends get out of the drift they're in and give something a chance to grow? They're all hanging around, the whole Beach is like that, hanging around."

Crow stopped suddenly, one finger raised. "Don't ever start hanging around, Kid. We have to be the canaries. You know, the birds they keep in the coal mines to warn the miners of poison. We have to be the canaries, Kid. There's lots of poison in the air."

4

"When one reads these strange pages of one long gone, one feels that one is at one with one who once was ..."

"That's crazy," Frankie said.

"No, it's Joyce," I said. "He's describing—"

"Oh, fiddledeegee Joyce! Ride in your own Rolls-Royce! You're always using someone else's voice." Frankie sneered.

I was hurt. We were walking through Chinatown, Frankie's arm linked in mine. My friend's girl friend's arm linked in my armlock. Milton is in San Jose selling dope. A dopey deal. Dealy dopey velly lisky Charlie sellum buyey whiskey. Under the wrought-iron dragon lampposts beside a laden garbage can I paused. I feel Frankie uses me to tease Milton. Friend of convenience. Convenient friend. I lifted Frankie's arm out of my arm and stepped off the curb.

"Let's go up to Nob Hill," Frankie said. "We can sit in the park."

Empty, the fogdamp street dappled lemon yellow under the streetlights. Reminding me of Paris, narrow corridors, subway grates, hunkered creatures craving warmth and solace from the underground furnaces. At Washington Street we turned right and started up. At a narrow doorway we stopped. A fumbling creature listed over, greatcoated, a bulging garbage can. "Kelly!" I cried.

Kelly Sam turned, smiling a rice paper-thin grin. Automatically I pulled a dime out of my jeans and crossed his palm. His hand, daggerlike, slipped scabbardwise, silently disappearing into the greatcoat pocket. Kelly Sam is an incredibly old, unbelievably thin Chinaman who wanders the after-hours Chinatown streets in search of sustenance, bound outward on his own ninety-year-old Hegira that links him to an archipelago of garbage cans, doorways, Mindanao-deep alleyways and heated laundromats. Kelly Sam is so bent over, his head appears to be coming out of his chest. Each year his head sinks lower, compensated for by the knifelike ridge of back rising above it. At night when he wanders through Chinatown's streets rummaging in the garbage cans for the leftover debris he lives on, I sometimes see him standing at the glowworm end of a darkened alley looking like a human question mark, the end of something philosophical and profound.

When I first met Kelly Sam, I wandered the Chinatown alleys with him, he gleaning the garbage cans and I him. Each doorway yielded up to Kelly Sam's vivid imagination incredible tales and stories, histories and myths left illustrated by the rifled garbage cans, the wilted bean sprouts and old lettuce leaves scattered behind us like Chinese ideograms.

I introduced Frankie to Kelly Sam. Kelly Sam held out his long thin fingers and grasped Frankie's hand, his eyes gleaming lecherously. "Herro, Flankie," he said.

"How do you do, Kelly Sam?"

"Velly fine, velly fine." Kelly Sam's toothless mouth gaped in a grin.

He was standing in a recessed doorway, the vaulted roof looming over his bent head. I wanted Kelly Sam to tell Frankie one of his tales. "Tell Frankie about the doorway you're standing in, Kelly Sam."

Kelly Sam turned and surveyed the arched doorway. His hand snaked out and tapped the ironclad door. He smiled. "Ho, this velly old entlance Six Tong Assassination Blureau. Blureau velly bad debbils in Chinatown rong time ago. Ober six tlousand assassinations in Chinatown 'tleen 1910 and 1925. Velly bad time."

Kelly Sam looked at Frankie. "You 'mind me of beauriful Plincess Chuy Fee Wong, pletender to thlone of China. She assassinated by Six Tong debbils with poison ammond cookie, velly bad debbils."

Frankie laughed. Kelly Sam laughed too and bent back over his garbage can. Frankie grabbed my arm and ran out into the middle of the street. "I like him," she cried.

"Kelly Sam's a great person," I said.

"You amaze me sometimes, Kid. Whenever I look for you to be out leading the pack, you're always trailing behind. And whenever I look back there for you, you always seem to be somewhere out in front of everybody else."

She danced forward a few feet. "Let's race. I'll beat you to the end of the block."

Frankie dropped my hand and took off, running wildly up the street. I held back a few seconds and then lagged behind her, puzzling in my mind what she had said. In my own mind I felt a stranger, and seeing Kelly Sam again had brought back for a moment all the anguish and lonely days I had spent on the Beach before I met Frankie. When I reached the corner, Frankie was standing widelegged, hands on hips, laughing. I reached out to touch her hand, but she was off again, racing wildly up the hill.

On top of Nob Hill we strolled hand in hand, looking at the city below. After midnight San Francisco looks like a bed of coals burning softly in a grate. The black perimeter of the bay defines the city and a warmth emanates up from the lights.

In the small park we sat down. I nudged close to Frankie and put my arm around her and felt her tit. She didn't move. Maybe tonight's the night. I moved my fingers slowly over Frankie's breast. She reached inside her pocket and pulled out her recorder. She blew into the recorder softly. I watched her fingers move like leaves over the instrument. It sounded nice. A childhood tune. I lost my grip on Frankie's tit and struggled to get it back. It was no use. She was intent on her recorder. I leaned back on the bench and listened.

The soft melodious music lifted up over the darkness of the park and hung in the trees, floating out over the city. Frankie played her music to the bay, to the water that flowed under the Golden Gate Bridge. On Alcatraz Island the ghosts of old convicts can hear the thin quiet sound of her recorder lilting down the steel halls of their prison. Terrible Louie, the murderer of five thousand, lifts his head up from his narrow mattress. The music is like angels' wings on his ears. He wonders if he's dead. "Hey, Max, what's that?" he cries to a friend in the next cell. Later, when Terrible Louie goes back to sleep, there is an unfamiliar wetness to his dream.

Toward dawn Frankie and I walked down Jones Street and then climbed the steps leading to the top of Russian Hill. We sat in the courtyard of an apartment building, under the gaze of a gilded angel. The water in the angel's fountain was still, reflecting back the light-reflected fog. Foghorns boom-boomed on the bay and the light on top of Alcatraz swept in circles, a solitary eye surveying the world. Under angel wings Frankie told me of her childhood: smalltown girl from Idaho, sweet, silly little lips that pucker when she talks, divorced parents, younger sister. The same old American dream broken down in the back seats of Greyhound buses.

"My mother spent the last five years running away from Bill. He was my daddy. He was a character, I guess. I never did get to know him very well. William Nobles, the greatest shuck in the American West. We'd move from town to town, Mama working as a waitress, a clerk, anything she could do to keep ahead of Bill, who always managed to sniff her out. Sometimes we'd even get sort of settled. You know, like once we lived in Texas—that's a crazy state. We had a house with a yard and a front porch and an icebox and everything. You know, real America, nasturtiums in the front yard. I really dug it. Glyn and I'd be sitting on the front porch and it's been so peaceful for so long that we'd say to each other, 'Well, it's about time for old Willy to show.' Bill had a system going. Whenever he found out which town we lived in, he'd go up and down all the streets knocking on all the doors asking, 'Does Mrs. Nobles live here?' Pretty soon we'd see a speck of dust and who'd be stomping up the road but old Willy, living and breathing just like a real human. Then it was nights in the backs of parked cars in the Panhandle of

Texas, outside truckstops in Waco. Ooo, cold like you've never seen. I was thirteen and Glyn was eleven. Then we'd help mother fight. It was nice."

Frankie gazed down on the glowing coals of the city. I sat glooping beside her. Her family. I pictured this small girl in Waco, Texas, at night, a truckstop.

"I was in Waco, Frankie, 1953. I bet I was in that very truckstop. Is that the one with all the pumps, the west side of town? There were deerheads mounted on the walls of the cafe. I probably walked right by your car, a 1941 Dodge. You were asleep in the back seat with your sister, or awake listening to the jukebox music, Mama inside drinking coffee, yass."

"The funny thing is, Mama really loved Bill. She just couldn't live with him. The same old story, I guess. He had some interior hangup, some streak that made him weak, restless, mean. He couldn't ever really stop, could never settle down. Then when Mama left him and started on her journeys, Bill just sort of went wild and spent the rest of his days following her all over America. He died in Denver in 1956."

Frankie and I walked down the thousand steps of Russian Hill one at a time. My hand brushed Frankie's hand. A hotel room in Denver. I know that room. My father too. The Grand Hotel. We have rooms with carpets, old age, and regrets. Noble William. Staring out blank windows on Larimer Street. I could smell the nap of the rug, feel the dust rise up to my nostrils. Some interior hangup that wouldn't let him settle down. What was it Patrick Cassidy said from his jail cell in Santa Cruz in 1959? "Outside my window there is a wall with a sign. The letters are faded. A neon sign flashing on and off somewhere in the free world. We see it through our barred window. It's as senseless as everything else, though; it will flash twenty-four times one minute and thirty-five times the next. The only pattern is its irregularity. The room is empty now."

"What about you, Kid? What's your story?"

"Oh, the same old shit. I was raised in Southern California. Colton, in the middle of orange groves. There was a mountain outside of town where my father worked, a cement mountain. Sometimes on summer afternoons I'd climb up there and smell the orange blossoms. When the trees were in bloom, it was like the whole valley was full of orange honey. You could stretch out your hand and almost touch it in the air.

"Every year the mountain got smaller and smaller because they kept blasting it away to get the cement. A couple of times I even went inside the tunnels with my father and watched him drilling. It was exciting and a little sad."

"It sounds terrible."

"It wasn't terrible. It was a job. Then my father got injured in a cave-in and couldn't work for a long time. That was bad."

"What'd you do?"

"I used to wander down to the railroad tracks and watch the trains. Colton is a big railroad town. I remember when we first moved to Colton, we came on a train. Me and my brothers spent days and days at the windows looking out at all the small towns we were passing through. Every time we came to a railroad station, we'd see the sign and say, Is this it? Is this where we're going? And my mother would say, No, we're going to Colton. Finally, after about five days we came to Colton. I was looking out the window and I could see miles and miles of railroad tracks stretching away on both sides—and the sign in the station said Colton. Then I knew we were where we were going.

"After my father got injured, I used to wander down to the railroad tracks and watch the trains go by. There were cottonwood trees on the other side of the tracks where we could collect mistletoe to sell for Christmas. Sometimes, every week or so, a special train would pass through town. It was called the *Cherokee* and it was pulled by a big sixteen-wheeled engine that looked ten stories high. Inside I could see all kinds of fancy people going to Los Angeles. Every time the *Cherokee* passed through town I'd go down to the tracks and watch it. I used to dream about the time I'd be able to get on it and it'd take me out of there."

Frankie was silent. We walked arm in arm. "How'd

you end up in the city, Frankie? What brought you here?"

"I took some tests when we moved back to Boise," Frankie said. "I got a letter from Stanford saying they would be delighted to have me. It was like a dream, me going to a bigtime school because my scores were higher than anybody else's. It didn't last long, though. I got mixed up with a fraternity boy. The school suspended both of us. I came up here on a lark. The fraternity boy brought me. That's when I met Milton. I've been here ever since."

At the bottom of the hill I held Frankie close. We kissed. Frankie and I walked down Columbus Avenue. We stopped. We held hands. We were lonely on the road together.

I let Frankie go at the door to Milton's pad and walked down Columbus Avenue toward Pacific Street. As I walked past Washington Square, I saw the spires of the Church of St. Peter and Paul, lonely, like Indian tepees made out of Italian marble and cherries in brine. In the middle of Washington Square I saw Charlie Running Dog pose his men. They stood silent along the edge of the park. Charlie Running Dog raised a hand, spoke: *"Ka'altcha nuima mo neutla wanto.* We are the last of the tribe. Here is our home. We will run no more. This is a peaceful place, full of water and good things to eat. We are the original people of this land and it is here that our tepees will stay and be a symbol everywhere."

Charlie Running Dog spoke and then was still. When his speech was over, I opened the door to my loft and climbed the stairs and lay down on my bed. The rafters crisscrossing my ceiling formed patterns like Egyptian hieroglyphics, and I read in them all the travails of mankind. The crossing beams carried the secret message of Larimer Street and Bill Nobles and the *Cherokee* and all the hotel rooms and every American dream broken down in the back seats of Greyhound buses. As I drifted to sleep, I could hear the taut cables of the Golden Gate Bridge singing in the wind.

5 I was loinlocked in an erotic dream when I heard the distant sound of drumbeats. My dream was delicious torture, like someone dropping two-pound pudendums on my forehead. Every time a pudendum dropped, drums banged. Pudom! Pudom! I blinked and struggled up from under the weight of descending pudendums. Hoya! Hoya! Hoya!

"Hey, Kid!"

On my white brick wall I saw flickering Indian shadows dancing.

"Hey, Kid, wake up!"

I was dreaming drumbeats, seeing Sioux fiercely painted counting coups against retreating bluecoats, repeating rifles repeating.

I staggered over to the windows. Feathers and drums. Taos Pueblo has invaded Roach Alley. Walter Chappell was sitting on the top of a jeep that was surrounded by four dancing Indians. The Indians in turn were surrounded by gaping lumpers and secretaries and truck drivers from the produce market. From atop the jeep Walter whooped, holding a bottle aloft. "Hoya, hoya, hoya," he cried as the Indians circled around the jeep. Walter rose unsteadily, cupped his hands, and aimed his voice at my window. "Hey, Kid, wake up!" He tipped the jug to his lips and slipped slowly down, his butt bouncing off the jeep top. The jug never left his lips. As he bounced off the roof, he continued beating his pudom! on the metal jeep.

I slipped on my Levi's. Jesus, what was Walter doing here? Walter's an insanely frantic genius with infinite capacities and insatiable appetites for everything— women, booze, dope, laughter, music, work, talk. When Walter comes around, he sucks you into his orbit and you start revolving like a minor planet around a hectic super nova. So intense and cataclysmic are his binges that stories about them reverberate up and down the California coast, assuming the element of mythology, even extending into other states, Arizona and New Mexico, where he's lived since fleeing Big Sur, moving onto the desert to be near Indians. When Walter goes on a binge, no one is safe and whoever is with him has to act as guardian not only of the wives and girls and the bar and the streets and the cars on the street but also of Walter himself and so on et cetera into the early morning dawn. Walter never gets tired and he never gives up. When he gets drunk, it's like standing beside an exploding mountain; all you can do is put out your hands and try to hold a volcano up.

I walked downstairs. The Indians were still circling the jeep. Walter was spread-eagled across the hood. He had on tight leather pants and was covered with turquoise, a huge concho belt holding up his pants, a Hopi bowguard on his wrist, bracelets on each arm, amulets, rings, necklaces, feathers, leather thongs, beads, a traveling medicine show rolling chaotically around on the jeep's hood, threatening to fall off. A truck driver who'd just pulled in from Modesto with a twenty-ton rig full of grapes gaped from the streetcorner. Walter struggled upright on the hood and then careened off, sliding like a sack of potatoes onto the fender, his stick bonging steadily against the hood, headlight, and bumper before plopping softly onto the pavement, flop! From the ground he continued beating his drumstick, accompanying with his metallic pudom! each shuffle of the Indians' feet. Two of the Indians stopped dancing and attempted to hoist Walter up by the shoulders. He wrenched himself loose and threw his drumstick into the air. "Kid!" he cried. "Hoya! Hoya! Hoya!"

He rushed forward and grabbed me, kissing me on the mouth. I stood as rigid as a pole in his arms. It's disconcerting to be kissed by a man. It's like being kissed by a hundred-year-old grandmother with thumbtacks on her chin. I eased out of Walter's grasp.

"Kid, it's you! You're here! I've come all the way from Taos! Hoya, hoya, hoya! What the fuck." Walter collapsed in my arms. I looked at the Indians helplessly. The four of them stared at me. "Ugh, you help-um carry upstairs," I said in my best pidgin Indian.

"Crazy, man, you lead the way," the tallest Indian said.

We carried Walter upstairs and put him in my bed. I went back down to find Walter's drumstick. When I climbed back upstairs, Walter was asleep and the Indians were swinging from the rafters.

JoJay, Jose, Joselito, and Trinidad Archelito have set up their hand-sewn deerskin tepee at the far end of my loft. It looks weird rising up out of the worn-out mechanical claptrap of modern America. The four brothers sit inside the teepee all day long beating their drums and drinking beer. Occasionally JoJay lights up a-joint and gazes at the wall with heavy-lidded eyes.

JoJay, Jose, Joselito, and Trinidad Archelito are four brothers from Taos Pueblo. JoJay says Mama Archelito loved the name Joe so much she couldn't stop naming her sons Joe. She named the youngest son Trinidad for effect. JoJay's the leader of the group, also the tallest, built with the plump, rounded, deceptively soft look of most Taos Pueblo Indians. Jose is next, his chubby face and slightly cocky smile setting off limpid dark eyes. Joselito is third, a short stocky man, the best dancer in the group. Then comes Trinidad Archelito, chief drummer, thin, wiry, the exception to the Taos Pueblo roly-poly rule. The four brothers have come to San Francisco with Walter to dance and make music. Walter has lined up a show at the Art Institute for his *America Needs Indians* sensorium.

"America needs Indians, Kid," Walter explained. "America doesn't know how much it does need Indians."

Walter was living in Big Sur taking photographs and one day while visiting Berkeley two thugs jumped out of a car and hit him in the face with a tire iron. As a consequence of that act, Walter lost his front teeth, moved to Taos, New Mexico, and started loving Indians. "I lost my teeth but I gained Indians," Walter said, smiling a smile with an edge to it. "I am very glad to have lost my teeth."

Walter's *America Needs Indians* sensorium is composed of JoJay, Jose, Joselito, and Trinidad Archelito dancing, drumming, singing, chanting, and blowing on an eagle wingbone whistle while Walter plays the piano. It's all recorded on tapes with overdubbings and redubbings and photographic slides and paintings and lots of feathers. "It's designed to get you into the Indian's mind for one evening," Walter explained. "An Indian's mind is a very curious place; it's full of magic."

"I believe what you are saying, Walter," I said.

"Hoya, hoya." Walter nodded in satisfaction.

JoJay starts each day by blowing on a whistle made from the hollow wingbone of an eagle. The piercing noise of JoJay's hollow wingbone whistle wakes up everybody in the loft. "It has to be the left wingbone," Walter explained. "That's the wing that points down toward the center of the earth when an eagle flies around in a circle. It's a holy bone."

After JoJay wakes everybody up with his holy hollow eagle wingbone whistle, Jose, Joselito, and Trinidad Archelito start in with their drums.

Each man sits with his goatskin drum tucked between his legs, Trinidad Archelito setting the beat, starting slowly in an age-old rhythm, "To welcome the sun," Jose explains, "and to give the day a good beginning."

The drumming starts off slow, almost too slow, then quietly accelerates, padum dum dum *doom!* padum dum dum *doom!* as JoJay's piercingly shrill holy wingbone of an eagle whistle cuts through the loft. When the room is full of drumbeats and the shrill singing of JoJay's whistle, Joselito, the official greeter-of-the-day dancer, jumps up and poom! hits his left foot down, poom! his left foot down in an off-beat shuffle, moving around the floor with a dignity and grace belied by his squat body. In a few moments the whole loft is affected, the sounds and rhythms beating into the old walls and bricks. When the official welcome-to-the-day dance is over, the loft is unusually quiet, like standing alone on top of Black Mesa with only the sound of the breeze blowing through the long grass.

JoJay's magic works. Yesterday Mr. Tagliani came by to investigate the reports of racket in my loft. He has had numerous complaints. JoJay took Mr. Tagliani by the arm and showed him the tepee and the drums. Mr. Tagliani touched the deerskin tepee with the tips of his fingers, then peeked inside the flap. At JoJay's urging he stepped inside and sat down on the sheepskin rug. Inside the tepee is a subdued light that is reflected from my white brick wall. The light envelops the interior of the tepee with a soft resonance, highlighting the pictographs Trinidad Archelito has painted around the base. Mr. Tagliani sat on the sheepskin rug for a long time. He reached up and touched the feathers hanging from a thong. He tapped his fingertips gently on Jose's goatskin drum. When Mr. Tagliani stepped outside the tepee, his eyes were shining. "How mucha you pay the rent here, Keed?" he said. "Never you mind. You no paya the rent here coupla months. Itsa good you feex uppa the place. You doa nice job."

He walked over to a window and stuck his head out. "Whatsamatta you people no likea the drums?" he yelled up and down. I feel secure because Mr. Tagliani owns all of Roach Alley.

JoJay feels good after his confrontation with Mr. Tagliani. He wants to start a new Indian campaign. He says the Indian wars were just the first skirmish.

"We have just been sitting out between battles," JoJay said. "The American cavalry better watch out."

"The American cavalry doesn't exist any more except in old men's heads," I said.

"That's where the next battle is going to be fought," JoJay said. "In old men's heads."

Walter has been carrying his equipment into my loft for a week, tape recorders, movie cameras, amplifiers, etc. The end of the loft looks like a recording studio. Wires and lights and drums litter the floor. JoJay and his brothers sit in their tepee drinking beer while Walter mixes his tapes. Walter's tapes are incredibly complex mixtures of atonal piano, Indian drums and bells, sticks, rattles, gongs, chants, and JoJay's shrill eagle wingbone whistle. Behind this is Joselito's and Trinidad Archelito's hoya hoya hoya, the whole effect being one of mysterious complexity and movement. This morning while Walter was playing with his tapes, Pippen tapped softly on my door. I let him in. He looked inside JoJay's tepee and listened to the tapes. "Very interesting," he said.

"It's magic music," I said.

"It does have a certain quality," Pippen said.

Pippen sat on the edge of my bed for a long time while the chanting, beating, throbbing, crashing music resounded throughout the loft. The walls vibrated with the drumbeats and Pippen sat quietly, holding his head between his hands. When the tape was over he stood up and walked out.

Walter's magic music is already famous. Outside my loft windows delegations of lumpers and secretaries and truck drivers stand around and listen. They lean on Walter's jeep and ponder my windows. Occasionally they circle Walter's jeep, peering inside it. The jeep is covered with feathers and mandalas and sheepskin upholstery. It has become Roach Alley's talisman. I asked Walter why he covered his jeep with feathers.

"JoJay and his brothers covered it," Walter said. "They covered it when Mama Luhan blessed it."

"Blessed your jeep?"

"Yes. This is the only jeep in the history of the world to be blessed by Mama Luhan, the high priestess of Taos Pueblo. Because of my blessed jeep we can go anywhere in it and we will never be in danger. That's part of the blessing."

"It sounds great."

"My jeep is the only jeep in the history of modern times to make it over the Canyon de Chelly quicksand during the height of the rainy season," Walter said. "Tons of forestry equipment, tourist campers, and old-time Conestoga wagons lie preserved under Canyon de Chelly's quicksand, but my jeep made it through because Mama Luhan blessed it. No vehicle could possibly make it without being blessed."

Last night Frankie came by and was mesmerized by JoJay and his brothers. Frankie stayed inside JoJay's tepee for hours and smoked marijuana with the Indians. Walter played one of his tapes and took photographs of Frankie. I got high and my head floated up through the hole in the tepee and drifted about in the loft's vastness. Outside I heard the sound of traffic. It was like being inside a hollow drum. At four A.M., when everyone else was asleep, Frankie came to my bed. Her body was like a drumhead. I played upon it until dawn.

I walked over to the San Gottardo Hotel to see Clementi. Clementi's an Italian photographer who has a room there. Clementi pays three dollars a week for his room. The room's just big enough for Clementi and his bed. "When I ball a chick, it's terrible," Clementi said. "But we manage."

As a photographer Clementi is recording the history of mankind as it pertains to North Beach San Francisco. "I am the Timothy O'Sullivan of my generation," Clementi said.

Clementi takes pictures of everybody in North Beach. "It's good to have a record of times gone by," he says. When Clementi develops his film, the San Gottardo Hotel is thrown into an uproar. Clementi uses the bathroom as a darkroom. Old Italian men waiting to pee pound on the door. Clementi's possessed, though; nothing will dislodge him until his photographic record is complete. One of the old Italian winos who lived in the San Gottardo Hotel got into the bathroom while Clementi was out on the roof drying a print. The old wino drank some of Clementi's developer and had a stroke. Clementi got a good picture of it. He calls it "The Tragic End of an Old Italian Who Drank Too Much Developer." He entered it in the Upper Grant Avenue Street Festival and won first prize.

The reason I went down to the San Gottardo Hotel to see Clementi is because he had taken a picture of Frankie. "It's a strange thing," he said. "I can never seem to get her. Every time I take a picture of that chick, she seems to be out of focus or something."

I looked at the print. It was Frankie and Milton in

Washington Square. Sure enough, Milton was sharp and clear but where Frankie stood was a dark blur.

Milton came by my loft, shuffling up the stairs. I don't know if Milton shuffles because he's a spade or shuffles because he's a spade who chips smack. When he chips heavy, his shuffle becomes more pronounced. At the same time it's a lethal shuffle, like a leopard wounded in one knee.

"How's business?" he said.

"Okay. I got rid of a few."

"Crazy."

Milton shuffled around my loft. He peeked inside JoJay's tepee. "What's the tent bit?"

"It belongs to Walter's friends. They're staying here for a while."

"Crazy," Milton said.

He sat down on a box by a window and looked down into Roach Alley. "How much you gettin' for the goodies?"

"Between twelve and fifteen. I sold a couple for ten."

"You oughtta get fifteen cents for 'em. It's bad business havin' different-priced ounces on the set. I sell mine for fifteen."

"You have different customers," I said. "There's not much bread on the Beach right now."

"You have the bread for the ones you sold?" Milton snuffed deep in his throat in a junkie snuff-lip way. He leaned against the wall with his eyes half closed.

"I gave most of them out front and I haven't collected yet."

"Oh, maan . . ."

I had fifty dollars in my pocket. I pulled out forty and gave it to Milton. "I'll give you the rest when I collect it."

Milton stared at me. The whites of his eyes were slightly yellow. "Maan, you shount give grass out front. Cats don' pay that way."

I thought of Linda Lovely and shrugged.

Milton sent Frankie over to collect the money I owed him. Frankie was angry that I hadn't paid Milton. "I don't have the money," I said. "Why doesn't that nigger collect his own debts?"

I said "nigger" to see Frankie's reaction. The word had no effect on her. I used the word a few more times. She narrowed her eyes and stuck out her lower lip, the way she does when she's angry.

I once had a friend who had a copy of *Nigger of the Narcissus* on his bookshelf. He was a college-bred liberal, and when I asked him about the book he said, "Yes, *Negro of the Narcissus* is a fine book."

I laughed my ass off. I couldn't stop talking about *Negro of the Narcissus* for weeks.

When I told Frankie that I didn't have Milton's bread, she said that I didn't have to take the grass from him. I said the big bastard forced it on me just like he forces it on everybody else.

"That's not true," Frankie said.

"You've got an ache between your legs for a big black dick, Frankie, that's all."

Frankie looked at me. "Where's your ache, Kid?"

Last night I had a dream of childhood. I was in Colton and I walked down to the railroad tracks where the *Cherokee* was due to go by. I stood beside the station. I stood for a long time and then I put my ear to the ground. I could hear the *Cherokee* coming. I had a red flag in my hand and I was going to wave the flag and stop the *Cherokee* when it came by. When the *Cherokee* stopped, I would get on it and it would take me away from there. I stood beside the tracks for hours and hours and I could hear the *Cherokee* coming and coming, louder and louder, but it never reached me.

6

"Hey, Kid," Little Joe said. "I've got a problem."

Little Joe and I are walking down Grant Avenue toward the Amp Palace. I'm looking in the shop windows. It's Saturday, a nice October morning.

"What's your problem?"

"I got to find a husband for Francesca. You know she's eight months gone. I told her I'd help her find an old man."

"What's she want an old man for?"

"Her parents. They're gonna institutionalize her and adopt the baby unless she gets married."

"Who's the father?"

"God only knows," Little Joe said. "And I wish to hell he'd tell Francesca."

Francesca. Everybody's baby. Francesca's a student at the Art Institute, seventeen years old, a very luscious little chick who leaves a definite impression on every man she meets. Half the Art Institute and all of North Beach has been impressed, including me. When I think of Francesca, I get a very definite series of images in my mind: Francesca lolling in Washington Square with her buxom belly and sketchpad; Francesca lying on the sand down at Aquatic Park, a scant patch of bikini over her loins, juicy and tender like frail pigeons; Francesca down at 72 Commercial Street lying on sheets of butcher paper while McCracken outlines her nude body in acrylics. Balling by the numbers, he calls it. "I want to get all the possible positions down on paper and then go from there," he said. Francesca giggles from under her butcher paper mattress.

Her baby could be mine—or anybody's. I couldn't get over it. I'd watched Francesca's belly grow for eight months, and pretty soon her baby would be playing in Washington Square along with the rest of the babies: Italian, Chinese, black, energetic little characters chasing balls across the park, running across the grass with squeals of delight, falling, crying, getting up, and hurrying on again, herds of little beings who in reality were wizened little philosophers—Kants and Hegels and Schopenhauers too small for words.

As we walked down Grant Avenue, in my mind's eye I could see Francesca strolling across Washington Square with her baby, perhaps pushing one of those fancy perambulators from Goodwill or St. Vincent de Paul, the sunshade lowered to protect the baby's eyes; Francesca strolling across Washington Square pushing the baby that could be my baby or Little Joe's baby or anybody on the Beach's baby that we had to find a father for.

Little Joe grabbed a corner table in the Amp Palace. Amp for ampule. Ampule for speed. Every slowdown hipster in North Beach connects in the Amp Palace. It's the only place on the Beach that stays open all night, and Monte, the proprietor, runs a tight little score scene. After two A.M. Monte bops around the place like a faggoty phantom hustling hard hipsters out the door, cooling everyone, saying, "It's all right to nod in the corner, but keep the aisles clean."

The Amp Palace is North Beach's favorite hangout for every stoned-out junkie with no place to go. Here they can connect and then hustle on up to a flop on Harwood Alley to fix and then stagger back to nod out. Dope is a very social scene. The nature of it is singular—it's a lonely bag hacking away at the vein—but nobody needs people like the junkie. He oozes into his corner carrying his napkin-cradled cup of coffee and then floats in the clouds of humanity around him, the conversation and warmth reassuring him that when he wakes up he will still be among other humans who speak and touch and turn. Communication is what he needs. The very act of fixing is his daily Reichian jack-off, a public orgasm with the drop of blood in the eyedropper becoming the minute seed that gives life to his ovarian fantasies. Best of all is to have someone participate in the ritual, tie him up and actually shoot the stuff into his veins. It's like an exquisite orgy that precedes the return to the nodders and freaks back in the Amp Palace.

Little Joe outlined Francesca's problem to Sandy, the counterman.

"I dunno, man," Sandy said.

"Me either," Little Joe said.

"What color is the baby gonna be?"

"Gee, I don't know."

"That will have a lot to do with who you pick for father."

"It might," Little Joe said.

While we were talking, Hube the Cube walked in. He sat down in the corner. Little Joe looked at me and I looked at Sandy and Sandy looked at Hube the Cube.

"Maybe it won't after all," Sandy said.

Hube the Cube sat at his table and stared. He stares all day in a kind of tunnel vision. When he walks down the sidewalk, it's like he's walking in his own personal subway, a private corridor as wide as the sidewalk. Hube the Cube's a guinea pig for the University of California Medical Center on Parnassus Avenue, taking every pill and every combination of pills that all the young intern innovators can push down his throat. The medical center has catalogued over five thousand different pills that should not be given anyone under any circumstances. An impressive list of forbidden combinations of drugs has been cross-filed because of Hube the Cube. Seminars are held with Hube the Cube as subject while batteries of interns, pharmacology students, doctors, and psychiatrists probe, punch, and interrogate him and inject combinations of chemicals into his veins. For all this Hube the Cube receives two hundred dollars a month plus side effects.

The side effects are generous. While Hube the Cube sat at his table, Sandy and Little Joe and I discussed Francesca's problem.

"All she needs is for some guy to go through the paperwork," Little Joe explained.

"I'll give Hube the Cube a cup of coffee," Sandy said. "Maybe we can talk to him."

Little Joe and I nodded. Sandy went behind the

counter and got a cup of coffee and took it over to Hube the Cub.

"Maybe Francesca won't want Hube the Cube as a husband," Sandy said when he returned.

"Nonsense," Little Joe said. "He'll make a perfect husband."

"Yeah," I said. "Francesca will never know she's married."

"You guys leave it to me," Little Joe said. "I'll talk to Hube the Cube."

"Be sure to stand directly in front of him when you talk," Sandy said, "or he'll never see you."

Little Joe went over to Hube the Cube's table to talk to him. He sat there for half an hour, then returned. "He says he'll marry Francesca if we score an ounce of crystal for him," he said.

"That's a lot of crystal," I said.

"It'll be worth it. What do you think?"

"I'll see what I can do," I said.

"Maybe you could talk to Milton, explain the problem."

"Milton and I aren't on speaking terms."

"What's wrong? Milton putting the jog to Frankie?"

"Fuck you!"

"Gee, we're pretty sensitive in that area, aren't we?"

"I'm not sensitive in that area. If anyone's sensitive in that area it's Frankie."

"Yeah, I guess she would be sensitive in that area"—Little Joe laughed—"with a jog like that flogging her."

Francesca has agreed to marry Hube the Cube as long as she doesn't have to live with him, and Hube the Cube has agreed to marry Francesca as long as we score him an ounce of crystal. I promised Hube the Cube that I'd personally stand behind the ounce of crystal.

"I'm trusting you, Kid," he said.

"I'll get the speed for you, Hube."

To show my good faith I scored a little crystal from Doorknob, a smalltime supplier on the street, and let Hube the Cube geeze a few times. When Hube the

Cube tied up, a look of ecstasy came over his face.
"Ahhh," he sighed.

"That snuff affects you like smack, doesn't it?"

"At first, then the trip starts."

"Why do you like it so much?"

"It makes my mind work."

"Yeah, but your mind can only take so much overtime, then somebody has to pay the bill."

"We use our minds at only one-tenth capacity.
Speed brings out the other nine-tenths that never
works."

"Then blows it out."

"Fuck you, Kid. What's your trip?"

Milton and I made up. Frankie said it was bullshit
what we two old friends were doing to each other and
she wouldn't stand for another minute of it. I was glad
Frankie intervened between us, because I like Milton
and the whole thing had been a bum trip. When Milton
came over, I gave him another fifty dollars on what I
owed him. We shook hands. "I'll peddle the rest of
those lids and get the bread to you," I said.

"Crazy."

"You coming to Hube the Cube's and Francesca's
wedding?"

"I wouldn't miss it for nothing," Milton said.

The wedding is to be in my loft. JoJay wants to offi-
ciate. He says he's endowed with an ancient ancestral
right to perform all kinds of ceremonies: marriages,
christenings, deaths, circumcisions. "My people have
been doing these things for centuries," he said.

"This marriage is for legal reasons, JoJay. It has to
be done with the right paperwork and everything so
Francesca's parents can't take the baby away and send
Francesca to an institution."

"There is no ceremony more legal than the Taos
Pueblo Unification Ceremony. Our laws were written
before the first white man set foot on this shore."

"I know, JoJay, but the great white father in city
hall might not recognize the Taos Pueblo Unification
Ceremony."

"Everybody recognizes the Taos Pueblo Unification

Ceremony. White men come from miles around to see
it. In our ceremony the bride dances around the groom
seventeen times, washes his feet in fresh mountain
spring water, and sleeps with all his brothers to remove
her vice. That way she vows never to be cross or angry
with her husband."

"That sounds like a wonderful ceremony, JoJay.
And part of the requirements have already been met.
Francesca has slept with all the groom's brothers."

JoJay and I compromised. Pierre from the Bread
and Wine Mission will marry Francesca and Hube and
Cube, then JoJay will perform the Taos Pueblo Unification Ceremony.

"That's good," JoJay said. "Double insurance. That
way it will be a perfect marriage."

"Yeah," I said. "It'll be a marriage made in heaven."

All of North Beach is preparing for the wedding.
The Amp Palace is humming with anticipation. "Aaron
says Saturday will be perfect," Little Joe said. "He
threw a chart on both Francesca and Hube the Cube
and the stars say both of them are overdue for a
dramatic event."

"Maybe Hube the Cube's going to have the baby,"
Jerome Kulek said.

Jerome's a cynical dark ex-Detroit streeturchin-
with-a-degree transplant who publishes a literary mag
called *Nexus*. "Nexus Plexus, you white Anglo-Saxon
motherfuckers," he'd say. "If God invented anybody
smarter than Nietzsche, he didn't tell me about it. In
fact, I think it was Nietzsche who invented God."

"The Beach has been needing something like this,"
Clementi said. "There hasn't been a good get-together
since Big Daddy Nord threw that party down on Battery Street and Bill fell out the window."

"More people should get married," Sandy said. "It
brings the family together."

"If somebody gave me an ounce of speed, I'd get
married too," Jerome Kulek said.

"With an ounce of speed you wouldn't know if you
were married or not."

"I know. That's why it wouldn't bother me."

I told Crow about the impending marriage. He said he'd like to come.

"You can take notes for your novel," I said.

"Fuck my novel! I just want to see that your Indian friend's ceremony is carried out properly. Seventeen times around the groom and then the bride sleeps with all the brothers."

"That requirement has already been carried out," I said.

"It hasn't been carried out with me," Crow said. "Or ain't I a brother?"

Three more couples have enlisted to get married. Pierre says he will perform a group ceremony. "Hell, we're legalizing the whole Beach," Little Joe said.

"We should have the wedding on Saturday," Aaron said. "All the stars are right. Jupiter is in conjunction with Mars, and Pluto is in the seventh house."

"And the sun is rising in Fresno," I said.

"Don't knock the stars, Kid," Aaron said. "According to their charts, Francesca and Hube the Cube will have lots of kids and live happily ever after."

"That's not exactly the plan," I said.

"You can't mess with it, Kid. This marriage was planned in heaven long before you were born."

"I just hope it takes place before Little Gus is born."

Little Gus is the name Little Joe has given to Francesca's forthcoming baby.

Wednesday evening Little Joe arrived with part of the loft-decorating committee from the Coffee Gallery. He flew up the stairs with three chicks and a half gallon of Valley of the Moon wine under his arm. The chicks floated across the floor into JoJay's tepee.

"What did you give those chicks?" I asked.

Little Joe held up a block of hashish and cackled. "Organic hash. Good old Nepalese health food."

I heard maniacal laughter from JoJay's tepee. JoJay stuck his head out of the tepee flap. "Hey, Kid," he said, "that Taos Pueblo Unification Ceremony includes the bride's sisters too."

"Wail, baby!" Little Joe cried.

"These beatnik chicks are going to ruin our Indian's morals," I said.

"Indians are the original beatniks," Little Joe said.

JoJay stuck his head out of the tepee flap. "Mind your own morals, Kid."

By nine o'clock Roach Alley was jumping. Half a dozen more chicks flew in with cans of paint and rolls of paper and thumbtacks to decorate the walls. McCracken and Arthur and Bowen burst up the stairs with coattails flapping and wine bottles in hand. McCracken rushed to the rear of the loft and was immediately scheming how to get some of the girls back to Walter's mattress. While jabbering with Silvia, he rubbed Mona's breasts and kept his eye screwed on Janey. Mona sighed and leaned against McCracken's leg. The three chicks giggled and headed for the mattress with McCracken following. They flopped down and started drinking wine.

While McCracken hustled the chicks in the back, Arthur and Bowen roared around directing the decorating. Bowen grabbed a large roll of butcher paper that Little Joe had boosted from a meat shop on Stockton Street and carried it over to the brick wall. "This wall demands a mural," he cried, unwinding the paper along the floor.

"Kid! You crazy motherfucker!" Arthur cried, slapping my hand. He danced around, cackling like a hen.

McCracken and Arthur and Bowen are a trio of insane painters who share a loft at 72 Commercial Street, a loft McCracken conned off a sweet young girl who found the place and paid the first two months' rent. McCracken is the Modigliani of the group, young and talented and mad and most doomed to an early death. Bowen's a superslick con-man hustler who has every cat and chick on the Beach doing his bidding, surrounding himself with a fleet of art patrons and lawyers and doctor types who buy his work. When he needs bread, he rushes out in the afternoon or early morning down alleys picking up bits of iron and scraps of junk and then rushes to a welding shop and cons the old Italian welder who's busy welding keels for boats or wrought-

iron fancy grillwork for Pacific Heights houses and
talks him into fitting together the pieces of scrap iron
into an artistic design that he, Bowen, directs, and always the old Italian—or Chinese, Russian, gringo, Ar-
menian, it doesn't matter—welder crustily and un-
willingly does Bowen's bidding, due to his really magical conning ability, and in a trice he has a "piece,"
which he rushes over in a borrowed car to Potrero Hill,
where an eccentric but astute doctor named Wenner
lives—who has monkeys, dogs, birds, kinkajous, everything, you name it, except cats, all shitting on the floor
at once, and who buys everything Bowen produces.
The doctor owns three houses on Pot Hill, each one of
which is a storehouse of art, Bowen and McCracken
and Arthur being three important artists in his collection. Bowen always approaches a sale with the doc as a
hustle, and so he always assumes he's conning the old
doc, when in reality the doc is getting a whole passel of
really remarkable art dirt cheap. The young artists
don't realize they're selling away their work for a song.

Arthur is strangest of all, though, and perhaps the
most serious and talented. Arthur is a black dude who
paints only in black and white. "Everything comes out
mulatto," McCracken says. Arthur is quiet and serious
and he speaks with a soft burr-like whisper that intones
shades of Oxford and Boston Common, a low, intellectual bzzzbzzz that you have to listen to with bated ears.
Arthur shares one corner of 72 Commercial Street,
Bowen another corner, and McCracken a third. The
fourth corner is taken up by Roosevelt Chicken, a
crazy hen that Bud Olderman, a poet, found one night
on Grant Avenue, an escapee from a Chinese poultry
shop which he picked up and carried back to the loft.

The loft Bowen, Arthur, and McCracken share is an
incredible tangle of junk, old picture frames, canvases,
bottles and cans of paint, a giant swing with a thirty-
foot arc hung from the rafters, paint-splattered wooden
floors, beamed ceilings, a skylight, a fifty-rung ladder
leading up to a trapdoor in the roof, rows of shelving
along the walls, paintings and drawings stacked three
deep, buckets for mixing plaster of paris, goodies gar-
nered from debris boxes, old doors, window frames,

lamps, radios, pieces of wood, hatch covers, barrels, rope, anchors, wooden boxes from Chinatown, rugs, filing cabinets, wicker baskets, bricks, books, Christmas lights, street signs, roadwork flashers, pots, pans, helmets, hats, clothes, old shoes, gunny sacks, posters, and in one corner a sack of chicken feed for Roosevelt Chicken. The front part of the loft, overlooking Commercial Street and the Mission Emergency Hospital, has a long row of tall windows that let an enormous amount of light in. Downstairs is a cabinet shop and next door is the hiring hall for the warehousemen's union.

The focal point of the loft—aside from the working areas where each painter keeps his tools, paint stolen from the Art Institute, and paper from the lithography plant on Battery Street—is the bed, a giant affair, two double mattresses really, placed side by side and covered with an enormous multicolored spread. Over the years the spread has assumed a weird pastiche of colors, having changed from a once bright paisley green and blue affair into a junglelike floral funk, an organic bedspread, constantly metamorphosing with all the food and come and wine and puke and tobacco and paint and dirt and dandruff and sweat and chicken shit ground in over the years. Every two or three months McCracken or Arthur will rip the sheets out from under the spread in desperation and sheer physical nausea (Bowen never does; for him the funk is part of the fun) and rush them up to the New Star Cleaners and Laundry on Grant Avenue. The spread itself is never cleaned though; to clean it would be like vacuuming the Pacific Ocean, an impossible task, and so the pungent odors from the spread permeate the loft, mixed in with the smell of marijuana, shellac, paint thinner, oils, and coffee. Everybody lives together in the bed, sort of a ménage à Beach where sex, dope, talk, booze, and art are consumed, consummated, consecrated, created, and carried over, sometimes separately, sometimes together, into the early hours of the dawn.

Whenever Roach Alley becomes intolerable with too much silence, I walk over to 72 Commercial Street, padding through the streets at night, touching the tops of crates of fruit, smelling bananas from Panama, stopping in the street below the windows and hollering up in the dawndark silence, "McCracken! Bowen! Arthur!" knowing that at least one of the trio will be home painting or balling or just sitting quietly by the stove listening to KJAZ on the radio. A head will pop out one of the windows and the door will open. It's kept locked for security reasons—underage chicks, dope, orgies, etc. When the door opens, I walk up the stairs and sit down in front of the fifty-five-gallon drum cut open in the front that serves as a great and comforting stove. Whenever I walk up the stairs, I get a great feeling of energy, madness, creativity, of color on canvas; the warmth of the loft after the silence and chill of the streets seeming so much like back home in Colton when I used to walk across the park after school and find pots of beans cooking in the stove, the smell warming me, wafting over the park like a spoor that I followed, that clung to my brain, leveling out the hardship of a child's day spent standing in the schoolyard against the fence, alone, thinking of the future.

The scene in my loft is growing quietly insane. I hear hooting laughter and turn around to see Zeke Tollerton fly up the stairs. "Whaaa whaaa haaa!" His great bellowing laughter reverberating through the loft.

"Kid! Gawdamn sonofacoonlickinbitch! Haw are ya?" Zeke stomped across the floor and threw his arms around me.

"Zeke! Jesus, where you been?"

"Whaaa whaaa haaa! I'd take a month t'tell ya an' I oney have an hour! What the fuck's goin' on here?"

Zeke flung off his coat and threw it into a corner. Under his coat he wore a black shirt and black pants tailored down over a size fourteen pair of black boots. His pants were held up by a four-inch-wide belt with an enormous silver buckle. The coat was a tailormade Nazi stormtrooper's overcoat made of black pigskin. Zeke had the coat redone to fit over his six-foot-three-inch frame. On his head he wore a high black Hopi Indian hat. A full black beard flowed down from beneath his high half-Indian, half-Kentucky-mountain-man cheekbones. Zeke and Patrick Cassidy worked the coast together poaching abalone, making illegal runs up to Tomales Bay and heisting the forbidden abs out of the water during heavy fogs.

Zeke was Patrick's third partner, having been recruited out of the Bagel Shop one night after Patrick roared in drunk with his pockets full of money. Patrick had just delivered seventy dozen abalone to Stagnero's on Fisherman's Wharf that afternoon, each dozen worth twelve dollars, and so he whooped into the Bagel Shop and jumped up on the bar tossing twenty-dollar bills around, kicking over sugar urns, dancing with a beautiful young girl, throwing money away like it was made in heaven. That night in the Bagel Shop continued on into the next day, Saturday, the day of the Grant Avenue Street Fair, when thousands of tourists and crazies milled around. Patrick was still drunk, drunker, Zeke and me drunk too, McCracken drinking hard to catch up (he did).

Later in the day Patrick discovered the young chick he'd danced with the night before and so hoisted her up on his shoulders. In his drunkenness he lost his sandals, so he ended up dancing in broken glass until there was blood and wine in the street, yelling, music, and wine bottles in alleys, Tokay Bill standing on the corner laughing, Crazy Alex calm and bemused for once and saying nothing from his corner under Ken's awning, all of us flopping together in a giant pile of drunkenness in the back of Patrick's gypsy wagon, careening among the diving gear, sleeping bags, air tanks, wine bottles, old clothes, rubber mattresses, our mirth and craziness infecting the whole Fair until cops came and we had to split up the street, rushing down Bannam Alley to Union Street, whirling through Varennes Alley and then back down Green Street to Grant Avenue and out on Fresno Alley and gone. Zeke decided at that moment that he wanted to be part of Patrick's craziness, garner some of that poaching money, lift girls up on his shoulders, throw wine bottles at shadows, and burn, burn like a meteor that dazzles everybody as it disappears out of sight.

Patrick had just lost Kell Robertson, his regular running mate, Kell being an old pokealong cowboy who never did like the sea anyway, at least the way it was manifested off the California coast. Together Zeke and Patrick made a mad duo, roaring around North Beach in the gypsy wagon, a '47 Plymouth station wagon with the top cut off. Patrick cut the top off so he could throw his gear in the back without having to waste time opening the door. Whenever they went up the coast, they'd lash a sixteen-foot skiff on the back along with an outboard motor, skindiving gear, and poaching apparatus, fur coats on and hats, great bundles of arms and sleeves and wine and sixpacks of beer, and maybe a chick or two along for comfort if any could be found as they were leaving. If no chicks were immediately available, they'd cruise the streets for half an hour. If they found none, it was tough shit! and off they'd go up the coast, alone with only port wine and bennies and beer for company—and Zeke's incredible whaaa whaaa haaa! roaring laughter trailing the gypsy wagon by four miles.

I had poached abalone for a time, the insane rides up the coast sucking me in with their crazy energy just as they sucked Kell and Zeke in. Tomales Bay is strictly off-limits for abalone, though. The bay is full of commercially farmed oysters and the beds are patrolled by the Fish and Game Department to insure that the oysters don't get pinched. Patrick and I weren't interested in the oysters, however. We wanted the abs that lay ten thousand thick on the bottom of the bay. When the fog moved in, we'd move in too, roaring up the coast highway in the gypsy wagon, stashing the wagon in a grove of redwood trees after plunking the skiff in the water, revving up the old thirty-horse Johnson that Patrick had bolted on the back of the skiff, and putt-putting out on the bay just off the point where the kelp beds yawned and waved over the house-high heaps of abalone.

It was weird out on the bay in the thick fog. The way Patrick dove was strictly illegal also, going down into the water with a set of aqualungs and prying the abs off the rocks with an iron, scooping them into his bag, and signaling me with two jerks on the line to haul them up into the skiff. In an hour or so we could get ten dozen, me dumping as quick as I could and sending the bag back down. If I heard the dut-dut-dut of the Fish and Game patrol boat I'd signal Patrick and we'd haul up quick as shit and make haste for the shore. In the thick fog it was dangerous as hell, but Patrick was insane. He'd pull the throttle back on the outboard and shoot off across the water at thirty knots and naturally the Fish and Game boat puttered along at a safe and sane old man's ten knots, listening wistfully as our pirate skiff slithered away in the fog. "Jack London, goddamnit!" Patrick would cry, and by the time the Fish and Game cops reached shore we'd have our skiff lashed in the back of the gypsy wagon, the abalone stored, the engine revved up, and be off down Highway 1 to a little cut of trees where a network of old logging roads began, pathfinding ditches and arroyos and old cow trails that led across the peninsula to Bolinas, where we'd stop and have coffee, laughing like idiots before making it into the city to sell our abs on Fisherman's Wharf. When I found my loft on Roach Alley, I stopped diving with Patrick.

Since Zeke and Patrick started working together, they'd become inseparable. "Where's Patrick?" I asked.

"Man, don' you know?"

"No. What happened?"

"Shit! Patrick's in the slammer. We got caught with a wagonload of illegal reds in Sanna Cruz. I thought ever'body knew that."

It was news to me. "How'd Patrick get popped?"

"Whaaa whaaa haaa!" Zeke's laughter bounced off the walls. "We were actin' like a coupla gangbusters on the boardwalk. We had sixty dozen reds in the back of the wagon that we was gonna peddle to Stagnero. A coupla tourists ast us if they could take pitchurs of us doin' the unloadin'. Hell, how was we to know they was Fish and Game? They let us unload those abs and the next day they showed up with all these nice eight-by-ten glossies—in color! They had us, man, in stereo. Patrick got a year in the county workhouse."

"Christ, a year in the slammer! Isn't that a little heavy for poaching abalone?"

Zeke squinted his eyes and looked at me, moving his face in close to mine. "Patrick din' get no year in the slammer for poaching abs," he said. "I was standin' right beside him an' all I got was a shitty little old two-bit five hundred dollar fine an' a month in County. Patrick got his year fer callin' the judge a political prostitute."

That was the kind of thing Patrick would do, sacrifice a year of freedom so he could call an asshole an asshole. I laughed with Zeke.

"Judge Franich was all set ta give Patrick the same thing he gave me when Patrick stood up and called him a political prostitute. 'Course, the bastard is, but Patrick shount a' called him that. He talked hisself into the workhouse."

"That fucking Cassidy's prison pent," McCracken yelled. He tucked in his shirt and slapped Zeke on the shoulder. "Who's got the dope?"

"If ain't nobody gonna bring out their stash, it looks like I'll have to unwind some of this Pontchartrain Poontang!" Zeke reached inside his shirt and brought out a silver cigarette box. Inside were ten elegantly rolled joints.

Zeke lit a joint and handed it to me. "Kid, this is reality weed. You put a lil bit of this mota in between these lil ole papers an' roll it up inna lil ole cylinder an' light a match to it and *pow!* You gonna have what they call in the trade a *high!*"

I smiled and handed the joint to McCracken. He toked on it and handed it back to Zeke. Mona smelled the grass and floated across the floor toward us. I toked on the joint again and handed it to her. She sucked on the joint dreamily. It was good grass. My head was already floating pleasantly up around the rooftops.

"I hope Patrick can take the slammer for a year," I said.

"Shit! Patrick can do it standing on his head," Zeke said.

"They'll make him shave his beard. I've never seen Patrick without his beard."

"Patrick ain't gonna shave no beard off. His beard's gonna be three feet long when he gets outta that joint."

"How about visitors? Can he have visitors if he doesn't shave?"

"Who?"

"Patrick, with a beard?"

"What's wrong with Patrick's beard?"

"Huh?"

It was good grass.

Thursday morning Little Joe and I walked up to Hube the Cube's pad to see if he was getting ready for the wedding. Hube the Cube lives on Meth Alley. Meth Alley is really Harwood Alley, but like so much else in this ephemeral world, usage has changed its name among the people on the street. Meth Alley is famous for its parties and for people jumping out of windows and other definite acts. When you turn off Filbert Street and enter Meth Alley, you discover suddenly that your feet are three feet off the ground. "It's a strange feeling," I said.

"It's the vibes," Little Joe said.

"Yeah," I said, sniffing the marijuana smoke drifting in the air. "I can smell the vibes."

Little Joe knocked on the door. I heard a startled rush of activity and then footsteps approaching. "Who is it?" Hube the Cube asked.

"It's me," Little Joe answered. "And the Kid."

"Wait a minute."

While Little Joe and I waited, strange tearing noises came from the other side. "What's he doing?"

"Untaping his door."

I looked at Little Joe.

"He tapes all the cracks," Little Joe explained. "He doesn't want anything to escape."

"Any what?"

"Any of the vibes."

Hube the Cube opened the door a few inches and pulled Little Joe and me inside. "Hurry up," he said, "you're letting too much air in."

Hube the Cube's pad was pitch black, every crack sealed with masking tape. In one corner a small blue lightbulb burned. Five watts. It made everything darker. The room had a mysterious womblike feeling. Cushions and pillows covered the floor. I instinctively hunched over so I wouldn't whack my head on something. After a few minutes my eyes began to adjust.

I sat down on a cushion while Hube the Cube retaped his door. Little Joe rolled a joint and gazed around the pad. The walls were painted black and were covered with hundreds of colored circles, large and small, intersecting and merging into one another. The circles were painted in brown and yellow, giving the effect of spiderwebs moving and undulating on the walls.

"Hube the Cube paints circles," Little Joe said.

"No shit."

"It keeps my mind occupied," Hube the Cube said.

"Which part of your mind?" I said. "The one-tenth or the nine-tenths?"

While we were getting high, Hube the Cube put some koto music on his record player. The knocks, clangs, and whacks lent a mysterious air to the pad. I was reminded of one of Crow's lines: "I want to go back to the womb, I do; any old womb will do; I must have left something behind."

"The wedding's set for Saturday afternoon, Hube," Little Joe said. "You gonna be ready?"

"How about my ounce of crystal? You guys get it yet?"

"Everything's set up," Little Joe said. "The Kid talked to Milton this morning and Milton's gonna score an ounce for you before the wedding."

"I'll try to have it for you by Friday, Hube."

"That's great, Kid. It's been so dry around here that I had to go boost some inhalers from Rossi's Market. You guys wanna share one?"

"No, thanks, Hube," I said. "This weed's fine."

Hube the Cube broke open one of the inhalers and dropped the cotton strip into a cup of tea. "If things don't ease up around here, I'm going to have to make it on up to Petaluma," he said.

Whenever things got tight for Hube the Cube, he

rushed up to Petaluma to score some LayPlenty. Lay-Plenty is a mixture of scratch and Methedrine used by chicken farmers as a stimulant for their chickens so they'll lay more eggs. "It's not what you'd call pure," Hube the Cube said, "but it sure as hell gets you off when there's nothing else around."

Before we left, Hube the Cube said he had something to show us. Little Joe and I followed him out of the back of the pad and up a flight of stairs to the roof. Sitting on the roof was a portable shower, tin, with hundreds of little holes punched in the top. "You guys want to take a sunshower?" Hube the Cube asked.

Hube the Cube stripped off all his clothes and jumped inside the tin shower. The light poking through the holes sprinkled over him, little dapples of sunshine. Hube the Cube rubbed himself furiously under the arms, across his stomach, between his legs, rubbing mightily, like he was actually washing. "It's a great invention," he said. "Sort of like Reich's orgone box, only better. This way I can get all the sunshine I need and not worry about sunstroke."

Little Joe and I looked at one another and walked back down the stairs.

7 Little Joe and I walked down to Washington Square. On sunny afternoons half the winos and poets in North Beach gather in the square to talk and drunk wine. One corner is the unofficial "poets' corner," foreign territory to all the Italian and Chinese grandmothers, who keep their youthful wards out of it; in the corner the poets gather, all clans and parties represented, hunkering together with their winewords and roaches.

Bad Talking Charlie and Bob Seider were passing a bottle and arguing about the artist's soul. They were always arguing about the artist's soul. That, and pussy. Bad Talking Charlie's a black sculptor who competes with Milton in scoring white chicks on the set. Bad Talking Charlie's even better than Milton at scoring white pussy, though, because of his bohemian artist rap. "The only thing that saves the rest of us from Bad Talking Charlie," Crow said after seeing him in action at Vesuvio's, "is his penchant for red-haired chicks. He refuses to fuck any chick who doesn't have red hair."

Bob Seider is a white jazz musician who, in temperament and sensibility, is blacker than Bad Talking Charlie. Bob plays tenor sax and is a veteran of every jazz, dope, lack-of-love, and heart-break-hope scene available in the world of small-club jazz, a sad-eyed, high-foreheaded, beaknosed dude with a wistful look and shy smile who is usually found hunched over his horn in the Coffee Gallery or Jazz Cellar, or alone in Washington Square blowing to the wind. "A man's rap's gotta back up what he is," Bob was saying to Bad Talking Charlie. "When a man's rap is just rap, that ain't where it's at!"

"You gotta remember in the extemporaneous existence in which an artist lives, the lives he gathers around him are just as important as the lives he leaves

72

behind. I mean, so what if I use people, people are here to be used. Artists have always done this—use 'em and lose 'em—it's part of the scene, using up lives like canvas, like marble, hacking images out of stone to leave the memory of what was there . . ."

Bad Talking Charlie got his name from his habit of latching on to a subject and talking it to death. He has a singular talent and an incredible vocabulary. Bob Seider uses slow-motion ammunition in self-defense, raising his heavy-lidded eyes whenever Bad Talking Charlie opens his mouth, peering into him with an I-can-see-through-you-you-fucking-oreo gaze. Bad Talking Charlie feels uncomfortable around Bob because Bob is into the being-black-in-America trip more than he is, and in self-defense always takes the offense.

I nodded to Bob and Bad Talking Charlie. Nobody listened to them. Their dialogue had been going on for years. At every party, every scene occurring on the Beach, Bob and Bad Talking Charlie would be getting it on, their voices a counterpoint to every other conversation.

I sat down beside Dick Moore. Milton and Frankie were lying on the edge of the circle. I nodded to them. Milton nodded back.

"Hube the Cube says he'll be ready," I said to Dick. "We just saw him."

"This wedding's going to be something else," Dick said. "Half of San Francisco's going to be there. I heard about it down at the paper. The society columnist wants to send a photographer."

"Christ, don't let any cameras in," Little Joe said. "Half the dudes on the set are wanted for one thing or another. It'll freak 'em out."

"What's wrong with your head?" I asked Dick. He had a giant bandage swathed around it.

"I got drunk with Crow night before last. We had a hopping contest."

"Who won?"

"Nobody. Crow slipped on a fire hydrant and got a hernia, and I hopped so high my pants leg got caught on a parking meter. I think I fractured my skull."

Dick Moore is the dance critic for the S.F. *Examiner*

and also the World Hopping Champion. One time Dick outhopped 427 army recruits when he was in basic training at Camp Roberts. Each recruit had to hold his left ankle in his right hand and hop until hopefully he was the last one standing. Dick hopped and hopped and hopped until the playing fields of Camp Roberts were littered with recruits. He even outhopped the base Boxing Champion, who had a longstanding reputation as an unbeatable hopper. "Where'd you get your talent?" I asked Dick when he told me the story. He shrugged. "I've always had it." With that—*sproing!*— he took a tremendous leap, straight up. I jumped back. "Do that again." "Sure, there's nothing to it." *Sproing!* Up he went, almost over my head.

While we were talking, Shoeshine Devine walked across the square, squatted on the edge of the circle, pulled a sixpack from his shoeshine box and popped open a can of Coors. At the pop, Phil McKenna, Pavlov-like, levitated up from amongst the park-edge rhododendrons. "Hark!" he cried, careening circleward. "Did not my government-trained tympanic membranes detect the unmistakable tintinnabulation of tapped beer cans?"

"Aha, the professional drinking companion," Shoeshine Devine said, holding a foaming beer can toward Phil's outstretched hand.

"Thank you, me lad," Phil cooed. He squinted dolorously at the can. "What, it's not Rainer Ale! You people can't be serious drinkers."

"Phil sleeps all day in the bushes and rises like a zombie at the pop of a cork or the tinny twang of a beer can." Dick laughed.

"Sleep is just another form of high," Phil hiccupped. Phil's an ex-undercover Hollywood scriptwriter cum alcoholic poet who dwells in various North Beach lofts and winedark doorways. Occasionally he takes a six-month cure at one of the local sanitariums. "One high is as good as another until you find Big Brother." He sipped from the foaming beer can and slipped lawnward.

"Speaking of highs reminds me of the time I was waiting for the man in Lake Pontchartrain," Reb Barker said. Reb's another poet who wears rimless specs and a professional paunch and collects obscure verse from the other poets, all of it ostensibly designed for the ultimate anthology, graffiti-begrimed, to be published in North Beach as *Fux: The New Bible.* "I'd been sitting three days in that swamp and the man musta had the wrong swamp, because there they just don't have no time sense."

Shoeshine Devine broke open the rest of the sixpack and handed it around. D'Artagnan Pig grabbed a can, licked his lips, rolled over, and poured a frilly stream of brew down his gullet. D'Artagnan was just up from Laguna Beach, having driven his '52 Chevy, the Caja Flash, up to San Francisco to be free. He had a sodden W. C. Fields voice, the sibilant ends of his syllables trailing away like foam from an open beer can. He even looked like W. C. Fields, a roly-poly dude with a whiskey nose and a cynical grin.

"People," he said, "I just want to warn you Laguna Beach . . . guys down there ain't human . . . everybody's halfway to being aquatic, they got gills growing outta their cheeks . . . there's one dude down there who deals horse, biggest dude I ever saw . . . he has muscles in his eyelids."

Reb scratched his belly and sighed. "Lake Pontchartrain's built on the mud, man. Mud bubbles up like a nasty sore on a whore's belly. I sat in that swamp for three days. It were awful."

"This dude has muscles in his feces, Kid . . . absolutely the biggest dude I ever saw."

"Reminds me of the time I was doing time in Philly," Bob Seider said. "Had a doctor there, real unethical cat. Used to hook little boys on bennies and then suck their dicks. He had a monkey he call Monkeyshit because that all he do, go around with a turd for a nose and bad habit."

"You just can't trust the professions no more," Phil said.

"He has muscles in his pubic hair, people, pectorals on the pubes."

On the far side of the circle Ed the Junkie took the joint Little Joe offered and spoke: "Over in the Fillmore the heavies cop and carry a balloon around in their mouth in case they're popped. They have a coupla filling stations where you can cop a clean outfit for a dollar. Couple faggots run one, and the other's run by a coupla old-time hustlers. Every five minutes the door opens and five cats walk in wanna use a clean outfit, that way they can shoot up and pay the dime and walk out clean. When an ofay walks in that door, every motherfucker in there gets his back up against the wall. Heh heh, I just raise my sleeve and say, 'Maan, I got tracks here longer than the Southern Pee, you cats can sit back down.' "

"Whatchou motherhumpers doin'?" Kell said.

"Kell baby, sit down!" Shoeshine Devine held up a beer.

"Shit, man, don't mind if I do." Kell stepped gingerly over legs and bodies and squatted down at the edge of the circle. "How ya doin', Kid?" He held out his hand.

"Good, Kell. How you been?"

"Oh, I cain't complain. Got a new woman and a new squaller and a new set of strings fer my gittar. I cain't say I'm steppin' in anybody's shit but my own."

Kell's a pokealong poet who lives on the fringes of North Beach, tumbleweeding it in from Phoenix or Santa Fe or El Paso every six months or so, setting up housekeeping in a cheap room with his at-this-moment wife and present child. He lived in the San Gottardo Hotel at present, with a hotplate, a guitar, and volumes of songs and poetry. His voice is part of every room. In the evening he sits in his room with the door open and plays his guitar, singing in a flat, dry West Texas twang. Kell's one of the few guitar carriers who looks natural carrying his guitar. In fact, Kell looks unnatural when he doesn't have his guitar on his back. That's because he was born with it, or got it early.

When he told about how he started playing guitar, he said, "My stepfather bought me my first guitar from a wandering bum who wanted a drink more than another song. It was scratched and chipped and cracked across the face. He thought it was a great joke but regretted it later when I stopped caring about school, about jobs, about anything but the music which I absorbed from the Grand Ole Opry every Saturday night. One night, whiskey crazy, he smashed the radio against the wall and chased me out of the house. I hid in a rabbit hutch and listened to his screaming till silence came and I knew he had fallen on the bed. The guitar came next, of course. He chopped it to pieces on a stump in front of the house, and although it was a year before I left home, I walked away inside then as he stood with the afternoon sun on his axe and the pieces of my guitar all over the yard. The last time I played for him he wavered on the edge of death, his teeth falling out, his body a frame of skin on bones. He invited the neighbors over. 'Listen to my boy play,' he said."

Kell's a cowboy poet whispering sensitive songs out of the anger and misery and loneliness of backroads America, a country-bred loner who was brooding over steelstringed flatpicked plywood J. C. Penney guitars long before it became fashionable, strumming chords like Jimmie Rodgers and Hank Williams, marrying a succession of women and carrying them around the country with him like blues on his back, fathering girls. "Nothin' but girls, Kid," he says with a grin. "I cain't see havin' anything but chicks around the house."

When I listen to Kell sing, I'm reminded of a certain loneliness, a desperation that seems to well up out of a space too large, too big, yet a space that seems incapable of holding anything. What I hear when Kell sings is his loneliness, a sad, flat Kansas wheatland loneliness that only boys born to those plains know, the sound, a certain sharpness of the wind at night. Kell was born in Kansas and later moved through the grace of long childhood days in the Southwest, a curious part of America, the only real part perhaps, the days remembered with wine and the stepfather who smashed his guitar and curled crusty fists around beer bottles and crushed peanut shells on the bar as he told his stepson of his own past life, a life whose agonies Kell remembers as he remembers the sound of train whistles at night.

Kell picked his guitar and sang of the stepfather who

drank Louisiana hot sauce straight from the bottle and
shot pop bottles off Kell's head for friends on weekends. "I still have scars on my head from flying glass to
prove it," Kell said.

Between sips of beer he strummed his guitar and
sang:

> "Under a watertank in West Texas,
> With a bottle of cheap whiskey
> And a package of damp Camels,
> Watching the lights of El Paso
> Behind a curtain of rain. . . .
> I shared my whiskey with everything."

"Hey, Milton, how much you getting for your shit?"
Doorknob circled the group's edge and sat down. He
flashed a thirteen-going-on-thirty-year-old grin.

"How many miles you got on that sleeping bag,
Doorknob?" Bad Talking Charlie asked.

"Twenty thousand miles." Doorknob smiled. "I'm
leaving for the East Coast tomorrow. Gonna catch a
fast freight, ride the everlovin' rods."

"I bet that sleeping bag could write a book,
Doorknob. You oughtta ask it . . ."

Doorknob is never seen without his bedroll and a
brass doorknob he wears on a chain around his neck.
It's his symbol of distance traveled and a personal door
opener; he's a floating member of that unique club of
American drifters: curve counters and railroad water-
tower watchers.

"I'm just looking for a room with a view,"
Doorknob said quietly.

"You're gonna fit that doorknob into the wrong door
one of these days," Bob Seider said. "You're gonna
walk into a room with a view of another room, and
that room's gonna have a view of another room . . ."

Doorknob edged circleward, smiling, temporarily
sane, stoptimed; took tenderlipped and passed the
sweet jug of rosé wine.

On the edge of the circle Frankie lay, Milton ath-
wart her, his long hand on her breast softly stroking. I
looked away, stricken, the moment gone and me here.

A staring, irate Italian grandmother walked by muttering, head shaking. I got up and walked to the square's edge, stood still a moment, two. Some secret whisper of regret. In my mind I slew Milton, my friend, a thousand Miltons, a Zulu war chieftain and me, alone, spears hefted ... thrusted ... ahhh ... and from forth Frankie's girlsoft womb, softflowering, a child erupts, greypearl softbrown ... a mixture of us both ... the new race ... Toynbee's solution ... a scattering clapplause from the silent park circle ... we both bow, the semen-scented leaves ripple lightly in the dusk. ...

8

Last night Walter brought a girl home to the loft. Or last night a girl brought Walter home to the loft. Walter staggered down Roach Alley at four A.M. and pounded on the door. Four A.M. is Walter's favorite hour. When I opened the door, Walter was sitting on the curb. The girl was standing beside him looking sweetsad in the dark. "Look what I found, Kid," Walter said. "An angel. I found an angel named Cornsilk."

"My name is Lady Blue," Cornsilk said.

"Cornsilk followed me home, Kid. Can I keep her?"

Cornsilk giggled in the darkness and helped me carry Walter upstairs. We dropped him in the tepee and Cornsilk climbed in beside him and stroked his forehead.

"I'm going to marry Cornsilk," Walter said. "She is a visionary wordweaver from Kentucky, and she is also an angel."

"What about your mama angel and three little baby angels in New Mexico?" I said.

"A man has to surround himself with angels," Walter said.

"I'm going to start charging rent for JoJay's tepee," I said. "At a dollar a ball I could pay three months' rent."

"It's the shape," Walter said. "Chicks are fascinated by this symbol."

Walter and Cornsilk tumbled in the tepee for two hours. Finally Walter crawled out on his hands and knees and staggered over to the sink to wash his dick. After drying himself he went over to his tape recorders and started fiddling with the dials. I laughed when I thought of what Frankie once said about Walter. Whenever he's in the loft, Walter has the habit of parading around nude—no matter who is present. When

I brought Frankie over to the loft one afternoon to listen to Walter's tapes, Walter was there with his dick hanging down eleven inches between his legs. "I like his style," Frankie said. "Bell bottom scrotum."

"I got a great idea for a new tape, Kid," Walter said. "I'm going to fuck Cornsilk while she recites her poetry."

"That sounds great, Walter."

"For a crippled waltzer, waltzing in the dust, I know you, Mr. Time," Cornsilk intoned from inside the tepee. "For the foghorn blind that brings us in brings us back to turn us under my Kentucky bosom."

"Cornsilk's from Kentucky," Walter said.

"Where even the grass is blue. Take me through this wound in the woodgrain wind ... where wagons are wheeled in wonder."

"See," Walter said, turning his front-teeth-missing smile to me. "With the sound of us fucking it'll make a great tape."

Cornsilk crawled out of the tepee. She stood up and arranged her clothes: blue hat, blue dress, blue shoes, blue eyes, blue lips. Everything blue except her hair, which was the color of cornsilk. "Blue is my color," Cornsilk said. "It brings out the true me."

"Blue's a nice color," I said. "Especially for a girl from Kentucky."

"Cornsilk wants to read some of her poems at the wedding," Walter said. "I told her about it."

"It will help sanctify the service," Cornsilk said. "Like the ancient Druid ceremonies."

"You better get together with our friend JoJay," I said. "He sanctifies things too."

Dennis the Booster came by to help me stock up on supplies for the wedding. Dennis the Booster is the uncrowned champion booster of North Beach. He can boost the wart off a cop's nose.

JoJay was interested in learning some of Dennis the Booster's techniques. "What is your secret, Dennis?" he asked.

"The important thing is to create a diversion. Always create a diversion and never stand out."

Dennis the Booster doesn't stand out. He's five foot seven, blond, blue eyes, bland, freckled, 100 per cent red-blooded American-kid-on-the-corner stock.

"I don't know if I go along with that one hundred per cent red-blooded American bit," JoJay said.

"It's a figure of speech, JoJay," I said.

"Always act natural," Dennis the Booster continued. "If possible, work in pairs. In some stores it's better to work alone, but usually it's best to work in pairs. That way one person can create a diversion while the other one takes care of business."

"That's the way Indians work," JoJay said. "We create a diversion and then move in for the kill."

"A German named Clausewitz wrote about it many years ago," I said.

"You're too well read, Kid. He must have picked it up from the Indians."

"As a matter of fact, JoJay, I think he did."

"Always wear something natural," Dennis said. "Don't wear any of those kooky costumes like a lot of the kids are wearing nowadays. Except sometimes it's good for the diversionary partner to wear a kooky costume because that creates a good diversion."

"Just like the Indian wars," JoJay said.

"It is a war, JoJay," I said. "Our empty bellies against the supermarkets."

"If you work in pairs, always enter the store separately. It's best to enter through different doors. Don't be seen together and don't nod or recognize one another. However, you don't have to conspicuously avoid one another if your business takes you down the same aisle. If there's a detective working the store, he'll keep his eye on the kook; that's the way they think." Dennis the Booster removed a carton of cigarettes from under his coat and passed it around. "Take a couple of packs. They're courtesty of Safeway."

"It's like the old-time Indians raiding the white man's stores," JoJay said, helping himself to two packages of cigarettes. "Does the store detective carry a repeating rifle?"

"I prefer to think of it in terms of poaching," Dennis

said. "The supermarket's the King's forest and we are lowly poachers forced to slay the King's deer."

"Those are reasonable terms to think of it in," JoJay said. "And if you change the term 'King's forest' to 'Indian lands,' then you will see that your work follows in a long tradition."

"You have a hangup, don't you, JoJay?" Dennis said.

"Only when I come to the big city," JoJay answered.

"What should you wear when you boost?" I asked.

"That depends on what you want to boost. Personally, I like to wear this blue flight jacket for a number of reasons. First, although it's relatively tight-fitting, underneath it is quite bulky. A lot of things can fit under here." Dennis the Booster opened his flight jacket and stuck his left hand under his right armpit.

"Never put anything in your pockets. That's the way an amateur boosts. Conspicuous bulges are dead giveaways and besides, if you're really serious about developing the craft, you'll soon realize that ordinary pockets don't hold much."

"What about unordinary pockets?" I said.

"Extraordinary pockets I like to call them," Dennis said. He removed his flight jacket and held it open. In the back there was a small slit in the lining.

"The whole lining is one large pocket. I've carried up to ten steaks at one time out of Safeway inside this pocket."

"Extraordinary," JoJay said.

Dennis smiled modestly. "When you're boosting, it's easy to walk by a counter and casually pick up a steak and slip it under your arm. The movement must be quick; hesitation at the counter might draw undue attention to you, especially if you don't look like a regular shopper."

Dennis stood up and demonstrated his trick with a book. He walked across the floor to my bookshelf and casually removed two or three books from the shelf. In a trice, without JoJay or I seeing, he had the books under his jacket and continued walking.

"Once you have the steaks under your arm, it's nothing to slip them around to the lining pocket. You can bend over to look at an object on a lower shelf and simply slide the steaks around. It's quite easy."

"You do it very well," JoJay said.

"A craftsman takes pride in his work," Dennis the Booster said. "If you're not going to boost many items, sometimes it's best just to leave the objects under your arm, always maintaining a freedom of movement so you don't appear suspicious." Dennis walked around the loft with a large book under his arm, swinging his arm back and forth as he walked. It looked very natural.

"One of my important rules is to always make a small purchase and go through the checkout line. That way you have justification for being in the store."

"You palefaces are smart," JoJay said. "An Indian could never learn these things."

"That's why the Indians are on the reservations," Dennis the Booster said. "They don't know how to steal properly."

JoJay elected to be the diversionary tactician. He went into his tepee to put on his diversionary outfit. When he came out, he was a new man.

"This is my costume," he said.

"It's not the vision I had," Dennis the Booster said.

"Do you think it will work?" I said.

"I could add a few bells," JoJay said.

JoJay was covered with feathers from head to foot. He had eagle feathers tied to his knees, his ankles, his belt, and his arms, and a feather headdress that trailed down his back to the floor. When he extended his arms, they looked like large eagle wings.

"These are sacred feathers," JoJay explained. "When I wear them, nothing can go wrong."

"Perhaps a few bells would add something," Dennis said.

JoJay got some bells from his tepee and tied them around his ankles. When he walked, he rang.

"It gives quite an effect," Dennis said.

"Do you think it will create a diversion?" JoJay asked.

"Yes," I said. "I think it will create a diversion."

JoJay, Dennis the Booster, and I walked down

Columbus Avenue toward Safeway. While we walked, Dennis the Booster instructed us further in his art.

"In a sense my art is the art of survival. It's a matter of finding out where the enemy keeps his stores, choosing the ones you need, and, wham! taking them. I always make it a policy of staying away from the small specialty items. Concentrate on things that are essential to your needs and that invite the least possibility of retaliation in case you're caught. For instance, if you boost a three-dollar can of escargots and are caught, you might have a hard time explaining to the manager of the store that you took it to feed your starving children."

"My children were raised on escargots," JoJay said. "Escargots have always been a necessary part of their diet."

"Keep him away from the escargots, will you, Kid?" Dennis the Booster said.

JoJay was already creating a diversion. Three Chinese kids followed us down Columbus Avenue. Each step JoJay took jingled.

"When boosting for parties, I like to concentrate on the meat department," Dennis the Booster said. "Meat falls into the legitimate food category and it's usually too expensive to buy. It has the further advantage of being a good excuse item if you're caught. You can always bring up the starving kid bit."

"How do you explain ten steaks?" I said.

"He has lots of kids," JoJay offered.

"Everybody eats meat," Dennis said. "It's one of the best things to boost."

"I like meat," JoJay said. "I want you guys to boost some buffalo steaks for me."

"That might be possible, JoJay. Safeway sells buffalo steaks. They buy them from a ranch in Montana."

"Wait'll I tell my cousin Tell Me Good Morning," JoJay said. "An Indian stealing buffalo from the white man."

When we reached the Tic Toc Drive-in across the street from Safeway, we stopped to reconnoiter. Six Chinese children sat down on the bench opposite us.

"Maybe they think it's Chinese New Year," Dennis the Booster said.

"It's going to be a good diversion," I said.

JoJay shook his feathers at the kids. They laughed and ducked their heads under the table.

"You go in first, JoJay," Dennis said. "The Kid can enter through the opposite door and I'll follow."

"You want me to do anything in particular?" JoJay said.

"Use your imagination. I'm sure anything you do will divert them."

"Maybe I'll do my rain dance. That's always a good diversion."

"That's a good idea, JoJay. Just don't dance by the escargots."

"Or I could do my buffalo dance. That one would do good with the buffalo steaks."

"You better do a plain old cow dance, because that's probably all you'll get," I said.

"Only old women do the cow dance," JoJay said. "What are you trying to do, insult an Indian?"

"It's time to go. You first, JoJay," Dennis said.

"EEEEEYYYAAAAAaaaahhoooooo!" JoJay cried.

"My god, what's that?" I said.

"A war cry. Don't you white men know anything?"

JoJay walked toward the east entrance of Safeway and I walked toward the west entrance. As I entered the store, I saw nine kids trailing JoJay. News of the crazy Indian had spread to the housing project down the street from Safeway and kids were running across the lot toward the store. As I pushed through the turnstile, Dennis brushed past me. "Maybe Safeway will hire him to give away balloons," he said as he walked by.

JoJay pushed through the turnstile at the opposite end of the store and stood in the area between the checkout stands and the food racks ringing his bells. A herd of wide-eyed kids surrounded him. Customers and clerks gawked as he whirled and thumped on his heels. The kids laughed and turned with JoJay, enjoying the performance.

While JoJay was diverting, I walked down the aisle

to the cheese display rack and casually grabbed two large Goudas off the shelf. I slipped one under my belt in back and the second one under my arm. I walked down and around the aisle toward the meat rack. I saw Dennis nonchalantly picking up his steaks, calmly examining the packages as he moved down the aisle. I adjusted the cheese under my arm and walked over to the wine counter and grabbed a small bottle of Cribari wine. Dennis was still standing at the meat counter. I walked to the front of the store with the bottle of wine in my hand just as JoJay wheeled down the aisle toward me followed by the laughing kids. One of the kids accidentally brushed against a display pyramid of coffee cans and the stack tumbled over, bouncing cans across the floor. JoJay and the kids wheeled past and I saw Dennis walk over to the checkout stand with his purchases. He had half a pound of hamburger and a jar of mustard in his hands.

When I reached the checkout stand, I felt nervous. The cheese felt huge underneath my belt. I was sure it bulged suspiciously large. The clerk rang up my wine and I gave her a dollar. "Anything else?"

"That's all."

She gave me my change and stared at JoJay as he wheeled around the corner and started back up toward the cash registers.

"Quite a gimmick," I said. "Safeway's really getting far out."

"It must be one of those beatniks," the clerk said. "They come in here looking like wild Indians."

"He does look like an Indian."

"They're all phonies. He probably gets an allowance from home."

"Yeah, I know. He was probably raised on escargots."

I walked out of Safeway and crossed the street to the drive-in. Dennis was waiting.

"How'd you do?"

"I broke my old record. I got twelve steaks and a fat slice of ham."

"I got two cheeses. I was nervous as hell."

"Shit, I could have walked out of there with a shopping cart full of food. JoJay's a gas."

We waited for JoJay. In a few moments he came out of the store followed by a gang of kids. "Go on, shoo!" he shouted when he reached our table.

"How'd things go, JoJay?"

JoJay shook his feathers and reached under his vest. He held up a small can. "Why didn't you guys tell me escargots were snails?"

9 Walter is preparing for Hube the Cube's and Francesca's wedding. He's on one of his magnificent drunks. I never referred to a Walter drunk as magnificent until Crow enlightened me. He was helping me carry Walter home from Vesuvio's one day. "It's a magnificent drunk," he said.

"What do you mean?"

"Some people get drunk to hide their cares," Crow said. "Others get drunk to forget. Walter, though, gets drunk simply because he drinks more than any other ten people I know, therefore it's a magnificent drunk."

"I'd never thought of it that way before," I said.

Everybody in North Beach is out looking for Walter. "I know he's around someplace," JoJay said. "I saw him this afternoon with Cornsilk."

"He bought a jug of Armagnac," Joselito said. "He said he was warming up for the wedding."

All the rumors are bad and Walter is nowhere to be found. "We have to find him before the police do," I said.

JoJay and I walked over to the Amp Palace and talked to Sandy. "He was here a couple of hours ago," Sandy said, "but he left."

"On his own feet?" I asked.

"Well, he had a chick under each arm."

In the Bagel Shop the same thing. "He ate four garlic sausages and three helpings of potato salad," Mark Green said. "Then he split."

"Which way did he go?"

"Every way."

In the Coffee Gallery Mike Kelly was pissed. "He brings in his own jug, demands a glass, then sits at the bar and guzzles his brandy. That's against the rules. If Leo hadda come in, I'd a had it."

I ran into Little Joe. "Walter's off on one of his

trips," I said. "Mike threw him out of the Coffee Gallery."

"Gee," Little Joe said. "I hope Walter's not eighty-sixed from the Gallery for good."

"Walter's been eighty-sixed from every bar from Klawock, Alaska, to Española, New Mexico, and he still drinks in them."

"He's a credit to the industry," Little Joe said.

Later that evening Cornsilk ran into the loft. She was crying. "What's wrong?" I asked.

"Walter said I was a country illiterate with an intuitive way with words."

"What's wrong with that?"

"I've never had a tutor in my life," Cornsilk said. "The words have always just flowed out."

"Where'd you lose Walter?"

"In Washington Square. He went behind some bushes to pee and I never saw him again."

"I'm surprised he bothered to go behind the bushes."

"There were fifty old Italian ladies chasing him. One of them had an umbrella."

"Oh, boy," I said. "This is a magnificent one."

JoJay found Walter. Walter was pushing Trout Fishing in America Shorty's wheelchair up and down the bocci ball courts at Aquatic Park. Trout Fishing in America Shorty and Walter were both singing selections from Italian operas in the bocci ball courts. Trout Fishing in America Shorty is another magnificent drunk who was named by the writer Richard Brautigan. Trout Fishing in America Shorty doesn't have any legs and he staggers around North Beach in a shiny chromeplated wheelchair.

I had an epiphany once and I saw that Trout Fishing in America was actually the reincarnation of Charlie Chaplin. I was asleep on the grass in Washington Square, and Trout Fishing in America Shorty was drinking wine under the poplar trees not far from me. This was before he lost his legs and was named Trout Fishing in America Shorty by Richard Brautigan. This was when he was named Raul, which was the name his mother had given him, or perhaps his father. Raul was actually Raul Vespartin, and I knew from talking to him in his sober moments that he had been a major in the Loyalist army fighting against Franco in Cordoba, Spain, in 1936. Wounded at the battle of San Martin Bridge, Raul was nursed back to health by a strong peasant woman who lived in the faella of San Geronimo, a woman who had three sons of her own who died in the defense of Madrid. Esperanza took Raul under her more than ample wing and made him well. She called him Raulito, or little Raul. When the Loyalists fell, Raul made his way to Vera Cruz, Mexico, on a cattle boat, and thence over the years to California.

In California Raul worked in the fields as a bracero, content to cleanse his body and mind of the past with the hard honest work of stoop labor. When the crops were picked in one section of the country, Raul would hop a freight train and move to another, going from the date trees in the Coachella Valley to the lettuce and strawberry fields in the Salinas Valley, then over to the San Joaquin Valley for peaches and almonds. The long freight-train rides were soothing to Raul and he began to take longer and longer rides, sometimes passing by the fields altogether, content merely to look out on them from the back of a flatcar of lumber, or pass by them during the night inside a boxcar with other hobos.

Eventually Raul stopped going to the fields altogether and he became a hobo. One day Raul was riding a freight train to Tracy. There is a particularly good jungle there on the outskirts of town, a jungle known to hobos far and wide, and Raul knew that he could stay there for a couple of weeks. The train got accidentally switched in Watsonville, however, and Raul ended up in San Francisco instead. When the railroad car stopped, Raul the Hobo stepped out and found himself standing at the foot of Telegraph Hill looking up at Coit Tower. "That looks like a good place to get drunk," he said, and he bought twenty-nine cents' worth of Valley of the Moon tokay and climbed to the top of Telegraph Hill and got drunk under Coit Tower. When he was sufficiently drunk, Raul the Hobo

staggered over to the observation plaza where the
statue of Christopher Columbus stares down. He stared
down too. That was his first glimpse of North Beach.
He never left.

Raul stopped being a hobo and became a wino in
Washington Square and Grant Avenue doorways. Raul
the Wino. There is an interesting causality in names.
Anyway, I was deliciously asleep on the grass in Washington Square when I suddenly had this urge to wake
up. Just as I did, I saw two policemen leading Raul
away. He stumbled and flapped his arms and flopped
his feet in that inimitable gesture of Charlie Chaplin's.
That's when I noted that Raul was really the reincarnation of Charlie Chaplin, wizened smile and everything, a sad, lonely figure flapping across the park.

Trout Fishing in America Shorty lost his legs in a
strange way. On one of his magnificent drunks he staggered down Davis Street and fell asleep under a produce truck. He didn't wake up until the produce truck
ran over his legs. It was a terrible way to wake up
from a magnificent drunk, but Trout Fishing in America Shorty didn't seem to mind. The city gave him a
shiny new chromeplated wheelchair and he learned to
stagger down Grant Avenue in it. He is very expert.
He even tosses himself in and out of it when he wants
to sleep on the grass. When he gets drunk, Trout Fishing in America Shorty shouts, "I'm only half a man but
I can drink more than you!"

Sometimes I have visions of Trout Fishing in America Shorty lying under that produce truck and having
his other half run over instead of his legs. I see visions
of those legs staggering down Grant Avenue in a shiny
chromeplated wheelchair. The leg half of Trout Fishing
in America Shorty wouldn't be the reincarnation of
Charlie Chaplin, though, because then there would be
no arms to flap or shoulders to shrug in that inimitable
way. I say all this because you never know what distances legless men have traveled.

JoJay carried Walter home from Aquatic Park and
put him to bed in the tepee. Walter knocked the tepee
down but JoJay straightened it up again and secured it

with a rawhide thong from one of the rafters. After Walter fell asleep, I played one of his tapes, the one with JoJay and his brothers chanting and beating their drums and Walter accompanying them on his piano. It was the Taos Pueblo houseblessing song. The music was soothing, reminding me of mesas and river bottoms and far distances. I lay down on my bed and closed my eyes and listened to the music. I heard the echoes of the drums resounding off my white brick wall. In my tiredness the white brick wall became the thousand-foot-high walls of Canyon de Chelly, and I saw the ancient Hopi pictographs painted on the cliffs come alive, the figures moving across the shadows. When the music stopped, I opened my eyes and saw that the day was over.

10 Saturday afternoon Little Joe and I put the finishing touches on the loft. JoJay and his brothers strung rawhide thongs hung with feathers from the top of the tepee to the rafters. Trinidad Archelito tuned his drums while Walter prepared his tape recorders. He was going to record the whole wedding. Every wall was covered with erotic paintings and drawings by McCracken, Bowen, and Arthur—long butcher-paper murals depicting orgies and dancing and sex. "It'll inspire Hube the Cube," McCracken said as he wielded his brush over one particularly pornographic nude. "We got to start this wedding off right." Dennis the Booster spread out the food he'd boosted from Safeway. The loft looked great.

At eight o'clock Little Joe threw open the door. "Yahoo!" he cried. "Let 'em come!"

Francesca immediately ran up the stairs alone and jumped into my arms. "I don't know if I can do it, Kid. Hube the Cube's so crazy!"

"Ah, c'mon, Francesca. Me and Little Joe worked hard on this."

"Do you think it's going to work out?"

"You've got to trust us, baby." Little Joe danced around Francesca. "Everything's going to work out fine."

Francesca ran toward JoJay's tepee, lifted the flap, and disappeared inside. Little Joe pounded me on the back. "Kid, this is absolutely great! This is going to be the greatest wedding in the history of North Beach. Have a snort!"

I grabbed a quick snort of wine and looked around. The loft was filling up, beginning to hum. Dennis the Booster stood beside the table proudly surveying the spread. He'd been bringing in steaks and goodies from Safeway all morning. Lady Joan and Abby had cut the steaks into thin strips and cooked them with rice on the hotplate. The table groaned under the weight of stacks of food and great polished bottles of wine.

Walter had his three tape machines going at once, one recording and the other two booming music throughout the loft. His glass of wine was empty, so I grabbed a jug and filled his glass and mine. Francesca was all right inside the tepee. JoJay held her close, the two of them rocking on Trinidad Archelito's goatskin drum. People were streaming up the stairs, spreading out against the walls and heading for the food table, picking up glasses and filling plates, munching food and loosening up. I heard a crashing barrage downstairs and saw D'Artagnan Pig fly up the stairs. He headed straight for the food table and grabbed a plate, swooping great handfuls of food into it, grabbing a bottle with his other hand and running to a corner. "Keed! Jesus Chriisss, how ya beeeennn?" he cried.

When he worked, D'Artagnan Pig was a bartender. When he wasn't working, he crisscrossed back and forth over America in the Caja Flash, his '52 Chevy. "I'm looking for the perfect bar, Keed; somewhere in America is the perfect bar, and I'm going to find it."

I asked D'Artagnan what were his requirements for the perfect bar. He looked thoughtful. "It's intangible, Kid. It goes beyond the perfect Bloody Mary I had in a bar at six A.M. in Generoso, Idaho, three years ago, and there'll be something more to it than the perfect preswingshift boilermaker a guy used to make for me in Chicago in 'fifty-six. It's something that you can't put into words, a quality, an ambiance, like light and shade."

D'Artagnan Pig is a huge hulking bear of a man with traces of every mahogany bar he's ever leaned against grooved permanently into his stomach, huge hurtling cannonball laughter, and sad eyes that darken whenever he thinks of the incredibly big overblown fuck-ups he's made with his ex-wife and now ex-kid too. He's been gone so long on his perfect bar odyssey that his little son Joaquin doesn't know him any more, a sad stranger appearing out of the night with a can of Rainer Ale in his hand, saying, "H'lo, Serena, my keed, how he . . . ?" peering over her shoulder in the blue TV twilight.

D'Artagnan Pig swallowed his food and slurped down his wine, quickly surveying the loft. Abby walked by in front of him. "Keed, that's femininity with a history behind it." He threw his plate down and rushed after her.

In the back of the loft Dr. Frick Frack and Barney Google were talking. Dr. Frick Frack is North Beach's foremost authority on movies. He spends all his time, when he's not recuperating at Napa State Mental Hospital, at the Times Theater on Stockton Street, three features for ninety-nine cents. Barney is a severe intellectual, wine-ridden, who is the only man I ever met who could recite the first ten pages of *Finnegans Wake* from memory. Dr. Frick Frack had Barney Google by the collar. "Now, Barney, you've got to see this flick, greatest prison flick ever made." Barney nodded sadly and fingered his beard.

Dean Lipton stood beside the food table. Dean is a tall, sad hawkjawed man with finely chiseled lips and dark brooding eyes. His strangely handsome face was later to collapse when an ear operation went wrong. A hospital goof left him with one half of his face sagging down in long lines, lending an air of impenetrable woe to the once handsome face, making Dean hulk around the streets, through alleys, every night making the rounds of the bars and cafes, into the Spaghetti Factory, where he eyed the girls, took quick walks to the men's room, where he paused momentarily in front of the mirror and gazed at himself, wondering what went wrong. Crow called Dean the Overcoat That Walks Like a Man because of the navy blue trenchcoat he always wore, a saggy affair that furled around his legs with the weight of books in every pocket. Dean was a writer who scribbled away every day in his room, and taught classes to budding writers at the library every week. He stood beside the food table with a glass of wine in his hand, surveying the room.

Next to him stood Richard Bloomer, serious and sad-faced. Richard was a Sephardic Jew with a black beard and brooding eyes who walked woeful and un-

understanding around North Beach streets ever since his brother Frank died in San Bruno, the county jail in San Francisco. Frank was the innocent victim of a police roundup in the Swiss American Hotel, incarcerated for being in a house where dope was being used. Frank was a sensitive, quiet man who moped into a corner of his cell and said nothing to nobody, not even his brother who loved him, and willed himself dead. When people in North Beach heard the news, they were stunned. Frank dead? Nobody could believe it, least of all Richard. They were closed to being twin brothers, and ever since Frank died, Richard wandered the streets, sad and unknowable, a poignant reminder of the brother who was gone.

In the back of the loft Crow and Joanie jumped around playing badminton with pieces of french bread. Crow leaped hippityhop toward Joanie in great jouncing jumps, catching the french bread between his teeth. Joanie laughed and skittered out of his way. The whole loft shuddered. Little Joe rushed up with his pipe and stuck it in my face. His "good old Nepalese health food." I sucked on it quickly and handed it to Zeke, who took a long toke. "Gawddamn, Kid, here I am at a highclass function in my four-hundred-fifty-dollar suit, my fifty-dollar shirt, my twenty-five-dollar tie and my two-hundred-dollar handmade boots, and if I step in shit, I'm in trouble. Lookit!" He held up his boot and fingered the sock showing through.

Shoeshine Devine ran up the stairs. "Kid, I was trying to make it with this chick in Gino and Carlo's"— he poked me in the chest—"you know, a nice little English bar type, not a heavy bar scene. Anyway, I realized it wasn't going exactly to be a timespan relationship, not too permanent in other words, but it did definitely have intensity, really intense if you know what I mean. Anyway, this very Anglo-Saxon-type dude sees me making it with this chick and comes over and cuts in ... definitely Anglo-Saxon, I wouldn't even call him minority. The chick had very pretty hair, you know, pretty wavy black hair ... I let Anglo-Saxon cut in because actually it's hard to talk a chick into going to your room when you don't have a room. After the cat cut in, I said to him in my Marlon Brando voice, 'Well, what are you going to do with the guys after you're done with the girls?' I really let him have it. You know what I mean?"

Zeke Tollerton laughed. "You gotta stay outta those bars, Shoeshine. You'll end up sleepin' in a Third Street mission. The New Bethel Home of Our Saviour and Grace, all colors admitted! I crawled in one the other night when it was rainin' and fell down on the floor. In the mornin' I woke up with a piano thumpin' in my head and my eyes all shot. Couldn't see nothin'! I moaned and closed my eyes but the piano kept talkin'! Up goes my head, thump! against the roof. I was layin' underneath a pew. And I open my eyes and look around—nothin' but gloom. I eased up over the pew and in front of me I see old Granddaddy Bop hammerin' away on 'I'll Meet You in God's Heaven By and By,' so I lower my head back down and commence crawlin' outta there, puttin' my hands out in front of me one at a time, gropin' towards the light which I assume is the door. I'm creepin' up the aisle tryin' to get away unobserved and all of a sudden I see a pair of the biggest flattest widest feet in alla Christendom. I move my eyes slowly up those two beat feet to two of the skinniest blackest legs I ever seen, and when I get to the top of the figure I see it's old Grandmammy Bop sittin' there in a ladderback chair. I change course and am makin' it towards the door still on my hands and knees and I hear after me, 'We Love you, brother. Come back.' "

The loft was jumping. Millie the Flower Lady puffed up the stairs. Millie was a North Beach institution. Four feet high and just about as wide, she trundled around the cafes and streets and bars with her basket of roses and cackling laughter. Millie was never seen without her flowers, a mop-eared figure bundled up in waterfront clothing and workman's boots, hawking her roses and goodwill to tourists and lovers. Behind her Don Graham slipped quietly in the door, nodded to me, and grabbed a Coke from the food table.

Don was a sad, moody orphan from Wisconsin, full

black beard, slow moving, a clerk at the Discovery Bookshop. Don was the unofficial greeter for every new kid off the street; half the denizens of North Beach had been taken in by Don when they first arrived, succored, fed, given two dollars, and told where they could find a cheap room. Don was addicted to Coca-Cola and mahabas, the long black Italian cigarettes, and a cloud of mahaba smoke accompanied him wherever he went. He was also addicted to religion, never going anywhere without half a dozen religious tracts, arcane documents, obscure Bible translations, and theological ruminations sticking out of his saggy corduroy jacket pockets. One time Don ordered a special limited edition of *The Exegesis on Rabbi Cornfeld's Theory of the Jewish Prerogative As Dealt With in the Lately Discovered Papyrus Index Papers, Annotated and Inscribed by Chief Joseph and the Two Hundred Disciples in Sanskrit,* or some such title, in twenty volumes. Don special-ordered ten sets at $120 per. When the books arrived, he unpacked them and quietly started giving them away to his friends. When Fred Roscoe, the owner, got the $1200 bill, he sat behind his desk stunned. "Don," he said, "these books ... what are they? Where are they? What's happening?"

Don puffed sadly on a mahaba, his eyes dark brooding holes. "The paucity of theological involvement on the part of the essentially religious kids around here is directly proportionate to their ignorance and lack of availability of appropriate material," he said. "I just thought I'd order some background."

Fred fired Don but hired him back the following week. Fred was always firing and hiring Don. Aside from his propensity for special-ordering his own arcane selections, Don also was a self-appointed censor, blatantly slipping volumes of dirty limericks and sexploitation books off the shelves and into the trashcan, much to Fred's dismay. The Discovery Bookshop was a battleground between Don and Fred, the one racing around looking behind shelves and display racks for the books Don had censored, the other quietly slipping what he considered "bad literature" into the debris box next door in Adler Alley.

At nine o'clock sharp Pierre walked in. Pierre is cool and concerned, ready to perform a regular mission-type beat regalia ceremony with ecclesiastical overtones. He's an Episcopalian leaning toward street preaching. In fact, his Bread and Wine Mission up on the corner of Grant and Greenwich is full every night with a similar scene as the wedding, only not as intense, where freeloaders and out-of-work poets fall by to gobble up the free spaghetti and wine, read books and talk talk talk into the early hours of dawn. Pierre handles it all with a cool aplomb, talking, listening, analyzing, psychoanalyzing, helping, lending, agreeing, fulfilling, making do, and cleaning up afterwards. It's hard on his wife, Lois, but she mingles and makes coffee, keeping quiet in the background, and like most women really running the practical aspects of the mission from behind Pierre's front-room props. Pierre ran over and whispered, "Kid, is everything set?"

"Everything's cool, Pierre. Hube the Cube'll be here in a few minutes."

"What about the other bunch? Are they ready?"

"Forget about the rest of them. If they don't get here in time, they don't get married."

"That's good, Kid. I like your discipline."

Pierre hustled off to the wine table. He sipped politely for a moment and then filled a glass. "Blood of the lamb," he said softly.

The party was getting wilder. Paddy O'Sullivan, the beat poet, whirled around the room in his cape and feathers. Paddy was a famous character on the Beach, making it up and down the avenues with *Weep Not My Children*, his volume of tenpenny verse under his arm, goosing tourists, reading extemporaneously from streetcorners, Maxwell Bodenheim reincarnated, only crazier, scragglier, with a Van Dyke beard and a plumed cocked hat and a long flowing cape under which he kept, as Shoeshine Devine said, his secret stash of condoms, Sheiks and Trojans, little rubber receptacles in which he saved his sperm for future generations. "We are the new race," Paddy shouted, whirling madly around, his cape and cane scattering revelers. "It is our genes from which the new mutant will issue forth!"

"Better he should keep his genes in his dork and his dork in his jeans if that's what the new race is going to act like," Crow said.

Paddy had an insane intensity. "Crazy for nothing," Walter called him, implying that the kind of craziness Paddy displayed really meant something only when it was crossed with genius. Instead, Paddy was a character, shouting, laughing, guzzling wine, grabbing chicks, pounding on JoJay's tepee like it was a drum, twirling his cane, and dancing around the loft. The noise was deafening.

I walked over to the windows and looked down into Roach Alley. The sounds from the party bounced off the walls of the buildings outside and rebounded inside the loft. People milled around, talked, jumped with excitement. I saw Little Joe and ducked over to his side. "Where's Hube the Cube?"

"I don't know. Haven't you seen him?"

"Oh, Jesus," Little Joe cried. He dashed for the door. "I'm going to make a run up to the Beach. Hold things together until I get back."

I circled the loft. Francesca was in a corner with McCracken. The long food table was packed with people. Dr. Frick Frack and Crazy Alex rummaged among the food. I ran over to the table and grabbed another glass of wine. Everybody was dancing and jumping to Walter's tapes. Trinidad Archelito and Jose were drumming like mad, dancing around their drums as they beat them with insane frenzy. Joselito was wearing JoJay's long feathered headdress, shuffling crazily around the loft, chanting and shouting, "Hoya hoya hoya," moving slowly and steadily in and out of revelers, back and forth from one end of the loft to the other. Dick Moore, the World Hopping Champion, was hopping. Periodically I would see his head and shoulders appear above the crowd, then sink down again like in slow motion. The noise was so loud, it all seemed quiet. More people ran up the stairs and dashed toward the food table. Suddenly someone stumbled and the whole table crashed to the floor. Nobody stopped drinking, they lifted the table upright and straightened glasses and went on with their shouting. I turned to the stairs when I heard Little Joe's laughter. He dashed through the door. "Kid, it's great! Hube the Cube's on his way."

I scanned the room for Francesca and Pierre, the two other main elements for the wedding. JoJay stumbled out of his tepee. The wedding was about to begin and he wanted to be on time for his part. Hube the Cube crept up the stairs. He ducked furtively toward the food table and poured himself a glass of wine. He looked askance at all the people. "Jesus, Kid, you didn't say this."

"It's okay, Hube, they're all your friends."

Hube the Cube shrugged. Francesca was inside JoJay's tepee. Little Joe pulled her out. She stood up and stared at Hube the Cube and burst into tears. Everybody was embarassed. I didn't know what to do. Hube the Cube looked unconcerned. As quickly as Francesca started crying she stopped, then suddenly she moved over beside Hube the Cube and grabbed hold of his hand. Hube the Cube squirmed. Pierre stepped in front of the couple with his book, and the loft went quiet.

"Now, my friends . . ." Pierre looked around the room. Zeke stopped in the middle of a great booming laugh and was still. Francesca stood beside Hube the Cube meekly, demurely holding his hand. Hube the Cube stood motionless, quiet, in a trance. His lips moved with Pierre's. Pierre opened his book and started the wedding ceremony. He read from the Bhagavad Gita. Francesca turned her face to Hube the Cube, a curious soft glow on her lips. Her belly moved under her dress, a soft, silky affair that seemed to have a life of its own, moving and settling around her firm round belly. I smiled and felt like crying. I turned my face away. Pierre murmured the litany and everyone listened. The loft was churchlike, the music soft, JoJay and his brothers tapping softly on their drums, Walter's tapes playing quietly in the background, Jose and Trinidad Archelito chanting. I bowed my head. Francesca's head was down, and when I peeped up to look at the rest of the loft I saw that all the other heads were down too. It was a quiet ceremony that lasted ten minutes. When it was over, Pierre closed the book and leaned over and kissed Francesca and Hube the Cube on the cheek.

"Yaaahooo!" Little Joe cried. He threw his wineglass against the white brick wall. "Yippeee! Whaaa! Hooray!" Other voices jointed in and a hundred wineglasses shuddered against the bricks. I flung my glass too. McCracken's orgy scene was dripping wine-red down the wall.

JoJay blew on his eagle wingbone whistle and danced around the couple, sanctifying the marriage. Jose and Trinidad Archelito beat on their drums. Joselito was too drunk to care; he splattered about in the back of the loft, rolling under the tepee. Cornsilk read her poetry, her voice lilting through the vastness of the room. Walter turned up the volume of his tape recorders and the music roared through the loft. The walls quivered; the bricks cracked. In the middle of it all Milton and Frankie walked up the stairs. I'd been wondering where they were. They'd missed the wedding. Milton immediately ran over and grabbed one of Trinidad Archelito's drums and began beating on it. Frankie settled down on a pillow next to the wall. She looked tired. Everyone was dancing and jumping, blasting weed in the back, drinking wine. McCracken was dancing with Linda, and Bowen was holding Francesca by the hand, maneuvering her toward the rear of the loft. He had one hand under her skirt feeling her belly. Bowen got his kicks running his hands over pregnant bellies. I looked at Francesca and decided I'd like to do it too. She smiled and lay down on the mattress.

Hube the Cube and Carl Eisenger, a poet, were talking in a corner. Hube the Cube was high on his speed, nodding rapidly as Carl talked. He leaned his head sideways in a peculiar way he had and turned his face toward Carl. Carl said, "Yes, yes!" punctuating his talk with stabs of his hand. In the rear of the loft Linda Lovely and Steve were groping. Linda Lovely smiled a beatific smile and curled up in Steve's arms. Abby was dancing with Crow, Jerome Kulek was rapping with Milton, Little Joe and Barney Google were drinking wine. I felt frantic. Arthur sailed past with Jean and waved his hand. "Great party, Kid." I nodded.

In the front of the loft a group of people were sitting in a circle, wineglasses in hand. Phil McQuire, a sketch artist and painter from Big Sur, told a story. It was about the time he was a powderman on a bridge job. He explained how one day he was ordered to blow a big rock that blocked the way. Phil set the powder out, strung the wire, loaded his primer, walked down the path to the plunger, and pushed it down. Poof! The rock exploded, showering the crew with bits and pieces. Inside the large twenty-ton rock was another perfectly round rock, laid bare by the blast. Phil took up the small circular stone that was the size of a base-ball and carried it home.

Somebody handed out a fistful of joints, they started around the circle. Bob Seider pulled his sax out of a beatup old case and started blowing melancholy riffs in accompaniment to Walter's music. Dick Moore's head and shoulders appeared and disappeared above the crowd. Dr. Frick Frack yelled movies, and Barney Google nodded sadly in the dark. Crow was balancing a wineglass on his forehead and dancing around on one leg. Crazy Alex was jabbering to Jay Hoppe, owner of the Bagel Shop, who looked skeptical from one corner. Jay viewed the world with a jaundiced eye. The joints were going around faster and faster and the talk in-creasing. I listened until it got boring, then walked to the back of the loft. Laughter and giggles from Wal-ter's mattress.

I looked for Frankie. She was asleep on her pillow, her head leaning against the wall. I got a blanket and covered her. She moaned softly. Behind me I heard Milton's booming laughter. He was rolling another joint and telling stories. Carl and Hube the Cube were still talking, their thin hands fluttering in the soft light. Hube the Cube's beret nodded up and down as he talked. I sipped from my glass of wine. Tokay Bill, a calm, bemused observer of the general calamity, moved by saying, "Well, well," heading for the wine table. Behind me the party went on. I heard laughter from JoJay's tepee. Linda Lovely and Steve were inside making love. On the other side of the loft Little Joe had a sweet young girl I'd never seen before backed up against the wall. She was smiling at him through tender lips and puffing on a cigarette. McCracken circled too. He had a chick's hand, holding on, leading her around the loft, looking for a place to lie down. I grabbed my coat and headed for the door.

It was quiet outside. I looked up to my loft windows. I heard the party sounds, rippling laughter and clinking glasses, occasional loud laughter from Milton and Zeke. For a moment I wished I was Hube the Cube, married to Francesca for one night so I could take her home and rub my face on her belly. I'd curl up beside her and put my cheek on her rounded belly and feel the life growing inside her, the life I helped make, that maybe was mine. Her belly would murmur under my hand.

I walked toward Grant Avenue. Halfway there I changed my mind and turned back toward the waterfront. Grant Avenue would be too much tonight; I couldn't take it. I walked down to the Embarcadero and stood on the docks listening to the sea. The sea was soft. I looked out across the bay toward Alcatraz. While I stood thus, a ragged man shuddered past like a ghost. I looked after him for a long time. Maybe he was telling me to go.

I walked after the shroud, following him around the Embarcadero. At the corner of Powell and Bay I lost him. I walked down Water Street and peered in a window where I knew a girl. Her window was dark. Water Street was deserted. Across from Ott's Drive-in I paused, the hot smells and bright lights holding me. Suddenly a car flew past. It honked its horn as it rushed by, then turned and rattled back by making a U-turn through a gas station driveway. It was Radical Mike. He screeched the car to a halt in front of me and jumped out. "Kid! Jesus Christ, let's go. The night, it's Saturday night. What you doin'? C'mon!"

I leaped in the car without thinking and immediately we were speeding toward Grant Avenue.

"Kid, I been meaning to tell you, I missed the wedding. It was tonight, wasn't it? Damn! I was coming too. Had my suit all dolled up, special order duds, I got fucked up. Meet this little girl here, Sue her name. Sue, meet the Kid. We're on our way, the Jazz Cellar, you know who's there, and I want to say, Kid, the times are fantastic, yaass, hup hup whaaa!"

With that, Radical Mike thundered down Columbus Avenue to Green Street and whipped left to an illegal stop in front of the Jazz Cellar. We all leaped out, ran down the stairs, and planted ourselves along the bar. Immediately we had three drinks in front of us and Radical Mike was running up to the bandstand to see who was blowing. Bill Wiejon and Max Hartstien were on the stand, Bill on the piano and Max on bass. Pony was blowing alto sax. I slipped into a corner near the bandstand and listened. Radical Mike and Sue were holding hands in front of Max. Radical Mike swayed to the beat and sweat poured off him. Max thumped his bass with a yowling beat that he echoed with his voice, groaning with each lick. Pony was sweating, jumping up and down on the bandstand as he reached down to ground level for a note, lifted it up with his knees, and blasted it out into the crowd with his gut, thump-thumping the blaugh blaugh screech into the smoke-filled crowd. The musicians were swinging and the crowd loved it, blacks and whites blasting back and forth with talk, swaying and singing, chicks and dudes along the bar hunched over as the music bit through the smoke above their heads. It was crazy! Meanwhile, cool Bill played his fingers over the piano like he owned the joint, which he did, and the soft rippling and then harsh disconsolate chords flipped back up under Pony's screeching rages, Max's determined thumps, and the slush slush of a drummer who was content merely to slide his brushes over the lip's rim to keep time.

I felt good. Sue sat down at my side while Radical Mike dug the jazz. I rubbed my hand along her back. She smiled and leaned against me. It was nice. Bob poured more drinks and we leaned together, digging the music. I ordered another round and Bob set it down quick and split to take care of business along the bar. People from the wedding party were streaming down the stairs; obviously the party was drawing to some sort of a close. I leaned into the music and dug what each cat was saying. Yaawheee! the horns cried. I shuddered under the weight of the music, downing my drink and wailing along with it. Pony pointed his sax at me and blasted. I moaned softly and lifted my glass up and leaped off my chair. The whole place was mad, me among them, dancing and jumping while the beat blasted out over the floor. Suddenly it was two A.M. and we were all heading for the door.

"Kid, I'll take you back to your loft," Radical Mike said.

"No, that's all right." I hustled off in the night, high, delirious, running giggling down the street. In Washington Square I stopped under the poplar trees. The statue of Benjamin Franklin stared down at me. "What the fuck's goin' on, Ben?" I cried. Ben said nothing. "Fuck you!" I yelled and ran raggedy-breathed across the square. When I got back to Roach Alley, I staggered up the stairs. The loft was a mess, remnants of the party, wine, paper cups and plates, broken chairs, and glasses. The place was quiet. I felt an ache in my loins. Suddenly I heard a cough come from inside JoJay's tepee. I looked inside. It was Frankie, huddled on the floor. She looked up at me. "Kid, I was wondering where you were."

I knelt down beside her, took her hand. "Frankie, what're you doing here? Where's Milton?"

"I don't know. He left."

Frankie looked small and cold. I grabbed a sheepskin blanket that JoJay kept in the tepee and spread it over her. It was warm and soft. Frankie looked at me.

"I wondered where you were. You've been gone a long time."

"I went for a walk. I didn't know . . ." I looked around for Milton. For some reason I felt he was still in the loft. There was no one else around.

Frankie huddled under the blanket, her eyes poking out from under the sheepskin. She smiled. I smiled back and she reached out her hand and touched my face. I was surprised. I put my hand over her hand and knelt beside her. She rubbed my face softly and I kissed her.

"It was a nice wedding," Frankie said. "I'm glad for Francesca."

"Everything worked out fine," I said.

Frankie put her her hand on my leg. It felt good. "I was waiting for you to come back," she said.

"I didn't think you were going to come here tonight."

"Milton had to meet some people; they were late."

I held Frankie's face between my hands and kissed her. She kissed me back, passionately. I moved my hands up under her skirt, rubbing them over her buttocks. They felt wonderful.

While we lay together, I took off Frankie's clothes. Her body was firm, her breasts like hard plums under my hands. She unbuttoned my pants and held my dick between her fingers. Her hands felt like butterflies.

"I've been so fucked up lately, Kid," she said. "I wish we could talk more."

"Not now, Frankie. We'll talk later."

Frankie pressed herself against me, holding on for dear life. I didn't want to talk, I just wanted to squeeze my body into her.

"I've been acting so crazy lately, insane almost."

"Shhhh, baby, don't say anything. We'll talk tomorrow."

11   When I woke up, Frankie was gone. I searched the loft—nothing. I debated running over to Milton's pad to see if she was there. I decided against it. I'd see her later, after she'd had a chance to rest. It was only eight A.M., so I went back to bed.

Little Joe woke me up at noon. "Wake up, you lazy bastard. I just had the greatest fuck of my life. If I don't tell someone about it, I won't believe it myself. Get up!"

I was dreaming. I was floating in a dreamhaven of rich red cunt, cunt that was comfortable and deep, with the smell of roses and pomegranates. Little Joe kicked my bed again.

"Wake up, Kid. I've got to tell someone."

I opened my eyes. "What's wrong?"

"What's wrong! What's wrong is I've never really fucked in my life until last night! Last night, all night!"

Little Joe paced back and forth at the foot of my bed. He held his hand over his crotch, moaning softly. I sat up. The sun slanted through the windows. "What time is it?"

"Time! Who the fuck cares what time it is? It's time for you to get up! I gotta tell you about this chick. I just met *The Chick,* Kid, you gotta meet her. She was here last night. Goddamn, you did meet her. I introduced her to you before we split. I took her over to my room at the New Riviera. She has arms, legs, thighs. Her ass is . . . magnificent! You should see her poozies. I can't tell—Here, I'll show you the bruises on my body." Little Joe danced around my room holding his crotch. "My prick is so sore I won't be able to use it for a week. It has teeth marks on it, ooohhh!"

I sat up and scratched under my arm. I tried to remember the girl. Shit! There were forty girls at the wedding party. I couldn't think of anyone but Frankie. "Who was she? I can't remember."

"Kid"—Little Joe sat down on the edge of my bed—"throw out every chick you have, every one! Get rid of 'em! Send 'em back to their daddies! I got The Chick! She's so far out it'll take a moon landing just to bring her back into fucking range. She's the greatest motherfucking lay that any man, beast, or dog ever had. If that ain't true, I'll personally cut off my own dick and feed it to the pigeons in Union Square!"

I got out of bed and walked over to the sink. Little Joe danced after me.

"Kid, let me tell you, this ain't no ordinary cunt. This chick's been trained. You know what she told me? She's the daughter of an army officer, a colonel or something, I can't remember. All I remember is her cunt. It's juicy, it's sweet, like ripe persimmons. Her old man was stationed in Japan. She lived with him— the whole family lived in Japan—she was there between the ages of fourteen and seventeen, can you imagine that? The most important years! A young American pussy over there in Japan where all those five-thousand-year-old sex traditions go down. I mean they train girls how to fuck in Japan! Nothing's left to chance. It's the same way they bend those little peewee trees into any shape they want. Those Oriental cats are heavy, man; they're years ahead of us, centuries, life- times! Shit! Have you ever seen pictures of some of those statues they have in India and places like that? They were doing stuff three thousand years ago that we ain't even got around to thinking of doing yet!"

"What are they doing?"

"Aww, c'mon, Kid. Those Oriental cats have sex practices. It's an art with them. American chicks don't know how to fuck, except this one I just met. You ever had an American chick grab your cock? Hell no, you haven't, except maybe some drunk bitch in a bar. In Japan it's different. Over there they come on, man, I know it! I've seen it. Here it's all straight, like your old lady lays down like a log on the bed and you have to build the whole fucking fire. You have to construct the whole fucking palace and then fuck her in it. Why do we have to do that, Kid? Why don't the chicks help build the fire? They act like we're nothing but human dildos, that's why! They haven't been educated in how to make love. This fucking country doesn't teach chicks how to fuck, it's all left to chance. We learn how to fuck in the back seats of Chryslers, you know that! There ain't no school or nothin'. Fuck. The first time I dipped my dick in a chick I had to ask the chick was it in. I couldn't tell. Of course, I have to admit that first chick's cunt was like a small manhole. In Japan the chicks know what they're doing, though. They're taken when they're small tikes and given lessons. Can you beat that? That's what this chick— Melanie, that's her name—told me. I met her right over there in the corner. She heard about the wedding party at Mike's Place and came on up. She was drinking wine and grooving when I met her. You were too fucked up to remember. Melanie's been trained, man. She said she used to sneak off and take lessons; she knew a Japanese girl, they were girl friends. It was a strange relationship anyway, with her family, I mean. Her old man was out at the base all the time. You know how those army families are; I never met one yet that isn't completely fucked up. Melanie had this Japanese girl friend who was being trained. Her mother was seeing to it that she learned how to make love properly so she could please her future husband. That's how the Japanese people are, they know the essential things. Can you imagine, they teach American chicks multiplication when they should be teaching them copulation. That's what I call civilization, man, teaching young chicks how to please their future husbands. Can you imagine that happening here? Shit! The only thing you learn here is what your little sister has between her legs, and to learn that you have to go out behind the garage. This chick Melanie went to classes with her Japanese girl friend, she took lessons. She told her mother she was taking Kabuki lessons or something. You know, Japanese culture. You've got to meet her, man. No, on second thought I want to keep her all to myself. She's an angel, terrific! I can't get over her. Whenever I think about her, I get this tremendous hard-on. I can't stop thinking about her. She almost fucked the end of my dick off. She uses little silk ropes with knots in 'em. Oh, man, I gotta tell you, I'll never be the same. What'll I do? Maybe I should marry her. If I don't, I may be fucked up for the rest of my life, victim of a magic fuck. I'll spend the rest of my life remembering that fuck. Knotted ropes up the asshole. Tell me, Kid, have you ever heard of that? When you come, she pulls it out. Oh, God, it's like your whole insides are coming out. I thought I was going to die. It's like making love while stoned but without the grass. It's better! You can see, taste, feel, smell everything! She has scents in her pussy, aromas, nothing is left to chance. Incense in her pussy. It smells like roses, sandalwood. I've been walking along all morning with my hand on my dick thinking about her. I've got a perpetual hard-on! It won't go away. Kid, you've got to help me reach a decision. If you don't, I may be fucked up for the rest of my life. If I don't marry her, I may spend the rest of my life looking for her. She's like dope, like smack! Once you're on, you don't want off. It's too good, too sweet. It's painful but it's a delicious pain. When I came, I thought I was going to die. I did die! That's what love is: death one fuck at a time."

Little Joe ran over to the window. "Christ, it's getting late. I'm supposed to meet Melanie at Mike's Place. She had to go someplace, had an appointment. Maybe she's preparing her cunt again. It's a ritual with her. Other women spend hours making up their faces and they don't realize that's the wrong end, they should spend their time working on that slit down there. Melanie perfumes it. Each lip is like a petal, perfumed and powdered. Kid, you don't know what I'm talking about. I can see that glazed look in your eyes. You think I've been dreaming. Well, I have been dreaming. The whole night was a motherfucking dream. What is it Lew Welch said? 'The most jaded Persian potentate can't imagine in his most voluptuous dreams what I experience every day!' "

Little Joe turned his face to me. I had never seen him so agitated, so delirious and excited at the same time. I tried to remember the girl he'd introduced me to at the party the night before. If she was as great as Little Joe let on, I wanted in. I started scheming immediately on how to get Melanie. I had my rights. It was my loft, the party was my idea, etc. Little Joe was a sly bastard, though. He knew what I had in mind. He paced back and forth in front of the windows, fingering the streamers from the wedding party. A content yet hungry look filled his eyes, like a dog who'd just copped the biggest, juiciest bone but was worried about the other curs in the neighborhood.

"None of your orgy trips either," he said. "I'm going to protect this girl. She's my own sweet little Melanie and I'm not going to let you and Walter go sniffing around her ass like a bunch of dogs. She's mine! I found her. She was in the corner drinking wine while you were getting fucked up. And anyway, she's meeting me tonight and we're going to cement our relationship."

I laughed and threw a bar of soap at Little Joe. "You can't lock something like that up in a prison. If she knows all you say she knows, you've got to let her out so she can educate the rest of us. You owe it to me especially, as a friend. Besides, how do you know she wants to be locked up in a single relationship?"

"I'm not going to lock her up in a single relationship; I'm just going to keep her away from you guys. Nothin's sacred around you cats. You're as bad as McCracken and Bowen except you're a little more subtle, that's all. You slip in like grease. I bring Melanie up here and before I know it you'll have your dick between her legs and she'll be living in Roach Alley. I've been hungry too long, Kid. I deserve this girl."

Little Joe paced back and forth and then turned. He had a determined look on his face, as if he was about to bare his soul. I sat back on the bed and relaxed, feigning boredom.

"Kid, I've got to tell you, Melanie is a cunt unlike any other cunt I've ever met. I could marry that girl, you know that!"

Seeing Little Joe married would be like seeing the Golden Gate Bridge pick up its trusses and walk across the bay.

"It's the wedding. It's affected a lot of people."

"Maybe that's it. God, I never thought I'd say the word marriage out loud. Jesus, it's horrible seeing those poor bastards plastered down with kids. Do you see them in the park on Sunday? It's like torture, herds of them screaming and bawling like the little monsters they are. That's why those cats work twenty hours a day, to stay away from those kids."

I laughed at Little Joe's vehemence. For some reason I had a picture in my mind of him being one of those guys with five or six screaming brats trailing him across Washington Square. He was the type, I knew. When his Beach days were done, he'd be selling insurance and feeding fifteen mouths and loving every minute of it.

"I know what you're thinking." Little Joe turned his eyes to me. He had a shitty grin on his face. "You think I'd secretly dig being married and having a pack of squallers. Well, maybe you're right." He kicked the bar of soap across the loft. "Shit, let's go to the Gallery. I'll buy you a beer."

Little Joe punched me as we walked downstairs. "You'll dig Melanie, Kid. She's a gas, but I ain't gonna let no one near her until I find out if she's real."

We walked down Pacific Avenue toward Columbus, Little Joe running on about Melanie and his night of extraterrestrial love.

"You know, Kid, what that chick did to me was absolutely educational. I didn't know people did those things. To tell you the truth, I was a little embarrassed. Some of those Oriental chicks take getting used to. You know, after we'd done it a coupla times, I couldn't get it up. You know what she did? She stuck her finger up my ass, and pop! The old soldier stood right up for one more salute. It was fantastic!"

At the corner of Grant and Green we turned up toward the Coffee Gallery. It was about six and the first evening flyers were out, streetcorner fixtures who assumed their posts at this time: old Italian news vendors, Chinese mothers hurrying home from the sweatshops to cook supper, late shoppers with packages under their arms. At Grant and Green, Crazy Alex chewed the wind, weaving a pattern of sound to the passing crowd. Nobody stopped; nobody listened. I handed Alex a quarter as we walked by. Little Joe rapped on.

"You know, Kid, I don't see how doctors can get hard-ons after inspecting cunts all day. I mean, when you really get down and look into one of those things, it loses all its mystery. I got right down there, Kid, and opened that damn thing up; it opens like a flower, each little petal. You know how a rose opens up one petal after the other, little drops of dew hanging on each lip? That's the way Melanie's cunt is. It smells sweet too, just like a rose. That's the incense she puts in it. Can you beat that, Kid, putting incense in her cunt! After I balled her, her cunt smelled sweeter than before. I fucked her real good right before I inspected it. After we balled, we were talking and I had this sudden urge to really inspect a chick's cunt. They're beautiful, but at the same time they're kinda ugly, you know what I mean? A little horrible like kinda, but at the same time sweet and necessary as hell, I'll tell you that. You know, if they didn't have all that hair down there, it'd be weird, that slit. Have you ever seen a chick's pussy without any hair on it?" Little Joe grabbed my arm.

"Seriously, Kid, have you ever really inspected a chick's cunt? Max told me that Bowen shaved a chick's cunt once before he balled her, that's the type of thing he does to get it up. Max says a regular cunt can't give Bowen a hard-on any more. He's had so many of 'em he has to shave 'em and put whipped cream in 'em and stuff like that. You know what else Max told me? He said once when Bowen was driving up from L.A., Skippy, that chick he was going with at the time, sucked his cock for four hundred miles. Through all those towns, hee hee, can you imagine that? Old Bowen, you gotta hand it to that bastard. I can just see him sailing through San Luis Obispo and Salinas cool as hell, pulling up at a stoplight, sitting back, and Skippy sucking away on that little two-bit dick of his. I gotta admit, though, Bowen uses what he's got. He's weird, though. I think he's perverted. You know, one time when we were both making it with a chick up at

Tahiti's place, he grabbed my balls. I had her on the
bed and Bowen was sucking her tits or something and
that bastard grabbed my balls and squeezed. I thought
it was an accident at the time, but now I don't know. I
think he digs that AC-DC trip. You can never tell
with a lot of those fruits, man; they slip in on you."

Inside the Gallery Little Joe continued. He was
wound up like a spring, he couldn't stop talking about
cunt: Bowen's cunts, Max's cunts, the cunts he'd seen
on the street last week, the cunt he hoped to crawl inside of tonight. I ordered beer.

"How's Frankie, Kid? She's pretty hung up on old
Milton, ain't she? I picked up on that first time I saw
her. Well, you gotta expect it. There's lots of emanci-
pated chicks hanging around who want a taste of that
black meat. You gotta wait it out. Besides, you know
the stories going around—every chick's gotta find out
for herself if black dick's any better than white dick.
You can't blame 'em. Shit. I'd fuck Frankie in a
minute if she'd open up but she's one chick on the set
that don't peddle it on the corner."

Little Joe ordered a beer and surveyed the chicks at
the bar. He nudged me and pointed at one of the girls,
a big bleached blonde with protruding teeth.

"See that broad there? Look at her lips, see how big
they are? Ten to one her cunt's the same size as her
mouth. They say that's the way it is. A chick's mouth
is shaped just like her cunt. If a chick has real big lips,
she'll have big lips on her cunt; if she has one of those
little grandmother mouths, then she'll have tight little
lips on her pussy."

Little Joe swallowed his beer and laughed. "That's a
strange relationship, ain't it, Kid? That must mean the
mouth and the cunt were made for each other." He
leered at me. "Do you remember when you ate your
first pussy? Were you scared? Hee hee, I thought it was
going to bite back. Or else pee on me. Some chicks like
that, you know, they dig being peed on. I had a chick
like that once, she said it turned her on. Weird, huh?
Well, it takes all kinds. I dunno, if somebody pissed on
me, I prolly wouldn't be able to get a hard-on. Melanie, though, now that chick, just thinking about her

turns me on. I got a hard-on right now like ten dollars' worth of jawbreakers. Melanie's the sweetest little twat in the world, an educated pussy. She can do things with that crack that most chicks can't even imagine doing with their tongues, mouths, hands, and assholes all together. It just goes to show you, Kid. What if you get married before you experiment around? Shit, a guy can die without ever realizing what's possible. I bet that's why all those Montgomery Street freaks go to those pornographic movies and buy all that paper pussy shit. They never see any of the real stuff. Listen, did I tell you? The other day I was walking down Columbus Avenue, you know, in front of Discovery Bookshop. I saw this beautiful blond chick, and man, I mean beautiful. She was sitting up like a nigger in this white El Dorado next to this cat. He prolly had his finger four inches up her snatch, they were sitting that close. She was looking at a magazine. I saw it. She had this pornographic picture book spread out in her lap. It showed a chick with straps and belts and whatever around her crotch. Her legs were wide open, man. Her snatch stuck out like a Fuller brush and she was stuffing a Coke bottle or banana up it or something. That's weird, huh? A beautiful blond in a Cadillac. Maybe the dude gave her the mag to turn her on; some people need that, you know. They have to have pictures to get inspired. They can't get it up otherwise. I think this country's perverted, you know that, Kid? I can't understand why they don't take off their clothes and see the real thing. I can't understand it. No imagination, that's why. Me? I live with those pictures in my head all the time. I don't need to pay no fucking four dollars to get a hard-on."

Little Joe tipped his beer and slid the mug across the bar toward Mike. *"Dos mas,* Mike." He eyed the big blonde who was sitting at the bar, leering sensually at her. He stuck out his lower lip in a particularly disgusting way he had and drooled. "Man, I bet she has a pussy you could stick your head in. Look at that mouth! I bet you could drive a Mack truck up that chick's snatch and unload four tons of tomatoes."

Little Joe grabbed the refill Mike planted before him

and downed it. "They're all too easy, though, that's the trouble. There ain't no sport in it. It's like chasing a streetcar. You know it's gonna stop at the next corner." Little Joe laughed. "That's why I like Melanie, she's different. She's something special. There ain't never been a chick like Melanie on the Beach before, I can tell you that. I wonder how long it's going to take to spoil her, turn her into a cow just like all the rest."

"There's a high mortality rate here," I said.

"You ain't shittin' there's a high mortality rate! Man, these kids come in from every little streetcorner in America and bam! They don't even know how to brush their teeth. It's terrible! Sometimes I think I'm contributing to it."

Little Joe paused and looked down at his beer. His tongue flecked softly out, licking his lips. I raised my beer and signaled for another one from Mike.

"Cats can handle it better than chicks, you know that, Kid? Chicks seem to be more vulnerable. They swing like they can handle it, but underneath, you know what I think? What they really want is that family scene with a house and kids and all that ordinary crap this country paints big pictures of. On the outside a lot of the chicks that drop onto the set say, 'Fuck me, fuck me,' but on the inside they're saying, 'Love me, love me. Carry me home and build a little nest for me.' You know, Kid, the other day I was pounding away on old Suzy, that chick Max's been fucking lately. I looked into her eyes. It was accidental, you know, and man, what I saw frightened the shit out of me. I saw hysteria! And, baby, you know there ain't a harder chick on the set than old Suzy Sheetmetal. Shit, she drinks like the cats, smokes dope like the cats, but when I looked into her eyes I saw hysteria! I jumped off that chick and split! I didn't even wash my cock, which is a cardinal rule with me every since little Janie gave me that dose. Suzy didn't know what happened. I saw truth in that chick's eyes, baby, and that truth spelled hysteria!"

Little Joe shook his head. "It's too much. Sometimes I feel like splitting the set, making it down to Big Sur or someplace; I feel like getting out of this jungle. I want to rest up by the seashore. The only trouble is it's probably the same thing down there, a lot of hungry people looking for a piece of flesh to hang on to."

I nodded helplessly. While Little Joe talked, an image entered my mind, the image of a tremendous machine on which we were all captives. We were trapped on a perpetual-motion treadmill that churned and clattered and tumbled human beings around in relentless circles, a treadmill of hopelessness and regret from which no one escaped. We were all locked on the flapping, rumbling mat that led us inexorably onward toward ... What? Surely, I thought, the feet on the treadmill must know what they are seeking.

I felt myself and everyone I knew trapped, desperate for a way out, for a bit of flesh to hold on to, a hand to touch, the warmth of another body. Everyone was afraid. They were searching, and when they found what they were looking for they were unsure. And so they tested, questioned, judged. I felt dizzy and leaned against the bar. Little Joe's jaw was still moving. I hunched over the bar and saw Milton and Frankie struggling. I saw Frankie's lips on Milton's lips. I cried out but the lips slipped away. Other lips slipped away too, mouths passed, arms and legs passed, people passed in one long, surging, droning, despairing blur.

I slipped off my barstool and stepped outside. It was evening; the streets were humming and the smell of wine and garbage reeked from the gutters. I reeled against the building and then staggered across Grant Avenue. Crazy Alex was jabbering on his corner, his hands weaving in the air, constructing huge buildings, suprabuildings in the dusk.

I climbed the stairs to Coit Tower, each step an infinity of distance. Above me the tower gleamed, its white sides brilliant in the spotlights illuminating its surface. The trees below were silhouetted, weaving and trembling in the breeze that swept in from the bay. When I reached the road that led around Telegraph Hill, I crossed it and jumped up on the stone wall. I edged along the wall for a few feet and then crawled under the bushes at the base of the tower. It was dark there. I felt suddenly guilty, as if I were a transgressor,

my presence off the beaten path making me suspect, a
fugitive from the tourists who climbed the road around
the hill and stood on the observation plaza and looked
down at the city. I listened. How many times had
Laury sat here under the bushes with his eyes closed,
listening? "The fog has its own sound; if you sit very
still and concentrate you'll hear it."

The fog moved among the bushes and trees. Its
silent hum accentuated the sound of my own blood
thundering through my body. Above the sound of the
fog, the din of the city, quiet at first, almost inaudible,
grew in intensity until it reached a deep, sensuous roar.
Below me, running like an artery through San Francisco, was Grant Avenue. I saw the lives of all my
friends spread out along the avenue, from Market
Street on up to Telegraph Hill and beyond, down the
north slope toward the Embarcadero, where the street
ended in a cul-de-sac above the bay, a cul-de-sac that
somehow signified the lives of all the freaks and beats
and hipsters on the avenue. I saw Little Joe and his
hapless cunts, Bowen and Crazy Alex, Dr. Frick Frack
and Bad Talking Charlie and Jay Hoppe and Paddy
O'Sullivan and Bob Seider and Frankie and Milton and
Hube the Cube and Walter and Doorknob and Shoeshine Devine and Don Graham on the avenue, rest-
lessly pushing forward, one more step. I saw Dean Lipton and Arthur and McCracken and Francesca on the
avenue, pushing and shoving with Jerome Kulek and
Zeke, D'Artagnan Pig and Dick Moore, the World
Hopping Champion, restless souls trundling forward in
lockstep, creating the real history of North Beach San
Francisco. The history of North Beach San Francisco
cannot be written in monosyllables or in English! The
real history is unique; it can only be recorded in the
language spoken here, a rhyming slang that's a cross
between a death rattle and the cry at orgasm time! Between those two parentheses the history is complete.

When I walk through the streets of North Beach, the
language comes back to me; old ghosts walk; it is
Vico's history repeating itself. The circles grow smaller
and smaller. Inside the last small circle is the true language I am searching for—the language of love. I see

Bob Seider with his ancient sax. No man can carry that instrument as long as he has carried it! I hear its wail along the avenue and see Bob's beaklike profile exposed to the elements and I realize that no one is spared. It is a face that has lived and died on all the streets, clear back to the 1950s, roamed every city, been stuck in Albany teaching Egyptian mathematics, and now owns this place on the alley where he talks with Gurdjieff and understands the system as he knows it. Bob walks alone except for those who remember. I sit and listen to his music. Who has ears? What do you hear? It is a bleak wind that blows down this street, and none of us knew so many would go mad. When I walk the streets at night I am an invisible shadow who knows.

Do you know why Dean's face fell? What gravity pulled that flesh down to that depth? Have you followed Dean down Third Street, waited with him for the number 15 bus at three in the morning, ridden down to Market Street to that old hotel? What stories could he write if he would write? What lonelinesses? You know nothing of despair until your face falls and words don't come. The Overcoat That Walks Like a Man, Crow called him. Yes. The Spy Who Doesn't Have Sense Enough to Come in Out of the Cold. Yes. Have you ever made love? Have you watched a girl as she rises, pulls off her clothes? Is that a ritual? Who fingers the window when it rains? Every pane displays an earthly haiku. Have you read them? When I followed Dean down Third Street to Market, on to that decrepit hotel, do you know what eons we traveled? Years and centuries passed in blocks—time meaningless, no one's there when we get home—and is that no small portion of regret? How many times have you returned to that room? The bathroom's down the hall, there's a path worn in the carpet. I hear his feet, see his shattered face, harbinger of every countenance: Richard Bloomer's and Frank's, who wailed death on Filbert Street and died in a cell in San Bruno of a broken heart. Who sings his Kaddish? What words do you remember?

I am on a voyage of regret that encompasses every latitude. All the storefronts are rented. You came too late. Nobody wants your products. It isn't sold here any more. There's no use for it. It's all over; you can't even buy the paper to write it down. They give free bread at the Italian-French Bakery on Grant Avenue if you ask for it. Mike's Place is open until three in the morning. It's warm in winter. There's a restaurant in Chinatown where you can buy a bowl of rice and a pork bun for twenty cents. Mr. Hum is his name, heaven his destination!

I am a recorder and nothing else. I offer no truths, only consequences. Anyone can walk these streets. I've been wandering a long time and my tape recorder is full. I have listened to every sewing machine in every sweatshop on Grant Avenue. It is a language of need. Your streets are not my streets. We sit at the same table, but your table is different from mine. I offer no excuses. The food is caked in the cracks of our table and sends up its own sweetsour aroma. With what magic did your parents bear you? Where is your place on the curb? Do you put a napkin in your saucer, under your coffee cup, the sure sign of a cafeteria sitter? Have you ever sat at the window and watched all those interesting aspects? Did you ever marvel in those days? Did it tug at your heartstrings almost when you saw those tables with chairs where you could sit down and look out at the sidewalk? I am trying to describe the simple sequence of a man—he is born, he grows up, he gets old and dies. Is it magic that makes me remember that gesture, the sequence you forgot? How can any movement be unimportant?

Remember that day in the park? Laury said, "I came up to you because you looked happy, you looked like a man who had solved most of his problems." The hand is raised, a child's gesture. A piece of sour rye bread. The unbelievable ecstasy of a child. Remembrance of things past. I walk the streets and the sound of that truck is still there, soft and sweet, heard over a long distance. Was that an epiphany? Was that what Joyce meant? The sound brings back universes, and when galaxies explode I hear the clatter of that scavenger truck and the wooden windchimes in Chinatown. It's the little things, like windchimes at night and arms

and legs from high bridges. Time is suspended like a
star and every face is lifted, every face foreshadowed,
every face assumes the quality of outright distance.
There are so many questions to be answered.

Are we travelers in the same stream? Do the gar-
bage-picking historians scoop up our debris with their
long poles and deftly toss it into their dugouts, fanning
the history in that deep blue water that sails so imperi-
ously past this sad continent? Histories that are as in-
transigent as worn-out electric lightbulbs? There are so
many histories floating in that stream; that wail you
hear is the child in the stream! the junkie in the
stream! the madman in the stream! the most likely to
succeed in the stream! Captain America in the stream!
the top ten in the stream! the most popular boy on the
block in the stream! I am floating down the stream and
the seafloor comes up to meet me—I am a victim of
shattering glass and toppling masonry—the cadence is
older than time; it encompasses all time. As we sink,
the palm fronds of our victories wave in the magnified
shadows of the lampposts. Grant Avenue is the same;
only the name has been changed to protest the innocent!

When I walk through the streets of San Francisco,
I look about me; the image is there for my eyes. It is
heartrending. I am a tracer of these corners. I have
stood on every one. The magic is a magic of numbers,
numbers enclosed in years, in lives and lives aborted.
As I walk, I try to picture who I am, what chronicle I
keep. It is *The Journal of Anxiety's Child*. It is *the*
book! And when I walk down Grant Avenue and see
the loungers outside the Co-Existence Bagel Shop, I do
not see loungers, I see poets and philosophers and children of the new age. And when I walk past the Amp
Palace and see Hube the Cube and Monte and Little
Joe and Joe DeLucca and Ella and Paddy O'Sullivan, I
do not see these people, I see mythological creatures
from another time, from another epoch really, biding
time, creating out of time a new solstice that will be
both the first and last day of winter. When I walk
down these streets and cross Washington Square, I am
transfixed by the pathos and beauty of the event, the

magicalness of the hour, the incredible surrealistic ecstasy of the moment. Time is surely a stream, and that voyage begun decades ago continues, recorded here, plagiarized and copied, imprinted and embedded, Xeroxed and stamped into each vortex of my brain. It is the image of a time and America I know nothing of; it is *my* America, timewracked and weary, straddling a fault that runs compass-perfect down to the deepest reaches of the human heart. How many of us have tried to pin her down? How many of us have hung our specimens on the wall and stood back, gazing transfixed? And when I write this down, I think, Is my America your America? Do you walk these same streets? You were beside me; did you see what I saw? Where were you when I walked across the park? Did you spend your afternoons at the Colton Public Library? Did you listen to what Crazy Alex said at his corner table? Is your alley my alley? What graffiti did you read as a child? I want to know that poetry.

I am trying to recreate the sounds of my childhood. I am trying to inscribe upon the head of a pin the entire history of a unique race—a race unique because it is so maligned, so egalitarian, so democratic, so perverse, so unimaginable that the pin itself must be withdrawn from the heart, the blood wiped off, the surface burnished, cleansed with a thousand incredible romances, a million walks, countless heartbreaks, recollections, and regrets. I am trying to describe the history of something I knew, make tangible a race, an idea conceived extraterrestrially, on the moon, in the farthest reaches of space! I am trying to set down the first blueprints for the age of rebellion, that heartless, unregenerative task of making memory ring true. When I look out of my Roach Alley windows I see the entire history of my race inscribed on the head of a pin. The pin is a point. The point is embedded in my veins, the veins of my childhood. What I see is the sweeping arc of a bridge, a city that doesn't exist, a race of men monstrous in their duplicity, a girl suspended like time between bridge and water.

I shivered among the bushes and listened: the traffic below me, cars on Columbus Avenue, and trucks thundering along the Embarcadero; the Beltline Railroad switching cars, making trains as they shunted flats and empties in and out of the barnlike piers; out on the bay the boats, mournful foghorns bleating like lost animals searching for their mates. The foghorn on the Golden Gate Bridge vented its roar, deep and moving like the mad bellow of a giant ship at sea. I thought of the city as a vast instrument, a million-stringed harp, and every soul living in the city as one of the strings, each being and baby and body part of the music and blood and song.

For a long time I shivered in the darkness, the warmth of the city protecting me from the damp ground and wispy fingers of fog that filtered through the trees. I lay on the ground listening, opening every pore of my being to the sounds and rhythms and roar of the life below me. When my body was completely filled, it seemed as if I was floating, still, quiet, a lone vapor borne upward over the wind and fog and darkness.

As I rose above the city, it seemed that the countless billions of antlike feet turning the cogs and wheels and gears of the machine ceased moving, and the treadmill stopped.

12 "Hey, daddy, you doin' with that jazz what you sayin' you waaazzz?" Milton slapped my palm and smiled, dancing in little jigaboo steps on the grass. I stood still. Milton spread out his arms in an exaggerated stretch. "Oh, maan, this weather. How you doin' with the shit?"

"It's all out on the street. I was just going over to see Groovy and get some bread."

"Crazy." Milton doubled over and touched his toes. "God, I feel great! I'd like to get the scene straight by this weekend. I'm going over to see Sam."

I shrugged. "I'll do what I can. Things are a little tight right now."

Milton laughed. "Things are always tight. You just gotta stay on top of 'em, tha's all. I'll catch you Saturday."

Milton jogged across Washington Square, swinging and stretching his arms. It was hard not feeling antagonistic toward him at the same time I felt foolish. I'd let myself get roped into dealing and now I was letting my end slide. I wasn't on my way to see Groovy; I had no intention of going there. The ten lids I'd given Groovy out front could rot for all I cared. The only thing I wanted was to get out. If I'd known what peddling dope on the street was going to entail, I'd never have agreed to do it. Even my rationale for agreeing to sell weed in the first place had backfired; Frankie was more aloof than ever, probably because I was dealing. It had been a tactical mistake getting involved in Milton's dope trade. Instead of maintaining an independence that gave me a little distinction, I'd become another asshole on the street who owed him bread. The whole thing was depressing.

Since I'd told Milton I was on my way to see Groovy, I decided to go over to his place after all.

Even my petty lies were beginning to get me down. My whole outlook on life had changed since getting involved with weed. I didn't even enjoy smoking it any more. Even the streets were a threat; I found myself slinking through them harboring a paranoia I'd never experienced before.

I headed down Columbus Avenue toward the San Gottardo Hotel. Groovy's a downhome hipster who makes the San Gottardo Hotel his little weed domain, servicing the place like the cleaning lady services the sheets. The San Gottardo Hotel is the end of the world, one room at a time, the last, beatest, loneliest, saddest, dreariest depository of despair in San Francisco, harbinger for every bo, bodiddly, bum, bindlestiff, bagman, bogey, bopper, and bomber in North Beach, dues-paying members of the human drift who are only part-time drifters. In reality they are Pulitzer prizewinning poets temporarily out of poems, down and out forecasters waiting for tomorrow, beginning and ending hipsters with cheap studio space, creeping octogenarians with monthly farewell checks, penniless prophets with lined notebooks and used library cards, unpublished writers with twenty-pound manuscripts of double-spaced personal apocalypse, word-weary winos inundated with nonreturnable bottles, rheumy-eyed old spinsters with leaking eyelids and dusty cunts, toothless watchdogs guarding abandoned foyers, decrepit dagos, demons, devils, daredevils, demonstrators, and the dead. They sit in their TV-lit rooms waiting for the sun to rise and the sun to set; that daily arc above their heads is their lifeline, a personal meridian stretching umbilicallike into every corner.

Every time I visit Groovy, I enter this miasma of gloom, a haunt of loneliness only the dead can understand. Salvatori, the four-foot-four-inch Italian winedrinker, shuffles through the downstairs bar, fingers the coin return slot on the jukebox, finds a dime, and plays a tune: "There's a Tule Fog Blowing through the Golden Gate of My Heart." Pearl, the three-hundred-pound hula girl, sways in obscene rhythm with the music, whirling voluptuously in her surrealistic dance, floating across the floor and pausing as she bows to the scattered applause from the lurching figures at the bar. Adolph the Harkener, as some call him because of his perpetual semistooped back and sidewise shoulder list, harkens at the door, then settles slowly into his accustomed place at the end of the bar. Each day the creatures from the numberless rooms above drift down to the bar, rattle their gums among old bottles, wheel barwise, and collapse. Johnny the bartender fills their glasses with thirty-cent shots of dago red and wipes the bar. On the walls the paint peels and fades.

I nodded to Johnny and climbed the stairs and walked down the long narrow hall to Groovy's room, number 26. I knocked on his door and waited for the inevitable doglike scratching on the other side to subside—the two-minute hide-the-stash panic. Groovy sighed visibly when he saw me. "K-Kid, c'm-m-mon in."

Groovy has a squint in his left eye that makes him look like he's about to be hit in the face with a hammer. His stutter tends to diminish when he's high, so he stays high all the time. When he isn't high, it's like listening to a Mexican machine gun, sort of an inconsistent cha-cha-chatter. Crow calls it "staccato hipster." "It should be recorded by the Library of Congress," he said, "just like Jelly Roll Morton. It'd be a shame to lose it."

The minute I walked in, Groovy whipped out a joint. He took a swift toke and handed it to me. I've never seen a guy so fast on the draw. If North Beach were the Old West and joints were Colt .44s, Groovy would put Shane to shame. As it is, he can sniff out, grade, score, manicure, roll, and smoke a joint faster than any other ten cats on the set. Groovy's specialty is rolling tight little numbers the diameter of a needle (part of his New York scarce-grass legacy) that if you suck too hard on will slip down your throat. More than once I'd dropped a Groovy joint and spent an hour trying to fish it out of a floor crack. Groovy's proud of his rolling ability, though, and even when he has weed to spare he always rolls his Harlem Toothpicks, he calls them. Next to Patrick Cassidy, who was born and bred in a weed patch and who rolls joints the size of small whale turds, Groovy's are the most famous joints on the set. Show me a head's joint and I'll tell you who he is.

I sucked lightly on Groovy's joint, not wanting to get high. I wanted to talk money. I saw "no sale" in Groovy's eyes, however, the lids drooping over the two eyeballs, making them look like cracked marbles in a mesh bag. Groovy sat on the edge of the bed and sighed. His squinty eye leaked and a tear puddle formed on his cheek. He wiped the tear away and looked at me. "How are things going?" I asked.

"Ah, man, y-y-you know ... I been j-j-jumpin' through a lotta s-s-strange hoops lately."

I nodded. Groovy's room is a little two-bit affair, eight by ten with a bed in the corner. The smoke from the joint drifted toward the ceiling. I opened the window. "I'd like to pick up some bread for those lids I laid on you. Milton's coming on pretty heavy with me."

"F-fuck Milton. He ain't h-hungry."

I passed the joint back to Groovy. He stared at the floor.

"I know he ain't hungry, but I do owe him the bread."

"M-man, things have b-b-been tough lately. You know h-how things are."

"Do you have any of the grass left? I'll return it to Milton."

"M-m-man, I don't have any of t-t-that grass. That g-g-grass is g-gone."

The joint had burned down to a roach. Groovy held the roach between his fingers for a long time, then pulled out a roach clip. He handed it to me.

"That g-grass is all over the B-B-Beach, m-m-man."

I took one last toke and handed the roach back. Groovy popped it into his mouth and chewed slowly.

"Can you collect from anybody? I'd sure like to get some bread."

"I dunno, m-m-man."

"How about Keith, doesn't he owe you some bread?"

"F-f-fifteen dollars. He ain't got no bread, though. He's s-s-strung out."

"Let's go see him anyway. I heard Rowena's working; maybe she has some bread."

Groovy sighed. It was a major effort for him to get up. It was a major effort for me too. The weed had gone into my body and touched each bone. I wanted to lie down. I felt terrible. I was turning a nice laying-back high into a work high. I prodded Groovy. He sighed and reached for his coat. We stumbled out of the hotel onto the bright sidewalks. Groovy shaded his eyes with his dark glasses. I had none. I held my hand over my eyes as we staggered up Filbert Street.

I felt better on the street. We headed toward Keith's place, Groovy walking with his peculiar shortjump shuffle that reminds me of a school of minnows in a pool, fluid and together but heading in every direction at once.

While we walked, I complained halfheartedly about the people I'd laid grass on who were burning me, sort of a gentle reminder to Groovy. He paid no attention, just kept shufflin' along. "You t-talk about bein' burned. I been burned by everyone—m-my parents, s-school, the slums, j-j-jail. Look at Bill. He's c-c-cold-turkeyin' m-meth an' he can't even f-f-find a place ta stay. He h-has ta sleep in laundromats because all the p-pads are full of m-meth."

We turned down August Alley and ducked into a little passageway. At the end of the walkway a dim light-bulb burned over a ragged door. Three busted steps led up to the landing. Groovy stepped up and rapped softly. The door swung ajar and he stuck his head in, peering back at me with a finger to his mouth. "Keith?" he said softly. I stood outside in the alley. Groovy motioned me inside.

Inside it was dismal gloom—the fetid-catshit, old-wash, sink-cooked-food, sweaty-body smell of a junkie pad. I stumbled against something in the dark and reared back. From the light of a window half covered by a torn shade I saw what had frightened me. A pa-pier-mâché horse stood on the table, one of Keith's sculptures, sad and bedraggled and forgotten among the stacked dishes and cups, empty bottles, and left-over food scraps. Keith "harrumphed" from the corner, lifting himself up on one elbow. He was lying on a mattress on the floor, empty cough medicine bottles and candy wrappers spread about him. His wispy beard hung in patches all over his face, and his eyes were so inset under his brow that I couldn't see them. Keith was an artist and sculptor, supertalented, with assemblage pieces in museums all over the country. Dr. Wenner had hundreds of his pieces in his collection and considered Keith one of the most talented artists he collected. Now he was strung out on meth. Groovy sat down on the edge of the mattress.

"H-how ya doin', Keith?"

"Hey, man, what's happenin'?" Keith drew the question out in a long Methedrine whisper. He sat up on the mattress and scratched himself slowly under the arm, glancing around the room. His sunken eyes gave his face the appearance of a skull. "You guys got any cigarettes?" He waved his long nicotine-stained fingers in the air.

Groovy lit a cigarette and handed it to Keith. He drew deeply on it, and I got up and opened the door.

"Oh, man, shut the door!" Keith held his hand over his eyes.

I closed the door.

"You f-f-feelin' all right, Keith?"

Keith smiled and scratched himself. "Well, man, you know . . . things are okay."

"H-how's Rowena? I h-hear she's been w-w-workin'. Is th-that right?"

"Ummm, yeah man, she got a gig. I dunno . . ."

Keith reached over and picked up a guitar lying beside him on the mattress and dragged his fingers idly over the strings. The soft rippling notes lent an oddly disturbing quality to the room. I was suffocating. I wanted to get out.

Keith's fingers stopped moving. He smiled, fondling the guitar. "Look, I made a stash."

He held the guitar up. I leaned down to inspect it. A little hole was carved into the side of the guitar, it had a door that closed tightly. "It's just big enough for one lid," Keith said.

"Hey, man, th-th-that's groovy."

"Yeah, that's nice, Keith. How long has Rowena been working?"

"Uhh, I dunno, man. Coupla weeks ... one. She's typing or something ... filing papers downtown."

I stood up to go. "We just dropped by to see how you're doing," I said.

"Yeah, K-K-Keith. You ready t-t-to go, Kid?"

"Hey, you cats got any speed?" Keith looked up from his mattress. His tombstone teeth gleamed dully in the light.

Groovy looked at me. "Ah, n-n-no, man, we ain't holdin' n-nothin' right now. We'll s-s-see you later, h-huh, Keith?"

"Ummm. You guys seen Rowena? She supposed to score some speed t'day."

"H-hey, baby, she'll probably b-b-be back s-s-soon. We'll see you later, h-huh, Keith?"

I stepped outside into the alley. Groovy came out and closed the door behind him. As we walked down the narrow corridor, I heard Keith strumming the guitar. The notes sounded distant, as if each note were separated by a hundred miles. Out on the sidewalk I breathed easier. "Keith's pretty s-s-strung out, huh?" Groovy said.

"I didn't know he was so fucked up."

Groovy shrugged. "P-p-people are jumpin' through a l-l-lotta strange hoops lately."

When we reached Columbus Avenue, I turned down toward Roach Alley. "I'll see you later," I said.

"G-g-groovy," Groovy said.

13 JoJay rolled five joints in preparation for a visit to his cousin, Walk in Many Suns. Walk in Many Suns is a plumber who lives in YumYum Estates. He has invited Walter and JoJay and his brothers and me to participate in the Bonanza Ceremony.

"YumYum Estates," Walter said. "What's that?"

"I think it's some kind of pueblo," JoJay said. He licked joint number five and placed it in his medicine bag. "Walk in Many Suns said that lots of Indians live there. It's in Oakland."

"YumYum," Walter said. "Maybe Walk in Many Suns knows something we don't know."

We drove across the Bay Bridge in Walter's jeep. JoJay lit a joint and passed it around. Jose, Joselito, Trinidad Archelito, and I sat in the back of the jeep behind Walter and JoJay. Between tokes on the joint, JoJay blew on his holy hollow left-wingbone-of-an-eagle whistle. His brothers pounded on their goatskin drums while Walter rattled his turquoise jewelry and beat on the dashboard with one hand.

"I feel like I'm taking a journey into a giant gumdrop," Walter said.

"Don't feel bad," JoJay said. "Walk in Many Suns said the Bonanza Ceremony is worth the trip."

JoJay was dressed in full Indian regalia in honor of the Bonanza Ceremony. I had on an ancient buckskin jacket JoJay had given me the day before. I was standing in JoJay's tepee admiring the coat when he told me to try it on. I tried it on. The coat was handmade, sewn with beautiful beads and porcupine-quill scrollwork, with fringes around the edges. On each breast were small blue and yellow feathers, woven in between the beads and porcupine quills. The coat was beautiful. "It's yours," JoJay said. "For a white man with an Indian's soul." I sat up in the back of the jeep in my new ancient buckskin jacket, proud to be a white man with an Indian's soul.

"This Bonanza Ceremony is a big thing," JoJay said. "Walk in Many Suns said it's the high point of the week. It's some kind of city Indian celebration."

"As long as Walk in Many Suns serves some of that wild rice and pickled moose-nose soup you told me about," Walter said. "I'll celebrate anything for some of that."

"Don't worry," JoJay said. "Walk in Many Suns said the Bonanza Ceremony wouldn't be the Bonanza Ceremony without the wild rice and pickled moose-nose soup."

We sailed across the Bay Bridge. JoJay's feathered headdress flapped and furled in the jeep's windstream. Passing drivers gawked and rapidly cleared a path for Walter's jeep. JoJay shrieked on his holy whistle and Walter sailed through the tollbooth.

"Uh . . . Walter . . . I think you're supposed to stop and pay a quarter at the tollbooth," I said.

JoJay screeched louder on his whistle and Walter pounded his open hand on the dashboard in time with the music and drums. The jeep was really swinging. I looked behind us and saw the black and white patrol car coming with red light flashing.

I tapped JoJay on the shoulder and nodded toward the patrol car. "Maybe we better swallow those joints, JoJay," I said.

By the time the highway patrol caught up with us, all the joints were swallowed except half of one which was lodged somewhere near JoJay's esophagus. It's hard swallowing four marijuana cigarettes on the spur of the moment. It's something that can be done with a bit of reflection, but on the spur of the moment it's very difficult. To be democratic, each of us should have swallowed three-fourths of a marijuana cigarette, but JoJay was holding, so he swallowed three and a half joints and was busy working on the last half of the fourth joint. The rest of us watched solemnly as JoJay's jaws worked overtime. The highway patrolman stopped his car behind us and walked around to the driver's side of the jeep. It seemed to me that JoJay's jaws were working in slow motion, but that was because JoJay was choking on the dry marijuana and was slowly asphyxiating in front of our eyes. It tends to make you slightly paranoid seeing an Indian in full ceremonial regalia slowly asphyxiating in front of your eyes while a highway patrolman is walking up behind you. It's hard to describe the exact feeling. It's like reaching for the husk of a dead sparrow and picking up a fifteen-pound bird.

The highway patrolman was very polite. He told Walter it was customary to stop at the bridge tollbooth and pay twenty-five cents.

"It's been the custom for a long time," he said. "People have been doing it for years."

While the highway patrolman was talking to Walter, JoJay was slowly turning blue. He was wheezing carefully somewhere down in his lower tract. It's disconcerting to see a redman turning blue right in front of your eyes.

"What's wrong with that purple Indian?" the highway patrolman said.

"He took some Indian medicine to prepare for the Bonanza Ceremony and he's slowly asphyxiating," Walter said. "That's why I didn't stop at the tollbooth. We have to find some water."

"Why didn't you say so?" the highway patrolman said. "I'll get my thermos."

The highway patrolman ran back to his car and returned with a thermos of coffee. By this time JoJay was turning a colorful shade of mauve. JoJay took the thermos from the highway patrolman and drank some of the coffee. It might have been his last act. Instead, the coffee washed down the last half of the fourth joint and saved JoJay's life.

"That's why I always respect the law," JoJay said later. "You never know when the law's going to wash down half a marijuana cigarette."

JoJay thanked the highway patrolman for saving his life and Walter backed up to the tollbooth and paid a quarter and then we continued on. YumYum Estates is in the hills of Oakland, but it is not a pueblo. Yum-

Yum Estates is a housing tract surrounded by Boca Raton Estates, Dawn Vision Estates and Sherwood Forest Estates.

"I wish I'd brought my longbow," JoJay said as we entered the development. "You never know who you're going to meet in Sherwood Forest."

Walter circled identical streets for half an hour before finding Walk in Many Suns' house. When we drove up in front of his house, Walk in Many Suns was standing in the driveway wearing a pair of hundred-pocketed Can't-Bust-'Em bib overalls and no undershirt. He looked like a Cherokee plumber. He raised his hand in the traditional "hou" sign as Walter stopped the jeep.

"Hou, cousin!" JoJay answered.

As we were getting out of the jeep, Neck Like a Swan, Walk in Many Suns' wife, and her five children came out of the house. Neck Like a Swan was shaped like a soft ball bearing. She was wearing a beaded buckskin dress, and her five children hid behind her. There was not enough buckskin dress to hide five children, however, so some of them spilled out.

After he and his brothers had made the traditional hand-upraised sign, JoJay introduced Walter and me to Walk in Many Suns and Neck Like a Swan.

"These friends are not tradingpost whites," JoJay said. "They are not cowshit white men."

Walk in Many Suns made the hand-upraised sign. "Welcome to my house," he said.

Inside the house were many Indians. Walk in Many Suns introduced us, and from each Indian we received the traditional handshake and sign. Jose and Joselito and Trinidad Archelito brought in their drums from the jeep and set them up in the powwow room. The powwow room was the den. Neck Like a Swan brought us beer and we sat down on the floor. The floor was covered with thick sheepskin rugs and colorful hand-woven blankets. When I asked about them, Neck Like a Swan blushed and said yes, she wove them.

At the far end of the powwow room was a giant television set, sitting in the place of honor. Against the walls were hundreds of old bottles, bones, rusty locks, and pieces of metal and artifacts Walk in Many Suns had dug up while working as a plumber. Walk in Many Suns was an amateur archeologist.

"I am glad you could come to our Bonanza Ceremony," Walk in Many Suns said. "It starts in half an hour."

"I never knew Indians had a Bonanza Ceremony," Walter said. "I have never heard of a Bonanza Ceremony in Taos."

"This is a private ceremony," Walk in Many Suns said. "I invented it myself. It's catching on fast, though."

More Indians arrived. We were introduced and Jose and his brothers started tapping softly on their drums. The Indians squatted on the floor and drank beer and nodded as Jose and Trinidad warmed up. Neck Like a Swan brought in large bowls of mutton and rice and a huge kettle of pickled moose-nose soup. Each of us ladled some of the soup into a cup and drank it. Plates were brought out by one of the daughters and we ate mutton and wild rice. The food was delicious.

"This is good food," an Indian named Face Longer Than a Stick said. "It is a long way from the mountains, and this food reminds me of the mountains."

"It's good mountain food," JoJay said. "Hey, Walter, what you say?"

"Hoya hoya!" Walter cried. The Indians laughed.

After the men finished eating, Neck Like a Swan and her daughters cleaned away the dishes. Walk in Many Suns brought out his pipe. While he was filling the pipe, JoJay told what happened at the bridge. Everybody laughed. Walk in Many Suns lit the pipe and passed it around the room. Each Indian took one long toke and passed the pipe on. There were twenty Indians in the powwow room. When the pipe reached me, Walk in Many Suns reached over and turned the television set on.

"Now the Bonanza Ceremony," he said.

While the TV set flickered to life, Neck Like a Swan brought in cans of cold beer. The Indians opened their cans and gazed intently at the TV set. Jose and his brothers tapped softly on their drums and sucked from their cans. I leaned back against the wall and watched the screen. The whole room had a musky Indian odor, an odor of sagebrush and outside. It was a good smell, reminding me of wide places and laughter. When the TV picture came into focus, I peered intently at it. It was *Bonanza,* the western serial. Walter and I looked at one another. The Indians stared intently at the television screen. From the shadows of the powwow room I heard an eerie sound, a sound like brittle wind off the plains. I looked around and realized that it was JoJay blowing softly into his holy wingbone-of-an-eagle whistle. Somehow the music was perfect, full and empty at the same time, like a lone bird circling high above flat tabletop vistas looking out upon the beauty and stillness of Black Mesa.

The pipe came around again and I toked from it. On the TV screen Hoss and the Cartwright brothers rode hell for home, and the Indians shouted in merriment. Beer cans emptied and others popped open and were drained in long foamswallowing gulps. Walk in Many Suns led the merriment as the Indians followed every incident on the screen with hoots and laughter. Every time Hoss or a white man came on the screen, the Indians hissed and booed, throwing empty beer cans against the wall. Jose and Trinidad boom-boomed on their drums and Joselito chanted. The other Indians shouted encouragement. I rocked on the floor in laughter as a commercial interrupted the performance.

"Hoya hoya! It's a good ceremony, huh, JoJay?" Walk in Many Suns shouted.

JoJay nodded his head. Tears were streaming from his eyes he was laughing so hard. Walter grabbed another can of beer from Neck Like a Swan and chanted with Joselito, each of his yelps drowning out the bikini-clad girl in the commercial. Everyone in the room hollered and swayed, completely mesmerized by the beer and grass and the action on the screen. I got on a laughing jag and rolled on the floor helplessly. The sound of Hoss bellowing and drums beating and the blue haze from the pipe and the drawn curtains of the powwow room and the sheepskin rugs on the floor and the chanting Indians intermingled with Walter's hoya

hoya! and JoJay's eerie wingbone whistle lifting up out of YumYum Estates and carrying over the Oakland hills toward the bay, all conspired to send me into fits of laughter. With tears streaming from my eyes and my belly aching, I rolled on the floor helplessly.

14 Walter and JoJay and his brothers have gone to Marin County for the day. After they're gone, I am like everybody else on the Beach, alone and searching for companionship—but more alive alone than with someone. After they leave, I rush to the windows and open them so the Roach Alley musk can enter, a combination of farm and asphalt and concrete and sperm and blood. It's the California environment, a weird projection that is really gristle I lay on each female companion I take. At times I feel perverse, running through the North Beach streets like a madman or satyr, a mythological beast searching out some maiden on which to lie, grope groins and lay on my Simmons mattress (stolen from the factory down on Bay Street) and slumber later in the musk. I told Little Joe about it but he doesn't understand. Or maybe he does. The need for me to lie alone and savor the smells of the city, of my bed. He doesn't know of my secret assignations, the girls I bring back to my loft after he is gone. He speaks of his fucks and their magical cunts and he doesn't realize that magical orifices gape open for me too, weave their patterns against my white brick wall and leave a scent like ambergris on my pillow. In the morning I wallow and delve like the white whale after a fuck too big to hold, it would take ships and ships to stow her. If Little Joe only knew. I'm perverse sometimes in my desire to tell him, but at the same time I know that in the telling I would lose all I have, a particular position in North Beach where female porpoises cavort and dive.

I was in City Lights Bookstore when I met Madonna Suddenly. Sitting at the table reserved for serious readers with books spread out before me when this cute young thing comes in. She has hips so nice, lips and looks that take my eyes away from the book I'm reading. I sat sad-eyed and looked at her and in a moment of courageous desperation asked her her name. She smiled and took my hand, led me up the stairs and outside. "I want to see your face in the sunlight," she said.

It was early evening by then and only soft glints of leftover sunlight gleamed off the Bank of America Building across the way. That was enough. She grabbed my arm and we hurried hand in hand up Grant Avenue to Gerke Alley. We climbed her stairs and inside she turned to the door and wrote a note in big hand on lined paper—STAY AWAY! with a big exclamation point—which she pinned on the outside door.

I sat down on her bed while she slipped into the bathroom and returned in a robe so silken and soft I thought it was her skin until I removed it. I looked at her. She had the sweetest body, skin so fresh, dimpled buttocks, and slightly rounded belly that makes me or anyone go all soft inside. Her between-legs V was so small, so neat, so tight little wiry and kind that I had to nuzzle my face in the fur and thank whatever gods there be who dwell in bookstores that girls like this sometimes do come out. They are not all dreams; life is not what it seems. We lay down and swapped skins. Madonna Suddenly. Later in Mike's Place over coffee I asked about her funny name. We sipped our coffee and she told me about herself. She'd lived in North Beach for years, father an Irish sea captain, worked and had an apartment and supported whole herds of people whom I didn't know and who took advantage of her (hence the door sign), was keen on jazz and in fact that very night was going down to the Jazz Cellar to dig Pony. Did I want to come?

I went with her. Downstairs in the Jazz Cellar she introduced me to Bill Wiejon, the handsome blond piano-playing proprietor who set up the drinks. Madonna Suddenly and I sat quiet, listened mutely as the jazz that she loved drifted out slowly from the just-warming-up players. Pony hadn't arrived yet, only Bill and Max and a drummer, Otto somebody, who rippled the skins with his brushes in warmup riffs and waited for the serious moment when Pony and the Crowd came in, all the preliminaries simply a beat to keep the others awake, me and Madonna Suddenly holding hands, sharing drinks, twining and smiling in the dark together.

I stayed in Madonna Suddenly's apartment for six days and nights and we drank wine, sipped tea, lay in bed and looked at one another, Madonna getting up every morning and going to work downtown in an insurance office, praying for me to be there when she returned. I was, waiting for her with hot tea and bed from six thirty until nine, then dinner and the Jazz Cellar till midnight, then home to bed again with a little weed and wine to make the nights curl by soft. After a week I was exhausted. Madonna Suddenly smiled and tweaked my chin. "I thought you liked me," she said.

"I do, I do. You're wonderful."

"Well, then, c'mon."

We climbed into bed and did it again.

When I met Maggie, I imagined virgin greenery. Nothing could have been further from the truth. I grasped her in front of the Amp Palace and spirited her home posthaste. Posthaste. Old-fashioned word. For an old-fashioned girl. When we got up to my loft, she rubbed her cheeks along my white brick wall and inspected JoJay's tepee. I watched her. Yes, I said to myself, I've found one. Maggie is a virgin angel striding the length of my loft, whispering and singing and understanding my wall and finally lying still on my mattress, her hair spread out across the pillow, each follicle the headwaters of a hirsute Orinoco. I stroked her velvet belly, so soft! Maggie crooned. I use these words purposefully, none else will do. I laid her back and bared her bodice. I stripped the cloth aside and felt her breasts. I mouthed first one and then the other and then grabbed both and tried to make one of two. Maggie yelped and squirmed and turned her back to me, lifting her bottom as she did. I let go her breasts and slid bottomwise, melding my lips over her mesial groove. Inside her cheeks I licked and lapped and bit. She squirmed and cried, wriggling her ass into my mouth.

The next morning I took Maggie to the U.S. Restaurant for breakfast. I liked the U.S. Restaurant. I especially liked the old Italian waiter who hunched over the tables with his beard stubble and gnarled hands. He reminded me of my father. When I looked at him I saw his whole history; it was the history of a million workingmen in America: linotype operator for *L'Italia* grown too old for the job, hands too shaky, eyesight gone bad. He lived in the San Gottardo Hotel and walked down carpeted hallways. Or else he was a longshoreman who couldn't make the shape-up any more; he hung around the waterfront for forty years of four A.M. shape-ups and now he shuddered coffee across linoleum tabletops. It was a process watching him, each delivery a question mark.

Maggie ordered a short stack and one over easy. I ordered some hashbrowns and fried eggs. I sipped my coffee and watched Maggie eat. She licked and lapped her victuals, opened her purse for lipstick, and put on her mouth.

"D'you have a pitchur?" she asked.

"What?"

"A pitchur of you. You know, a photo."

"Oh. Not with me," I said.

"I always like pitchurs of guys."

Maggie unstrung her purse. A thousand-compartmented wallet unfolded. In each compartment a picture of a guy. I looked at her. She smiled.

"It's nice to remember what they looked like," she said.

Frankie and I met for coffee at Mike's Place. The billiard tables were empty. Charlie Wong, the ex-death row cook for San Quentin, wiped the bar and read the paper. Frankie looked glum.

"Milton and I are going to Big Sur tomorrow," she said. "We're going to spend the day on the beach."

"Where on the beach?"

"I don't know. Milton has friends."

"Is he going to score?"

"I think so. Milton doesn't tell me much."

"Milton's starting to hit that shit pretty hard, isn't he?"

"Milton's business is Milton's," Frankie said. "I don't run his affairs for him and he doesn't run mine for me."

"It's good to know you've got a nice arrangement," I said.

"It's nice and I intend to keep it that way." Frankie glowered at me.

"Just tell him to be careful. I hear it's awful tight in Big Sur right now."

"Milton's always careful."

"I know. Milton will still be peddling his shit when all the rest of us are in the joint."

"He got you your ounce of crystal, didn't he?" Frankie said. "You should be more appreciative."

"It wasn't my ounce of crystal, it was Hube the Cube's. Besides, he charged enough for it."

"I don't think he made much money off it. It wasn't easy to score."

"Milton always makes bread off what he sells, and it's never easy to score."

Frankie sipped from her cup of coffee. She looked out the window. "It's really a drag with you sometimes, Kid."

I didn't say anything.

I walked over to the register and paid Charlie the bill. Frankie and I walked outside.

"I'm going over to Muir Beach next week. Would you like to come?" I said.

"I think Milton has plans to go to Berkeley next week. I'm going with him."

"I'll see you later," I said. I split down the street.

15 I walked down Columbus Avenue, past the Italian newspaper stands and pastry shops and bars and shoeshine stands and the five-and-dime. The statue of Ben Franklin brooded under the poplar trees in the middle of Washington Square. When I reached Aquatic Park, I strolled along the sand and then walked out to the end of the long curving concrete pier. I stood on the end of the pier and looked at Alcatraz. Inside the concrete and steel rooms the convicts were lining up for breakfast. They would eat mush and toast and jelly and stewed prunes on a cold tray. I could hear the din. The din was inconsolable.

I walked back along the pier and watched the Chinese children and ancient Fillmore spades dangling their lines in the water, casting for tonight's supper, or jes passin' time, naathin' t'do. I sat on one of the benches and looked at the city, gleaming white and pure in the early morning sunlight. The shadows of the buildings blended together like ethereal vapor into an image of crystalline tenderness. The whole city was one beating, breathing, vibrant structure, an edifice rooted so deep into the eleven gray hills that it was the hills themselves, its towers the hilltops from which men gazed longingly toward the sea. The atmosphere around me was so quiet I could hear the tiny bullheads and lingcod as they bit the children's lines, feel the delicate jaws break as the children pulled the lines taut. Above the city shone a light so pure I thought my heart would break, a sky so brilliant I was blinded.

I walked along the pier's edge and rubbed my hands against the rough concrete pillars, imagining the pillar ends down among the detritus and ooze of the bottom, felt my face scrape against the surface of mollusks and stone. Dismembered fishes lay on the pier, staring heavenward drunkenly. I walked through gaggles of screeching, scolding seagulls who opened and closed around me in waves. I watched the fishermen untangle their lines, bait their hooks, and toss the whole thing—hook, line, and sinker—into the sea. The sea accepted all without a ripple.

On the sand again, I dragged my feet and laughed when I thought of Walter. One evening when he and I and Cornsilk were walking here at Aquatic Park, he perched on a rotten piling below the Maritime Museum and pissed out magnificent scrolls and whirls, writing his name in the sand. "I'm looking for the artist who has the courage to paint his pictures in the sand," Walter cried. Cornsilk protested, so Walter pissed her name out too, joining both their names with a beautifully symmetrical heart ten feet wide. Walter had the biggest bladder I ever saw.

On the ampitheater steps adjoining the Maritime Museum a group of black conga drummers beat time on their drums and shared a jug of red wine. I stood among them and tapped my foot. The jug came around to me and I swallowed the spit and piss and blood-red port of a hundred lips as I let the cool flaming liquid flow down my throat. I saw Tambourine, young North Beach spade, weaving among the conga drummers. Tambourine looked old, but he was young. He smiled and waved, his huge body moving gracefully with the music. Tambourine had the biggest feet in the world and a gold tooth shone through his sad Agnew mad-house smile. "How many died, Maxwell?" he said when I walked up and stood next to him. I shrugged my shoulders and tried to remember. Tambourine held out his hand and I gave him a dollar. It was a ritual between us. He smiled and slapped my hand. "Thanks, Maxwell." He called everyone Maxwell.

During the Monterey Jazz Festival in 1962 Tambourine took off his shirt and swung from a tree outside the gates, preaching to the thousands of people congregated there. "I'll stop dropping pills when you stop dropping bombs!" he cried, and thousands cheered. Later a group of us went up to Gene Flores's house on Pacific Street. During the party Tambourine cried,

"Did you all see me swinging from that tree like a monkey?"

"I didn't see no monkey swinging from that tree," Zeke cried, "but I sure as hell saw a big black coon!"

Everybody cracked up.

A large crowd gathered around the conga drummers, so I turned and headed toward Fisherman's Wharf. I saw the small boats bobbing at the quay, trim Italian fishing craft that left each morning before light and returned each evening, their one-cylinder Hicks engines put-put-putting across the bay. Farther on, at the end of Pier 45, the *San Cristobal*, late from Genoa with a cargo of Italian marble and cherries in brine, unloaded. Small figures of men ran around the ship as they operated the winches, hoisting huge loads of cargo onto the docks. What were they thinking, now, at this time, in this place?

The Kid turned from the wharf and walked down the Embarcadero past the *Balclutha*, a three-masted sailing ship, to where hustling, crushing, booming trucks and forklifts hooted and thumped and jockeyed their loads dockward, the bustling madness becoming a longshoreman's symphony, enveloping the whole waterfront. Across the Embarcadero from the docks, inside the U.S.S. Eagle Cafe, the Kid stood behind longshoremen as they pushed and shoved and shouted their way through the serving line, staggering under the heaps of eggs and bacon and potatoes the countermen ladled onto their trays, scurrying to their tables and shoveling it down and returning for more. Food! Food! Good American meat and potatoes and milk and coffee, along with mugs of beer, the foam from the glasses strung over the bar like confetti, long trailing wakes of golden liquid awash on the tables. The black frisco jeans and loose-fitting hickory shirts stretched taut over midmorning breakfast guts, the older dock workers pushing their food down stoically, noiselessly, laughing and guffawing, bellowing jokes and hammering one another on the back while the younger new-to-the-trade rakelike handsome blacks and Italians caroused at their tables, secure in their youth, a fraternity of workers, dockmen, longshoremen, whose work was out there, visible, piled up on the docks and disappearing into the holds of ships, the smells and languages and distances seeping into the U.S.S. Eagle Cafe, enveloping it and making it foreign, alive, peculiarly unsophisticated and untamed, fists hammering on the bar as business agents and union representatives cursed and laughed and tossed down Bloody Marys and boilermakers in their more sophisticated dress-up suits, their hands soft next to the longshoremen's, although some double-breasted gentlemen at the bar had spatulalike fingers and hamlike upper arms, attesting to earlier days on the waterfront among cranes and boxes and whining belts and winches and booming madness. The Kid got his coffee and joined the men at the formica-topped tables, cupped his mug in his hand, felt the energy reverberate over the rooftops, sat quiet and listened and gazed around the room, smokedense, noisy, crazy, alive. On the wall of the restaurant, over the clock, was an eagle carved in wood, symbol of America and the U.S.S. Eagle Cafe.

Outside again, crossing the Beltline Railroad tracks, the Kid jumped aside just as a chain of cars crashed by, shunting a string of open-doored boxcars full of merchandise into the barnlike sheds covering the piers. Inside the piers the trucks and tractors and machinery were pushed out onto the loading ramps, hoisted up into the air by giant winches, and dropped into the yawning hatches of the merchant ships. On Pier 37 the *Canberra* docked and hundreds of passengers streamed down the gangplank, jumped into taxis and waiting cars. The Kid saw them gape and gaze as they got their first close look at San Francisco, watching reunions and handshakes and kisses and lovers' clasps and families together again, sons and daughters returned, visitors and strangers, old and young.

The Kid walked down the Embarcadero past dingy restaurants and two-bit bars and rattling buildings as old as the bay itself, refuge for every tired drifter and desperado America had ever produced. On Steuart Street he stopped and shared wine with a trio of ancient veterans, soldiers of Skid Row who showed their scars and medals, bandages and crutches and pisspainted overalls and blood, all the cast-on garments of regret, every second of life gone bad as they tipped their tokay wine toothless to the wind and whispered to each other trying to remember. The Kid laughed with the wino soldiers and whispered too, tipped the wine and pissed against the pierhead wall. "You 'member that time in that jungle near Tracy?" Slimjim cried. "Kid, this is the truth. Musta been forty bos round that stew an' we had ten gallons of good ole Valley of the Moon redeye . . ." Hawkeye laughed and slapped his pissstained knee. "Shuck huk, waal shore. Pass that jug, Harvey, hyaw, hyaw, 'member that time . . ."

The Kid crossed over the road and stood on the railroad tracks and looked up at the Bay Bridge. The bridge was so big it seemed like a dividing line, a marking-off place separating the city from the country. "This is the line, boys, and this bridge is here to prove it." Under his feet he felt the earth move.

As the longshoremen and truck drivers scurried to and fro under the bridge, the Kid wondered at their indifference. How could they live and work under the shadow of such a giant sculpture and not be affected by it? Then he realized that the men were affected by it, each and every one. The bridge had gone into their blood like some poison or drug that when taken over a long period of time is assimilated, goes into the bloodstream, and changes the body without the body being aware of it. Not only had the bridge entered the people's bloodstream, the city itself and the bay and the mountains surrounding the bay had all gone into the bloodstream of the people living here. They were all addicts, all of them hooked on the insane magic of the city. The Kid looked up at the huge bridge arching over the bay and felt his own body change, felt himself addicted, knew that he too was a helpless victim borne along in San Francisco's stream.

The Kid walked for hours. He covered all the Embarcadero, walked down Third Street to the China Basin drawbridge, stood still while the drawbridge lifted slowly for a family of fishing boats to pass. He walked out Third Street to Butchertown and breathed

deep the smell of dying animals and burning cars in the
wrecking yards and dead fish from the catfood facto-
ries. On the edge of the bay at Hunters Point he
watched as men shot hot bolts into the sides of huge
steel-hulled ships, climbing over the scaffolding like
ants as they pounded their hot rivets in. Beneath the
smokestack on Potrero Hill the Kid turned and headed
back, walked along Army Street to Iowa and then
down Iowa Street to Third Street again, to the saddest
corner in the world. The corner of Eighteenth and
Third is one of those corners where everything ends
up. All the debris and dirt and trash and old newspapers in the city congregate on the corner of Eighteenth
and Third, blown in by every ill wind and disturbed
eddy the city can provide. The Kid stood on the corner
and felt himself part of it, another piece of grime blown
onto the streetcorner. He rested on the corner with a
seventy-year-old Negro named Henry. "I'se jest waitin'
fo' a bus to take me home," Henry said.

The Kid walked down Third Street, past the Cameo
Hotel and Jimbo's Oh Boy Liquors and Acme Loan—
"Any Amount Loaned from 5 dollars to 5000"—and
lines of torpid winos standing three deep on the sidewalks, their cracked bottles in brown paper bags
clutched like rosaries to their chests, guiding them from
storefront to storefront at Third and Howard. I salute
the puke and piss of San Francisco at Third and
Howard. Men stand on the curbs and they fall, their
heads cracking like eggs against the pavement. When
they fall, it is in slow motion, their fall taking them
through years and centuries and lives they never understood.

The Kid walks through the streets of San Francisco
and is struck by the history of the city. There is so
much to see, so much to understand and put down. Dig
down into the ground and you will discover the relics
of lost civilizations. San Francisco is the new Bonam-
pak, a curious display of frescoes and wall paintings
dug out of the lush tropical jungles of the modern age.
The city's streets and alleys are a mystery to everyone,
a giant riddle carved along the continent's westernmost
edge, a riddle that can be understood only by a race

from another planet—with that vision—like the Nascan script that's drawn along Peru's forgotten steppes, a sign language decipherable only from the distance between stars.

When I wander through the streeets of San Francisco, I think of what Jack Micheline said. "This city ain't America, it's Baghdad! It's Shangri-la! It's perfect and I ain't perfect. I gotta go back to New York, back to the pit where people are human, where they hate each other. It's the only America I understand."

Jack is right. San Francisco is not America; it's what's left of America. It's Custer's Last Stand at Land's End! It's the Great Wall of China of America's forgotten promises! Here in San Francisco have gathered all of society's children, space-age dropouts from the American dream, Horatio Algers in reverse, descending from riches to rags and gathering now on the corners of Grant and Green in their beads and spangles and marijuana smoke to watch the entire structure crumble. Here the last battle will be fought; here the machines will descend to commence the Psychedelic Wars. San Francisco is a modern-day Peloponnesus and the Psychedelic Wars will be a modern-day Peloponnesian Wars. Here in San Francisco the children with their expanded minds and psychedelic rayguns will stand up with their potsmoke against the teargas and napalm and olivedrab steel of the Establishment. The distant rumblings are already heard, the tanks are gathering on the outskirts, the police squads command the corners, barbed wire unwinds across the parks; the teargas and potsmoke mingle and float out under the Golden Gate Bridge with the afternoon fog.

On Market Street the Kid renewed himself. He ate a hotdog and followed a wispy-eyed girl until he lost her in the crowd. People were everywhere. Market Street was the crossroads of San Francisco, heartline where every beat hipster and lonely soul in the city gravitated to find solace, warmth, hope of love. A wide thoroughfare of rinky-dink shops and shooting galleries, hotdog stands and all-night restaurants, alongside giant department stores and fancy establishments, it stretched from the Ferry Building on the Embarcadero straight through the heart of the city to Twin Peaks and beyond, a throbbing, vibrating artery packed solid with cars and streetcars, buses, people, derelicts, drifters, and dreamers.

On Market Street were hustlers from everywhere, bums with no arms and winos with wheels for feet, the walking and rolling wounded holding tin cups up, the bottoms ringed with dimes, accordion music and the sound of violins accompanying their sad laments. Everyone ended up on Market Street, especially the poor. Armies of bedraggled blacks and ancient Chinese and poor whites mingled, sniffed the air, and swallowed. One old woman with collapsed shoes and twenty layers of clothing rummaged in a trash can. All the good trash was gone, scooped up by earlier rummagers. Gum wrappers, cigarette packages, torn-off labels, bits and pieces of old newspapers littered the sidewalks, forming a tramped-on mosaic of money spent, news read, gum chewed, cigarettes smoked, insides spewed out. Every window offered something you couldn't afford not to own; every doorway promised excitement, sex, memories, companionship.

The Kid saw a theater marquee that promised part-time deliverance from this place. Dream palaces of gloom for all the city's drifters. He paid a dollar and went inside and sat down and laughed until he cried, and when the cycle of moving blurry figures started repeating itself he got up and walked outside into the late afternoon. The sun gone down behind the buildings and late shoppers hurrying home. The Kid was late too. He rushed into the crowd, got caught up in the bustling elbows and backs and shoulders of shop people and business people and executives and laborers and bums and drifters and rounders and loafers rushing to and fro along the streets. He followed old men and pretty women and young girls along the city's streets and alleys. On the corner of Stockton and Post he saw a beautiful society lady and headed after her, following her through the streets block after block, waiting outside fancy stores while she shopped. When she came out, he followed her again, keeping discreetly behind so she wouldn't notice and be afraid. The Kid wanted only to look, to smell, to feel the presence of the voluptuous flesh enclosed in fabulous furs and wraps and expensive garments. The Kid was a voyeur of the streets, and while he followed the woman he fantasied. The woman was in her mid-thirties. She had long black hair done up in a fancy Gibson Girl style. She had on a chic outfit, a belted suit with a fur-collared jacket and shoes that looked sexy as hell as she minced across the street and stopped in front of a store window. The Kid panted after her, dreaming in his head of the moment when she'd turn and see him and get that electric sexual shock. Zzonck! The woman was a rich, bored society chick out on the make, wealthy as hell, and she lived in a fabulous house up on Nob Hill. She crossed the street and he followed her, walking a little ways behind; then she turned and bang! there it was. The Kid gave her the glad eye, the sex eye, and the woman smiled. "C'mon, follow me, if you dare," she seemed to say. The Kid danced after her like a puppy on a leash, lapping up the sex smell that spilled out from between her legs and lay like musk over the sidewalk. The woman stopped a few doors down the street, pondering an article in a window. The Kid stood beside her so she could see his reflection in the glass. Their eyes met. He smiled, a shy smile, but not too shy. He held his head sideways so she could see his rugged profile. The woman took a few steps and gazed into another window, and all the time the Kid's eyes and her eyes were locked together in the window's reflection, their eyes two instruments absorbing the shock of one another. The Kid broke the silence. He stood beside her and admired the handbag she was inspecting. "It's a nice bag." Or perhaps he came right out front and said, "You're a very beautiful woman." The statement didn't frighten or shock the woman at all. She was relaxed as hell, at ease, an aura of big-city sophistication hung over her. She looked at the Kid, moved her eyes slowly over his face. "Would you like to have some coffee?" he said. "I'd love some." Together they went to a coffee shop, the Kid smiling at her, then reaching out and holding her hand. She didn't move; she placed her other hand on top of the Kid's hand. While they sipped coffee, the Kid talked, told her of the city, the streets, his plans. The woman listened and then told the Kid of her life, past histories and stories that mingled and became current, like two old friends making the past the present by remembering it.

Later they went home together. The woman was the wife of a successful lawyer or doctor, or perhaps her husband owned a large business and was away most of the time. Her house was empty, or perhaps she lived alone, a divorcee or a young widow. The house was incredibly palatial with voluptuous rugs and drapes and furs thrown on couches and a fabulous sound system with speakers in every room. There were stained-glass windows in every corner of the house and a huge picture window looking out over the bay. The Kid gazed out the window and saw the Golden Gate Bridge, a long glowing arc in the late afternoon dusk. The woman—Alexy, that was her name—poured the Kid a drink and held it out toward him. "Excuse me while I change." She walked upstairs and disappeared from sight. While Alexy was gone, the Kid explored the main room, reading the titles of books on the shelves, examining maps on the walls. He gazed at exotic fish swimming in a lighted aquarium built into the wall. He turned on the hi-fi and listened to music he'd never known.

Alexy returned and stood for a moment at the head of the stairs. The Kid gasped. She was beautiful. She paused, then walked slowly down the thickly carpeted stairs, moving softly over the plush white rug into his arms. He took her willingly, pulling her toward him. It was like waves coming into shore, inevitable, with a blending fierceness he barely fathomed. The Kid took Alexy in his arms and carried her to the middle of the room and laid her down on the rug. He undid the snaps of her gown, a long golden affair with a white fur ruffle around the neck. Underneath the gown her small white breasts gleamed lustily in the pale light, white as pearls and firm as bullets. They stood up like puppies as the Kid ran his fingers across their tips, cupping his hands and caressing them softly. Alexy cringed as the Kid's rough hands flowed gently over her. She grabbed his belt, unbuckled it, and pulled his jeans down over his hips. As they fell, she leaned forward and brushed her lips across his stomach, breathing in the rich smell. For a long time they lay together, feeling the surge and flow of blood and flesh through one another's body. The Kid had a hard-on a mile long, it was standing straight up against Alexy's cheek. She leaned over and placed her mouth against his dick, molding her lips over it like rose petals brushing a thorn. He cried out in pain, grabbing her buttocks in his hands and squeezing them fiercely while her mouth played with his dick. When the aches became intolerable, the Kid flipped Alexy over and buried his face in her, kissing her lips and hair, her eyes and mouth and body. The Kid swallowed Alexy's breasts, taking a whole breast inside his mouth, one at a time. She kissed back, crying softly as she did so. When she cried, the Kid kissed every orifice of her body, lapping and sucking at her navel, her mouth, licking her mound of belly and darting into the little web of hair that covered her sweet undersea lips. Alexy moaned and bit and chewed through the tangled hair on the Kid's stomach, grabbing his cock between her teeth. She lapped and sucked on it like it was a delicious lollipop. The Kid cried in delight. Everything was white, a blinding light that exploded in his head as he dove between her legs with his mouth and kissed and licked and suffocated in the sweetness of her body. Alexy spread her legs out in one long arch that opened her innermost being to the Kid's darting tongue. Nothing was sacred. He dove in and took everything, chewing and biting and sucking and drowning in the sea of white rug. Alexy's cries became moans of delight as the Kid opened her up, spread her out and entered her in one long hot flash that bruised the soft, forgiving flesh. Standing, the Kid turned and held her riveted on the end of his cock like a piece of meat spitted over an open flame. She sucked his tongue into her mouth and twisted about on the end of his dick. Her body was stiff, rigid, and limp at the same time, a fish on the end of his line, wriggling and curling in that magic tail-out-of-water dance. He twisted her around on the end of his cock and bit her tits, nibbling and chewing on them, sucking and swallowing as if he would never taste breastmeat like hers again. Alexy cried as the Kid wrenched away and flipped her like a dime between his hands and buried his lips in her muff. She smelled like a combination of seasalt and woman and perfume and ambergris. He felt as if he were devouring the Mindanao Deep of cunt, as if he had plunged to the very bottom and found still further crevices to explore, new flora and fauna hibernating in the inner folds of Alexy's labia, as if her twat were the hothouse of the New World, a deepsea settlement housing secrets only the Kid could understand. He sucked and sucked and he grew young, his body died and was reborn inside Alexy's cunt, a cunt that spread over him like Lake Erie, like a sea, the Red Sea, as it wept and flowed and wallowed in waves against his cockhard shore. His coastline stood up to meet her and their two seas met, became one, subsiding afterwards in exhaustion and foam.

It was all a dream for the Kid, a dream while rushing home along the avenues of late-afternoon San Francisco. Part of that parcel of loneliness handed out to him at birth, that loneliness angel riding shoulder over him, soft, like the whispered wings of dreams one wakes from but can't forget.

When I got back to the Beach, I went over to Milton's pad to see Frankie. A note on Milton's door said, "Gone to Big Sur, back Saturday." I walked back to Roach Alley. The clock on the Church of St. Peter and Paul said midnight. Out on the bay the foghorns boom-boomed softly.

16 JoJay wants to fuck a Chinese whore.

"Take me to a Chinese whore, Walter."

We are drinking espresso in the Caffe Trieste. Walter keeps his eyes on the *Chronicle*. He's reading Herb Caen. Herb Caen has some interesting things to say this morning.

"I have been told that a person does not really know San Francisco until he has fucked a Chinese whore. They say that fucking a Chinese whore is an entirely new experience, like learning to eat food with chopsticks."

JoJay stole a pair of chopsticks from the Universal Cafe and now he wears them tied to his medicine bag on his belt. JoJay removes the chopsticks from his belt and drums them on the table under Walter's *Chronicle*. Walter pays no attention.

"They say that Chinese women are built very interesting. I have heard that said many times."

JoJay drums his chopsticks on the table and Walter reads his *Chronicle*.

"They say there are certain anatomical differences between Chinese women and"—JoJay looks around the Caffe Trieste—"and Indian women. I want to know if that's true, Walter."

Walter turns a page of his *Chronicle* and sips from his espresso.

"Indian women are very good to fuck but they are like elephants. I am tired of fucking elephants."

This interested me. "Why is fucking Indian women like fucking elephants, JoJay?" I asked.

"Indian women and elephants never forget," JoJay answered. "I am an unforgettable man all over northern New Mexico. There are so many places in New Mexico where I am unforgettable that it is getting

157

hard to live there. I want to fuck a Chinese whore because I have heard that they do not remember."

Walter turns a page of his *Chronicle* and JoJay drums his chopsticks on the table. The chopsticks make a small tattooing noise over the din of the coffee drinkers.

"Some Indian women are not like elephants, though. Some are like horses. You know that don't you, Walter?"

JoJay's tabletop tattoo rattles faster. He places both chopsticks between the fingers of one hand and continues the beat—rhythmical, fast, like tiny horse feet racing rapidly over a flat plain.

"Remember that Indian bruja I took you to in Santa Fe? What was she like, Walter, an elephant or a horse?"

Walter pays no attention to JoJay; he turns a page.

"Walter was very borracho when we were in Santa Fe." JoJay turns to me. "When Walter gets borracho he gets borracho like an Indian. An Indian with no sense, as the white man says."

JoJay fidgets with his chopsticks and Walter turns another page. I sip my espresso and say nothing.

"Tell me, Kid, do you not think that it would be a good idea for Walter to take me to a Chinese whorehouse?"

"I think it's an excellent idea, JoJay."

It was true. I thought the idea of Walter taking JoJay to a Chinese whorehouse was an original idea. It had never occurred to me to go. I had often followed wispy-eyed Chinese girls across Washington Square but they always seemed unattainable. They seemed like a closed race with no use for the white man. The idea of a Chinese whorehouse where you could pay money to fuck somebody in a closed race was appealing.

"I have heard tell when you fuck a Chinese whore it is like riding a new pony," JoJay says. "It's like breaking in a new pony, that's what I have heard."

JoJay separates the chopsticks and holds one in each hand. He continues his rapid staccato stampede on the tabletop.

"My cousin Tell Me Good Morning fucked a

Chinese whore in Flagstaff and he said it was like riding a new, unbroken pony. It was a very pleasurable experience. A new, unbroken pony speaks to your whole body, does it not, Kid?"

"I have never ridden a new, unbroken pony, JoJay, but I imagine it would speak to your whole body."

"When you come to Taos, I will talk with my cousin Tell Me Good Morning and get a new, unbroken pony for you to ride, Kid. You will see that what I say is true."

"That will be a pleasurable experience, JoJay."

"I will also take you to the Imperial Hotel in Santa Fe and find you an Indian woman, although an Indian woman is not a new, unbroken pony. An Indian woman is an elephant; she never forgets."

"Perhaps a new, unbroken Indian woman is like a new, unbroken pony, JoJay," I say.

JoJay looks at me for a moment. "That's a thought. That is a thought you have there, Kid."

JoJay drums his chopsticks on the table. Walter reads.

"When a man has an Indian for a friend, that man has a friend for life." JoJay looks at me but aims his voice at Walter. "An Indian would give his last pony to his friend if the need arises, and that is not cowshit talk, do you know that, Kid?"

"I know that an Indian friend is a friend for life, JoJay, for you've told me that many times."

"I have told you that many times because it is true. An Indian will give his last pony to a friend if the need arises. A white man does not understand that because a white man will not even take an Indian to a Chinese whorehouse."

"Perhaps there are no Chinese whorehouses in San Francisco," I say. "The Chinese are a very closed race. Perhaps they don't allow their women to work in that way."

"Cowshit!" JoJay says. "Every race allows its women to make an honest living. Besides, even in Taos I have heard stories of Chinese whorehouses in San Francisco. My cousin Tell Me Good Morning told me. He has been around."

"Maybe we could go out to Fillmore Street," I say. "A nice black whorehouse. I have a friend who knows many black whorehouses."

"It is not the same. Black whores do not fuck like new, unbroken ponies. Besides, I fucked a black whore in Albuquerque."

"A nice white girl. There are lots of nice white beatnik girls on Grant Avenue and you can fuck them for free."

"No," JoJay says. "White beatnik girls are like chop suey. A half hour after you're finished you're horny again. I want to go to a Chinese whorehouse. I want to see if Chinese women are built the way they say. Walter told me they are built very peculiar."

Walter folds his paper and looks at JoJay. "JoJay," he says, "I will take you to a Chinese whorehouse before we go back to Taos."

"Good," JoJay says. "For a while I thought the white man was going to break another treaty."

17 Tuesday night I walked down to 72 Commercial Street and hollered up at McCracken's window. "Hey, McCracken!"

McCracken stuck his head out the window. "What's happenin', mon?"

"Let's take a walk."

"Hey, you crazy? Come up here and get high. I just finished 'The Revolt.' "

Upstairs McCracken is standing in front of the painting he'd sketched out briefly on the wall of my loft as part of the decoration for Francesca's and Hube the Cube's wedding. He calls it "The Revolt of the Martyrs." McCracken isn't actually standing in front of the painting; he's dancing in front of it. The painting is immense, spreading out twelve feet in length. It's somber, muted, yet at the same time fiercely aflame, a flight of people carrying torches across the length of the canvas, half impressionistic, half realistic, the running people blending into the flames and the flames themselves dissolving into the air to become dark, somber clouds.

"Well, what d'you think?" McCracken flung his brush into the corner. "Twelve fucking feet of visual poetry! It's the biggest painting I've ever done."

While we were looking at the painting, Roosevelt Chicken flapped up and perched on the edge of the canvas. "Get the fuck off there!" McCracken yelled, throwing a bottlecap at the bird.

Roosevelt Chicken is the nemesis of 72 Commercial Street. The bird belonged to Bud Olderman, a poet on the Beach, but he stays at the loft because Bud can't keep him in his hotel room. Not even the San Gottardo Hotel will accept Roosevelt Chicken. The trouble is Roosevelt Chicken shits on everything in sight. When Bud first brought him down to the loft for safekeeping, his favorite perch was on the bedstead above the pillows. He also explored the rest of the loft, however, spreading his mark over everything.

"One of us has to start taking Roosevelt Chicken out for a walk," Arthur said to McCracken one day. "There's chickenshit on every one of my drawings."

"I like that," McCracken said, pointing to a drawing of Arthur's that Roosevelt Chicken had criticized. "Roosevelt's definitely trying to say something."

"He does have a certain style, doesn't he?" Arthur said. "Maybe we should let him have some paper of his own."

"You're right." McCracken grabbed a sheet of drawing paper and spread it out on the floor. He lifted Roosevelt Chicken off the bedstead. "Go on, do something for us, Roosevelt."

Roosevelt Chicken cocked his head at McCracken and Arthur and stared with doleful eyes, one eye at a time.

"Maybe he needs something to inspire him." Arthur grabbed a can of paint. He dribbled it around Roosevelt Chicken.

Roosevelt Chicken pecked desultorily at the paint, then stepped in it and walked across the paper.

"I think we should give old Roosevelt his own canvas so he can work things out," McCracken said. "It looks like he has something going."

Roosevelt Chicken became King Chicken at 72 Commercial Street. McCracken and Arthur and Bowen encouraged him, providing paint and canvas and a space for him to work. Soon Roosevelt Chicken had a whole collection of paintings. Dr. Wenner, Bowen's patron from Potrero Hill, visited the loft to look at his work. "Well, what do you think?" McCracken said.

"I think it's the beginning of the San Francisco School of Chickenshit Art," Dr. Wenner said.

McCracken locked Roosevelt Chicken in the bathroom and we covered "The Revolt of the Martyrs." He grabbed a bottle off a shelf. "I got three inches of port left. Goddamnit, Kid, I feel like celebrating. Let's go over to Spadelee's and buy a jug!"

We shared the three inches of port as we walked

down Drumm Street toward Spadelee's. McCracken was excited, painting giant pictures with his hands, weaving images in the air. I felt good too. The sweet port tingled in my throat and the frenetic atmosphere of the produce market excited me. The streets vibrated with the noise of the big rigs. We dodged in and out of crates of vegetables and fruit, grabbing fistfuls of grapes, cramming them into our mouths along with swallows of wine.

"Goddamnit, I'm the best fucking painter in San Francisco!" McCracken cried.

"Better not let Bowen hear you say that."

"Aw, Bowen's good too, him and Arthur. We're all brothers, the Three Musketeers of Painting, yaheeee!"

I tipped the port to my lips and handed the jug to McCracken. He swallowed the remaining inch and then ran forward a few feet and hurled the empty jug over his head with all his might. "Yahooo!" The bottle sailed over the top of an abandoned warehouse and clattered on the rooftop, tinkling as it broke into little pieces.

We turned down Jackson Street toward Spadelee's. Spadelee is an old black wino who runs a decrepit little hole-in-the-wall grocery store smack dab in the middle of the produce market. Spadelee's store is stocked with a few cans of sardines, some milk and crackers, and a full wall of wooden shelves containing Valley of the Moon wine. Spadelee is famous for his Valley of the Moon wine. Valley of the Moon wine is an institution in San Francisco among a certain coterie of serious wine drinkers. The wine has an aura about it, a certain tangible ambiance that, when one consumes it long enough, becomes part of the drinker. Whenever I drink Valley of the Moon wine, I think of Jack London. Valley of the Moon wine leaves a literary aftertaste in my mouth, an aftertaste that reminds me of crumbling stones and flames at night.

When you enter Spadelee's grocery store, a little bell that's attached to the door rings to warn him that he has a customer. When the bell rings, Spadelee shuffles out from the back room where he sits all day drinking wine and watching television. It's like a scene out of *Let Us Now Praise Famous Men,* with *I Love Lucy* blaring.

When Spadelee shuffles out of his back room, he smiles a sad smile and hunches his shoulders up in a peculiar way he has, and he always says the same thing: "How's things going, boys?"

"Great, Spadelee. How's things going for you?"

"Oh, fine 'n' dandy, fine 'n' dandy. You boys want to buy a little old spodi-odi?"

"Yeah, give us a jug of that old spodi-odi."

Spadelee reaches behind him and takes a pint of sweet tokay wine off the shelf and carefully wipes the dust off the bottle. McCracken pulls twenty-nine cents out of his pocket and lays it on the counter.

"You boys want this in a paper bag? I can put this in a paper bag if you boys want me to."

"Yeah, put it in a paper bag, Spadelee."

Spadelee reaches behind him on the shelf and picks up a used paper bag. He smooths the wrinkles out and then carefully places the pint of tokay inside it, elaborately twisting the top of the bag around the neck of the bottle.

Outside on the sidewalk McCracken broke the seal of the jug of tokay wine. I like the cracking sound the seal makes when it breaks. It's like a signal that something good is about to happen. McCracken held the jug out to me and I hit it lightly and handed it back. The sweet tokay wine was a nice warm red river sailing down my throat. When the river hit the sea, which was my stomach, I felt at peace.

McCracken and I stood under the streetlamp outside Spadelee's grocery store and emptied the pint of sweet tokay. The banks of my river were well formed and a little silt was gathering on the bottom. "This is good wine," McCracken said.

"Umm." I nodded. I felt foxtails and pussywillows growing alongside my river.

"I think it'd be a good idea to go back inside Spadelee's and buy another jug," McCracken said.

We walked back inside Spadelee's grocery store. The

little bell attached to the door rang. Spadelee shuffled out from his back TV room.

"How's things going, boys?"

"Great, Spadelee. Can we have another jug of that old spodi-odi?"

"Sure, boys. You want me to put it in a paper bag?"

I pulled the twenty-nine cents out of my pocket and laid it on the counter. Spadelee carefully polished the jug with his rag and then put the jug inside a paper bag. He twisted the top of the bag around the neck of the jug.

"You boys be good now, hear?" he said as we walked out the door.

For me Spadelee's little hole-in-the-wall grocery store is a shrine, a consecrated temple for all the down-and-out humanity floundering in the streets. Sometimes when I pass the store on my solitary walks, I see the wrinkled bums sitting on the curb in front of the place, their empty or half-empty jugs of Valley of the Moon wine standing like discarded chalices on the cracked sidewalk. Inside, Spadelee's grocery store reeks of dust and time and old age. The tiny pint jugs silent in rows on the shelves cast an imperious soft glow in the late afternoon sunlight. I see the sun's rays shining through the bottles, casting shadows on the floor like stained-glass windows in a wino's house of worship. Sometimes the sun glints off the bottles with such a brilliance I am blinded, and when I see Spadelee shuffling among the rows of bottles I feel like weeping, seeing him and time mingling, holding hands as it were, as they walk together toward empty shelves.

Before he fell asleep under the produce truck on Davis Street and lost his legs, Trout Fishing in America Shorty came by Spadelee's store every day to buy his wine. Even now he sometimes wheels his shiny chromeplated wheelchair down Jackson Street to buy his Valley of the Moon tokay, carefully avoiding the sidewalks so he won't have to go up and down the curbs. When he reaches Spadelee's store, he rattles the screen door with his fist so the bell rings. Then he hollers, "Hey, Spadelee, bring me out a jug!"

When Trout Fishing in America Shorty shouts out his orders, Spadelee shuffles out of his TV room gloom and goes behind the counter and gets a jug of tokay wine off the shelf and carefully polishes it with the rag he keeps on the counter. Then he shuffles to the door and opens it slowly and hands the jug out. Trout Fishing in America Shorty grabs the jug with a fierce scowl and breaks the seal and takes a long snort, then he thrusts the jug in his coat pocket and wheels away, never bothering to pay. From his doorway Spadelee watches him go, his expression never changing, an expression so ineffable and sad that it seems to be part of the storefront itself, created by an architect who understood the nature of the essential impermanence of all mortar and stone. To me the jug of tokay wine that Spadelee takes from his shelf and Trout Fishing in America Shorty's shouting cry are like a talisman between vendor and vendee, a link that's ageless, each of them part of a mathematical equation that would be incomplete without the other. I mentioned this to McCracken and he laughed. "You're a romantic sonofabitch," he said.

"But don't you see? It all means something ... I don't know . . ."

"It's an old spade wino with a two-bit store and a wino bum with no legs and in a few years the fat cats will come in and buy it all up and erect one of their superbig shit-yellow apartment buildings, that's all it is!"

"But there's more to it than that." I stopped talking because I didn't know what to say. All I know is that there's a certain wall on Commercial Street, wooden, part of a building that's incredibly old. The colors in the wood are like amber mixed with blood. I once took McCracken down to Commercial Street and showed him the wall. I wanted to know if he felt about it the same as me. I turned to him. "Do you remember that wall I showed you, the one I had Clementi take a picture of? Do you remember that wood?"

"Oh hee hee hee," McCracken laughed. "Fuck yes I remember that wall. Clementi and I laughed about it for weeks afterwards. The Kid and his crazy walls, Clementi said. Didn't you know that?"

We shared the jug of tokay wine as we walked through the produce market. On the corner of Sansome and Clay we stopped to read a plaque affixed to the side of an old building.

SITE OF SHIP NIANTIC

The immigrant ship Niantic stood on this spot in the early days when the water came up to Montgomery Street! Converted to other uses, it was covered with a shingle roof with offices and stores on the deck, at the level of which was constructed a wide balcony surmounted by a verandah. The hull was divided into warehouses, entered by doorways on the sides.

The fire on May 3, 1851, destroyed all but the submerged hulk, which was utilized as the foundation for the Niantic Hotel, a famous hostelry which stood until 1872.

This tablet was placed by the historical landmark committee of the Native Sons of the Golden West, September 19, 1919.

"Did you know the water of the bay used to come right up to here?" McCracken said, his little-boy mouth pursed out. "Goddamn! That's when I would've liked to have been here, back when San Francisco was alive! Man, the city was wide open. You could screw and fuck and live! You weren't safe on the streets during the Barbary Coast days, man. Walk down a back alley and bam! The next day you're on a square rigger heading for Singapore. That's chance! That's what's missing nowadays! Chance don't stand a chance any more."

We strode on up the sidewalk heading for the Coffee Gallery, passing the jug back and forth as we walked. "Cool it with the vino," McCracken said suddenly. "That guy's the heat."

I looked around. I saw an ordinary-looking guy in a business suit crossing the street. Nothing irregular. The guy approached us. "Can I see you boys a minute?" he said, flashing a badge.

"What'd we do?" McCracken said.

"Where do you boys live?" the cop asked. "D'you have ID's?"

"Hey, what's going on?" McCracken protested. "We live here, in a loft on Commercial Street. We're just walking around."

McCracken and I go through interrogations like this all the time, especially when we walk at night. People who walk at night are suspicious. "Why're you walking?" the cops ask. "Where's your car?"

"I ain't got a car," McCracken spits back. He always explodes with anger at these interruptions. The cops can't understand the need just to walk. One night we were stopped and a cop asked us the inevitable question, "What are you doing walking the streets at night?"

"I'm listening to the sounds," McCracken said.

"Shut your ears or I'll run you in," the cop said.

McCracken has the outsider's instinct for survival. "My hands are always in and my antenna's always out," he said.

Further on we stopped at a laden debris box. During the day the boxes are filled with all the junk and paraphernalia from the various buildings being remodeled in the area, and during the night the artists and writers and denizens of North Beach come out to retrieve what's useful. Some of the debris boxes remain parked beside construction sites for months at a time, much to the annoyance of the debris box companies who make their money by hauling full boxes away. It's like the boxes have a life of their own, though, metamorphosing from empty to full to empty time and time again, like strange North Beach cultures growing alongside the streets, providing sustenance for the people living around them.

McCracken is a master debris-box scavenger. As soon as we spotted the box, he clambered in and started rummaging around. This one was full of all kinds of stuff—crates, paper, old furniture, couches, clothes, toilet bowls, shoes, bathtubs, scrap iron. "Man, they throw a lot of good stuff away," McCracken cried.

He pulled a solid oak door out of the trash. "Hey, man, this'll make a great table. Help me carry it back to the loft."

Carrying the door between us, we walked homeward. On Commercial Street a prowl car pulled up alongside us. There were two cops in the car. One of them trained his flashlight on us. "Hey, what're you guys doing?"

"We're just taking this door home," McCracken said.

One cop got out of the car and walked around to us. He shined his flashlight first in my eyes, then McCracken's. "Where'd you guys steal that door?"

"We didn't steal it, we got it out of a debris box."

"What debris box?"

"The one back there on Washington Street."

"You guys got permission to take stuff out of that debris box?"

"Man, it's there for the taking. Everybody gets stuff out of debris boxes."

"What's your names?"

The second cop got out of the car and backed us up against the wall while the first cop checked out our fingerprints, driver's license, adoption agency, dogtags, auto certificate, gas bill, social security number, library card, draft notice, laundry tag, bill of sale, grocery slip, vaccination mark, rent receipt, and number of cavities. We stood on the sidewalk holding the door between us, working through the whole identification routine, foot-shuffling and nervous, leaning against walls, etc. When the report came back that we were clean, the two cops got back in their prowl car. "Keep off the streets and don't take any more stuff out of debris boxes."

"Fuck you!" McCracken gave the cops the finger as they drove away.

After depositing the door in McCracken's loft, we headed back toward the Beach. When we passed Fresno Alley a voice called out. "Psst, hey, Kid, McCracken."

Tokay Bill stepped out of a doorway and sat down on the edge of the curb. He was holding a jug. We sat down beside him. Tokay Bill's a wanderer of the streets like us, only he has his own streets that neither McCracken nor I know. Most of the time Tokay Bill hangs around the Beach, but occasionally he disappears for a week or two on a mysterious mission of his own to another part of the city, a mission no one ever asks about and that he never volunteers any information on. When he's on the Beach, Tokay Bill can always be found in an alley not too far from Ken's Grocery Store, where he sits in the shadows drinking. Ken's Grocery Store is Tokay's filling station. Whenever his jug gets empty, he wanders back up Grant Avenue to the store.

Tokay Bill's jug was full now and the neck stuck out of a twisted paper bag. He handed it to me and I hit it and handed it across to McCracken. The jug went around and ended up back in Tokay Bill's hand.

"It makes a nice fire inside," I said.

"Best heater in the world," Tokay Bill said.

"It's good wine," McCracken said.

"After a couple of hits, it's good even if it's bad," Tokay Bill said.

The jug circled again and then Tokay Bill stood up and held it in his hands, rocking back and forth on the balls of his feet. He moved in a slow fluidlike motion, up on his toes and down on his heels, as if he remembered. Tokay Bill wore a full beard and he had a gold earring in one pierced ear. As he moved back and forth, he looked like an African chieftain, noble and alone in Fresno Alley. Rocking slowly, he put the jug to his lips, his teeth flashing in a great wide smile. "Heh heh heh," he chuckled, deep sonorous, like all of Africa laughing. "Whoooeee!" he said, "this is some fine wine, yeah!"

I took the jug and hit it. The alley lights flashed behind my eyes like neon butterflies.

"Pass that jug, you bastard," McCracken said.

I handed him the jug. I let my own hit flow down my throat without swallowing. When the wine hit bottom, it lay there, eating a hole through my stomach. I felt the walls of my stomach churning together, like huge gloved hands congratulating themselves. The wine made me feel giddy and level-headed at the same time.

"Its a good winedrinking night," McCracken said.

"Every night's a good winedrinking night." Tokay Bill nodded in the dark. "I have yet to meet a night that wasn't a good winedrinking night."

"Some nights are better winedrinking nights than others. Some nights are superwinedrinking nights."

We talked like this for twenty minutes. Wine talk. We didn't care. When the jug was dead, we'd walk up the street to Ken's and buy another pint. It was that kind of winedrinking night.

"A Fresno Alley winedrinking night," Tokay Bill said.

McCracken and I nodded our heads in unison. We knew what he meant. Fresno Alley winedrinking nights are nights to remember. They are nights to remember because in the morning you can't remember them.

"One more jug and I'll be ready," I said. "My head'll be set on jus' about right."

Tokay Bill nodded. He hit the jug again and passed it to me. "One more jug and your temperature'll be just right."

"It's a drag being cold," McCracken said.

"Nobody likes to be cold," I said. "Here, warm yourself."

When the jug was empty, we staggered out of Fresno Alley. I saw Frankie on the corner. She was leaning against the window in front of the Coffee Gallery. She looked sad. I walked over to her while McCracken and Tokay Bill went on to Ken's. They returned with a jug of wine. "Have a shot of this," McCracken said. He popped the top of the jug and handed it to Frankie. She took the jug and sipped from it.

"Where have you been?" I hadn't seen Frankie for a week. She looked gaunt, thin. She handed the bottle back to McCracken.

"I've been around."

"Where's Milton?"

"Around. Taking care of business."

We walked back to Fresno Alley, passing the jug on the way. In the dark Frankie looked small. I sat down on the curb and pulled her down beside me. I had an edge on, was feeling goofy, and laughed. "Gee, Frankie, it's good to see you. I haven't seen you since the wedding."

"I've been home," she said.

"I dropped by a coupla times; you weren't there."

"We went to Stinson."

"What's this, the morgue?" McCracken cried. "Where's the jug?"

Tokay Bill handed the wine to McCracken. He tipped the jug, then held it out to Frankie. "Drink this, it'll make you feel better."

"I feel fine," Frankie said.

"This'll make you feel superfine."

Frankie took the jug and sipped a little more. She handed the jug back and wiped her mouth.

"Let's go down to my place," McCracken said. "Fuck this alley shit. We can sit around a fire and get fucked up."

"Do you have any speed?" Frankie said.

"What d'you want speed for?" I said. "Are you shooting speed?"

"No," Frankie said. "I've just been chipping a little."

I had a sudden flash of dismay. Frankie's face had an edgy, empty look. The baby fat was gone from her cheeks. Her eyes were darker and her lips thinner. "Is Milton shooting you full of speed?" I said.

"Oh, fuck you! You sound like an old grandmother."

"That motherfucker's shooting you full of speed, isn't he?"

"Hee, hee, hee," McCracken laughed. He was sitting on the curb with his elbows on his knees and his head hunched down between his legs, slowly shaking his head.

"You two are too much." He lifted his head and looked at Frankie. "I've got some speed. Come down to my loft and I'll give you some."

Frankie got up and walked back toward the Coffee Gallery. "I'll see you later," she called to McCracken. She didn't look at me.

"You going to give Frankie some speed?" I looked at McCracken.

"I'm going to fuck her," McCracken said. "I'll put a little speed into her."

The nice wine-edge I had was gone. "I don't want you to give her any speed."

"What's the matter with you, Kid? You getting religious or something? You bite once in a while, don't you?"

"Some people can't handle it."

McCracken looked at me. "Shit, you scored for Hube the Cube, didn't you?"

"Hube the Cube's not Frankie."

"Frankie can take care of herself," McCracken said. "She's been geezing smack with Milton for quite a while now."

"Has Milton strung Frankie out?"

"Fuck, ask her. I'm not her keeper. What's wrong with you, you bugged 'cause Milton's fucking Frankie?"

"I didn't know she was geezing smack."

"Everybody geezes smack. Frankie only chips now and then."

"She's strung out, I can tell. That asshole Milton got her on speed and now she's chipping smack."

18 I got up and walked out of Fresno Alley. I looked back and saw McCracken and Tokay Bill still sitting on the curb. Fuck it! What was the use? I'd let go and float like everyone else I knew, drifters and drunks, speed freaks and addicts, children and wastrels, who moved up and down Grant Avenue like strangers, people no one knew. I kicked at the curb. I felt an incredible desire to reach out and touch something, and more and more it seemed impossible to touch anything. There was no touchstone, there was no one to touch!

I walked down Columbus Avenue and headed back toward the produce market. My head buzzed with the residue of tokay wine. The good feeling was gone and only the bad feeling remained. I walked toward the Embarcadero. The streets were empty, like brick canyons, cold and lonely, the dark warehouses looming over me like forbidding tombstones. I was full of bitterness toward Milton and McCracken. Both of them were using Frankie for their own ends. Hell, when it got down to it, I was too. We were all a bunch of hungry people out to satisfy our own pitiful desires.

My mind whirled as I walked along, full of an exasperating windmill of thoughts that seemed phony and juvenile. I realized that most of my actions weren't actions at all, but reactions, animal responses to the stimuli surrounding me. I didn't even know why I dug Frankie. She was just another chick, another chick on the set with eyes and mouth and ears and veins open for anything that could be stuck into them. The very idea of being on the Beach was crazy. Why was I here? The life I was leading seemed empty and useless; I felt like a parasite sucking sustenance from a city and an area that promised nothing but despair. Yet I loved North Beach. It was a community, albeit a community of hopelessness. Even hopeless people are better off when they are together, even strangers are better off when they touch. "How many died, Maxwell?" Tambourine said. Years later when all the corpses were stacked and counted I would be able to tell him. Now, at mid-century, everybody seemed to be standing on the corner waiting. "Why don't your friends get a decent pad, and a bed, get some basis they can build upon. They're always hanging around, they're always standing on the corner," Crow said.

For me the meaning *was* in the people who hung around; the streetcorner sitters and winedrinking circles held more promise than anybody else. Frankie was my touchstone; she was my promise. But Frankie loved Milton. Milton was once my good friend and now I was beginning to hate him. He wasn't even Milton any more, not the Milton I'd known on the Beach. Somehow he'd become something else, a symbol, a degeneration of friendship, an old pal gone wrong, become the reality of himself. I was beginning to hate Milton. I was even beginning to hate his blackness, a blackness that consumed and followed me down the streets. What right did that big black bastard have to Frankie? I was white, goddamnit, and I loved her! When this thought struck me, I laughed out loud. I was nothing but a white nigger. Worse than Milton, because at least Milton was out front with Frankie. Frankie knew exactly where she stood with Milton. With me she dealt with a weasel, a sly weasel. Her heartbreak with Milton would be no more and no less than her heartbreak with me. It seemed we were all destined for heartbreaks. With one hand we accepted, grasped for strangers, and with the other hand we rejected them. I saw this in myself, the inability to sustain a relationship beyond the first few sexual thrusts. Frankie was just another chick whom I'd set my eyes on, just like I'd set my eyes on others, girls who, after they were hooked, were thrown back like small fish in the sea. I didn't understand this part of myself any more than I understood the sea. There is the need, there is the person who will fill that need, but when the stranger is no longer a stranger there is still that need.

I turned down the Embarcadero and walked in front of the looming piers. The fog tunneled into the bay like columns of an intangible army, absorbing everything by its presence. I stood between two piers and watched the fog trace its way over toward Berkeley, a silent advance, no noise from the battalions, no clatter of tanks or shouts of artillery. It was a dreadnought whose very silence lent it a feeling of impending calamity. Shrouding myself in the fog, I continued walking. I stopped beside the *Balclutha*, listening as the wind played through the rigging of the old three-masted sailing ship. That's what it sounded like out at sea, I knew, back in those times when sailors stood on deck or lay half asleep in their bunks listening to that sound, the devil's breath, the whip and whir of wind lashing the rigging, of movement, of going and coming, and it was strange to them in those days as it was to me now.

The *Balclutha* sat ghostly in the dark, her shrouds and furled sails seeming to hold communion among themselves. I looked for phantom sailors in the rigging but saw only fogswirls sweeping between the masts, the dew glistening from the hawsers and the old steel hull gleaming dully in the dark. I listened for Stubb's call, but Stubb didn't call; I listened for Ahab's ivory clack, but heard only the echo of the foghorn on the Golden Gate Bridge weeping mechanically in the night.

At Aquatic Park the lagoon was still. I stood on the steps above the beach. On the sand a figure nursed a small fire which flickered silently. Beyond a small jug of wine lying half buried in the sand was a small bundle of clothing. I recognized Pluto, the Aquatic Park madman. Pluto is a leftover from the Bataan death march and he spends his days and nights here in Aquatic Park, stepping off those days left him as if Japanese soldiers still held bayonets to his head. Pluto lives on a military pension and has no place to go so he goes everywhere. A hundred times I've run into him on my sojourns through the city, hurrying along, long scarf and flappy coat flying. Pluto always wears an old GI overcoat buttoned up to his chin, two or three pairs of trousers, a couple of battered sportscoats under his overcoat, and three or four pairs of socks inside his flappy highbutton shoes. He always has a pipe stuck between his teeth and he moves his head neither to the right or left as he walks, always forward, marching on and on.

I never speak to Pluto, have never, in fact, heard him speak. Every day Pluto comes to Aquatic Park and every day he takes off his layers of clothing, burying the items one by one in the sand as if to prevent them from being blown away by the wind. He takes his pipe out of his mouth, burying it stem-end in the sand, along with the little bag of Bull Durham tobacco he always carries. After disrobing down to his final pair of ragged shorts, Pluto strides up and down the beach on his magnificent legs. Pluto's legs are the color of deep mahogany; the muscles ripple in them like demon tendons struggling to break out of the skin's hold. Sometimes when he's striding over the sand, he'll make a sudden dash for the water, hurl himself over and over in the waves, then stand waist deep splashing himself, scrubbing his body down. Then he'll literally leap out of the water and roll on the beach, covering his skin with sand, the grainy hide somehow looking natural on him, as if his skin had metamorphosed back into some primeval foreskin that mankind must have had during some phase of its journey out of the sea.

After lying and rolling in the sand for half an hour or so, Pluto leaps up and continues pacing the beach, moving like a dancer up and down the strand, striding in and out of knots of bathers, pacing off in incredible strides the whole length of Aquatic Park, up to the tangled pieces of rotting boards that mark one boundary, then back to the bathhouse that marks the other.

Pluto sat hunched over his fire this night, gazing out over the dark water. I couldn't see his face but I knew he was grinning, a craggy grin with a question mark. Pluto's face always carried the same quizzical grin, a grin I knew was simply the burnscarred skin pulled back tight around his lips, baring his teeth in such a way as to leave him perpetually smiling, day and night, sun down, moon down, and finally earth down too. I paused for a moment, wanting to share my night with Pluto, and have him share his night with me. In the end, though, I passed his campfire and walked slowly up the strand to the sidewalk and climbed the concrete stairs to the top. For as long as I stood there on the steps, Pluto didn't move, just stared out over the darkened bay.

The night was getting cold, so I pulled my sweater up around my neck. Frankie was probably at McCracken's loft by now. The thought made my heart swell with bitterness. I wasn't angry over the fact that McCracken was going to give Frankie some speed; if she didn't get it from McCracken, she'd get it from somebody else, from Milton or any number of people on the Beach who'd gladly supply her. I'd even give some to her myself if she really wanted it. What really bothered me was my inability to control things, my own life, Frankie, the set. We all seemed to be victims, and I knew that I was just as much a victim as anyone else, the only difference was that I felt I had a faint understanding of my disease.

The knowledge didn't seem to help me, though; it brought no solace. All it did was make me anxious, more aware of the dilemma surrounding me, surrounding all the people on the Beach. And not only the Beach, but all over, everywhere. We were all victims of a crazy malaise that seemed rooted in our bones. What was it Scott said? "I'm keeping a journal, Kid, *The Journal of Anxiety's Child*. I'm not going to last long, so I want you to take it up. I want you to have it, the title's yours. You can finish it when you're ready. You have a strength the others don't have, a practical strength. It comes from your background. You're still rooted to the soil. Even though your family hasn't been on the land for years, you still have the strength of the ground. Everybody else on the Beach has some defect, a flaw somewhere. So do you, but yours isn't fatal. I want you to take *The Journal of Anxiety's Child* and finish it."

A few months after showing me his *Journal of Anxiety's Child*, Scott stripped off all his clothes in the Bagel Shop and ran screaming to the piano and climbed on top of it. "I can't stand the dishonesty!" he cried. "Take off your clothes! I want the coverings stripped away!"

I went out to the county hospital to visit him. When I walked into the psychiatric ward, he looked small and defenseless in his white bed. He didn't look at me, just stared straight ahead, his eyes boring into the white wall in front of him. "How are you, Scott?" I asked.

"The eucalyptus leaves are very delicate, aren't they?" he said.

A few days later I heard that Scott had been transferred to the Agnew State Hospital. I never saw him again. When I inquired about him, I heard that his mother or aunt had come and taken him away, back east, to a sanitarium for the insane.

I don't even remember how I met Scott. It must have been in City Lights Bookstore, downstairs, among the volumes of poetry and small magazines. All I can remember is the insane reality of his presence. He was there, in my loft, in the streets, a cataclysmic eruption of language and movement. Before Scott flipped out, he and I walked constantly. It was as if we were drawn to one another. Of all my walking companions, Scott was the most intense. McCracken was an artist, energetic, boyish, brash, cocky, alive; Crow was calm, conservative, intellectual, though given to extraordinary bursts of Irish ragman humor; Scott was feverish, wild, frenetic, unstoppable! When we hit the street, Scott plunged forward like a long-distance runner. Although I was a good six inches taller than he, I had to run to keep up—and me a walker! The trouble with Scott was that he didn't walk, he thrust himself through the streets. I panted after him and finally cried out, "For Christ's sake, Scott, slow down!" He stopped and whirled around. "It's good to walk, Kid. It's good to get out into the night. You've got to feel it, see it, get back to nature, back to growing things! We have to get close to the earth so we can maintain our reality! See growing things, touch them, smell them!" With this he turned and ran to the side of the road (this at three A.M. in a black old town searching out the reality of a leaf) and touched a tree growing beside the road. Telegraph Hill hovered over us. I stood in the middle of the street watching. "We have to keep close to the earth, remind ourselves that it exists, touch it, remember who we are!"

During the time I was with Scott, I was never so unattached to myself. My own little rituals and life patterns that I'd worked out to lend coherence to my days were changed to suit Scott. He'd come down to Roach Alley at night, stand under my loft windows yelling up at me, "Kid, Kid! Let's walk!" I'd open the door and Scott bounded up the stairs four at a time. "Let's walk, Kid, walk, walk!"

Our walks became ritualistic; they had a soothing quality about them. Scott needed to walk, to talk, to have ears that were open so he could loose the torrent in his soul. His voice was magnetic, vibrant with imagery and poetry. Scott was mad with talk, alive with it, so full of words that even his fingers spoke, weaving conversations in the air as he walked. Often when he was talking, he seemed to disappear before me; I would blink and there he was standing in front of me again. I had a premonition during these times that Scott would be dead before he was twenty. If not dead in fact, then dead in spirit. He was only nineteen now, but there was too much tension inside him, he was incapable of a peaceful moment, he thought too much!

Scott lived in a tiny dressing room behind the Hyde Street Playhouse. In his room one night he showed me his journal. He kept it in a large lined notebook, each day delineated by a brief, sad entry. He curled up in his small bunk and handed the journal to me. The writing was chaotic, slanting furiously across the page as if it were running a race with life—words tumbling over words, lines obliterated, pen and ink sketches bordering every entry. It was full of notations, thoughts, observations, outlines, poetry, drawings, questions: Man will be a spirit, an electrical force. If we push ourselves far we'll be Prophets and die like Artaud! We must go as far as our courage will allow us to go. We must train our senses, and the only real sense is the moral sense. Man is more honest than dishonest, more moral than immoral! Fear breeds immorality! Man can become God if we teach him not to fear. If you find yourself being mediocre, go out and commit suicide! Prize yourself! The morality of today is not the morality of tomorrow. Our mind is always ahead of us. We are good, we know that we are good, but we have to be told so! We need immortality! We have to have our pictures on the wall, our names in books! The work is the man! Realize this! Put it down on paper, touch it, hold it, and you will live forever! Approach the limit of yourself, push, push yourself right off the page! The fact that you are worried about where you are going will make you go there. I know I shall write it. I am writing it now! I prolong the pleasure of putting words down on paper. I am alive! Every second must be art! That's the trouble with North Beach, there is no morality in this new movement. All of them will die. They will kill God, all of them, uselessly. Every moment is serious. Don't dig everything—live it! Artaud went too far beyond himself, he went mad. If you don't think you are perfect, you won't be perfect. Imagine yourself to be what you are—and you will be it!

Among the notations in Scott's journal I found a poem:

> And then she asked me
> What is God?
> And I replied,
> God is religion
> And religion is morality.
>
> And then she asked me
> What is life?
> And I replied,
> Life is the organic time
> We have for morality.
>
> And then she asked me
> What is truth?
> And I replied,
> Truth is the courage we have
> To seek morality's morality.

And then she asked me
What is art?
And I replied,
Art is man's expression
Of morality's morality.

And then she asked me
What is love?
And I replied,
Love is God, Life, Truth, Art,
Morality's Morality—Man!

"I'm looking for a concrete reality," Scott said while I thumbed through his journal. "Man is essentially moral but he's afraid of his morality."

Scott grabbed a book of poems from the shelf above his head, opened it quickly, and quoted a line to me. He threw the book down on the bed and grabbed another and read from it also. "Read this when you have the time, Kid," he said. He tossed the second book down and grabbed another. "This play, Artaud, you have to understand . . . no—come here next week and you'll see it, they're going to act it on the stage." He grabbed another book, a book of drawings by Picasso. "Here, you must have these. Hang them in your loft." He ripped a picture from the book. I took the picture and folded it into the book he'd given me, a book of poems by e. e. cummings. "Here, take this!" He grabbed a metal box and unclasped it. "It's a safe. It's waterproof and fireproof; it will protect the journal. I want you to have my journal. I'm not going to write any more. I want you to take it, Kid. The title, everything's yours. You'll finish it for me."

A few days after giving me his journal, Scott and I were walking and we met Frankie. Frankie was in a hurry to get somewhere and she rushed off after a few words. "She has a basic malady, a flaw somewhere. She's doomed," Scott said.

I laughed. "Frankie's not doomed. She's a little hung up, that's all. She's no more doomed than anyone else."

"She has a flaw," Scott repeated. "A weakness."

"We all have weaknesses. I don't think Frankie's any more doomed than you or me."

"She's not if she finds the right person," Scott said. "But she won't find him, because she doesn't want to."

When Scott said that, I had a sudden premonition of his own doom, of mine, the doom of all of us. "Frankie doesn't want to find the right person, because some people are destined to failure," he said.

We hurried on through the streets. "The stars are out," Scott said. "Andromeda is very bright tonight."

I looked up and saw stars I'd never seen.

In physical appearance Scott looked like a small boy, an elf, one of the twelve wise old men, an ancient, a genius, a demented soul, an encyclopedia, a comic book. "How old are you, Scott?" someone once asked him. "Age!" he screamed. "Inevitable question! I'm as old as you think I am!" He was ten, he was a hundred, he was ageless; he was old when he was born; he will be zero years old when he dies.

I was shaken by my friendship with Scott. Whenever he burst into my loft on one of his three A.M. interruptions, I was aroused, but at the same time as mad as he was in my desire to hear, absorb, and record the calamity brewing in his breast. To me, Scott epitomized the Beach in its most unknowable form. One time as he and I passed the bird-dappled railing along the pier at Aquatic Park, I saw a seagull perched on one leg on the balustrade, one of its eyes filmed over in sleep.

"And smale fowles maken melodye / that slepen al the night with open yë . . ." Scott said, quoting Chaucer. "Anyone who can describe birds that way saw the truth," he said.

I suddenly felt very good walking along the pier with Scott. He grabbed my arm suddenly and looked into my eyes. "Listen, Kid, you've got to read Nelson Algren. He has something important to say. Promise me you'll read Nelson Algren. He's one of the few writers in America who hasn't sold out."

"Yes"—I nodded—"I'll read Nelson Algren."

The lightness in the dawn sky and the feeling of immensity all about me caused me to draw closer to Scott. In the bay I saw a million fishes dive, spinning in whirling circles out of sight into their own dark world. I felt myself descending into a similar maelstrom, caught in a whirlpool of words and madness. I struck Scott on the shoulder to say something, my hand resting there a moment past striking, then I drew away sharply. The sea is dark.

For me the night streets are a benediction, a ritual and renewal that cools or inflames the blood—whichever is needed. When I am alone, my walks are peaceful, invigorating, curative. For the desperately lonely only the streets hold solace. I can walk for miles, through whole cities, at a slow, leisurely, fluidlike pace, mesmerized by the block after block of absolutely incredible reality surrounding me. Sometimes when I walk through the streets at night, it is as if I am really walking undersea, and the buildings and structures and people that surround me are lost continents of Atlantis and Mu inhabited by strange species of flora and fauna, underwater kingdoms whose existence is entirely unknown except to those who, by accident or design, break through the barriers between worlds and descend to the subterranean levels of human existence. Sometimes I feel I am living in a dream, that I am as Pluto is, seen from behind by ragged adolescents as just as insane, just as intent, just as eccentric in my nightly perambulations. When I see Pluto, I feel like a fellow conspirator, member of a secret fraternity that has worked out an elaborate ritual, a system of codes and signals that we flash to one another telepathically, as if the streets we walk are in reality a labyrinth of mazes and tunnels in which we are carrying out some secret mission, a mission that will eventually lead us together—or separately in our own ways—toward some ultimate fulfillment.

It never ceases to amaze me that wherever I go on my walks—to the Tenderloin, Aquatic Park, even all the way to Butchertown—I always run into Pluto or Tambourine or some lesser-known desperado of the streets, as if we are the anointed, the streets for us alone. While others may think the streets are for transportation and commerce and the movement of traffic, we know that they are really designed for the secret communion of night-time walkers, solitary souls who seek solace in the back alleys and byways where clattering scavenger trucks rock the early morning stillness. Even as our streets are thoroughfares tunneling through the elaborate façades of our existence, we know that somewhere along the Embarcadero or Mission, or perhaps down at the end of the smallest, filthiest, most graffiti-strewn alley in the Tenderloin, we will cross paths for a moment, and for that moment our loneliness will be assuaged.

Walking up Columbus Avenue under the haloed streetlamps, I thought of Scott and Frankie and Pluto and McCracken, each in their own way lost, each struggling to find that elusive portion of their lives that was missing. The pattern of my own life had the same gaping emptiness, a pattern as mysterious as a Chinese ideogram, with each of the lines having a meaning, a meaning as old as language itself, but none of us knowing how to read them; somehow our education is not sufficient, it's the wrong education, it has no meaning for our real lives. And so we end up being philosophers and students and children and bums and dope addicts, tracing each part of our own individual ideogram, covering every stem and crosstree with our walks and parties and incessant chatter. Nothing will be solved until we understand that calligraphy, until the meaning is clear and the story complete. Somehow in my deepest heart I know that life itself *is* the meaning; the search is life and life is the meaning. We are the ideogram, and when we cross all the tangents, explore every stem and crosstree of our life, reach the end of ourselves, then we will explode into beautiful sunlight, brighter than a thousand suns, the ecstatic nuclear energy of LIFE, and that life will be us alone, perfect, content, beautiful, full. We will be the thousand-petaled lotus expanding forever into the universe, we will be the universe, we will be *free*.

When I reached Roach Alley, I heard the bell in the tower of the Church of St. Peter and Paul strike three. I opened the door to my loft and climbed the stairs and fell down on my bed to sleep.

19 Milton knocked on my door early the next morning. I got out of bed and let him in. He followed me up the stairs and I got back into bed. I didn't want to see him. I knew what he wanted. He crossed over to the windows and peered down into Roach Alley. "What's the story with the weed?" he said.

I had one hundred and fifty dollars in my pants pocket. I got the money and handed it to him. He counted it slowly.

"I owe you sixty bucks. I'll pay you as soon as I collect from Groovy."

Milton shook his head. He made a neat pile on the table and counted the money again. "You really hangin' me up, Kid. You was s'pposed to have this two weeks ago."

I walked over to the sink and splashed water on my face. I had worked my ass off to get the hundred and fifty. I was in no mood to listen to Milton's bullshit.

"You're lucky to get that. There's no money on the Beach right now."

"When you goin' to have the sixty?"

I dried my face. "Groovy said he'd give it to me as soon as his boys paid him. When he lays it on me, I'll lay it on you."

Milton looked skeptical. He pulled a chair out from the table and sat down. He lifted his feet up on the table and pulled a thick wad of bills out of his coat pocket. He added the money I'd given him to the roll, holding the money out in front of him so I could see it. I paid no attention. I lit a fire under my hotplate and filled a saucepan with water. "You want some coffee?"

"Crazy."

Milton stared at me while I fixed the coffee. "How's Frankie?" I asked.

"She's okay. She's visitin' Wenner."

"What's wrong with her?"

Milton shrugged. His manner seemed feigned, bored. He walked over to the windows and looked out. The water was boiling so I filled the cups. "Why's Frankie seeing Dr. Wenner? Is she sick?"

Milton sat down and stirred sugar into his coffee. "How do I know what's wrong with her. Maybe she got the clap."

"How long has Frankie been geezing smack?"

Milton laughed. "Frankie ain't geezin' smack no more'n anybody else on the set. You gettin' to be an old maid in your old age, Kid. What's wrong with the chick gettin' a little buzz now an' then if she feels like it? You ain't no virgin, are you?"

Milton and I stared at one another for a minute and then I turned away. I knew Frankie was strung out. I could tell by her appearance the night before. What bugged me was that I was incapable of doing anything about it.

"It's stupid for Frankie to go to Wenner if she's strung out. He'll find out in a minute. What's she gone for, to score some pills?"

"Fuck pills!" Milton yelled. "How the hell do I know why that chick's gone to see the doctor. Maybe she's fuckin' him! Frankie can take care of herself, and if she can't, I can! You can rest your sweet ass about Frankie!"

I stood up. I had a strange feeling in my head, and an almost uncontrollable desire to hit Milton. To think that Frankie could live with him and not shoot smack was absurd. Only my own stupidity and blindness prevented me from seeing it. Milton used smack occasionally, Frankie lived with Milton, therefore Frankie used smack. It was as certain as a mathematical theorem. Just like the axiom that says a friend who becomes a junkie is not a friend any more, he's a junkie. No one, nothing counts except his daily fix. And if the daily fix is missing, nothing is sacred until the junkie gets it. A junkie will steal from his own mother for a fix. Not only will a junkie steal from his own mother, his mother is usually the first victim.

I walked back over to the table. "How long has Frankie been using junk?"

"Oh, fuck, man, get off it! Frankie ain't strung out on junk! She chips a little on weekends now an' then jus' like ever'body else. A little weekendin' never hurt nobody."

"Man, what do you mean, a little weekending? You start chipping smack on Saturday night, and before you know it you're strung out eight days a week! That shit don't take no holidays; it works all the time, weekends and overtime!"

Milton jumped up. "Fuck you, man! Don' you start preachin' to me!"

"Fuck you! What're you getting Frankie strung out on that stuff for? She doesn't need that stuff. That's a death trip, man! What do you want to haul her down to your level for?"

"My level? What do you know about my level?" Milton glowered at me.

"Oh, fuck it, man. I can see it in the way you carry on with her. You're more interested in the scene you create than you are in Frankie. Your mind's always thinking about what those pricks down at Mike's Place think, the way you strut around the Beach with her on your arm. You're always checking out to make sure ev-erybody sees you cuttin' it with a white chick. Don't give me any of that shit. I've watched you, man. You're just as bad as the people you're always putting down, more interested in the image you create than you are in Frankie. How come I never see you with a black chick? There's lots of black chicks around. How come I've never seen you with any of them?"

Milton's eyes narrowed, his lower lip was trembling. "You don't know what I do off this set, baby, an' you don't know shit about what goes down *on* this set ei-ther! What's wrong with you? You want me to bring some black pussy on the set for you? You wanna taste some black meat? You tellin' me how I walk down the street with Frankie, you the expert on my feelin's? Maan, you don't know nothin' but that shitty little tribe of assholes that hang around the Coffee Gallery and the Amp Palace! You don't know shit how I feel! You don't know what hassles a black dude goes through just gettin' up in the mornin'! You been brought up in your lily-white trip for twenty years an' you think you know what goes on in my head. You don't even know where my head's at. You don't know what emptiness there is, Jim, silence, nothin'! Maan, when I hit the streets I know there ain't nothin' to say, it's all a zero, a big fat goose egg! That's what's in my head. You come on with your claptrap friendship shit that don't mean shit the minute some white pussy comes in between it. Maan, I'm sick of hearin' your white bullshit! You say you dig the streets? You don't dig the streets. You been watchin' TV, man. You never been out in the streets!"

"Oh, fuck it, man, don't lay that shit on me! We both have our hassles. You cover yours and I try to cover mine, that's all there is to it. It isn't black and it isn't white. It's just hassles all the way down the line. You hassle with a white pussy and the vibes in the street, and I hassle with the same vibes. The vibes don't disappear just because I'm white!"

I sat at my table for a long time after Milton left. I got up finally and walked outside. There's a peculiar aura in the produce market in the early morning. The streets are quiet and it seems as if the empty warehouses are waiting. I walked down Davis Street looking at the buildings. Some of the buildings have ornate cornices that are very interesting; other buildings are plain, unadorned, either brick or wood or stone. The residue of stacked-up fruit and vegetable crates still littered the streets. As I picked my way through them, I thought of Frankie. I walked the streets all day looking at the buildings. No matter how many buildings I looked at, I couldn't get Frankie out of my mind.

20 Walter is trying to con D'Artagnan Pig into driving us to Big Sur for the weekend. "I want to ride in the Caja Flash," Walter says. "We'll have a ball! I want to soak my body in those tubs all weekend."

"It'd be good to get away from the Beach for a while," I say.

"C'mon, D'Artagnan, crank up the Caja Flash. I'll buy the gas."

"Perhaps a medicinal soak in a rural spa would be beneficial," D'Artagnan Pig says, huffing up his belt.

Two hours later we're tooling down Highway 1 in the Caja Flash. We're all sitting in the front seat, D'Artagnan Pig behind the wheel, me in the middle, Walter next to the window. The back seat is full of wine bottles and bennies and a little weed to keep us going when our bones get weary. The Caja Flash speeds through Westlake and Pacifica and drops like a light down Devil's Slide, flashing toward Half Moon Bay. I feel happy, really crazy all of a sudden, the soft Central Coast rhythm quickening my blood. "Whaaa-hooo!" Walter cries, cracking the cap on a jug and handing it to me.

I feel insane. The joy of Big Sur lies ahead of us, a magic juxtaposition of mountains and sea that sets up an energy cycle no one can explain. The Caja Flash's engine hums and brussels sprout plants ripple by while D'Artagnan Pig and Walter burp and laugh, point and stare, and cry aloud at each knot of hitchhikers passed, slowing down for some, stopping, backing up for the girls, picking them up and cramming them onto laps and back seats, stopping farther down the road for more, a crazy hipster wagon making it down the coast along the fast rugged no-nonsense craggy western edge of America; alive, alight, away and gone like a light toward Davenport, Santa Cruz, Aptos, and Freedom, through little California coastal towns with no names, just wide spots in the road where strangers stop their cars and get out to stare into the gloom, holding on to hats as the Caja Flash's windstream rushes by.

Walter and I share the jug while D'Artagnan drives. I look out the window. I always get the same feeling on the road, how many times now, always and forever the journey down the road becoming like a dream, a strange feeling sweeping over me, the way the road turns and dips along the sea's edge, the musky smell of the brussels sprout plants, the Japanese farmers who always seem to make such a success of their farms, at the dunegrass blowing across the bluffs above the sea, the plowed fields manicured carefully as back yards, stretching away for miles and miles toward the sea.

Walter yips and shakes the jug while D'Artagnan laughs and whips the Caja Flash around the bends. I fall deeper into my coastal dream, reverent and afraid at the same time, knowing this is both the way toward and the way away from where I want to go. Inside the car there is a warmth that soaks into my blood, yet outside there is a road and a road edge that seems more mine, like a heartstring tied through all the places I've ever been and will ever go. . . . Perhaps I should explain:

I have never understood my feeling for America. Something in the roads, the way the land smells at night, an overwhelming sadness about my friends, those in this book and others, a genuine feeling of loss, a mysterious lessening as one grows old—all part, perhaps, of a realization that something in our heart is sick, something in our backbone not quite right, a loneliness all out of proportion to its pain, a devastation that seems somehow so overwhelming as to be inexplicable, a passionlessness that exudes the smell of prisons, emptiness and decay like a light over the land that showers the soil with dread.

I love America and yet am so alone in it, so cut off from everything, so panicked by the strangeness, aloofness, costliness of its life. On the road all this is assuaged. Perhaps it's the movement, maybe the stillness, but somehow the highway leads me to a fullness, a completeness that is unattainable on any streetcorner, in any room. It's the link between places that makes these places livable, that gives them content, that sends us down them with such hope, such expectancy, such emotional wishfulfillment that we imagine on the long dark silent stretches of beribboned concrete that the next town will really be the America we are taught to believe in.

"We need mammoth hunters!" Walter cries, tossing the empty wine jug in the back seat. "What we need are more mammoth hunters, people with bows and arrows, spears. We need people who are after something big!"

Entering Highway 1 is like a dream. I am on the westernmost edge of America, speeding along Land's End. Beyond the car window just a breath away is the sea, and nothing beyond but sea, the continental shelf snaking down into fathomless depths, depths, though, that are never deep enough. I gaze out the window as Walter sings and laughs. I can see his mammoths— farmers plow furrows over their bones.

On the outskirts of Santa Cruz we let the young girl hitchhikers out, watch sadly as they wriggle their sassy little asses across the road, turn to smile, wave, toss their hair happily, and bunch together in fits of laughter at the mad trio in the crazy '52 Chevy. We want to take them with us, but no, Walter scares them with his crazy laughter, his hooked teeth. Me, too, with my lecherous hands and mouth that cause them shrieks of mock fear and self-protective legcrossings all the way down the coast. Walter sits sadly and smells his fingers for four miles. I look at my hand that for forty miles tried to slip into a fourteen-year-old's thighs while D'Artagnan Pig gnashed his teeth, cursing and sighing as he held the Caja Flash steady with only one eye on the road, the other in the rearview mirror pinning the succulent plum-pudding breasts, the loinlocked loveliness.

In Santa Cruz we stop at the county jail to visit Patrick Cassidy. D'Artagnan Pig parks the Caja Flash in the street behind the courthouse and we walk inside.

We inquire at the desk, and a bull-necked sergeant stops us. "Come back at one o'clock. That's visiting hours."

We go outside and wander around the town until one o'clock. When we return, we're led into the visitors' area, a wire-mesh room separated from the prisoners' cells by a glass and wire wall. Patrick is brought in on the other side of the wall and sits down opposite us, looking young—maybe thirteen years old—and different without his long hair and beard. For five months he hadn't shaved and so had no visitors. Finally he shaved off his beard and cut his hair so he could see his friends. We suppress titters when we see him, but then all of us feel bad, knowing his anguish and guts in having held out so long. D'Artagnan sneaks a nip from his jug and tries to slip Patrick a joint, but jailers' eyes are everywhere. We weep over old stories, chat for twenty minutes, and then walk respectfully out of the steel room and down the stairs into the sunlight of the street. Outside as we lie on the grass in the park giving thanks that at least the sidewalks are free, running straight and true to the end, past life's cells and steel rooms, two big cops approach us. They ask the usual questions—names, dates, serial numbers, etc. We answer like the desperados we are. When they leave, we jump into the Caja Flash and hurtle away from Santa Cruz town.

In Monterey we stop at a liquor store. Walter buys a quart of Armagnac brandy and some wine and six-packs and chips and paraphernalia for the weekend. I take over the wheel while Walter and D'Artagnan Pig swap stories down the coast. Walter cracks the cork on the jug of Armagnac. "I was dying of TB in the General Hospital in San Francisco, winter of 'forty-eight, and I had a friend come by one dark night and rescue me. That hospital was killing me. This friend had a V-twelve Lincoln, one of those old jobs, rode up in the back of it like a maharaja on an elephant. He came by one night and spirited me away, down this very same road, to Anderson Creek where Henry Miller lived. Convict shacks and everything. It was the only thing that saved me. I was dying in that hospital, ex-wife blues and all. They wanted me dead. I got my friend to come down and I slipped out the hall in borrowed clothes and lay down in the back of his old—let's see, what was it? Yes, a 'thirty-nine Lincoln, all twelve cylinders purring, it was like a Pullman railroad car, all shiny and black. I died in that back seat and was resurrected in a convict shack in Big Sur, winter of 'forty-eight."

"Strange you should tell such a tale." D'Artagnan Pig speaks in his W. C. Fields voice. "I myself was engaged in captaining a certain bark by the name of *Esperanza*, sweetest little ship that ever sailed the Main. Yessirree, ummm, we were becalmed seventy miles off this very same coast ... hadn't had a bite to eat for thirty days ... I was down to a nerve-wracking two twenty. We were eyeing one another for edible portions when a typhoon lifted us up and deposited us three days later right off Point Sur light. Yessir, that was a memorable winter."

While Walter and D'Artagnan Pig talk, I watch the road, hear occasional snatches of conversation, see the sea take shape and roll, hear waves whip windward, watch them fall in foaming funnels of spray against the bright black rocks. The road curls along the sea's edge and I curl with it, the white line and me connected by invisible sensors reaching up out of the ground in embrace. Each time I enter Big Sur, a magical grace envelops me; in my body there's a balance and completeness I realize nowhere else. As I guide the Caja Flash around the curves, a tenderness comes over me, a fluid consciousness more attuned to the cliffs and road and the sea below than my waking consciousness; it is as if I am *Spirit* floating along the sea's edge, a spirit contained in a tiny mechanical shell that is imbued with spirit also, and together we are traversing the incredibly wild and rocky cataracts of a dream.

As we hurtle past Thurso's Landing, where Ferlinghetti has a cabin and Jack Kerouac sat in the outhouse and scribbled graffiti on the walls, the sun is just beginning to stretch out over the sea. At Hurricane Point we all jump out, the wind rushing over the

lee of the point almost knocking us flat! Walter grabs
the jug of Armagnac and we all drink from the bottle,
holding our dicks tightly in our hands as we piss over
the edge. The wind whips our piss back in our faces
and even our piss feels good! The sun melts out across
the sea's flat edge and drops, like a fifty-year-old whore
plopping down on an old divan. The time is magic. As
we stand still, even the wind stops, hushed for an instant while a calmness envelops the whole panorama.
The Indian-fingered night creeps up the cliff, and Walter and D'Artagnan Pig and I rock slowly on our feet,
lifting the jug of brandy to our lips and praying. We
zip up our flies after making our offering to the elements. When night is on us, we creep inside the car
and continue carefully down the coast. What was it
Jack said, dead now of the madness ringing in his
brain? "The waves are Chinese but the earth is an Indian thing."

In the Big Sur valley the road curves lazily between
trees and meadows, motels and stores, an insulated
community bounded by mountains on each side, open
only to Highway 1 running north and south. A few
miles beyond the post office is Redwood Lodge, a favorite hangout for locals. When we reach the lodge, I
swing the Caja Flash into the parking lot and we all
jump out. Redwood Lodge is swinging.

Inside an Okie band from Seaside is stomping out
their twang-twang blues. We rush in and immediately I
am dancing with a fine little chick with shoulder-length
hair and wistful eyes. When I rush onto the floor, she
is with another dude, but in my state I just rush out
and grab her and the other dude stumbles away. I'm
feeling wild and the chick feels my wildness, holding
on and letting go as we whirl around in circles across
the floor. Out of the corner of my eye I see sullen military types from the Point Sur Naval Station getting hot
and unhappy because of the three wild men from the
city who are spoiling their Friday night fun. I toss my
chick over my shoulder and people laugh, Big Sur locals guffawing and shoving beer down their bellies with
both hands as the music blasts out of the corner of the

room. Walter and D'Artagnan Pig don't care either. It's Friday night and the girls are pretty, and besides, D'Artagnan weighs two hundred and forty pounds and is mean, I am six four and ornery, and Walter is six three and wiry as a lynx. In our bravado we clap the girls on the ass and buy more beer to save our stock in the car and whirl around in bigger and bigger circles, the madness of the road infecting the whole room and soon everybody is dancing and hollering like lunatics.

It's a wild Friday night, a couple of good fights bound to happen. D'Artagnan Pig and I bump together in the middle of the floor and start to arm wrestle, knocking the other dancers away, while outside Walter moons over a little filly in the back of the lodge. Willy and Ron Lussier, two Big Sur locals who have a rep for breaking in every new gal on the coast, come in from their mountain hideaway and start dancing too, mustaches armed with spittle, drunk as we are, wild and happy in the late night. During the dancing I creep out with Willy and Ron into the parking lot to smoke some weed, passing the joint between us from finger to finger. While standing in the parking lot, Sheriff John, the local Big Sur authority keeper, drives by on his way to Nepenthe. We stoop down behind the Redwood Lodge sign. When we re-enter the lodge, the music is wilder, more insane, most of the sailors dancing, everybody friendly now, relaxing when they see we mean no harm, just down for a little fun and romp to wash the big city coal dust off our backs. During the course of the dancing I take my little angel out back of the lodge and we kiss and I have my hand up under her blouse and her sweet little paps feel ghostly soft. I lift her skirt and smell her virgin thighs, pick her up and carry her down an embankment behind the lodge and lay her gently on the grass. Under the redwoods we roll and laugh, swimming into each other's bodies, tadpoles in a sea. . . .

Back inside Redwood Lodge, Walter staggers from wall to jukebox to Okie band to sailor to wall. The manager's keen to have him out before Sheriff John returns. Walter doesn't want to go and D'Artagnan Pig doesn't want to go and the music goes limp while the drunks take over. Only for Walter it isn't a drunk, it's a release and an incredible sundering of his talents, the alcohol moiling up in his brain to produce effects not found in ordinary drunks. "It's a way we have of finding ourselves," Walter said when I asked him about it. Finally D'Artagnan Pig helps me carry Walter Chevywards, the three of us staggering out the lodge door amid hostile sailor stares. As I plant Walter in the back seat of the Caja Flash, little angel wings decides to come with us, so we all pile in and head down the coastal road.

It's a full moon, the huge golden globe floating softly over us as we flit mysteriously in and out of the canyons. Past Deetjen's Big Sur Inn I turn off the lights of the car and we drift silently down the road in the moonlight, the highway silver before us, only the sound of the tires and the sea's soft swish as we float southward, not talking, just quiet stares out the windows as the ghostly sea edge ripples silver across the way. In the moonlight the Caja Flash floats past deer families grazing at the side of the road, gazing nonchalantly as we slip past, deft and silent.

At Big Sur Hotsprings I park behind the silent buildings. Amid hushed laughter and giggles we stagger down the path to the baths, peeling our clothes on the way. When we enter the baths, we discover others already there, slim, cozy couples embracing in the candlelight. We're welcomed and with shy dances doff the rest of our clothes, stand around for a moment, and then drop into huge concrete six-by-six tubs full of hot sulphur water fresh out of underground mountain springs. Every ache and pain is anesthetized, the sulphur water and the heat anointing you, evaporating all the beer and wine and alcohol so you can pour more in.

We rub toes with strangers. My little angel child snuggles up against me and rubs her bottom against mine. I lay still, slip under the water and listen to the moan of the sea shuddering through the rocks, hold my breath for incredible long minutes until Walter pulls me up, not knowing that this is an old trick of mine from younger hours-in-the-water days of my youth. I sit up and Maureen, the little angel child, snuggles into me. I put my arms around her and cup her breasts, little nipples standing out like beacons in the dark. She turns her head and I rush my tongue down her throat searching for the bottom. I find it. Even in the hot sulphur baths I have an erection a good nine inches (six and a half?) long. Maureen slips up a mite so I can slide inside her. We sit quietly for a while, not moving, the slow rhythm of the water soothing us, the hot blast of the tubs slowly softening me.

After a few minutes I get out of the tub and dash myself with cold water, shivering excitedly. I walk toward the wooden railing, lean over it and listen to the sea. I gaze out over the water and watch as the waves lash the flint-black rocks. The moon is so bright I can see every detail with perfect clarity; I can see *into* the sea, see the sawtooth edges of the kelpgrass, the moon glinting on the rocks under water and far below, discern the moil and roll of the longlimbed seaweeds as they sigh tenderly over the lips and ripples of white sand. The kelp flutters and then is still, silent for a moment, then moves upward over the crest and down again in long swinging arcs, revealing bobbing otters as they rise and dive, shining octopi and abalone shivering softly in the moonlight. I stand at the railing for a long time watching, then reach over the wooden banister and grab handfuls of fresh mint. I rub the mint vigorously all over my body, under my arms and across my shoulders and back until it stings. I breathe in the sweet tangy smell of the mint as the fragrance fills me. My body tingles with warmth, I feel as if I have shed all my weight, as if I am completely empty. It seems to me that with one intake of breath I could be borne upwards. In a few moments the feeling of weightlessness leaves and I hear chattering laughter from the others behind me.

I turn and walk through the portals of the bathhouse up to the rocky path above the building. Outside in the fresh air the breeze licks my nude body, causing me to shiver with excitement. The breeze reminds me of the top of Telegraph Hill. Once Frankie and I climbed the hill and I took off all my clothes and ran nude around Coit Tower. It was three A.M. and I was so full of energy that night that I knew if I spread out my arms while running I would have lifted off the hill and floated out over the bay. Frankie sat on the steps and laughed. She played her recorder as I whipped around and around the tower, each of my circles making me feel more powerful. Tonight up here on the cliff the wind off the sea is cooler, soft, angelic almost. I feel immensely happy. Then, tired from the long day, the drive down the coast, the booze and dancing back at the lodge, I have a vision.

I hear the laughter and singing from the tubs below, my little kitten must be in Walter's arms by now, but I stand on the seashore. An old man approaches me. He is anciently old, yet curiously young-looking, as if the lines of his age reach within him and are etched on his bones. He smiles at me, a sweet sad smile that seems to contain within it all the warmth and sadness of mankind, and says, "I am very thirsty. Will you bring me a glass of water?"

I say yes and hasten to do his bidding. I run up the seashore and cross the road to the nearest house and knock on the door. When the door opens, Frankie is standing in the doorway, young and lovely, with a beatific smile on her face. "We've been waiting," she says. "It's time to start."

There's a wedding in progress. People are standing around, sitting; there are bridesmaids and flowers. It is my wedding. Frankie stands smiling beside me. She is dressed in white, her face hidden softly by a veil, her long black hair forming a halo. When she smiles, her eyes flash and I see into the depths of her soul, and what I see is peace.

A man in a saffron robe stands before us. He smiles and moves his lips silently, first at me and then at Frankie. I cannot hear a word he is saying, but I feel at great peace. I nod, then turn to Frankie and she nods also. Frankie lifts her lips to mine and we kiss. When I feel her lips it is as if immense mountains of soft white foam were surrounding me. We turn together and walk slowly through the smiling throng. Everyone is happy—Walter, JoJay, Little Joe, Milton. I smile at Milton and hold out my hand. "No hard feelings, brother," I say. Milton smiles.

Frankie and I are married. I love Frankie with all my heart. I am tremendously excited about our prospects. I rush to find a house so we can start our life together. I find a small cottage beside the sea. In the fields surrounding the cottage I work furiously with a shovel and hoe cutting furrows in the fields, planting corn and wheat. Frankie and I make love. Her belly grows large and I place my hand on it in wonder. In the fall I harvest the crops. A daughter is born. We name her Amy and she curls her fingers over mine. Our fields prosper. I plant larger and larger fields on the cliffs above the sea. I buy a house and cut furrows deep into the rich earth. The plants grow luxuriously. Soon Frankie is pregnant again and when she cries in the night I help her give birth to a son. I name him Max, and he is strong and healthy. Max grows up quickly. Soon he is helping me in the fields, his tiny hands curling around the stalks of corn like gossamer threads. At noon we go into the house to eat the food Frankie and Amy have prepared. Amy is a young girl and she wears long skirts and works beside her mother. I love my family and there is nothing I wouldn't do for them. I would stand on the cliffs and hurl myself onto the rocks below for my family if it were demanded of me.

Then one day the sky blackens. Clouds rush out of the west and pile up over the cliffs. The land grows dark, the wind rises and whips over the fields. Trees bend to the ground, the sea thunders up in huge breakers, the cliffs crumble under the fierce pounding, and the water rolls over my fields. The house shudders. My children wail in the darkness. We huddle together against the madness and I scream in agony as Max and Amy are torn from my arms by the wind. When I look around, Frankie is gone, swept away like a rag in the darkness of the storm. I stumble about in the wreckage of my house and scream for my children, my wife; I weep and fall exhausted into sleep. When I awake, the sun is shining, the sea is calm, and my fields are gleaming in the sun. The old man is standing beside me. "Where have you been, my son?" he asks. "I have been waiting for my glass of water for over half an hour."

Sad nostalgia and my vision. I stood up and leaned over the rocks and looked down at the sea. Below me Walter and D'Artagnan wrestled with the girls in the tubs and I shivered involuntarily against the sea's cool breeze. The dull red moon floated out over the sea like Shiva's eye. The rolling waves and dark rocks reminded me of a lover's face, but which lover I couldn't remember.

D'Artagnan Pig drove the Caja Flash back to the city, wheeling the car around the curves as only he could, up and down and over the hump to the lights of Monterey, out through Seaside and past the spectral sand dunes of Fort Ord, whirling past the queuing soldiers, me and Walter jabbering in the back, sharing the last bottle of wine, the dregs of the weekend. On the way Walter said, "Having a woman is like having a disease. It eats part of you away every day, yet we're lost without it, dead, a husk, capable of nothing."

"We spend all of our time looking for it," I said.

"And when we find it, we find our chains. We're the victims of that old snare. It's an elaborate trap, that's what it is. It's like they stick a knife into your chest; it hurts like hell and you know it's killing you, but you don't want them to pull it out because you know if they do you'll bleed to death."

I told Walter about my vision.

"That's because of the vibes from Huge the Cube's and Francesca's marriage, that and your own particular hangups with Frankie. She's not going to be happy, you know, neither are you. It's the same old weary triangle."

"I love her," I said.

"Yeah, and Frankie loves Milton and Milton loves Mabel and Mabel loves the man in the moon. What it really is is that everybody's in love with the idea of love; love loves to love love. The minute anybody says I love you, though, you throw up a shield. It's like putting up a brick wall between you. I love you, you say, and the chick says, I love Sam. Sam doesn't love the chick, though. He loves the girl who's in love with you. The truth of the matter is everybody is afraid to be loved. They want love and they want to be in love but they don't want the responsibility of being loved. It's too much of a responsibility; it's too much of a downward path to not being loved any more."

"Akk!" I said.

"Frankie wants her tragedies. The few times I've seen her, I've seen that need to fulfill her failures. She picks demons; she has to have them to pay for some unforgotten woe."

"Maybe her father, William. He died in Denver in 1956, a strange dude, Idaho cowboy with sad chaps." I recounted to Walter what Frankie had told me of her family.

"Her father, her mother, her great grandfather, who knows? She mistrusts you because you represent something she knows she has to surrender to."

"She is so much a woman. Her eyes, they frighten me sometimes."

"She's driving herself to Milton because Milton will make her feel as low as she wants to feel. She gives love no chance. It's the hardest thing, two people together, and when it works it's stronger than atomic bombs."

We swept through dark apple orchards, past Aptos and Santa Cruz, where Patrick dreamed behind steel walls, up the road to Davenport, dusty musty cement town shining in the night. When we stopped for gas, we staggered into the dim cafe. Walter and D'Artagnan ate pie à la mode and I sipped black coffee. Outside the sea roared and salt-gray whales passed in the night bound southward toward Scammon's Lagoon in the Sea of Cortez, there to roll and tumble in that ancient dance, feel each other's blood, and make baby whales grow.

On the road again Walter told Indian stories.

"The Hopis have a fetish, a small leather bag they keep tied around their neck, into which they rub blood from their wounds and sweat and semen from their bodies. It's part of the Ghost Dance, part of the ritual. The Ghost Dance was the ceremony that helped Crazy Horse defeat Custer. The dance is outlawed now. During the last Ghost Dance in the late eighties the men and women and children were shot down by the soldiers. Gatling guns were brought in. The white man knew the Indians had some magic, but they didn't know what it was; they just knew it had something to do with the Ghost Dance. The Indians use their fetish to keep their minds focused on reality; they don't focus on the exterior shit like the white man. We focus on everything exterior—cars, TV's, all that crap. The Indians go inside to where the juices are, into the blood and sweat and semen. Nothing the Indian does is done without reason; everything is thought out. That's why to the outsider their lives appear so ritualized, unbelievable really. Anthropologists go and take pictures and notes, and all they can do is describe. They can't tell what one gesture means, and every gesture means something. When Indians cut down a tree, they bless the tree and use every part of it. The same with hunting. When an Indian kills, it is with a sacredness. Every sentient being is his brother; his clans are named after the animals; he is reverent. He doesn't fight nature like the white man. He knows that nature is the only friend he's got.

"That's the great difference between the white man and the Indian. The white man fights nature, wants to conquer it; the Indian lives with nature, knows it can't be conquered. To conquer nature is to commit suicide. It's taking the white man a long time to learn this. We'll suffer a long time for winning the Indian wars."

"Maybe we haven't won," I said.

"Yes, that's what I think," Walter said. "The Indians are a patient people. Maybe we won the first skirmish and the Indians are waiting like JoJay says. The next battle will be fought in men's heads. You know, the Hopis have a prophecy. They say when the blue star appears, the final cataclysm will be launched, the United States will be reduced to dust, all except Hopiland. Those who flee there will be saved, those who are

pure of heart, with no malice, those who have God in
their eyes."

"Do you believe in the prophecy?" I asked.

Walter nodded.

"Me too," I said.

As we approached Half Moon Bay, D'Artagnan
slowed the Chevy and we slipped through the silent
town. We soon passed Princeton. I remembered the
times diving for abalone with Patrick Cassidy and Jim
Fish. I thought of the coast swept by the Hopis'
prophecy. It could happen. I knew the people who
would go—crabby storekeepers and officials, lonely
and bitter souls who leased no portion of another life,
who spent all their dread and anger here in tightlipped
meanness and woe. I could see the cliffs raked bare
and the coastal watchtowers swaying and crumbling in
the blast, the green fields emptied and the waves running red. It was our own madness doing it, our own
hypocrisy building bonetomb islands in the sea. As we
rocked up Devil's Slide, I leaned forward to the city,
intent on the lights shining before me.

21 Sunday I slept until the sun went down. I woke up when Walter kicked my bed. He was dressed in his pearl-gray Hopi fedora and a sheepskin jacket. JoJay was with him. "Hey, Kid, wake up! You've got to help us celebrate our last night in San Francisco."

Tomorrow Walter and JoJay and Jose and Joselito and Trinidad Archelito were returning to Taos. Nancy, Walter's wife, had been frantically calling from New Mexico for a week trying to locate Walter. She had finally run him down. Walter wanted one more bash in the city before returning home. I dressed hurriedly in my Levi's and the buckskin jacket JoJay had given me and followed JoJay and Walter out into the street.

We stopped at Coit Liquors and Walter ran inside and bought a fifth of Armagnac. "Where we going?" I asked.

"Chinatown," Walter said. "Our last night in San Francisco has to start at Sam Wo's."

Chinatown sounded fine to me. So did Sam Wo's. Edsel Ford Wong, the crazy Chinese waiter who ruled Sam Wo's, was bound to start things out right. We sipped the Armagnac slowly as we walked down Grant Avenue. The streets were crowded, and even though Walter and JoJay and his brothers were leaving in the morning, I felt happy. When we walked under the Chinese dragon lampposts, I yelled with joy, "Eeeyaa!" Startled tourists turned around and stared.

"Goddamn, I hate to leave this place," Walter said. "I've had a good time."

"It's been a good six weeks," JoJay said.

"I should buy your tepee, JoJay," I said. "Half the chicks in North Beach are going to miss it."

"Hah! You can't *buy* tepees, Kid. Come to Taos and my woman will make you one."

"I should go with you so I can learn to ride one of Tell Me Good Morning's ponies."

"Speaking of riding ponies"—JoJay turned to Walter—"I haven't forgotten your promise. An Indian is like an elephant; he never forgets."

"What promise?"

"The Chinese whorehouse. You promised you'd take me to a Chinese whorehouse before we went back to Taos."

Walter laughed. He raised the jug of Armagnac to his lips, then handed it to JoJay.

"Tonight would be a good night to go to a Chinese whorehouse," JoJay said. "We can celebrate our last night in San Francisco in real style."

"I don't know, JoJay. Going to a Chinese whorehouse is a religious experience. You have to be spiritually prepared for it."

"I can understand that." JoJay nodded gravely. "I can understand being spiritually prepared."

Thinking of young Chinese girls caused a murmuring in my loins. Walter handed me the brandy and laughed.

"The spiritual preparation is very difficult, JoJay," he said. "Some men are unable to make the sacrifice a visit to a Chinese whorehouse calls for. That's why I've hesitated taking you to such a place."

"I will make the sacrifice, don't worry. What do I have to do?"

"It's called the Great Chinese Whorehouse Sacrifice," Walter said. "I learned of it when I was in the Far East. It's spiritual, very Zen. Gurdjieff talks of it in his conversations with famous Chinese whores."

"It sounds like a wonderful experience," JoJay said, sipping from the Armagnac.

"It's a great experience," Walter said gravely. "If your body is spiritually attuned and you make the Great Chinese Whorehouse Sacrifice, you will then experience what is commonly known in the trade as a Zenfuck."

"I just want to fuck a Chinese whore. I don't want to start a religion." JoJay handed the Armagnac to me.

"The only reason I'm telling you all of these things

is because you're an Indian. Because you're an Indian, you can understand rituals and sacrifices. Nothing can be taken lightly in a Chinese whorehouse."

"Good," JoJay said. "Indians don't take things lightly either. I want to fuck a nice heavy Chinese whore."

On Washington Street we turned right and walked up to Sam Wo's. Entering Sam Wo's is like entering a Chinese opium den, only the aroma of sweet smoke is replaced by the smell of exotic fish and fried rice and noodles and ginseng. The restaurant is seven feet wide and three stories high. To get to the dining areas upstairs where Edsel Ford Wong reigns supreme you have to walk through the kitchen where wiry Tong cooks stand around with chop suey smiles on their faces and razor-sharp meat cleavers in their hands. Every time I enter Sam Wo's, some ancestral blood inside my bones causes me to unconsciously cross myself. When I walk up the stairs to the dining room, I feel like a condemned man climbing the thirteen steps to his last meal.

Edsel Ford Wong is the ruler of Sam Wo's. A demented waiter who not only sets you down where he pleases but takes one look at you and decides what you're going to eat. He orders for you, dictates to you, and generally makes your life as miserable as you'll put up with. For me Edsel is exasperating, but others dig his dictatorial manipulations. After Walter and JoJay and I climbed the stairs to the second level, Edsel grabbed my arm and yanked me back toward the rear of the restaurant, past the crowded tables. I didn't mind, since the rear of the restaurant is actually the front and I could look out the one big window to the street below. When a restaurant is only seven feet wide, I like to be able to see the street.

Edsel brought a pot of tea and danced an exaggerated two-step around our table as Walter poured dollops of brandy into each of our cups. Edsel's eyes gleamed and he shook his head in serio-comic gestures; his hand darted out and grabbed Walter's cup, which he emptied in one gulp, dancing out of the way as Walter grabbed at him. I sipped my tea, holding the hot liquid in my mouth, savoring the flavor before letting it sail down my throat. The brandy gave the tea an exotic flavor, and my head buzzed slightly as the comfortable aroma of the room filled me. All the tables were jammed and everyone was having a great time. Edsel jumped from table to table ladling out noodles and rice. When I half closed my eyes, I could imagine myself in the hold of a strange Chinese slave ship, all of us prisoners, a multiracial crew enjoying a hearty meal after a hard day in the galleys. The confines of the narrow restaurant, the brandy, and Edsel's piercing laughter as he scampered back and forth yelling down the dumbwaiter to the kitchen contributed to the illusion. It was only when I looked out the window behind me and saw the fog-dampened streets that I brought myself back to reality. I leaned back in my chair and enjoyed the comforting illusion.

"You know, JoJay," Walter said, "if you really want to visit a Chinese whorehouse you shouldn't eat. The Great Chinese Whorehouse Sacrifice demands that a man fast and cleanse his body to insure absolute clarity of mind before entering into the ultimate act. You remember that time I took you to that restaurant in Japantown, they made you take off your moccasins when you sat down to eat? Well, there are customs in Chinese whorehouses that must be adhered to just as rigidly."

"That sounds okay," JoJay said, shoving noodles into his mouth with his chopsticks. "If I decide to eat the Chinese whore, I'll take off my moccasins."

"That's not exactly what I had in mind. In Chinese whorehouses there are certain prescribed rituals, ways in which the act must be performed. It's all worked out according to thousands of years of tradition, just like in the Indian snake dance."

"I never fucked no Chinese whore at no snake dance," JoJay said, diving into the raw fish salad.

"Chinese whores don't fuck like ordinary whores," Walter continued. "Chinese whores have a very special way of fucking. They have a way of fucking that is unique. If a man is not spiritually and mentally prepared, going to a Chinese whorehouse can be a very dangerous experience."

"Why, do I have to fight the pimp afterwards?"

"No, I'm not talking about danger in the ordinary sense. I'm talking about an inscrutable danger. Most people will agree that the Chinese people are inscrutable, almost as incrutable as Indians. It's the same when they fuck."

"I've never had an inscrutable fuck," JoJay said. "I've had it every other way, though."

"The mysteries of the Orient are many." Walter chewed his salad.

"I'd like to fuck a mystery," JoJay said, pouring another dollop of Armagnac into his tea.

"Besides, there are complications if you fuck a Chinese whore," Walter said between chews. "There is the distinct mathematical possibility that if you fuck a Chinese whore, you will be remotely fucking a cousin twenty million times removed. That is a distinct mathematical possibility."

"What do you mean?" JoJay looked at Walter suspiciously.

"There are anthropologists who claim that the American Indian originated in Asia and came to this country across the Bering Straits. I can see it now: if we take you to a Chinese whorehouse you'll end up fucking your sister."

"I already fucked my sister," JoJay said.

"Don't ruin my theory with facts."

"I'm sorry," JoJay said.

We finished eating and Walter called Edsel over for the bill. Edsel jumped around our table. He elaborately toted up the charges and handed the bill to Walter, poking him in the ribs as he did so, feeling for the brandy.

"You got blandy for Edsel?" he asked.

Walter hauled out the brandy and poured Edsel a teacupful. Edsel peered around the room like an Oriental Buster Keaton and then downed the cup in one quick swallow. "Ahh, blandy go down good with Chinese food, huh?"

"Blandy go down good with any food, Edsel," Walter said.

Edsel shrieked with laughter and hurriedly cleaned the table.

As we were leaving, Walter turned back to Edsel. "Edsel, tonight's our last night in San Francisco and I have a problem. I promised my friend I'd introduce him to a nice Chinese girl before we left, one that didn't cost too much. You know what I mean?"

Edsel's eyes lit up. His round face spread out in a grin. "Ahh, you likee nice Chinese girl fo' last night in town, huh? That velly selious ploblem."

He thought for a moment. "You visit fliend of mine in Waverry Prace. He have lots nice fliends just in flom Hong Kong, not cost velly much."

Walter removed a couple of dollars from his pocket and handed them to Edsel. Edsel squeaked his laughter and repeated his little hoplike dance around the table.

Outside in the street it was damp. The fog filled the alleys and the sidewalks glistened. Walter grabbed JoJay by the arm and led him up Washington Street. Under a streetlamp glowing with an aureole of mist Walter paused, pulling JoJay back against a building.

"I've found you a Chinese whorehouse," Walter whispered in JoJay's ear. "Edsel says it's a first class joint."

"I want a young whore," JoJay said. "None of those sowbellies."

"Edsel says these chicks are straight from Hong Kong. They can't even speak English."

"Good"—JoJay nodded—"I never did like that language."

The Chinese whorehouse was at the end of Waverly Place, a narrow dark alley deep in the heart of Chinatown. Walter stopped at number 36. A real red light glowed above the door.

"This is it," Walter said.

"Are you guys coming in too?" JoJay asked.

"No, this is your night, JoJay. We're going to treat you to a Chinese whore."

"This makes up for that Indian whore I got for you in Santa Fe," JoJay said.

Walter handed JoJay ten dollars. "Say Edsel sent you," he said.

Walter and I stood on the opposite side of the alley while JoJay knocked. There was no answer. JoJay looked at us. He knocked again and the door opened slightly. A wizened head thrust itself out and JoJay spoke softly. An arm yanked him inside and the door closed swiftly. Walter and I looked at one another. I felt kind of sorry I hadn't accompanied JoJay inside the whorehouse. The night was beginning to get chilly and Walter and I kept warm by sipping from the almost empty bottle of brandy. Walter chuckled under his breath and laughed softly. I said nothing. An old Chinese news vendor hobbled by, his back so bent over his head appeared to be coming out of his chest. He reminded me of Kelly Sam, the Chinese philosopher. He neither looked at us nor said anything as he passed by. He was inscrutable, unconcerned, as meditatively immune as a stone rolling down a steep hill.

It was getting late. There was an inch or so left in the brandy bottle, so I wet my lips with it, saving the rest for JoJay. I glanced toward the door. The red light glowed dully.

"How long's he been in there?"

"Half an hour," Walter said. "Maybe longer."

We watched the door. It remained closed. "Maybe we should go in," I said. "I could go for a nice warm Chinese girl."

"Are you spiritually prepared?" Walter asked.

"I've got half an erection."

"That's a beginning."

Just then the door opened. JoJay stepped out and the door closed behind him without a sound. Walter and I stepped out to meet JoJay. I handed the bottle of brandy to him and he raised it to his lips, silently. When he finished, he dropped it into a trashcan as we walked by.

"How was it?" Walter asked.

"Good brandy."

"I mean the Chinese whore."

JoJay said nothing. We walked down Waverly Place

to Washington Street and then turned right. The traffic on Columbus Avenue was light as we walked across.

"Did you have a good ride?" Walter asked softly.

"What do you mean?"

"The new, unbroken pony. Was it like your cousin Tell Me Good Morning said?"

"It was better. When we rode, it was like we had rainbows between us."

22 The next day JoJay and his brothers took down their tepee, carefully folded it, and carried it downstairs to the jeep. Walter started packing his equipment. I helped, lugging tape recorders and sound equipment down the stairs and piling it up beside the jeep. While we were carrying stuff down, Walter ran down to Spadelee's and bought six pint jugs of Valley of the Moon port, "for the loading job," he said. "We'll get our serious road booze later." Serious road booze for Walter meant nothing less than half-gallon jugs, the little two-bit pint jugs weren't fit for inclusion in his jeep.

The loading took an hour, with me and the brothers carrying the stuff down and Walter fitting it into the jeep with the precision of a German mechanic. First the tape recorders, speakers, cameras, and toolbox, then the suitcases. The tepee went on top of that and then finally the sheepskin blankets, nice for burrowing into when Walter's jeep whipped down the freeway at seventy miles an hour.

By ten A.M. everything was loaded, tied firm with special Taos Pueblo rawhide knots, each knot accompanied by a special Indian incantation to tightness. "That way nothing comes loose on the road," Joselito said. "We don't want to have to stop halfway to Taos and redo the whole thing."

After the jeep was loaded, we retired to my loft to drink the last of the port. The place looked empty without the tepee, kind of sad and lonely. I mentioned this to JoJay.

"Yeah, it looks bare," he said. "But like I said, Kid, you come to Taos and I'll have my woman make you a tepee. Of course, you have to track down and kill the bucks for the skins, but that's no problem. You belong in a teepee anyway, not in this crazy building."

213

"This is my city tepee, JoJay. When I come to Taos, I'll live in the special tepee your woman makes for me."

We sat quiet for a minute, everyone sipping his port. JoJay's eyes darted around the loft. "Yeah, I got to admit I'm going to miss this place. First time I ever felt good in a white man's pad."

What JoJay said made me feel good.

"I never met so many crazy white men in my life," Jose said, his chubby face wrinkling with laughter. "These crazy whatchoucallem beatniks, they act like Indians."

"They are Indians, Jose," I said. "It's the lost tribe of Indians America never knew it had."

"Hoya hoya," Joselito shouted, stamping his foot down on the wooden floor. "Crazy damn white man Indians. I'm glad Walter brought us here."

We sat around waiting for Trinidad Archelito to speak. Going-away tradition said that each man had to say something of himself before departure. Trinidad Archelito sat, thin and wiry in the shadows, holding his pint jug of port between his knees with both hands. "Damn, damn," is all he said, shaking his head slowly back and forth.

"How long's it going to take you to get to Taos, Walter?" I asked.

"As the crow flies or the buffalo wanders?" JoJay asked in return. "Walter never goes anywhere direct. It's a thirty-hour trip from Taos to San Francisco with no stops for rest, but it took us ten days to get here."

"Walter always finds lots of diversions," I said.

"They're not diversions, they're appointments," Walter said.

The small dark jugs lifted and fell like pistons generating energy for the trip back down the stairs, into the jeep, and out onto the great highway.

"Damn, I hate to leave," JoJay said once again, gazing around the loft.

"Think of Albuquerque and Santa Fe," Jose said, "and Gallup on the way."

"You always bring up places where I've been in the hoosegow," JoJay said. "Why don't you say, 'Think of

Española, think of the banks of the Grande River, think of Taos Pueblo'?"

"I would say, 'Taos Pueblo,' but I know that Gallup and Albuquerque and Santa Fe come first, and the hoosegows are still there," Jose said.

"You sound like an Indian with a smart ass," JoJay said.

The talk went on this way for twenty minutes. Road talk. Nobody wanted to go and I was sorry I wasn't going. The departure could only be delayed so long, though, and finally we all traipsed down the stairs. JoJay and his brothers climbed in the jeep and Walter stood beside it. "Come to Taos, Kid," he said, taking my hand. "There's lots of squaws and clean air and silence."

He climbed behind the wheel. "Hoya hoya, Kid." JoJay, Jose, Joselito and Trinidad Archelito raised their hands in the traditional salute.

"Hoya hoya, amigos." I made the sign back.

Walter started the jeep and moved slowly down Roach Alley, around the leftover produce crates and empty fifty-five-gallon fire drums. At the corner all of them waved and I heard the piercingly clear call of JoJay's holy hollow left-wingbone-of-an-eagle whistle rise above the "hoya hoya hoya" of the vanishing travelers.

23 Little Joe came by the loft to me about Little Gus. Francesca had Little Gus in the apartment on Harwood Alley, and Hube the Cube delivered him. "Jesus, Kid, it was a sight." Little Joe shook his head in wonder. "I couldn't believe my eyes. For a while I thought it was going to end in a big stinko, you know, one of Hube the Cube's fiascos, the way he does things."

Little Joe rolled a joint and lit it and sat back and laughed. "You never saw such a sight, Kid. I wish you'd been there. Everybody else was. Clementi even got some pictures of it. Ask him to show you. He was clicking his camera all night."

Little Joe puffed on the joint and sighed. "I can't believe it happened, Kid. Hube the Cube was absolutely crazy. No wonder he works as a human guinea pig out at the hospital. They must have stuffed something in him to twist his brains around. The way he sat over Francesca. Had her do it Indian fashion, he calls it. Can you beat that? Can you imagine Francesca squatting over the mattress on the floor and pushing Little Gus out? That's the way she did it, though, no shit! Little Gus wouldn't come and Hube the Cube made Francesca squat and, plop! out he popped right out on the mattress just like Hube the Cube said he would."

Little Joe smiled and leaned back on the edge of my bed. He toked on the joint and handed it to me.

"Hube the Cube's pretty smart, though, you know that, Kid? He's read all the books. He said he knew how to do it and he did. He spends lots of time out at the UC Medical Center. He sneaks into the obstetrics ward. He's hung up on that ward. There's a peculiar kind of torture that goes on there that he likes to see the people go through. He says it's good for chicks, brings 'em close to the elemental aspects of life. You

216

know, pushing babies out of their guts and lying around in the slop and ooze.

"Francesca almost killed Hube the Cube, though. She was in there on the mattress panting and moaning and he was out in the kitchen preparing himself for the ordeal. He couldn't find his outfit. He looked in every stash place in the pad and he couldn't find it. Hee hee, you should have seen him, tied up with that scrawny blue arm of his with no veins left and running around like a chicken looking for his point. Francesca was in the other room on the mattress, moaning to beat hell. 'Oooh, oooh,' she said. Hube the Cube would dash in, dash out, fling open drawers, look in cupboards, under the table. He's always hiding his outfit in new places because of his paranoia, then he can't find it when he wants to fix. Francesca always has to find it for him. She's good at that. But she's in on the mattress looking like a small peak in the Himalayas and Hube the Cube's all frantic 'cause he can't find his point. McCracken finally found it under a bowl in the cupboard. Hube the Cube jabbed it around in his arm two or three times, you know, then he hit and you shoulda seen him. 'Ahhh, that's good!' he said. You know the way he gets when he sticks that shit in his arm. He smiled, real beautific, and rubbed his arm. His arm has ten thousand little chicken tracks in it. 'I got to start fixing in my leg!' he said. 'It's getting hard to find a vein in my arm.' Haw haw. Old Hube the Cube don't have any veins left in his arms. All he got is those chicken tracks. Chicken tracks with chicken tracks on 'em!

"That dude's strong, though, you know that, Kid? I wouldn't believe it, seeing how small he is, those thin arms and all, but he's strong as shit! I saw him arm wrestle Roxie once and, man, Roxie had to fight like hell to keep up. Hube the Cube's a strange cat, I'll say say that for him."

Little Joe sucked on the joint and passed it back to me.

"How's the baby?"

"Oh, all right, I guess. I don't know how babies are supposed to be. It came out okay. It started screaming as soon as it hit the mattress. Lady Joan was there. She wrapped it in a towel and cleaned it off. I've never seen anything like it before. When Francesca was lying on the mattress trying to push Little Gus out, you could see right up that big snatch of hers. It looked like the top of the baby's head was sticking out. I guess it was. Shit, it was a big baby, nine pounds or something. I've never seen a snatch look like that. It was weird, man. It kind of takes the thrill out of pussy, you know what I mean? Seeing that big crack gaping up at you like the Grand Canyon. I'm going to be celibate for a year. I don't know what to do. Every time I get in the rack with a chick now, I see Francesca's big cunt staring up at me and that little head pushing out.

"Now I know why the Indians do it the way they do. They send the chicks away, did you know that? They say, 'Get the hell away from here and go have your papoose!' It's a chick thing. Even in their monthlies they have special tents. The squaws live in a special monthly tent until their period's over. That's smart, man. That way the braves don't have to see that and have it around; they can maintain their illusions. It's debilitating to have to look at a snatch with all the illusions stripped away. You know, Kid, you were smart not being there. You still got your illusions. To you pussy's still a little slit down there with curly hair growing all around it. For me, man, it's a big gash all bloody as hell with a little head poking out."

I laughed and Little Joe toked on the joint and laughed too. "Man's a funny animal," he said. "We spend the first nine months of our life working our way out of that snatch and then we spend the rest of our lives trying to get back in. That's what life's all about, Kid, you know that? I think all the theories and all the philosophies in the world are giant cover-ups for pussy. They're camouflage for the real meaning of life. Everything we do, everything we eat, sleep, shit, talk, think, make, create, build, destroy, fabricate, illustrate, conjugate, and inhabit is a giant cover-up for that little gash down there between those two legs. It's terrible when you think about it.

"Did you ever read that story by Hemingway, 'A Clean, Well-Lighted Place'? That's what it's all about! We all want a clean, well-lighted place. We ain't never going to find it, though, because we keep building these big constructions. We keep building these huge buildings that block out all the light. All we want is a clean, well-lighted place and a glass of brandy. That ain't too much for us to want, is it? Shit! There ain't a man in the world who don't deserve a nice pussy to come home to. A nice warm pussy that don't snap at you like a snapping turtle. I'm tired of all those pussies with teeth in 'em, Kid. Too many of the chicks line their pussies with bricks like it's a church or something, a sanctuary! A lot of 'em walk around with a sign hanging out of their twat that says, 'Don't touch! It's holy!' That's a bunch of shit, Kid, you know that?

"Did I ever tell you about the cunt I had the other night? Oh, she was an angel. I did tell you, didn't I? I don't even know what happened to her. I wanted you to meet her. She had a beautiful cunt, like it was lined with diamonds. She put incense in it. She was too much. I wanted to crawl inside that pussy with a few books, a little weed, pull the vulva over me and spend the rest of my days in there. Oh, it was nice."

Little Joe relit the joint and smiled. The roach was small, so he took out his roach clip and held it delicately between his fingers. The smoke from the roach curled up around his face.

"It's a funny thing, Kid. I can remember a piece of ass I had five years ago with perfect clarity. Man, I have crystalline vision when it comes to that, but I can't remember a damn thing about the piece of ass I had last night. What does that mean, Kid, am I sick? It's funny. I can remember every word from five years ago. I remember the way the rug curled on the floor, the pattern on the wallpaper, I even remember the smell of her cunt. She had a special smell. She smelled like axle grease. Don't laugh! Axle grease don't smell that bad. I even remember what we talked about. You don't believe me, but it's true! We were talking about Playland, you know, out there on the beach. I was trying to describe the mad woman's laugh at the entrance to the funhouse. You know that laugh, it's weird. Funny but weird. It sends chills up your spine. That's what it's supposed to do, I guess. Anyway, I was describing the laugh of the mad woman and trying to laugh it for her. She had this axle grease cunt and I remember she had this wen on her breast. I kept playing with it with my fingers. It was a big wen. It had a coupla hairs on it, growing out of the top like on a wart. I asked her why she didn't cut 'em off. I didn't like the idea of fucking a chick with hair on her chest. She laughed. She said they'd grow right back. Then suddenly I liked the hairs. What's wrong with a few little wen hairs! She was a Jewish chick, you know, one of those sexpots with a sloppy cunt and lots of hair. Not really my style but I liked her anyway. It's damn strange, though, I can't even remember the name of the chick I fucked last night."

The roach was dead and Little Joe looked at it reflectively. Outside it was quiet, the sounds of the street distant and soft. Little Joe removed the roach from the roach clip and put it in his mouth. He chewed slowly, as if he were masticating his words.

"You know, sometimes I think it's not worth it, all this exercising we do to keep our weenies oiled. I spend all my bread on cunts. If I don't spend it on 'em, then I spend it trying to get 'em, buying drinks, dope, money for shows. Sometimes I think it ain't worth the time going out and trying to groove with a chick. You buy her a beer, you hold her hand, you tell her she's beautiful, and what do you get? A pocketful of shit, that's what you get!

"Sometimes I'd rather go home alone, you know that? When I think about it, I'd rather walk outta here by myself and go home alone. There's no hassle that way. You don't have to worry about catching the clap, coming down with a case of the crabs. You don't even have to take 'em to the U.S. Restaurant in the morning and give 'em a feed to get rid of 'em. It's lots easier just going home alone—no hassle, no shuck, no nothing. D'you ever feel that way? You just want to be left alone?

"It must be a good feeling to have your own pad. A

place to come home to. That's the way I feel when I ship out, almost like the ship's my home. It's lonely, though, you know; that's why we spend all our time looking. When you got it, it's a drag and when you don't got it, you're out looking for it. That must be what love is—really finding it! I've never met a chick I could look at and say to myself, I want to spend the rest of my life with her. I don't think it's possible. I don't see how anybody can. I think people shuck themselves when they say that. They're lonely, Kid, that's what they are. They say, 'Ah, fuck, I'll take a chance. If it don't work out I can always go back to being lonely.' I know cats on board ship like that. They're absolutely lost when they get on shore. That ship's their security! It's like a big womb for 'em, a protective covering they can nurse off of until they're too old to worry about it. That's one of the reasons I dig the Beach. It ain't so lonely here. There's people you can talk to. A lot of the kids on the Beach are fuck-ups, but a lot of them are trying. A lot of 'em ain't had no one to teach 'em, so they have to do it on their own. You know, they have to start all the way down at the basics, like learning how to brush their teeth, how to keep their dorks clean, everything! You know, I didn't realize it at first, but one of the problems with most of the kids on the Beach is that they've had too much and at the same time they ain't had nothing, you know what I mean? Most of the kids here are from rich parents, you know, reasonably rich anyway, taking things relatively. I mean they've been showered with all kinds of shit when they were kids but they ain't had any love! That's why they're on the Beach in the first place. They're looking for love. I hope some of 'em find it. I think the whole thing's a practical joke, though. That's why when I think about Francesca and Hube the Cube as fucked up as they are, I think they have as much a chance as anybody on the set."

Little Joe mused and cracked a smile. "That grass really makes me rap."

I said nothing.

"Hee hee," Little Joe laughed. "Sex is a funny thing. When you think about it, it's heaven and hell at the

same time. I think the practical joker who made this
place put both heaven and hell right down between our
legs—and he knew what he was doing! You know,
they had an expression for balling in the old days—
putting the devil in hell, that's what they called it. Boc-
caccio or somebody. When I saw Francesca's big twat
staring up at me like the Grand Canyon, I was looking
right smack dab down into heaven and hell! You laugh
at me, Kid, but I know what I'm talking about."

Little Joe was silent for a moment and then he
looked up. "You know, the funniest thing of all about
Francesca having Little Gus over there on Harwood
Alley was old Hube the Cube. You know how he is,
crazy as a damn loon with all that guinea-pigging out
at the UC Medical Center. Do you know what he did
the next day? He was working on a big collage when
Francesca went into labor. You know what that
bastard did? He took the afterbirth and used it in his
collage. No shit! You go over there and see it. It's the
craziest thing you ever saw."

24 I walked over to Milton's pad to get some more grass. I still owed him sixty bucks, but if he wanted his bread he'd have to front me some more weed to sell. In the back of my mind I hoped he wouldn't be home, just Frankie, so I'd have a chance to see her alone. I knocked and waited. Nobody answered. I left a note on the door and walked back downstairs. At each landing I stopped and gazed at the bay. The bay was calm. The sun glinted off the water next to Alcatraz. Between Fisherman's Wharf and the island prison, small sails dotted the bay, white, like the wings of miniature birds who were resting before continuing their journey.

On the corner of Columbus Avenue I caught a number 30 bus for the SP depot. Since Milton wasn't home, I'd go see Sam the Fatman. I had to get some more weed to bail myself out of the bind I'd gotten into.

As the bus made its way down Stockton Street, I looked at the people hurrying along the sidewalks. Everyone was intent on their chores, old people and young, buyers and sellers, we were all caught up in the day's business. I wondered what the people would think if they knew my business. Most of them couldn't care less; they were busy peddling their own dope in one form or another. The bus sailed through the Stockton tunnel with a whoosh and passed Union Square, packed with midday idlers. On Fourth Street I changed buses for the Mission. The bus was packed with old people hanging on to the straps for dear life. All the buses were packed with old people. When you grow old, you go live on a bus. When you stand up to get off, the driver slams on the brakes and you lurch to the front, fighting for a handhold. When you get old, the curbs are too high and the steps are too steep and nothing fits any more, not even your skin.

I turned my face to the window. I thought about the incredible lives we live, all the little lies and hypocrisies we weave around ourselves in order to survive. When I thought about it, I got depressed. When I thought about the alternatives, I got even more depressed. I slumped down in my seat and watched the street go by. Mission Street was a blur of bargain basements, army surplus stores, typewriter repair shops, and fleabag hotels. Past Ninth Street it changed character, giving away to automobile garages and decorative lamp establishments and unemployment offices. Training for the untrainable, skills for the skillless, lines for those used to waiting. Under the freeway the street changed character again, to corner hamburger stands and neighborhood bars and raucous jangling mariachi madness.

I liked Mission Street with its frenetic Mexican excitement, the young tight-assed pochas gumsnapping along under their ridiculous temple-high Aztec bouffant hairdos, curls black as midnight, jaunty alive on the sidewalks, thigh-confining close-kneed skirts mincing from window to window in their cockatoo-preening cha-cha sidewalk shuffle, cocksure and aloof until sudden shrieking laughter throws them in fits against walls, bouncing off to stand in front of other store windows, lacquered inch-long lashes flashing like rows of miniature scimitars over sacrificial well-deep eyes gazing miraculously agape at Pedro Enfante hit records, comic books, plastic statuary Holy Marys, their Coca-Cola complexions burnt desert soft by the Mission Street sun.

On Twenty-second Street I pulled the buzzer and got off the bus. For a moment the lifting vibrancy of the street lifted me, the razzle-dazzle tempo of canciones blasting out of music storefront speakers, eyewrenching theater marquees announcing *La Muerte de Zapata* in burnt-out lightbulbs, gyrating candystriped barber poles twisting up and down crazily, plunging buses starting and stopping inches away from calamity, cars' horns honking, and people hurrying. For a minute I debated plunging into the Mission Street madness instead of visiting Sam the Fatman. Mission Street wouldn't solve any of my problems, however. I'd only get lost in the shuffle.

I walked down Twenty-second Street to Sam's alley and knocked on his door. A thin-faced junkie with hollow eyes opened the door a crack and stared out at me. "Wha' you wan'?" he said.

"Is Sam home?"

"Wha's your name?"

"I'm a friend of Milton's."

"Hol' on."

The junkie closed the door and locked it. I heard his feet padding back up the stairs to the apartment. In a few minutes I heard his footsteps coming back down. He opened the door and checked the street. "C'mon in." I followed him up the stairs.

Sam sat at his ornate table, fatter than ever, drumming his fingers on the mirror-polished surface. "Kid, what's happenin'?" he said.

"Nothing much, Sam."

"Crazy. How's Milt? You seen him?"

"He was okay the last time I saw him. I went over to his place today but he wasn't home."

"Prolly out scoring pussy. What can I do for you?"

"Well, I've been selling grass for Milton and since I can't find him I wondered if I could pick up a key or two from you. You know, sell them and pay you a little later."

Sam's sausage-thick fingers drummed on the tabletop and a grin spread over his face. There was a package of cookies on the table and he picked one up and pushed it into his mouth. "You got any money, Kid?"

"I don't have any money right now, but I could sell a couple of keys in a few days. I could have the bread back to you by Thursday."

"I thought you was working for Milton?" Sam grabbed another cookie and shoved it into his mouth.

"Well, I am, sort of. This is just temporary, until I find Milton. There's lots of cats on the Beach want to score right now. I could pay the bread to Milton and he could pay you if you want."

Sam was laughing. He hit the table with his open

hand, pounding on it until it shook. The thin-faced junkie laughed too, like the sleazy bastard he was.

"Kid"—Sam laughed through a mouthful of cookie crumbs—"one of the first rules of this trade is you don't deal out front. Didn't Milton tell you that? Dealing out front is like giving your weed away. The day I start giving my weed away is the day my connections start giving it to me, and when that happens, ever'body's gonna have it for free."

"It'd only be for a couple of days."

"Haw haw haw," Sam laughed. "And then you're gonna traipse right on over here and lay that money out on the table, ain't you Kid, just like you did with Milton. Haw haw haw."

I looked at Sam. He really was a fat old asshole. I'd like to take his kilos and stuff them down his slimy throat.

"Milton got his money. I only owe him a few bucks."

"That's not what Milton says. He says you copped out on him. He says you were givin' that weed away for spare pieces of ass, ain't that right, Buzz?"

"Fuckin' right." The junkie nodded in agreement.

"I agreed to pay Milton three bills for that grass, and he's gotten two hundred and forty dollars of it."

"Oh, is that a fact now?" Sam's blubber body shook.

"Hyuh, hyuh." Buzz imitated Sam's laughter.

"When you want to deal with cash money, Kid, I might be willing to lay out a few keys on this table." Sam thumped the table with his hand. "Until you learn that this ain't no amateur night, though, you ain't gonna get no grass offa Sam the Fatman."

"I'm sorry you feel that way, Sam. I was sure we were going to have a profitable relationship."

I said this as I walked toward the door. When Sam the Fatman said no, there just wasn't any more.

At the head of the stairs I turned and surveyed the scene: the overstuffed room, the ornately carved table, the elaborate paintings and gold-leaf ceiling, a subdued light filtering through the baroque stained-glass windows. Sam sat at the table and Buzz, the sallow-faced junkie, stood beside him. As I headed down the stairs, Sam spoke: "You're just too uncool, Kid."

"Yeah," Buzz agreed. "Too damn uncool."

"You got too much trust, too much mush in your gizzard," Sam said.

I said nothing. Just walked down the stairs and unlocked the door and stepped out into the alley. I heard Buzz lock the door behind me.

25 It was four o'clock when I got back to North Beach. The note I'd put on Milton's door was gone. I heard laughter from inside the pad. When I knocked, Frankie opened the door. "Who is it, Frankie?" Milton yelled.

"It's the Kid."

Milton came to the door. "What's happenin', baby?"

"I came by earlier. I left a note."

"Yeah, I saw it."

"I wanted to make arrangements to get some more grass to pay off the rest of that bread I owe you."

Milton smiled. Frankie walked back inside the pad. I felt stupid. "C'mon in," he said.

I walked inside and sat down on the mattress on the floor. Milton sat down in front of his coffee table. He reached under the table and brought out a cellophane bag. "How've things been going for the Kid?" he said.

"Oh, up and down. I have a lot of guys who want to buy grass."

"Oh, yeah?" There was a mocking ring in his voice.

"Yeah. You haven't been on the set for a while. Nobody's been able to score."

"You don't saaay." Milton ended his words with the soft hipster trail, the inaudible sibilant. I never did like the sound. I felt it was phony and affected. "You ever collect for those ozees you gave Burkhardt?"

"Burkhardt's a fink. I don't want to have anything to do with him."

Burkhardt was a queer spade who'd once been a big customer of Milton's. I never did know their connection, but whatever it was it wasn't any more. One of the ten ounces I'd laid on Groovy had ended up in Burkhardt's hands. At the time I thought it was cool because Groovy said it was cool. It wasn't cool, though. Burkhardt had been busted and the rumor was out that he was working for the heat. He wanted to score for the man real bad so he could pull a few dudes down and lift himself up.

"How come you deal with a fink?" Milton said.

"You know him better than I do. Was he a fink when you dealt with him?"

Milton clicked his tongue and smiled. "You didn't answer my question, maan. I asked you why you deal with a fink."

"I didn't deal with him. I dealt with Groovy."

"So why don't Groovy go collect?"

"Nobody wants to go near the guy. He's hot. Forget about Burkhardt! I'll get your sixty dollars for you."

"How you gonna get my sixty dollars?"

"All I need is a little more grass. I can have your money in a day or two."

Milton's gold tooth flashed. He unwrapped the cellophane bag and spread the contents out on the table. There was an ounce or so of white powder in the bag. Milton scooped a spoonful of the powder up and let it fall back in the pile. "Nice, huh?" he said.

"Nice for what?"

"Haw haw haw, that's what I like about you, Kid, you're always so goddamn righteous!"

"I'm not being righteous. I just don't like that shit."

"You ever try it?"

"I don't have to try it. I can learn from the experiences of others."

"You don't know shit from others! You smoke a little weed, take a little speed, why are you so righteous about this stuff?"

"Carol," I said, "Artie and Betty. Bill, Mike, Ed. Who else do you want to hear?"

"Haw haw haw." Milton doubled over the coffee table laughing. He straightened up and stared at me. "Carol didn't OD, man, she did herself in. Everybody knows that. Artie and Betty are in just as good a shape as you an' me. What kinda shit are you tryin' to lay down?"

"I just don't dig smack. Everybody involved with it is slimy. They burn their friends and they rip off their own mother if they need a fix."

"Who're you? You the expert on smack all of a sudden?"

"I'm not an expert on anything. I just don't like that shit."

Milton played with his heroin, scooping spoonfuls of the white powder up and letting them fall back into the pile. "You don't know what you're missin', Kid."

"Tell me about it."

"Hey, baby, you got a hard-on for somebody?" Milton stared straight at me. The whites of his eyes looked slightly yellow. I felt depressed suddenly, depressed and tired. What the fuck was I doing here, uptight over a little weed and an ounce of smack? The whole scene was a stone drag. Sam the Fatman and Milton, the whole fucking scene was stupid. I wondered how I got myself into it, two-bit peddling on the street, and all it comes to is friends fucked up and bad feelings between everybody. It was time to go.

I looked at Milton. He spooned the heroin into little piles. "I don't have a hard-on for anybody. I came over here to see about straightening out a debt, that's all. As far as I'm concerned you can take the sixty bucks I owe you and shove it. It's not worth the hassle."

"You wouldn't have no hassle if you didn't give shit out front."

"Fuck it! I don't want to become a used car dealer with dope. A dude wants a little weed and he says he'll pay me for it, I believe him, especially if he's a friend."

"You must not have many friends, Kid."

"I guess not. I'm beginning to see that now."

"Hee hee hee. You so fuckin' square sometimes, Kid. That's what I like about you, you a fuckin' weed-smokin' square. Don't you know there are no friends when it comes to weed? A dude got bread, you give him grass; he don't got no bread, then he don't get no grass. It's simple as that."

"For you. For me it's not that simple."

"Crazy." Milton's eyes narrowed. "You got it all worked out. Maybe tomorrow I come over to Roach Alley an' score some gold from you, huh? You're the bigtime cat on the set."

I said nothing. Milton was right. The rules in dealing dope were down, everyone knew them. Only assholes gave grass out front. Part of the game, though, was everybody trying to make an asshole out of you. I was the Beach's biggest asshole and I didn't even care. I heard Frankie cough from the back bedroom. Milton measured his balloons of smack out on the coffee table and the room smelled of old mattresses and gloom. The whole apartment reeked of dismalness. I couldn't get over the fact that every pad where smack became the reason for being assumed the same sad atmosphere of wretched coughs and incessant scratching and that empty snuff-lipped hipster drawl. And waiting. Everybody is always waiting, waiting to go, waiting to score, waiting to deal, waiting to wait. Waiting for tomorrow, as Walter said.

Milton snuffed deep in his throat and rubbed his nose. His nose was runny; a small drop of snot glistened on the end of it. His smile was macabre, sinister almost, and I felt a shiver run up my spine. I realized suddenly how far away I had grown from Milton. It seemed strange that such distance existed between old friends.

"You wanna pay off that debt, though," Milton said. "I can lay a little of this blanco on you. It's good shit."

"Aw, man!"

"Don't knock it till you try it. Some of my best friends are junkies, hyaa, hyaa, hyaa!" Milton rolled over on the mattress, laughing at his joke. I couldn't help smiling.

"Good bread in it too. See this little balloon?" He held up a small condom-packaged pinch of smack. "Fifty cents, baby, an' if I want to cut it down more I can peddle it over on Mission Street for six bits. That's good bread."

I looked away. I knew the whole operation. Buy an ounce and cut it ten times with powdered sugar or talcum, sell each balloon for seventy-five dollars, and then sit back and groove. Every junkie on the set can nurse his sugar habit, and then when some real shit comes into town, two or three cats will trip out behind it and you'll read about it in the paper the next day.

Only you don't read about it in the paper; it isn't even news worth printing.

I knew that's what happened to Carol. I knew Keith and Artie spent all their time hustling for bread to buy shit. When I thought about it, it made me feel bitter. What made me feel even worse was the fact that I was part of it, in there with the rest of them cutting and chipping and nickel-and-diming my ounces. Even though I only dealt grass, I still felt wretched and stupid and unclean. I felt as if I were covered with the pervasive smell of Milton's pad, the smell of catshit and unwashed dishes and empty time.

"Besides," Milton said, "this is real good stuff. It makes you feel good."

"I feel pretty good most of the time anyway."

"Hayaa, hayaa." Milton lay back under the coffee table. "Well, I guess you do if you say you do." He tied another balloon and smiled. "But you gotta take in consideration all the cats that don't feel good! You gotta think of them dudes!"

"I do. Every time one of them comes around my loft and steals something to buy his next batch of 'feel-good,' I think about them all the time."

"Ah, fuck." Milton threw a balloon on the table. "You talk like the fuckin' man! Baby, there's things goin' on out there that if the ofays glued to *Bonanza* ever got out of their suburbs, they'd shit! There's a world down there behind the barbershops, pool halls, and broken-down sidewalks that if they ever got out of their wall-to-wall dreamworld it'd blow their mother-fuckin' minds."

I stood up. The whole trip was useless. When I felt this way, I said things that even I didn't believe. Who the fuck was I to preach to Milton, or to anyone else for that matter? If they wanted their smack, let them have it. It didn't mean shit to me. If it wasn't smack, it would be booze or speed or whatever. I moved toward the door. "I'd like to see Frankie," I said.

"Frankie!" Milton yelled.

"What?" Frankie answered from the bedroom.

"You wanna talk to the Kid?"

"No."

Milton looked at me. He didn't say anything.

"I'll see you later," I said.

"You sure you don't wanna try a little this shit?"

"No, I don't want any of it."

"Okay, maan, I'll catch you later."

I felt relief on leaving the pad, yet a curious heaviness seemed to have lodged itself in my chest. I felt as if someone had stuffed something down my throat and it had stuck behind my sternum. I leaned against the wall, breathing deeply. The fetid catshit smell of the hallway was sickening. The three flights down the stairs seemed interminable, so I walked down the hall to the stairs that led up to the roof. I stepped out on the roof and the fresh air hit me with a blast. I sucked in deep lungfuls. The late afternoon fog was moving in under the Golden Gate Bridge. I leaned against the parapet watching it. Then I closed my eyes, letting the cool air play over my face.

What the fuck was happening? I thought. Here I am in the most beautiful city in the world and I'm caught, trapped in a cycle of shit and junk and wasted friends. That feeling I had about smack, the feeling that a friend on it was a friend lost, as if the very touching of the stuff was fatal, was unshakable. I tried to shake it by remembering my own first experience with marijuana. Dennis the Booster and Jane and I had ritualized together one night on the rooftop of Dick Moore's pad on Greenwich Street. Dennis had a little hovel on top of the pad that Dick let him stay in as long as he was cool. Dennis had a couple of joints and he invited Jane and me up to join him in a smoke. We all toked away and I remember thinking at the time that I was going to get addicted. I had to laugh when I thought about it. As funny as it was, though, I had the same feeling about smack, one taste was enough, even more than that, just being around the shit was enough. There never seemed to be any addicts in a nonaddict pad, nor were there any nonaddicts in an addict pad—the two just didn't go together. I thought of what Milton had said and he was right. There is a whole world out there, a world that didn't exist for all the day-to-day freaks who sat glued to their TV sets, a world of poverty and disease and hardship and neglect and futility that made the escapist world of heroin livable.

I sucked in the fresh sea air, looking across the bay toward Sausalito. The russet hilltops gleamed above the fog. Alcatraz looked like a mirage as the first columns of fog wrapped themselves around the rock. It was chilly, so I stepped back through the landing door and started down the hall. As I approached Milton's door, I heard him laugh and saw the door open. Milton closed the door behind him and walked down the stairs. He hadn't seen me. For an instant I wanted to call out to him but I didn't. I listened as his footsteps echoed down the stairs and the street door opened and closed. I stood in the hallway for ten minutes, listening. Nothing. I wanted to see Frankie. I walked quietly down the hall and rapped on her door. "Who is it?" she called hesitantly.

Frankie unbolted the safety chain and opened the door slightly. "What do you want?"

"I want to talk to you."

"Go away! I don't have anything to say to you."

"What the fuck's wrong with you, Frankie? I want to talk to you."

"No!" She started to close the door.

I kicked the door with my foot. "Goddamnit, Frankie, I want to talk for a few minutes."

"I'm not going to open this door. Go away."

I had my foot between the door and the jamb so I pushed hard. Frankie pushed on the door, but she didn't have the strength. When she relaxed, I put my shoulder against it and shoved. The safety chain ripped off the wall. Frankie ran back into the kitchen. "Goddamn you!" she said.

"What the fuck's wrong with you? Are you so fucked up you can't even talk to me?"

"I don't want to talk to you. Not you or anybody."

She stood next to the refrigerator glowering at me. Her face was tight; rigid dark lines had appeared under her eyes. I stood in front of her for a long time and then shrugged. Her face held nothing, no warmth, no love, nothing. I turned away and sat down at the kitchen table. Frankie stared out the window. I felt a hundred years old.

Neither of us said anything. I rubbed my finger along the oil tablecloth and looked at her. I felt empty, the whole scene was insane. After a few minutes Frankie turned to me. She rubbed her nose, sniffing. "D'you have a handkerchief?" she said.

I gave her my handkerchief. "What's wrong with you, baby? What are you doing?"

"I'm not doing anything. Why do you always have to think I'm doing something?"

"Hey, baby, I'm not blind. What are you letting yourself go for? What are you doing?"

"I'm not letting myself go. Nothing's wrong with me! Why are you always acting like some old grandmother with me? You're always laying some jiveass miserable shit on me."

"I'm not laying any jiveass shit on you, Frankie. Where'd you get this hard hipster shell you're wearing? You don't even listen any more. I can't talk to you, say a soft word—"

"You don't have to be soft with me. You can be hard with me. I don't care."

"What do you mean?"

"I don't know. I mean, I don't care what the fuck you do. You can do what you want; it makes no difference."

"It makes a difference to me."

"Not to me it doesn't."

"Well, I'm sorry."

"Don't be sorry for me."

"How can I help not feeling sorry for you when I feel sorry for you?"

"That's your fault. I don't ask you for anything. I don't ask anybody for anything."

"What about Milton? You ask Milton for anything?"

"Nothing! I ask Milton for nothing!"

I looked at her sunken eyes. She flipped a nervous finger to her chin and wiped her nose. Hummmm. She was on the junk frequency, the death frequency, the junkie no-mood frequency, toetapping silence of wallpapered rooms and staring at her shoe.

I walked over to the record player and thumbed idly through the records. "Who Can I Turn To?" by Billie Holiday. I put the record on and waited for Billie Holiday's voice. Frankie raised her head, looked; the silence was a song. She sang with unmoving lips. Outside it was getting dark. The evening song.

The record turned and the evening darkened. I looked out at the bridge. I could hear the voice of the night tapping at the sill. I turned from the window and looked at Frankie. She was leaning against the refrigerator, the thin line of her shoulder a point in the dusk. Milton's shadow permeated the room. I was the white American lost in savage kitchens, ovens blasting loneliness and departure.

At the door I turned. Frankie was staring at the floor. Saddened, I walked down the stairs to the street. On Broadway I stopped at the dirty bookstore. I stood in front of the racks reading the headlines of the newspapers, flipped through *Time* and *Playboy*, then walked down toward the Embarcadero. I felt weightless, a husk walking along dirty sidewalks. When I passed Front Street, I stopped opposite the Evans Hotel and pissed against some boards leaning up against a fence. Everything was dank. A newspaper blew along the fence and wrapped itself around my legs. I kicked it away. The headlines spelled doom and Hemingway was dead. Who cared? Half a dozen large produce trucks were parked on Davis Street with their reefer motors running, waiting for midnight so they could unload. Trout Fishing in America Shorty had lost his legs under a reefer truck on this same street. The Kid hadn't lost his legs, but he felt as if he'd lost something else, something no chromeplated wheelchair could ever replace. He pounded his fist into his palm and felt the tears swell up into his eyes. The loss left a knot in his stomach that doubled him over, an intangible pain wracking his body. He walked behind a truck and tried to vomit, but nothing came, just bitter bile that soured his nostrils.

The Kid suddenly felt old, decrepit; he had visions of himself staggering down Grant Avenue with all the other misfits, a battalion of glorious failures marching up and down the avenue like destitute angels. He thought of old Pete Spears on the street with his dog Queenie, his baggy coatpockets full of yesterday's literature and tomorrow's throwaways. He thought of Keith Sanzenback dead in a canyon in Big Sur, of Ella and Mike gone from an overdose, poor Carol on the front pages of *¡Alarma!*, her dead eyes staring from a Tijuana motel room. He thought of McCracken dying in London's Bedlam and Don Graham ground to death in the county hospital's meatgrinder. He thought of Sammy and Tambourine and who else? Strangers all, gifted children fallen out of step, marching to that mad amphetamine drummer, the drug parade. It was a parade without drumbeats, only heartbeats, hearts that beat and then were still.

For a long time the Kid stood beside the produce trucks and thought of Frankie. He thought of her eyes and her lips and of her hand when she touched him. It was the thought of her touch the Kid liked best of all. Standing in the middle of Davis Street, the Kid thought of everyone he knew. It was a rich panorama, and it all appeared as ephemeral as vapor, as unbelievable as the week-old newspaper that blew against his legs. He walked down Pacific Street to the Embarcadero and walked out on an open pier and turned around to look at the city. The panorama was spread out over the whole city. No one was immune, everyone was part of it. It was a panorama of old days past and new days coming. Tomorrow was coming, happier, grander, livelier than all the rest. Tomorrow would be here soon; tomorrow was just around the corner.

26 I climbed the stairs to 72 Commercial Street and found McCracken fucking a chick. He got off and motioned for me to get on. "Fuck her," he said. "She can't get enough of it."

The chick smiled with the eyes of a sixteen-year-old suburban whore. God, I thought, can this really be? The girl was young, sixteen at the most. She was stretched out on the bed with her legs wide open, giving me a full view of her cunt. Her cunt looked like a bed of roses.

"I ate it for an hour before I even stuck my dick in," McCracken said. "You can eat it too if you don't mind seconds."

Finding a sixteen-year-old chick in McCracken's loft with her legs wide open didn't surprise me. Seventy-two Commercial Street was always full of chicks, but this one affected me in a wild way. I had an uncontrollable urge to leap on her. McCracken hustled bare-ass naked over to his drawing table and rummaged around in his papers. He had a knack for enticing all the unattached pelf on the Beach down to his loft—so he could sketch them, he said. The stupid little chicks fluttered around him like bees, waiting on him hand and foot, running out to Spadelee's to score wine, cooking soup, being the little homemakers all of them really wanted to be. McCracken made them take off their clothes so he could sketch them, sometimes getting right down into their cunts with a pair of calipers. "Scientific investigation," he said, dancing around the chicks with a ruler. "Every true artist is a scientist at heart." Look at Leonardo da Vinci." The chicks loved it.

Looking at McCracken's latest chick made me suddenly realize how tense my dick was. I hadn't fucked anything in a week and I wanted to jump on the chick and fuck the shit out of her. I felt a little depraved

thinking about it. I wanted McCracken to leave the
room. It was his loft, though, and I knew one of the
reasons he wanted me to fuck the chick was so that he
could watch. I took off my clothes. McCracken
grabbed his sketchpad. I felt slightly embarrassed, then
suddenly I didn't give a damn. The idea of being
sketched while I fucked the chick gave me a bigger
hard-on than ever. "Go ahead, get on her,"
McCracken said. "Her name's Ginger."

Ginger grabbed my cock and squeezed it. She looked
at it like it was a lollipop. She smiled when I put my
hand on her breast. Her breasts were little round vegetables, hard as turnips and just bitesize. Jesus, it was all
I could do to keep from coming in her hand. Suddenly
Ginger leaned over and licked my cock. She placed her
mouth over the end of it and sucked away, rubbing her
tongue all around it. I felt like screaming. I grabbed
both of her bitesize tits and bit them. Raspberry tarts,
that's what they were. Ginger wriggled her body under
me like an eel and I rubbed the head of my cock along
her belly. She had a nice rounded belly, a sixteen-year-
old belly as hard as a rock. McCracken sketched rapidly while I rubbed my cock along Ginger's belly. I
sucked on her tongue and she rammed it down my
throat. She was incredibly strong and she wriggled her
ass around so my dick slid across her cunt. I wanted to
stick my dick back in her mouth but she would have
none of that, she wanted it inside her cunt as far as it
would go. She lifted her belly up a bit and my dick slid
into her pussy like it was a greased pole. Ginger
moaned when I went inside her, rocking, crying and
laughing, and digging her fingernails into my back. Her
nails felt good on my back, adding a delicious pain to
the ecstasy I felt down below. I fucked her frontwards
for a while and then pulled out and flipped her over on
her face and jammed it in assbackwards. Now she
couldn't scratch me, so I really plunged in deep.
Ginger panted like a horse as I threw it into her, down,
down, deep into her body. My prick felt like it was
knocking up against a wall inside her cunt and she
screamed and wriggled her ass higher up into my face.
I knew I was going to go to prison for this, so what the

hell, I plunged in all the deeper! McCracken was right,
the little bitch couldn't get enough. I looked over at
him while I was pumping away and saw him throwing
paper out like a printing press. It turned me on even
more. I had a giant hard-on that wouldn't quit. The
heat of the stove, the audience, the little round ass
sticking up in my face—all of it combined to make my
blood rockhard, nothing could stop me now, not even
the sheriff beating on my back with his sap. Seeing
Ginger's little ass sticking up in my face made me want
to bend down and ram my tongue up her asshole, stick
it so far up her ass she'd scream. Instead I lifted her up
and held her on the end of my dick. Ginger screamed,
crying, "Yes! Yes!" I screamed too and jammed my
dick in and then pulled it out clean to the tip and then
plunged it all the way back in again, clean to the wall.
Ginger's come was running down her legs and then
suddenly I felt myself coming. I concentrated on it and,
whoossh! it was like a 150-millimeter howitzer blasting
off across the room. The jolt straightened out my
whole body, from the tip of my toes to the end of each
hair on top of my head. "Oh, Jesus!" I cried, forgetting
McCracken. I didn't care if the whole Art Institute
were sketching me.

Ginger sobbed and collapsed on the bed. She rolled
over smiling and stretched up to kiss my lips. When I
opened my eyes, I saw a little girl and a grown woman
in one body. She giggled and sat on the edge of the
bed. God, what am I doing? I thought. McCracken was
still sketching. "Fantastic!" he said. "I want to do a
portrait of both of you sitting there. I'll do a series of
erotica, I'll catch every move. It'll be great with a
soundtrack. We'll have a show of the drawings and
make a tape of the sounds of you making love. Fantastic!"

Ginger leaned over and licked my chest. I felt like a
wounded water buffalo, the scratches on my back
stung. I was beat, although my dick still had a hard
edge to it. Ginger grabbed the corner of the blanket
and wiped my dick off and then leaned over and kissed
it. She was crazy! A crazy runaway chick from the

suburbs. "Is this what they're producing in Westlake?" I asked.

McCracken laughed. "Ginger's not even out of high school yet."

"She's probably not even in high school, and her daddy's probably the sheriff."

"He's an accountant." Ginger smiled.

"I'm going to do a plaster cast of her body," McCracken said. "It'd be great to do both of you together, *Kama Sutra* in plaster of paris."

"You're insane!" I said.

"So is Picasso and look where he's at."

McCracken threw down his sketchpad and walked over to his workbench. The bench was covered with his tools: knives, paintbrushes, pots, paints, papercutter, press, ink, etc., all filched from the Art Institute. "Fuck those bastards up there," McCracken said when I asked him about his source of supply. "They're nothing but a bunch of Sunday painters anyway!"

One end of the bench is McCracken's and the other end belongs to Arthur. McCracken's end is full of color, pots of paint and bright acrylics and oils and watercolors. Arthur's end is black and white. The Mulatto Kid, McCracken calls Arthur. "He's been working in black and white for five years, refining, refining, refining. I wish I could draw like that bastard."

It's generally conceded by Bowen and McCracken that Arthur is the best draftsman of the three. McCracken and Bowen are wild action painters, while Arthur settles into his highback stool with his rulers and paper and heavy books on Peruvian and Egyptian and Sumerian art and draws diagrams and makes notes and then sketches black and white portraits and designs that are only the beginnings of elaborately worked out Mayan codices-type paintings that look like stone bas-relief figures that have lain in the jungle and been rained on for ten thousand years, all the lines delicate and soft, the figures' details almost dissolved, only the barest traces and shadows remaining to show the subtlety of Arthur's art.

Ginger was up and in the shower. She was singing

under the water. "An amazing ball, ain't she?" McCracken chortled.

"Where'd you find her?"

"Hee hee, that's an artistic secret. I'm going to do a whole series of sketches of her pussy. I want to get every hair just right. I want to do the definitive statement on cunts."

"That'll never be done," I said. "You better talk to Peter LeBlanc. He's been searching for the perfect pussy for that woodcut he's been doing for five years and he still hasn't found it. He says the perfect pussy is like a fine sable brush; it snaps back into place after it's been used. All you got to do is lick it."

"Hee hee." McCracken danced around his studio.

"Besides," I said, "every time you think you've found the perfect cunt, something new comes along."

"I guess you're right," McCracken sighed. "They're all the same but in some weird way they're all different, you ever notice that?"

McCracken hustled about mixing his plaster of paris. He stirred a big tub of the stuff like one of Macbeth's witches, bubble, bubble, toil and trouble. "When Ginger gets out of the shower, I'm going to cast her body in plaster of paris." He laughed gleefully.

I felt both elated and spent, thinking of Ginger. I felt a little sorry because the fuck I threw into her seemed to be just that—a fuck and nothing else. It had none of the grace, none of the tenderness, no passion I could call my own. It would have been just as well to have stood in the shower and flogged myself for all the meaning it had. It was just an animal release in a loft on Commercial Street. It wasn't even commercial. At least commercial fucks have some finance behind them. My fucking Ginger was simply a zero, a dead zero at that, an act of nihilism that produced nothing, created nothing, made nothing grow. I masturbated into Ginger's cunt, that's all there was to it. I thought of what Crow had said: "More than two is perversion." I wondered what the act of love was anyway. Was it the word itself? I love you. I fuck you. I want to make love to you. I want to make fuck to you. Fuck seemed more honest. When I thought about my bout with Ginger, I

felt incomplete. I felt unfulfilled. I felt less than unfulfilled, I felt empty.

Ginger sounded happy. Her voice lilted over the
shower walls, filling the loft. Maybe all it took to make
her happy was for someone to stuff a dick into her, it
didn't matter whose. I could probably have stuffed a
broomstick up her cunt and she would have been just as
happy, as long as that hollow space was filled. I knew
that wasn't true, though. Even Ginger, the sixteen-
year-old Madonna of the Alleys, needed more than
that. Down deep inside her, Ginger had crevices and
crannies that had never been touched. Yet she was
singing in the shower. Rock around the clock, baby.
Maybe she had had all her crevices filled. Maybe my
dick filled them. She had had McCracken's dick too.
Maybe she was singing because McCracken's dick
filled her up. Or maybe she was singing because she
had had both our dicks inside her and she knew she
was going to have more, an endless stream of dicks
moving in and out of her until she was too old to hold
them any more or too tired to care.

Ginger's beautiful voice floated over the loft. I felt
restless. The drawings on the walls, the figures hacked
out of stone and wood, the plaster of paris molds of
bodies and torsos leaning against every wall seemed to
be figures in a pantomime; and I too felt like a figure
in the show. Followed by the sound of Ginger's singing
and the slump-slump of McCracken stirring his
witches' brew of plaster of paris, I imagined myself cast
in a rigid, immobile mold, my white body leaning
against the wall with the rest of the crew. I walked
over to one of the plaster figures and inspected it
closely. It was the headless and armless torso of a girl,
a voluptuous beauty with chalky breasts. I touched a
breast. It seemed alive in a mysterious intergalactic
way. McCracken was a sorcerer, carving and dismem-
bering the girls he slept with. It seemed sacrilegious to
me, walking around in a mausoleum of old loves, only
the forepoints saved. There were no arms to grasp, no
legs left to tighten around your own. Above all, there
were no heads, no voices, no eyes left to look into to

catch the reflection of your own eyes. It was the perfect body bank.

Ginger stepped out of the shower and stood before me, her velvety young body steaming from the hot water. The sight of her caused a lascivious reaction in me. She stood before me rubbing a towel languidly over her breasts and immediately my dick was leaping against my leg, throbbing like a tuning fork. It felt as if we had piano wires strung between us. I moved toward her involuntarily and McCracken laughed. "Hee hee, you'll have to wait, Kid. I'm going to cast her now."

McCracken led Ginger over to his worktable and made her lie down. She complied, stretching out luxuriously as he began rubbing Vaseline over her body. I watched closely as McCracken spread great globs of Vaseline over her arms and breasts, across her abdomen, and down around her vagina, slipping a finger in "just for fun." "I put the Vaseline on to keep the plaster from sticking to her skin," he said. "It gets pretty hot as it dries."

I took a shower while McCracken finished his preparations. When I got out, Ginger was ready. McCracken scooped handfuls of plaster of paris out of the tub and spread them over the Vaseline. In a few minutes Ginger was covered from neck to crotch. She lay still under the coating of plaster, her eyes staring straight up at the ceiling.

"It gets firm in about forty-five minutes, then I can take it off."

I looked at Ginger. "How does it feel?"

"Oh, fine. It feels warm." She giggled softly.

"If it gets too hot, let me know," McCracken said.

While the plaster of paris was drying, McCracken picked up his sketchpad and thumbed through the drawings he'd made of Ginger and me fucking. I looked over his shoulder. Lines of energy and force, curious representations of the act of love. I tried to picture myself as the artist, a voyeur in a sense, as all artists are. I wondered if McCracken picked up on my feelings. Then I remembered that my own feelings were afterthoughts, thoughts after the event, while McCracken had sketched the moment itself. Despite the multiplicity of McCracken's series of drawings, somewhere in the back of my mind I knew that every act of love was singular, separate, like no other, and when that separateness was transgressed, then the coming together was not a coming together but a splitting apart. In McCracken's drawings I saw arms and legs and cocks and cunts. Thinking of Ginger and me together, I felt that we had raped one another, we had assaulted one another with permission, used each other's bodies, but we had not touched.

I looked more closely at McCracken's sketches. Somehow there seemed to be more life in the drawings than there was in the memory of the act itself. I told McCracken what I was thinking.

"Coming together," he said, "no matter how you do it, is never wrong."

"But what if the act leaves you empty rather than fulfilled, what then?"

"It's a physical trip and it doesn't have to be anything else. A temporary joining with no aftereffects, no remorse, no regret, nothing but the act itself. It's like two ships passing in the night. All you feel is the wake."

I walked over to Ginger's side. "How is it?"

"It feels heavy. It's getting pretty warm."

"That's the chemical reaction in the plaster," McCracken said. "It's getting hard. I'll take it off in another twenty minutes."

Under her coat of plaster of paris Ginger was beautiful and young. She smiled. I thought of the chemical forces churning inside her young body. Sixteen years old, with a cavity that would probably never be properly filled. I wondered what she was thinking. I would never find out; she probably didn't know herself. I picked up McCracken's sketchbook and looked at the drawings a second time. I saw the sensual line, the young girl caught between two worlds, a world of adolescence that was just emerging from the shadows of childhood, and the young woman, the young burgeoning woman with juices beginning to flow from her cunt, like ripening fruit dripping nectar. McCracken's drawings caught the moment of Ginger's ripening;

other drawings he'd made of her lined his walls, in
them the young girl flourished, vibrated with the magic
and grace of childhood. I looked at her and realized
that there *had* been a touchstone reached, somehow
within our coupling there had been that unfathomable
bit of grace, despite me, despite everything. What
Ginger needed, I needed, without any preamble of pain
or pity or self-doubt. Somewhere deep within mine and
Ginger's bodies our juices had mingled, only temporarily perhaps, but that was enough. The meanings we
give to the act of love—or the act of fuck, call it what
you will—are the meanings we ourselves create. The
meanings live and die with each of us individually; they
are ours alone.

I walked to the front of the loft and looked out over
the city. The lights from the buildings glinted in a
thousand crystal rays over the windows and the muted
clamor of the city reached me as though vibrating up
through a vacuum. Below me, across the street, the
Mission Emergency Hospital ambulance hovered, a
giant animal ready to pounce on the next victim of the
city's heartlessness. As I stood there, it leapt from its
moorings and hurtled into the dark alleys of the city.
The strangled breath of the wounded and dying as they
sprawled painwracked on the dismal sidewalks was all
around me. I heard McCracken and Ginger laughing,
and it was as if the whole city were here, in
McCracken's loft, listening to their laughter. I felt as if
I were a vague presence looking in on the scene from
another world. It was as if I were standing before a
fortuneteller's globe, or rather, I was *inside* the globe
itself and future, past, and all the secrets of the universe were spread out around me. A giant eye looking
out on the world, I saw reality, drawings pinned on a
wall, plaster of paris torsos, and ambulances hurtling
away through the night.

I thought of my own presence among the cacophony
and madness of the city and realized that all my yearnings and heartbreak and lonelinesses were mirrored in
a thousand similar lonelinesses, a hundred million
heartbreaks, yearnings beyond reckoning. Behind me I
heard McCracken working with the plaster mold on

Ginger's body and I heard her cry out and her cry mingled with my cry, though mine was silent, and the cries of both of us mingled with the night and the night's cry became Bob Seider's tenor sax in Washington Square, Bob Kaufman's jaw-wracked Methedrine madness down Grant Avenue, Kell Robertson's sad Okie lament, old Padraic Seamus O'Sullivan's feathered hat, Crazy Alex's whispered truths, JoJay's Taos Pueblo legacy, Frankie's tortured innocence, Little Joe's suffocation in the Grand Canyon of Cunt, Noble William watching death from a window in a hotel room on Larimer Street in Denver, Bill Wiejon dead at Point Sixteen, Carol Joseph resting at last on the front pages of ¡Alarma!, Don Graham hopeless in room after room, Dean Lipton waiting for the Third Street bus, Dr. Frick Frack gathering dust at last run movies, Hube the Cube taping furtively each crack in his room, Richard Bloomer chanting Kaddish over his lost brother, Keith Sanzenbach washed away in Willow Creek's flood, McCracken himself molding beautiful young Ginger's body on his way to Bedlam.

My view of the world isn't unique. It's a view available on any streetcorner; the voices I hear are the voices of the people who pass. The echo is taken up and reverberated through the night. And in this echo-driven night that I come home to, my vision out the loft window is like the mirror image of my soul; I can see myself in the window reflected back, the realizer realizing his dreams. It's a far cry from back home, that old Coltontown desperateness, those sad lost souls left pumping gas, the switch-engine roar of the going; it's all a loneliness now in the American dust. And who among us understands? It's like a dream dreamt once too often, the dream finally comes around full circle and then it's gone like dust devils that fade and die like the memory of lost dogs. As I looked out the loft window—my glass eye on the world—I realized that space is all we need, a little openness that allows us to be friends. Sometimes when I walk down the street, the realization comes to me that despite all our woes a magic pattern governs some lives—perhaps all—and especially I feel that a magic pattern governs my own life. Each mistake and each departure from the rules I make was somehow worked out in the cosmic scheme eons ago, and all I have to do is get up in the morning and brush my teeth and walk out on the street and there Destiny will meet me and take my hand. Sometimes I feel that this pattern is so inviolable that I must break it, go directly contrary to my own wishes. And when I do, even the farthest-out scheme comes back around like a celestial cog and takes me one step higher in that dream.

"The plaster's hard. I'm going to take it off."

McCracken lifted up one edge of the plaster cast and peeked under it. "How's it feel, baby?"

"Okay." Ginger stared out from under the white sheath. I watched her.

"Groovy. I'm going to lift it off real slow. Yell if it hurts."

McCracken lifted the plaster cast up slowly. Ginger's eyes were closed. Big tears spilled out from under her eyelids. As McCracken lifted the cast up, Ginger lifted up too. Her buttocks were four inches off the table. "It hurts," she cried.

"Jesus, it's stuck." McCracken let go of the cast. Ginger settled back down on the table, heaving a sigh of relief.

"What's holding it?" I kneeled down on the floor and stuck my nose one inch from Ginger's breasts. I peeked under the lip of the plaster mold. I could see nothing.

"I think her pussy hairs are caught in the plaster." McCracken gently lifted the edge of the mold. "It happened once before with Mona. I didn't use enough Vaseline."

McCracken and I both peeked under the edge of the mold. Ginger lay still. The plaster was hot, like an electric blanket turned up to ten. I tugged gently on one edge of the mold and Ginger's ass jerked up off the table. "Oh . . . oh," she cried, tears rolling down her face.

"What're you going to do?" I looked at McCracken.

"I'm going to have to cut her pussy hairs. Find me a razor blade, will you, Kid?"

I got a razor blade from Arthur's workbench and handed it to McCracken. He held the blade between the first and second fingers of his right hand and gently lifted up one edge of the plaster mold with his left hand. He slid his right hand in under the cast. Tears streamed down Ginger's face but she said nothing. As the plaster lifted up, Ginger's ass lifted up also.

"You're going to have to lay still, baby." McCracken edged his hand farther in under the mold. Ginger made short little gasping noises.

"Maybe we should break it off. You can always make another mold."

McCracken looked at me in disgust. "This is a good casting. I don't want to ruin it."

Ginger turned her big eyes toward me. I shrugged. McCracken moved his right hand back and forth in a sawing motion. Little squeals escaped from Ginger's lips. I held her hand tightly.

"It's coming. I can feel the hairs."

McCracken sawed away, moving his arm farther in under the plaster mold. Ginger was rigid on the table. Suddenly McCracken stepped back and jerked the plaster cast up with both hands, causing Ginger to shriek.

"Perfecto!" he cried, carrying the cast across the loft and leaning it up against the wall. "This is my best one yet, look!"

I walked over and inspected the mold. A perfect reverse representation of Ginger's body, each line and detail exact. I bent down and inspected the plaster cunt. Wiry little hairs protruded from the plaster.

"This one's a classic!" McCracken cried, rubbing his fingers over the pudendum. "Real live pussy hair. I bet I can sell this one to Dr. Wenner for a hundred bucks."

Ginger took another shower to clean off the Vaseline and plaster of paris, then she fell asleep in the big bed. McCracken and I sat around drinking wine and talking. We reminisced about the city, remembering friends who'd gone, either dead or disappeared; we didn't know. McCracken turned on KJAZ and we listened to the radio. The three A.M. fog swirled through the streets and I stoked the oil-drum fire with rolled up newspapers. Just before dawn we walked up to the Star

Cafeteria on Kearny Street. The Chinese cook behind the counter ladled out fried eggs and coffee and looked at us as if we were samurai warriors doomed to eternity, scraggly veterans of some feudal lord's lost battles. As we walked back, the sky was just beginning to lighten in the east, a pale glow that left each alley darker, every empty window emptier.

In the loft McCracken unveiled "The Revolt of the Martyrs," the big painting he'd done. He wanted me to help him deliver it to a buyer later in the morning. "It's the best thing I've ever done," he said.

I agreed. The painting was impressive.

"I've got to deliver it at nine thirty. I made a deal with a lawyer. I'm gonna give it to him so he'll get Patrick out of jail."

"What kind of deal did you make?"

"Well, the deal's not actually firm. I told the lawyer I'd give him a great painting if he'd help out a friend of mine who was in trouble. He hasn't seen the painting yet."

"Why don't you have him come over here and look at it?"

"I don't want to lose the initiative. Once the painting's inside his office, I know he'll fall in love with it."

"The Revolt of the Martyrs" was twelve feet long and four feet wide. We carried it down the stairs. As we edged it out the door into the street, a group of warehousemen lounging around the hiring hall next door walked over. They craned their necks to see the painting. "Hey, are you guys real artists?" one of them said.

McCracken said nothing. He pulled his end of the painting up off the sidewalk and started down Commercial Street. "Hey, you guys paint nekkid girls up there?" the warehouseman called. He made a jacking-off motion with his hand and the rest of the men laughed. I ducked my head. All along Commercial and down Battery Street early morning shoppers and office workers stared as "The Revolt of the Martyrs" went by. McCracken trudged on, shouldering his way through the crowds, wispy-bearded chin held high. I felt ridiculous and happy at the same time. McCracken's bizarrely checked pants that he'd dug out of a debris box on Drumm Street a few months before were three sizes too small for him. The pants were covered with months of paint and his ass was caked with plaster of paris. On his feet were a pair of sandals that Rowena, a chick he'd harbored in his loft for a while, had made him, the pitiful leather thongs struggling to contain his size fourteen feet. When we passed a store window, I saw myself, a hulking six foot four with ragged seaman's cap and flappy frisco jeans. My hickory shirt was gone at the elbows, and when I looked at our reflections and the reflection of the painting passing the plate glass window, it seemed that McCracken and I were two of the martyrs come alive, our torch the painting itself, which we bore bravely above the heads of the teeming multitudes.

The lawyer's office was in the Aetna Building on Market Street. We maneuvered the painting through the swinging doors into the lobby. The doorman approached on swift suede feet. "MayIhelpyousirs?" he said.

"We're delivering a painting to Mr. Allen," McCracken said. "Of Allen, Crankshaw, McDougle, and Fiber."

"Mr. Allen's on the fifteenth floor. You'd better use the freight elevator."

The doorman scooted ahead of us and punched the button with a gloved hand. The freight elevator arrived. McCracken stuck his end of "The Revolt" in and I maneuvered my end around, twisting to make it fit. It was stuck. The doorman took hold of one end of the painting while McCracken pulled and I twisted, I pushed and McCracken shoved. It was no use. "It's too long," Mr. Doorman said. "You'll have to carry it up."

We followed the doorman across the lobby to the door leading to the stairs. He held it open and we started up. At each turning, one corner of the painting scraped a wall. Climb-scrape-turn, climb-scrape-turn for fifteen flights, marring walls, scratching handrailing, chewing the corners of the painting, cursing and sweating our way up to Allen, Crankshaw, McDougle, and Fiber. When we reached the fifteenth floor, we leaned the painting against the wall and knocked on the lawyer's door. A secretary with hair two feet high invited us in.

The office smelled of thick rugs and fat fees. The walls were paneled in oak and money. McCracken and I sat down on a large black leather couch between two man-eating potted plants with leaves thick as wrists. I edged toward the center of the couch. The leather wheezed and I sank slowly in. We smiled. The receptionist smiled back. Her mouth looked like the front end of a 1956 Cadillac. McCracken sprawled back and spread his legs. His balls strained to burst out of his too-tight debris-box pants. I looked at his size fourteen sandaled feet and unconsciously lifted my boots off the rug. I tried to imagine plaster of paris molds and beautiful young Ginger's body. Suddenly I started laughing.

"What's wrong?" McCracken said.

"Nothing."

"No, tell me, whaddayou laughing at?"

I leaned over to McCracken. "Remember that time you fucked Choulos's secretary?"

"Yeah, what about it?"

"I was just thinking of her hair."

"Oh, yeah." McCracken tittered.

One afternoon Bowen had brought one of Choulos's secretaries down to 72 Commercial Street. Choulos is a high powered lawyer associated with one of the most successful law firms in the city. The secretary had hair like this one, and when she fucked McCracken her hair caught fire. McCracken had lit a candle and set it on the bedstead so he could fuck by candlelight, and Roosevelt Chicken knocked it off. When candle met hair, whoosh! Half her hair fizzed away before McCracken could put it out. She wasn't even hurt though. The plastic hair went so fast the flames didn't have a chance to reach her scalp. I rolled over in tears remembering, trying to hold on to myself. McCracken laughed loudly, hammering his feet on the floor.

Suddenly the inner office door opened and Mr. Allen walked out. He was accompanied by several secretaries, the informal art-judging committee, obviously. We shook hands all around and then Mr. Allen, urbane, casual, trim, suntanned, bounced over, the spring

in his step landing him first in front of me, then
McCracken, then the painting. "Aha," he said cheer-
fully. "So this is what I've been hearing so much
about."

The minute I saw Mr. Bounce I saw "no" writ all
across his Mantan face. McCracken moved over beside
his painting while Bouncy checked it out. The gaggle
of secretaries moved in behind him, cooing and ahhing.
McCracken explained his painting to the lawyer, dog-
gedly answering questions tossed out by a couple of
secretaries. Bouncy looked at the painting for a long
time and sighed. "What do you call it?" he said.

" 'The Revolt of the Martyrs,' " McCracken answered.

"It's rather large, don't you think?"

McCracken said nothing.

"What do you think, girls? Do the colors match our
decor?"

The girls tittered.

Bounceman stood in front of "The Revolt" for a
long time and then turned to McCracken. "Do you
think you could cut it in half? I don't believe it will fit
on my wall."

I looked away. McCracken was so enthused with his
work of art and his mission to rescue Patrick that he
failed to pick up on Bouncy's reluctance. I took
McCracken aside. "It's useless, McCracken. He doesn't
want your painting. Let's take it back to the loft."

McCracken was dumbfounded. I picked up one end
of the revolting martyrs and motioned for him to grab
the other. Together we carried it out of the office. We
lugged it down fifteen flights, descend, scrape, turn,
and out the front door and down Market Street
through the same early morning workers who craned
their necks to look at the painting. Inside the loft
McCracken leaned his painting against the wall and
looked at it. For twenty minutes he just sat and stared
at the painting. Then he got up and started stalking the
loft, like a lion in a cage. Again and again he returned
to his painting, occasionally casting glances across to
where I was sitting. The noon whistle on the Ferry
Building bellowed and traffic rushed by outside.

McCracken looked at me and cracked a smile. "Well, fuck! That damn Cassiday's gonna have to rot in jail a little longer. We haven't got our formula down yet."

I walked down the steps and whistled in the noon-time air. The sun was shining and the warehousemen lounging outside the hiring hall smiled and pitched dimes against the brick building. They nodded and passed a paperbagwrapped jug of sweet wine between them and laughed in the sunlight. "Hey, beatnik, have a snort!" one of them said, holding out a jug. I smiled and took the jug and tilted it up. The warehousemen laughed and slapped their knees and pitched their dimes. I handed the jug back and continued up the street toward the Beach, thinking of Patrick. I knew he would survive his prison and I knew McCracken would survive Mr. Bounce who wanted him to cut his painting in half so it would fit on his wall. What was it Jack Kerouac said, he who described so well this army of misfits and failures who snatched laughter from the mouth of calamity, who spit in the face of adversity, who reeled and hollered down the road in paroxysms of insane mirth? As I crossed Montgomery Street and joined the army of graysuited warriors returning to their concrete fortresses with their stock portfolios underarm, I remembered what Jack said: "Prison is where you promise yourself the right to be free."

28 That night I went up to the Spaghetti Factory Cafe and got terribly drunk and became such a mess with myself, leering over husbands' shoulders at wives and winking and licking my lips so lewdly, that Gary, the bartender, had to tell me, "Cool it, Kid. You're really making an ass out of yourself."

I was so drunk I didn't know what he was talking about. In fact I didn't remember the night at all except for walking home to Roach Alley later—that being the time my head usually clears up—or else much later and I'm in bed and some sound awakens me and I wonder where I am and what? Oh, yes, I remember, Lawrence was making fun of me. I was talking about poetry, about *On the Road* . . . about the way Neal Cassady died when his heart gave out along that railroad. Lawrence said about me, "And here I sit in the Spaghetti Factory Cafe in the American night, an American drunk who's been in all the American Slim Galliard scenes from top to VD bottom and Neal really didn't know shit, and he was impotent too, he told me so one dark American night drinking tokay in a gondola from Needles to Fresno. So, so . . . it's all emptiness filled with desperate bullshit. So I put my X here. Lawrence Bucker."

I staggered through the streets remembering Lawrence's quip and stumbled over the Beltline Railroad tracks thinking of Neal and that spot outside San Miguel where he died, where the memory of his death and the soft damp curve of his body lie still along the tracks, the curving rails running past saguaro cactus mounds and rippling cactus apple winds and baseball diamonds where sadfaced but joyous Mex kids batter balls around the field and scatter leaves the way Neal did along the same spot. I slept there once, a mile outta town alongside an arroyo. When the next morning sun and cows awakened me, I found I was beside a ragged poorboys' playing field a few feet from where Neal later died, his body blending into the dust and cinder of a life that ain't no more, only a memory, sad, bedraggled, but somehow not wanting, the lean body wracked weary with his ancient young man's face, the earth settled now in the shape and form of a man . . . soft . . . silent, in Mexico, small things squealing, growing, dying alongside the wailing tracks where 1940s railroad cars hurtle by. The next morning in my loft I wondered what punishment I'd have to assume to atone for last night's drunken bleary beery sins.

Before I got drunk, though, and was tossed if not literally then figuratively out on my ear, I met Arthur and we talked. I told him of McCracken's plight with Mr. Bounce, the neat-necktied lawyer, and "The Revolt of the Martyrs" and we laughed over it and agreed it was funny, especially the way the painting wouldn't fit on the wall and we had to wind it down all those stairs again and carry it back to the loft.

I got in a long conversation with Arthur revolving at first around the inconstancy of chicks and how they have that thing down there that drives men wild, how we need it and spend all our waking moments and half our nights searching for it, in essence giving it the stature of the Kohinoor diamond, so big, so bright, so glittering in its amber setting of legs, thighs, lips, the little twists and sins devised to torture us and burden our wet nights.

Arthur laughed at my merciless condemnation, which of course was the right thing to do. I bleared more and slopped the chablis wine that Gary kindly gave to quiet me and murmured "Frankie" on my sleeve like a litany. That partly explains my leering lippiness over other husbands' wives. (And not a few of the wives whispering behind their husbands' backs, "If only," "But how?" "Not now but later," and other such sad things that one hears in bars on weekends when families prepare for nights out with the kids at home and a sitter and then sit around and realize how old, we don't have anything to talk about any more, nothing but our love, which is deep if we only knew.)

It's always easy for barslobs to hold promise of strange, interesting, and not-experienced-for-a-long-time excitements that they use to take advantage of this woe that drifts over some tables—not all, thank God! So naturally the Supercock Kid picks up on those tables that have this sad vibe sight and zeros in like a hornet, a guided missile zoomed by heat and drowned in chablis wine and the natural wonder of someone new.

That's when Arthur started talking about Charlie Parker. His sad travails. I nodded majestically in my glass and harked to those sad remembrances of that strange cat. It seemed weird that Arthur would bring up Charlie Parker in all this din, the memory of those Kansas City afternoons, the sad coffin home on a train. "There's nothing inside," Ginsberg said. "Touch it." I touched the coffin. When I raised the lid, I heard the mad sax sound that only Bob Seider in Washington Square understands, him carrying that same burden, the wrath of instruments and secret melodies that die between uneventful heartbeats.

Mike Bloomfield and Nick Gravenites listen to those same tunes. Chicago Military Academies do not reek of that same sadness, though; the melody they play in the virgin greenery of Mill Valley has nothing to do with the sweet sad times that Charlie Parker stumbled through Arthur's doorway, sad, drunk, armwretched and weary, dismembered by the frozen dope in his veins.

I stopped in my chablis blindness for some reason. Suddenly I knew that I was being told some tale. The meaning not apparent to my ears at first because epiphanies come when I'm least expectant, caught with my pants down, as it were, which was unusual, because the Kid always wanders sobersided and serious about the Beach's bent streets listening for any secret sidewalk whisper. Now here drunk over a bar whole unrecorded scores were being played for me, riffs from inscrutable Arthur, the painter who is exploring the relationship between black and white. "Everything comes out mulatto," McCracken said. I hulked over the mahogany bar of the Spaghetti Factory Cafe and hushed as Arthur's wizened wispy voice recounted a life that somehow—don't ask me—had meaning and lent justification to the one I myself was leading. This true in the sense that how Charlie Parker lived and died is not a Standard Oil roadmap but a darkened plain that cartographers know nothing of. I shut up and listened. It seemed to me that I was hearing of my own unrealized life. The heavy bop riffs careened off my skull like the sad reminders of back home, all sixteen wheels of that old *Cherokee* thundering into history to settle years later onto sidings in Kansas City with the remains of that incredible black clay.

Arthur was speaking of Charlie Parker. Arthur knew Charlie Parker. Charlie Parker slept off a hundred drunks and bad heads in Arthur's loft on East Forty-second Street in New York City when the streets were full of snow and sooted sorrow. While Arthur talked, I pictured in my mind's eye Charlie Parker's trajectory from Kansas City dusty-lane tennis-shoed back porches with flapping screendoors to East Forty-second Street lofts with dark bricks and cold water and I suddenly remembered what it was. All this time I didn't know and then I suddenly knew what it was that sends you away from home: you're walking across the park maybe, the trees are the same, maybe losing some leaves is all, suddenly you're older, the municipal plunge doesn't hold you any more, a train whistle sounds closer—or farther away—the library's closed, the streets empty; everything happens and nothing happens; friends are gone, jobs, married; doors are shut, season's ended, it's time to go.

I heard the knock on Arthur's door. It was Charlie Parker. He was standing outside in the hall—the rug nap worn old with centuries, so old even time was frozen. When he stepped inside it was like a revelation. He didn't even set his case down; he held it like an emblem to his breast. Rainbows poured from it, the lilting sweetness of his silence so overpowering that I turned my sadness to the wall. It was like the leaves I heard fall in the park. They made no noise. The din was inconsolable. Somehow while Arthur was rapping I got Charlie Parker and Dr. Sax mixed up in my mind. I nodded. Maybe it was Charlie Parker's sax. The old slouch hat. When Arthur spoke, I heard that old melody. The mad cadenza. Yass. Dr. Sax, I know him well. Never knew he carried that black case, though. He only deals in glee now. In Arthur's telling, Charlie Parker became that old black magic. The sad, pitiful, yet wondrous tale of Charlie Parker's brief trajectory becoming in my chablis-stained brain an epiphany linking together the two mysteries: old gleeful ghoul Dr. Sax of Kerouacian backstreet Lowells and Charlie Parker, black sax-carrying niggerboy from flappy Kansas City afternoons. It was all one—or two—or three—the third becoming me, the Frisco Kid, because without the personalization none of it is meaningful. The whole sad drunk-over-the-bar tale really a message to me because of my bleariness and overt drunken helplessness and because I was reading Dr. Sax and all those facts—facts! facts! What do they have to do with this dream? I hunched over Arthur's shoulder and listened while he told me the story of Dr. Charlie Parker Sax. It's a strange tale. Listen:

"Bird was lonely, man, the loneliest cat I ever knew. When I opened the door, he'd walk in carrying that beat-up old case and walk over to the stove—I had a fifty-five-gallon drum cut into a stove, just like the one we got down at Seventy-two Commercial Street—and he'd stand beside the stove and smile. He'd hold that black case *(Dr. Sax have symbols, formulas, he carry magic in that case)* to his breast, just stand there and nod like he was keeping time to some rhythm only he could hear *(yass, I know, Jack tole me so. Dr. Sax have special hearing aid and senses, yak!)*. He was wasting away on junk. He used to come up to my place to rest; he'd sleep on the couch and in the morning he'd be gone to score or gone to scare up some bread to score. He never asked me for any shit. He knew I didn't hold. He'd just come in and flop and the next morning be gone *(through the window, black cape flapping, yeah!)*. Next week I'd hear another knock and there he'd be, rumpled suit and all *(Dr. Sax sleep in his suit, no time for amenities, nightflights across the shadowed river, Dr. Sax knows)*, had to make a gig and wanted some rest. He'd lay down on the couch and be out. I helped when I could, gave him a place to sleep and something to eat. When he wanted to stay straight, he always came to my couch. He was like Slim *(ex-partner Dr. Sax, carry the case for him, not as wise or strong but good sense of humor)* when Slim did cold turkey. Slim couldn't stay at any of his friends' pads because there was too much junk around. He had to make it in the laundromat and doorways, sleep on the benches so he wouldn't be near the junk that was stashed behind every dresser.

"Bird was on the downhill run bad and all of his friends knew it. He had too hard a time, it was too much, he was tired, not mad tired like he used to be but sad tired, tired of putting down all those sounds, telling everybody what it was like, you know *(yass!)*, the bad end of town, the bad head, the bad junk, the whole myth and ritual of Charlie Parker *(Dr. Sax)* America. Bird was sick, man, though nobody knew how sick until right at the end. He had no moderation *(moderation stinks! Mhee yee haa!)*. He fucked off twenty, thirty good years on all that bad shit and sleeping in gutters and no rest or moderation or peace. He had too much to say and nobody wanted to listen. Bird was on the way down the first time I met him. It was in Chicago. I was only seventeen at the time but tall, you know, all straightened out in my rag coat with the arms hanging down to my knees *(shroud over head too, Dr. Sax long cape flying, him making it down to the castle, gloom parties with Count Dracula, old mate of the Southern Mystic Hollywood Paraphernalia set, he whoop over that bridge)*. It was cold, man, freeze your ass off! I was class though—Slimjim tie and Mr. B collar, ofay chick on my arm. We was makin' it down to the South Alameda Arena, a skating rink, they had a dance there lasted from nine in the evening until six the next morning *(Dr. Sax hours, only he start a little late)*. Man, I plunked my three skins down and cut inside with this cute little chick, flash, you know? I was tough! That whole night was tough! I never seen so many people in my life. That's the first time I ever saw Bird, didn't even know who he was till later. I got to

know him after all his hospital trips and kicks and
lying in the gutter; I used to visit him in his pad on Divi-
sion Street *(same old Dr. Sax pad, little one-room
out-of-the-way place to store clothes, condiments,
secret black satchel)*, he had a little room there. Bird
was a sweet cat, man, he dug everybody. The night I'm
talking about he played 'Confirmation' for one hour,
man, one solid fucking hour! We danced fifteen, sixteen dances while that cat blowed! Everybody was
feeling titties and rubbing crotches and havin' a ball!
Chicks was dancing with chicks and cats was dancing
with cats and one stud was balling his old lady right
out in the middle of the floor! It was wild, man! And
old Bird was up there on the bandstand playing 'Confirmation.' I'll never forget that night. *(The night Dr.
Sax born in his shroud, known only to Kansas City and
Lowell, Massachusetts, boys, sapping marbles 'cross
the floor, and lil boyos going down to trainyards, winter in our youths, sad only that they pass, end on
bridges, heights, depths, not all reach them lads, it take
more than "Confirmation," mhee yaa weee!)*

"Bird was on the skids then but I didn't know it. He
was a heavy cat, he made all the scenes, went through
some boss shit. Whenever he was straight, though, he'd
lay down some heavy shit. Nobody was listening,
though; they didn't have ears, his stuff was too ...
heavy.

"I remember the last concert I saw Bird. It was Stan
Kenton's concert in Carnegie Hall. Bird showed up in a
Robert Hall summer suit and sneakers. Hee hee, you
know Robert Hall, two suits for a fin and five pair of
pants thrown in—but dig, Robert Hall summer suits
was *in* in New York. You paid a dollar down and another dollar when they caught you.

"That was a night, though. They was cats grooving
in the grandstand and cats bopping on the floor! Everybody stomping feet and telling those cats to *blow!*
When the concert was over and everybody was walking
off the stage, every cat in that place started screaming!
You never heard sounds like that night! And there was
old Bird in his Robert Hall summer suit and sneakers.
They had Oscar Pettiford on bass and Kenny Clark on

drums and Gillespie on trumpet and Bud Powell on piano. Powell can't play no more 'cause he's had a lobotomy and he can't play for shit; they cut all the muscle out of his brain, but man, that was a set! Bird was the greatest I ever saw. The whole place was pandemonium! When the cats got up to leave, we wouldn't let 'em go! We stomped our feet and raised such hell you shoulda seen old Kenton. He had to call 'em back. Bird didn't even miss a beat. He just kept wailing, sweat flying off his nose and sounds coming outta that horn. I never heard music like that in my life! That was *jazz!*

"That was the fall of 'fifty-two, a long time ago. Bird really started fucking up after that, stoned out of his mind all the time, alone, fearing the streets. He'd miss dates or come on too wild, scaring people. And the parasites were fucking him, sucking his blood like they always do when you start down. They made all they could out of his genius and now when he was slipping they dropped him. The last time I saw Bird, it was a drag, man. He even said so himself. 'I can't play like I used to,' he said. And what you gonna say? You gonna say, 'Ah, Bird, you doing all right!' Shit! Only Bird knows what he's doing and nobody else don't know! *(Dr. Sax know.)* Nobody can make the sounds Bird made. He was hitting the booze pretty hard by now but nobody knew the end would come so soon. He made all the scenes—Lexington, Bellevue, Camarillo. He rested up after Bellevue and that kept him from dying for a while. He kicked the habit, though, that's one thing I know. He was too sick from all the other shit to bother with smack. He had pneumonia and ulcers and cirrhosis of the liver and every fucking thing else you can think of. He made all the scenes but nobody was prepared for that final scene so soon.

"I had my own thing going by this time, just beginning to make it as a painter. I was on the road at the time, seeing the land. I didn't even hear of Bird's death until I got slammed in L.A. Man, when I heard it, it was like a bolt of lightning struck my head. Bird dead? What you sayin', man? I was doing a gig for vagrancy in Lincoln Heights. Those fucking L.A. fuzz! A cat told me. He came in on a narco beef and said, 'Bird's dead, man.' I got out a week later and looked it up in the newspapers. I remember I sat on a stoop in Watts and cried. I really cried, man, bawled like a baby. I just couldn't believe it. And already the bloodsuckers were out yelling and setting up memorial concerts, praising Bird the way they never bothered to do when he was alive. Ah, man, I couldn't take it. I hung around Central Street for a while and then made it on up to Big Sur. I wanted to look at the sea for a while. I hitchhiked up Highway One and when I passed Camarillo a funny thing happened. I was out on the road and when I passed that place it was like I could hear this strange music. I stood there for a long time digging the sounds. Like maybe it was those nuts in there laughing or something, maybe the waves, I dunno ... it's the same sound you hear when you walk out on the bridge *(heemhee wee)*, like some mad horn, only different, you know, like a horn that hasn't got any limit to it, none at all, you can stand there for hours and listen to that insane music. . . ."

While Arthur rapped, I was rapt attention at the bar. The floozies were gone, the chablis a dim memory in my glass. I hunched in my greatcoat and whispered, "Tell me more about that night!" Arthur said nothing. I looked up. Those cables, the bridge ... I looked at Gary busy wiping his bar and thought, What great souls in the night. Dr. Sax is still here. I will have to tell Jack. That's why they're here, to remind us. They are the language we forgot. The swoop poop plim and whim of oldtime dying. The taut timetwisting strands that weave my lover's body home to me *(mhee waa haa heee smeee!)*.

I rushed out of the Spaghetti Factory Cafe without adieu (That's what happened last night! No remorse and rushing out and accused of drunk! It was the tale, boys! I had cables to mend!) and rushed down Grant Avenue. In my sudden maniacal frenzies I had this urge to see Frankie. Tell her I loved her! You will come to no harm, child, I will see you, the night is young, the shroud will come, I will save you from the darkie! I rushed madly down Grant Avenue to Union and down Union to Columbus and down Columbus to Powell and down Powell to Francisco and up Francisco to Milton's pad and fast up the three flights of stairs to Milton's door and knock-knock-knocked. Nobody answered. I looked in the window and hollered at the door. Only the sea whispered to me. Dr. Sax hid in his shrouds and whispered glee in the lousy dusk.

So in my North Beach sorrow I trudged slowly back down those bleak stairs … each stair a creak … catshit hallways hollowed out in smells … the sea black in its silence … only a footstep between me and those sad piers where dip the bamboo rods of children, the Chinese Gods of Yum and Yee … seen through the eyes of late October rain *(the go-home-easy month, Dr. Sax's month, he only on the wing in October, April he's in a daze),* a still wind wisping listlessly in off the bay, earthshrouded, me, a wrinkle in the flat pavement, a piece of tar on the bridge (the bridge, the bridge, the stupid bridge!) whose cables I have sought, a sad dim gleam of rosy diamonds in the dusk. I walked down Powell Street to the wharf, silent in my dreams, Charlie Parker dead, the dark mad riffs only ripples now, the wind a crazy muffler to his soul. At Mason Street I crossed under the gloomy spectral awnings of Fisherman's Wharf gimcrackery and saw Pluto, master mariner, late of the sea, sandwrapped and weary, wending waveward as he tacked starboard on his own mysterious (Maybe he Dr. Sax?) voyages. He sounds seas only he sees sound. I moped along the wharf and spit, plop! into the creamy froth. My spit sat silent, sent ripples out in ripples, the prick-prowed Monterey double-enders bobbled in the mist, my own sad glob was gone, swallowed in the moving tide, a thousand fishes dive.

29 Next day I was sitting in my loft when Little Joe walked up the stairs and broke my heart. I was still reeling from my Dr. Sax Charlie Parker dream and wanted to tell someone, opened my mouth to speak when Little Joe opened the door, and he spoke first. "Hube the Cube sold Little Gus," he said. My heart stopped.

Ah, what anguish. Everything seemed so futile, so nothing.

Little Joe told me the story, talking in his usual beery-cheery way, the news just more North Beach gossip to him, the births and deaths of children making no more impression in his scheme than rain on the sea or volcanoes underfoot. This not true, though. Little Joe felt the loss as keenly as I; he sat sad-eyed and told me. The evilness of my thoughts was just part of the general gloom I felt as I thought of Frankie and Francesca and Little Gus, the baby sold for his small baba's bones.

Hube the Cube sold Little Gus to buy more speed. He talked and rapped and whipped weak Francesca (That bitch! What tenacity some mothers have! Don't give up the chip!) into submission and made her contact the doctor (not Dr. Sax?) who deals in babies' bones. Another couple from down the peninsula unable to breed their own small child will gladly pay for a nice white Anglo-Saxon (Sax, Sax, is that you?) baby. (Little Gus was white after all, important in adoptions.) The baby will bring six hundred on the market, no one has to know, it's all legal anyway, mother-father incompetent, child better off with adoptive parents, no sad chariots across Washington Square (I had visions of pushing Little Gus's perambulator across the square —foolish vision!), the Chinese and Italian papazzini

266

must play alone. Little Gus will grow up in Redwood City or some such place.

I listened while Little Joe talked. Dr. Sax flew out the window. This was just the kind of news Goodnews Gary would bring. Goodnews lured bad news. He loved to bring unhappy tidings. A messenger of laments, he'd sit before you with his hyperthyroid eyes and let you have it with both barrels, the juiciest low-down on the latest calamity: Russia finally dropped the bomb, the deathclouds were heading this way right now. Goodnews was harbinger of every catastrophe on the Beach; his scene was depression. Anguish caused him joy. If Goodnews could hang around Western Union and garner a few death notices, it made his day. He'd deliver them for free, singing songs to the bereaved. Goodnews was so joyous in bad news that people avoided him on the streets. If they could avoid Goodnews Gary, at least the bad news didn't come special delivery. With Goodnews Gary the news was there the minute it happened. It only took time for him to hear about it with his special accident-tuned ear and he'd rush it over first class. Goodnews was a real stickler for detail too; he included all the blood, all the guts and thunder. While Little Joe talked, I could hear Goodnews giving out with all the details of Little Gus's adoption. He'd know every detail about the couple that bought him. The dude would be a cop and he's already shaved Little Gus's head, he doesn't like long hair, Goodnews would say. The old lady's an alcoholic with infantile sexual infatuations. Gus's gonna grow up to be a faggot; he's already in military school. Two months old and the little bugger's got a shaved head and he's in school with uniforms and guns. Plus his new daddy has penis problems. Why do you think he ain't been able to have a kid of his own?

Little Joe wasn't Goodnews Gary, though, he was just another sad cat sitting on the floor, sorry for the news. I lay on my bed and looked out my windows toward the sea. My view was blocked by the buildings outside, but behind the buildings I knew the sea was there. I saw it shimmer in the quays, heard it meep and weep against the scrotum-tightened surfers, slip and furl onto the rocks, saw Dr. Sax floating above it. He scanned my bed and laughed: *All's hell in love and war.*

"Little Gus's probably better off anyhow," Little Joe was saying. "That damn Francesca's bad as Hube the Cube when it comes to serious things. Besides, he had her strung out inside of two weeks after they was married. Little Gus was just a rag on the floor."

I said nothing while Little Joe talked. My vision was lost to me. I was looking for those cables that held my vision up.

"Everybody on the damn Beach is strung out," Little Joe said. "They can't find nothing t'do but shoot shit into their veins."

Mhee hee yee hehaaa! Dr. Sax is on the bridge.

"I dunno what's gonna happen. Drugs are going to kill everybody. Why they don't blow a little weed and let it go at that, I dunno."

The cables twanged. The whole monolithic structure wheeled in the void. A North Beach San Francisco harp tuned to death flat!

"I don't even keep count any more," Little Joe said. "Everybody on the Beach is strung out—Hube and Francesca, Keith, Groovy, Carol. It's like a big circus, I don't even try."

There are one thousand cables on that bridge. I have counted every one.

"I'm gonna ship out for a while ... get off the Beach ... go to Hong Kong and marry a Chinese whore."

Little Joe stared glumly at the wall. Outside the sound of traffic was muted and dim. I looked out my Roach Alley windows and felt my street, ankle-deep in undeliverable wombs. Somehow the sad nostalgia of regret brought solace, the pain of silence was a song. I put my ear to the ground and listened to the rumbling of the *Cherokee*—sixteen wheels churning into history—and I knew the *Cherokee* was gone. It had always been gone. I realized that the sound of coming had, after all, always been the sound of going.

After Little Joe left, tears milled up behind my eyes. For a long time I was ashamed to let them flow. Then I wept. It felt good to let everything out, all the bullshit and jive and madness that had been building up inside me for weeks. I wept for Little Gus, I wept for the Beach, I wept for Francesca and Hube the Cube and Paddy O'Sullivan and Frankie and all the rest. I won't name them again. Yes I will! Their names are riveted on my brain, symbols that evoke memories too dear to keep. *This book is a book of names.* I wept for Dean and the way he holds his hand over his face when he talks to girls. Dean's desperate to talk to girls and he never does. I wept for Wheeler Tippet, who died a seventy-year-old faggot. Why do I say faggot? He died a seventy-year-old English gentleman with elegant manners who liked to hold on to my balls when I drove him home on his motorscooter. Why begrudge Wheeler Tippet my balls? My Levi's were too thick for him to feel anything anyway. I wept for Bob Kaufman and Bob Seider and Red Fred and Pete Spears and Bernie Uroniwitz and Little Joe and Walter and JoJay and Shoeshine Devine and Crow and Richard Bloomer and Carl Eisenger and Crazy Alex and Dr. Frick Frack and Charles Olson and Jack Kerouac and Malcolm Lowry and the little guy with the useless arm—what was his name—Abby, that's right! I grieved for all of them. Little Gus, who was he? A bastard child with nowhere to go. So he goes to San Jose. There is something indescribably sad about San Jose. As my tears erupted, I felt as if my heart had been ripped out of my body. There was nothing left. The crotch and pube shops could move into North Beach now, the neon signs go up, the fatcat caterwaulers take over with their doormen and debris.

Exhausted and desolate, I opened the door of my loft and walked down the steps. I stood in Roach Alley as the night moved in. The streets! How many times have they been my solace. There is no misery, no unhappiness, no heartbreak that cannot be consoled by the streets. I looked at the alleys and sidewalks and gutters littered with garbage and I felt clean. If I could have had my wish, my feet would have become roots reaching under the cobblestones, stretching through the rocks and dirt and sand seeking the bedrock of North Beach. My feet weren't roots, though, so I started walking.

Rudderless, I floated up Pacific Street to the heart of the Beach, moving with the crowd, but curiously suspended, afloat. People moved about me like water. I wanted to stretch out my arms and touched them, take them in—all of them—and hug and kiss them!

On the corner of Grant and Vallejo I stood in front of the Caffe Trieste. The air was vibrant and alive. Suddenly I felt horny. I had an erection in my Levi's that frightened me. It was as if my dick had developed a mind of its own and I was a robot following helplessly along behind it. I was so excited I trembled. I knew it was futile searching for a woman; nothing ever comes to you when you're desperate. I had to relax, amble along with the crowd and hope someone would find me. I had to be found by a girl who was as desperate as I!

I moved up Grant Avenue with the crowd and ducked into the Coffee Gallery. Inside it was pandemonium. Mike and a helper were frantically passing glasses of beer over the heads of customers at the bar, reaching for those in back, dudes and chicks stacked three deep along the wall. I squeezed in beside the bar and made my way toward the back room. Bob Seider was screeching out a long solo on his saxophone in the entertainment room while a Ray Charles song blasted out of the jukebox. The two sources of music blended together in a cacophonous atonality that hovered over the conversation, which was completely unintelligible. It was like standing in the mouth of a tunnel with a gale howling out of it.

In the toilet I relaxed while an incredibly drunken black dude pissed in and out of the urinal. He sang to himself while he pissed. Two musicians were tuning up their instruments along the opposite wall. The smell of twenty years of piss and beer and vomit and cigarette smoke was embedded in the walls like paint, along with a hundred years of disinfectant. The drunk finished piss-ing and then stood at the sink and elaborately washed and dried his long black hands. When he was finished, he turned slowly around and stumbled out the door. I stepped to the urinal. Whenever I stand at a urinal I remember what Crow once said: "There are two kinds of people, Kid—those who spread their legs at a public urinal to protect their neighbors, and those who don't." I smiled and spread my legs. I idly scanned the walls on which all of the Coffee Gallery's regular customers are dissected, their various sexual apparatuses assayed, the length of Joe's cock, the condition of Mary's cunt, the availability, mobility, utility, fuckability, accessibility of various well-known folk personages, the information exhaustively illustrated with drawings utilizing knotholes, woodgrain, nails, etc.

Countless times I've hurled myself into the street and ended up in the Coffee Gallery amid the stink and noise and smoke in the hopes of finding an angel among the dirty ashtrays and beer glasses. No angel ever materialized, though, except that time with Linda Lovely. She was going with Steve again, and the rest of the chicks were taken, branded by a dude's arm-over-the-shoulder embrace, or finger-along-thigh tattoo. In one corner Dr. Frick Frack was laughing, rapping with somebody about the latest flick he'd seen. I leaned against the wall a moment listening to Bob blow, then pushed my way out the door.

Inside the Spaghetti Factory Cafe it was the same, crowded beyond breathing, only here everybody was eating or waiting to eat. I edged myself in between two barstools and nodded to Gary. He brought me a glass of chablis. I pushed a dollar toward him and he pushed it back. I nodded thanks. I gazed around the room and saw Peter LeBlanc, the woodcut artist who'd spent the last five years looking for the perfect pussy for his masterpiece, a life-sized full-face nude painstakingly carved on an assortment of handmade cherrywood blocks, each block meticulous, each hair and each color months in the making. Peter was short, with a shaved head, intense, trucking no nonsense, built like a wheelbarrow full of set cement, two-decade habitué of North

Beach, bemused now at the bar with his glass of white
wine and newspaper while the crowd roared around
him. I nodded to him and he nodded back.

There was no one here for me. I downed my glass of
wine and pushed my way outside. Everyone had someone and I had no one. My hard-on still beat against my
leg. Self-conscious and at the same time titillated, I
rubbed it gingerly. As I crossed the intersection of
Grant and Green, I imagined every eye on the street
glaring at me. Fuck it! I walked past Gino and Carlo's.
Cavernous gloom with poolhall murals and jukebox
neon sadness. I continued on down Stockton Street to
Washington Square. The square was deserted except
for a couple sitting on a bench opposite the church. I
stood for a moment in the middle of the square breathing deeply, then sat down, stretching my legs to give
my dick breathing room. I felt perverse. I debated taking my cock out of my pants, letting the night air cool
it off. I laughed when I thought about it. I remembered
the story Anno, a girl I'd once gone with, told me
about the man who exposed himself in front of her
when she was riding home on a bus. "What'd he do?" I
asked.

"He waited until everyone got off, then he unzipped
his pants and waved it at me."

I burst out laughing.

"It's not funny," Anno said. "It happens all the time
with girls."

"Well, there's nothing wrong with a guy waving it at
you, is there? Maybe he was lonely."

"He was sick. The way those guys get their kicks is
by exposing themselves. Most of them can't make it
with a woman."

"Well, what'd you do?"

"I turned my face away and pretended I didn't see."

I sympathized with the old flag waver. Maybe I'd
end up like him, a pathetic old liplicker standing on
dark streetcorners waving my banner at the moon. According to Walter our dicks were in the wrong place
anyway. "Our balls really should be on the top of our
heads, Kid. Any good medical encyclopedia will tell

you that your balls create more cells than your brain. Man doesn't realize that he should be walking around with his dick sticking up in the air, a giant hard-on going beep! beep! beep! instead of those fucking police sirens all the time."

I cracked up when Walter told me that. "How about the cunt?" I said. "Where does the cunt belong?"

"Ahh, the cunt. Let's not change that, Kid, that's Mount Popocatepetl. Put your hand down there and you can feel it, that soft warm rise; it's a dormant volcano, that's what it is."

It was chilly in the square so I got up and walked down Stockton Street, heading back toward Grant Avenue. How many times had I made this solitary journey, back and forth, back and forth from loft to street to cafe to bar to park bench to loft to street? It was like a disease, a sickness that awakened me in the middle of the night and sent me out into the street, privy to all the scavengers, winos, hard hipsters, cops on prowl—the whole midnight-to-morning crew. I had to be out with them, fifteen or twenty miles a night, prowling corners of the city the rats didn't even know. Sometimes I felt I was trapped on a merry-go-round, a desperate carrousel geared to so many bars and cafes, a few joints and streets, a walled-in Deer Park of loneliness and frustration. At times I felt as if I were an inmate in an elaborately designed insane asylum, a do-it-yourself torture chamber whose walls are covered with thousands of crazyhouse mirrors, mirrors that projected fantastic images of success and fame and fulfillment. Only when I looked into the cracks of the mirrors did I see the truth.

I walked down Stockton Street, my dick feeling like a twenty-pound lead weight with wings on it. I thought of all the times I had been successful when I was horny and realized they were accidents, all of them! Carla, the English professor's wife, was window shopping on Grant Avenue when I saw her. I walked past her and her sex smell hit me like the heat blasting out of a Bessemer furnace. I zeroed in like a guided missile. Inside of two minutes I had her by the arm heading up to Coit Tower. Ah, Coit Tower, the ground below you is saturated with sperm! Under the trees I laid Carla down on her coat and pulled down her panties. She took my dick gently between her fingers and put it in her mouth and swallowed it. Later I took Carla down to Mike's Place. We had coffee. While we talked I wanted to fuck her again. "My husband has this theory about *Moby Dick*," she told me. "He says the homosexual ambivalence between Herman Melville and the white whale is manifested in Pip's relationship to—"

"I'd let my white whale dive in your sea anytime, Carla."

Carla sniffed over her coffee and looked miserable.

If I had Carla right now, I'd take her down to Mike's Place and spread-eagle her over a pool table and rivet her to the felt while the black pool hustlers and pimps aimed for the corner pockets! I'd fuck another Little Gus into her! My seed would swim into Carla and fertilize her egg, her egg would swell up and grow and be nourished by all the ambiance of Mike's Place, by the old-time calendars on the walls, the pool tables, the ancient Sicilians who totter gravely across the floor, the black pushers and pimps and prostitutes, the hustlers and dandies who cluster at the tables, the long bar and the sweaty reek of armpits, the food and vomit and sputum, the gloom and sadness, the ancient jukebox, the whirling fans and cracked linoleum, by the incessant parade of humanity that gathers at the door. I'd fuck Little Gus into Carla and watch him erupt out of her womb and grow to manhood along Grant Avenue, a real Child of the Century, harbinger of a new age! Every gene in North Beach that I had swept up in my wanderings would be synthesized in Little Gus, every deformity and every spark of genius! After I fucked Little Gus into Carla, I'd watch him emerge, progenitor of a whole new phalanx of beings who would spread out over North Beach San Francisco, inundating the city, covering the bridges, wiping out America! The new Little Gus would be the real Frisco Kid! Kid of a thousand sorrows, a million heartbreaks and joys, of uncountable aches and tendernesses. The new Frisco Kid would issue out of the sweetsad womb of the streets, out of Grant Avenue and Columbus Avenue and Broadway and Francisco Street and Roach Alley and Battery Street and every tangled alley of the city. The new Frisco Kid would be the child of the new America, child of the revolution; the new Frisco Kid would be the stoned-out sibling of the new age!

I didn't have Carla, though. I didn't have anyone. Suddenly the reeking humanity thronging Columbus Avenue sickened me and I wanted to get away, to be alone. I turned my back on the streets and headed for Aquatic Park. When I reached the beach, I took off my shoes and dragged my feet in the sand. The sand felt alive, gritty, and cold under my feet. I gouged out long swirling whorls until my toes stung, then sprinted down the beach to the end of the steps and then turned and sprinted back. I ran back and forth until my heart throbbed painfully in my chest. I sat down on the steps and rested. The waves lapped on the shore. For a long time I listened and then put on my shoes. The old circle, from loft to Beach to Aquatic Park to Fisherman's Wharf to loft. The night was cool, so I jogged toward Fisherman's Wharf, holding my hand over my beating heart. Suddenly my heart didn't hurt. Wind on my face, I ran with no effort, swinging my arms and legs out in giant strides, leaping curbs, each jump greater than the last. I was intoxicated by running, delirious and crazy, hurtling down Bay Street toward the cable car tracks. I could run all night! I dodged between people on the sidewalk and thought of Scott. In what insane asylum have they locked away his magnificent eyes? Tonight I could keep up with him!

At the corner of Powell Street I whipped left and jumped on a packed cable car that was just departing. I squeezed myself in between passengers. I didn't even excuse myself, just shoved in and grabbed a handrail and hung on. I felt invulnerable, like the time I'd stayed high on bennies for a week just to see how it was and ended up feeling omnipotent, powerful, fearless! While I'd been high, I'd walked into the middle of Columbus Avenue on Saturday night and held out my hands and the cars stopped, waited while I conducted them, moved them forward and backward with my hands. It felt magnificent! I had the power so strong that the next day when I was walking down Grant Avenue in Chinatown I plucked a plum from a fruit-stand and stood on the corner of Washington Street eating it as a girl walked by wearing a bikini bathing suit. I held out my half-eaten plum and she took a bite. When she bit into it, the juice ran down my fingers. I started walking toward Roach Alley and the girl followed me. We walked for seven blocks, me in front, the girl behind, without saying a word. When we reached Roach Alley, I opened the door to my loft and we climbed the stairs. Inside she unwrapped the towel from around her middle and stepped out of her bikini (this really happened, you guys!). Naked, we lay down on the bed together. She had spent the day at Aquatic Park. That night I discovered every grain of sand in her body.

When the power comes to you, don't question it, just use it! Tonight I felt the power. I squirmed in among the passengers and leaned back against the railing next to the conductor. A boy and a girl were wedged in beside me and my lips were one inch from the girl's nape. She had soft hair down on her neck and I blew it gently, stirring the filmy hairs with my breath. The girl turned her face to me and smiled. I smiled back. The cable car shot up the hill. We all clung together, a human mass sweeping skyward in an antiquated jaunting car. At the top of Nob Hill I jumped off and ran ahead of the car down Powell Street. The cable car caught up with and passed me in the middle of the block. I ran joyously onward. At the next corner the cable car stopped to let off more passengers. I overtook it, laughing and waving at the crowd. They laughed and waved back. They thought I was drunk. I was drunk! I was drunk with the idea of everything that lay before me. Insanely drunk and crazy and alive and laughing and running with the wind in my face, with the memory of warm lips and the smile of a pretty girl, with the reality that I was alive and had another day to live! Everywhere about me was death and turmoil and sadness and despair and sold babies, but I was alive and had another day to live!

30 It was three A.M. when I got back to Roach Alley. When I opened my door, Milton was sitting at my table. His outfit was spread out around him. He was cooking a spoon of smack.

"Where the fuck you been?" he said.

"What are you doing here?"

I felt something ominous in the room. A creepy stillness emanated from the walls. Milton held a match under the spoon of heroin and looked at me.

"You can see what I'm doin'," he said. "Where the fuck you been?"

I walked over to my bed and sat down. My euphoria vanished instantly. I felt venomous.

"You know I don't like that shit. Why are you fixing in my pad?"

" 'Cause I'm here, that's why, an' I been waiting three hours."

Milton extinguished the match and set the spoon down carefully on the table. He picked up his eyedropper and dipped it in the white liquid. As the bulb sucked up the heroin, his face assumed an intent, mesmerized look. Milton's hands shook slightly as the eyedropper slowly filled. When it was full his whole body relaxed.

"Tie me up. I can get a better hit if someone else ties me."

I sighed and took off my belt. Milton flexed his upper arm and I tied my belt around it. He clenched his fist once or twice and probed with the point. After two tries the eyedropper started to fill with a deep red—almost black—liquid. Milton let the blood run into the eyedropper and then he slowly squeezed the bulb, tapping the end of it with his finger. An audible sigh escaped from his lips as the smack took hold in his veins.

"You really need that shit, don't you?" I said.

Milton's eyes were closed. He licked his lips, clenching and unclenching his fist. He sat still for a moment and then nervously slapped and scratched his thighs as the heroin filtered through his system.

"Just a pinch to get straight," he said.

I put on my belt. Milton looked at me for a moment and then slowly wrapped up his outfit. I had an irrational fear that somehow the shit in Milton's veins was going to infect me, like a medieval plague.

"I been waiting for you a long time, Kid," Milton said.

"What are you waiting for me for? Leave a note on my door. I know where you live."

"I been burnt, baby. I need that bread you owe me."

"Jesus Christ, Milton, it's three in the morning. I don't have sixty bucks right now."

"Hey, baby, I need that bread." Milton narrowed his eyes and looked at me. His pupils were dilated and he rubbed his nose nervously. "Lisson, maan"—he eased his words out in a long junkie sigh—"I been burnt! That motherfucker Burkhardt set me up an' I ain't gonna be burnt twice. I want that sixty bucks!"

"Well, fuck, what am I supposed to do? I can't get sixty bucks at three in the morning. Nobody has any bread right now."

"Lisson, motherfucker, I need that bread! I ain't interested in your problems. I want that bread!"

I pulled out what money I had in my pockets and threw it on the table. Eight bucks. "That's all I have," I said.

Milton grabbed the eight dollars off the table and waved his fist in front of my face. "You asshole, you had three weeks to get that bread and you come up with this shit! Get up! I'm gonna take you over t' Groovy's an' get that bread!"

"Oh, fuck, man, you know Groovy doesn't have shit! What the fuck's wrong with you? Neither Groovy nor Keith has a dime. Why the fuck don't you cool it!"

"Cool it? I got the man on my ass and you say cool it! I like to see you cool it with the man breathin' down your ass!"

Milton paced nervously back and forth across the

floor. His eyes darted rapidly around my loft. I had never seen him so fucked up.

"What happened, anyway?" I said.

"That fucking Burkhardt, he set up a deal with some fag friend of his out in the Fillmore. Maan, that dude's been suckin' a cop's dick! Ever'thing about it told me not to go. Ever'thing was too smooth, y'know, on time. It never works that way! I shoulda paid attention to my vibes. I walked right into it!"

"You must not have walked right into it. You're here, aren't you?"

"I'm here, baby, but not for long. Every narc in the city's gonna be down my neck by tomorrow mornin'. I gotta get out of town!"

"Does Frankie know what happened?"

"Fuck that bitch!" Milton yelled. "I don't have no time for no ofay chick to be on my back. What d'you have around here that's worth fifty bucks?"

Milton walked quickly from one side of the loft to the other scanning my belongings.

"Goddamnit, Milton, why don't you cool it! You're running around like a goddamn madman."

"You say what? Madman? You fuckin' right I'm runnin' around here like a madman! I *am* a madman! You sit here all day bleedin' over this shit an' try 'n' tell me how I feel? You don't know shit how I feel! You can't even peddle dope an' set up a man straight! Maan, I'm tired of you livin' off my black ass!"

"Hey, it's not like that. I only owe you sixty bucks. I paid you a lot of bread."

"You paid me shit!" Milton yelled. "All you white motherfuckers think you gotta do is sit around puffin' on my weed that ain't paid for. I'm tired of that shit!"

"Hey, Milton, you're the one who came to me to sell your grass. You kept insisting on it. The only cat who hasn't paid me is Groovy, except for the ounce I laid on Linda Lovely, and you sure as hell can't call Groovy a white motherfucker."

"Fuck Groovy!" Milton yelled. "You gave that grass out front an' it's your responsibility! Where the fuck's your typewriter?"

Milton grabbed my typewriter and held it under his

arm. He glanced around the loft looking for the case. He was shaking.

"That typewriter's not worth shit, Milton. The most you're going to get for it is fifteen bucks. Why the fuck don't you cool it and I'll try to get the bread for you in the morning. Maybe Crow'll loan it to me."

"I need that bread tonight! I'm not gonna be able to set my black ass on the street tomorrow. I gotta get over to Mill Valley so's I can hide out."

"What about Frankie? You just going to split without telling her where you're going?"

"Hey, maan, that chick's old enough t' take care of herself. I ain't gonna be no nursemaid t' no cunt!"

I looked at Milton. For a moment I felt like bursting into laughter. Then I felt depressed. It always seemed to come to this, hassles over cheap shit and bread. I tried to feel some concern for Milton's problem but it was impossible. I wondered about Frankie. The whole thing was a drag. I was tired. Milton flung himself down in a chair and glowered at me. I felt numb, as if a heavy weight were passing down on my head.

"Maybe it's not as bad as you think. Maybe Burkhardt didn't really set you up."

"Oh, maan, lisson." Milton snuffed deep in his throat and laughed bitterly. He got up from his chair and walked toward me with a sick expression on his face. "What does it take for a little whitey to know he's steppin' in shit, when he's up to his nose in it? Baaby, I just busted my way out of a set-up, a clean, cold, nigger-faggoty set-up, an' you stand there an' tell me maybe there's nothin' t' worry about."

I said nothing. I was thinking of Frankie. If Milton did split, maybe I could convince Frankie to straighten out. Without Milton she'd have no source of supply and she'd have to clean up. Down deep inside I was glad that Milton was in a bind. It was his own doing anyway. At the same time I felt a twinge of guilt for not feeling more compassion toward him. I watched him pace back and forth across the floor.

"What about Sam the Fatman? Couldn't he lay a little bread on you?"

"Fuck that cocksucker!" Milton yelled. "He's like

every other white motherfucker, out for him! I made over fifteen thousand dollars for that asshole and he don't care shit! He don't give a roachclip out front!"

"Well, you always say that's the only way to do business."

"That's right! Sam the Fatman takes care of *his* business! No credit, no deals, no nothin' out front, just business! If I dealt like Sam, I wouldn't be in this bind right now."

I felt perverse. It pleased me to see Milton so fucked up. I did owe him the sixty bucks, but his behavior seemed all out of proportion to the amount of bread I owed him. His usual pioneering black watch-me-handle-this cool seemed ridiculous now. The Milton I saw pacing back and forth in front of me was the true Milton; the other Milton was an elaborate cover-up that he'd devised for the sake of his scene. It suddenly occurred to me that I didn't really know Milton. Our friendship had been so spontaneous when it began that questions of who and what and where had never occurred to me.

The first time I met Milton I was standing in the basement of City Lights Bookstore scanning the racks of Indian literature. I was holding a book in my hand with a small biography of Bras Coupé, the famous black outlaw, a six-foot six-inch runaway slave who'd lost an arm to marauding whites and revenged himself by leading forays into New Orleans and the Natchez Trace, killing and robbing white people. I was fascinated by Bras Coupé and deeply involved in the book when I looked up and saw Milton walking down the stairs. It was like Bras Coupé himself was coming down the steps, although Milton wasn't as tall as Bras Coupé, only six foot two inches, but he looked just as imperial, just as stately as I imagined the black renegade to be. The synchronicity of the moment was too much for me, so when Milton walked past me I held the book out to him, saying nothing, just nodding to the sketch of Bras Coupé. Milton glanced at the first few pages and then, looking at me, sat down at one of the tables reserved for readers. He read the whole biographical sketch, all the while his booming laughter blasting out in City Lights' basement. When he finished, he stood up and stuck out his hand. "My name's Milton, man, what's yours?"

I told him my name. "Let's go have some coffee," he said.

We went to Mike's Place. "Man, that shit about Bras Coupé is too much. Where'd you find that?"

"I'd just picked it up when you walked in. It was strictly a coincidence."

"Haa haa haa," Milton boomed out his great laugh. "Shit! That old mutha dancing around Congo Square shouting badoum! badoum! I can just see him. Thanks, man, for turning me on."

After our first meeting neither of us bothered delving deeply into the other. For some reason it seemed unnecessary, it was as if we had known one another for years. When I thought about it, though, I realized that it was as if we had purposely avoided any responsibility in really getting to know one another. I thought of Scott and Little Joe and others I'd gone out of my way to get to know, continually probing them with questions until they got tired of my inquisitiveness. I'd never asked Milton anything about his background aside from a few references to his family and where he was from, all of which he ignored. In a sense Milton's and my relationship was strictly on the surface, in the here and now, like both our previous existences were really irrelevant to what was happening right now, at this instant. I realized that not only did I not know anything about Milton's background, I had never told him anything at all about mine; he knew nothing of me save what he saw every day on the street. I watched as Milton strode across my floor scratching at his legs and snuffing deep in his throat. As he moved, I had the feeling that I was observing a stranger, someone I'd never seen before.

Milton paced nervously about and then he sat down. He sighed deeply and then laughed. The laugh was harsh, rasping, like a cough coming from deep in the throat. I knew that if anyone was going to help Milton it would have to be me. My only possibility was Crow, and I didn't know what Crow would do. I felt

Crow didn't like Milton, so I'd have to fabricate some story to get a loan. It seemed that I was constantly bailing friends out of jams, out of binds, jail, abortions, bailing them out of situations they had entered on their own accord.

I suddenly felt weak, tired. Any decision I made about helping Milton seemed inherently prostituted because of Frankie. If I helped him get away, it was so I could have a clear field with Frankie; if I refused to help him, it was because I knew Frankie would go with him if I did.

Milton's head jerked once or twice as he nodded off. I could sense the smack filtering through his veins. When I thought about my ambivalence about helping Milton, I had to laugh. If Milton was my friend and he was in trouble, everything else was irrelevant. I remembered Harry Balmer—incredible Harry, we called him—saying to me once, "There are no moral, ethical, or value judgments allowed! Don't call the sunrise beautiful, that's qualifying it. The sunrise doesn't care if it's beautiful or not; qualifications have no place in the scheme of things."

If I was going to help Milton, there could be no qualifications. Milton was in trouble. If he asked for help, it was my duty to help him, just as I would help a dog caught in a trap. Right now the only thing I could do was to contact Crow. Crow might lend me the fifty dollars. If I could get fifty dollars from Crow, that would absolve my responsibility toward Milton.

"Listen, Milton," I said, "cool it here until morning and then I'll go see Crow. If he doesn't have fifty bucks, maybe he'll let you stay in his pad until I can raise it—or you can stay here. Then I'll drive you over to Mill Valley tomorrow."

Milton's head snapped up. "Maan . . . I don't want my car seen on the streets. It's around on Battery Street right now."

"I'll move it. I'll take it down and park it at Fisherman's Wharf. Nobody's going to notice it in that parking lot for one day."

The fact that I had suggested something seemed to

relieve Milton. He sat up at the table. "Oh, brother," he said. "That fuckin' Burkhardt!"

"Maybe he has his hassles," I said.

Milton looked at me and shook his head in silent laughter. "Kid, I'll never get over you. You bleed over everybody on the Beach, even when they're pissin' in your shoes. You're *dumb*, baby."

I smiled. I wondered what Milton would feel if he knew what I had just been thinking. Maybe he did know. The truth was that I really was interested in what prompted a person like Burkhardt to go against his friends and fink on them. I knew Burkhardt was a smalltime dealer who supported his own habit by procuring for his friends. I'd always avoided him, though, because of his faggoty mannerisms. The one time I'd gotten close to Burkhardt, he'd tried to grab my ass and tell me how much he wanted to touch me. When I told Scott about it later, he said, "Watch out for him, Kid. His weakness will do him in someday and when he goes down he'll take a lot of people with him." I wondered about Burkhardt's weakness. I also wondered if I would betray my friends if I were faced with a long prison term. If Frankie wasn't involved, would I feel differently? I'd always considered myself a person who could be counted on when someone was in trouble—but was I really? I had helped Francesca with her marriage, but even that was questionable. Little Gus would have probably been better off if Francesca's parents had taken him. At least Hube the Cube wouldn't have married her and dragged her down into his dopey paranoia. All of my help seemed to go the wrong way. It started out good, but it all got twisted around so that in the end it was no help at all. I looked at Milton. I really *was* dumb. I should know better. I knew that Frankie loved Milton. I could see it in her eyes whenever she looked at him. Her feeling for me was something I had invented, was really *my* feeling for her, was a fantasy that in fact didn't exist.

Milton hunched over the table asleep. I was tired too, exhausted. I undressed and lay down on my bed. For a long time I lay there thinking. Outside, nearby,

Pippen's music roamed the streets. Farther away the foghorns on the bridge moaned softly.

Milton was shaking me. "Hey, Kid, get up!" He was staring into my eyes. "Get up, it's daylight."

"Jesus, what time is it?"

"Maan, it's morning, get up!"

"Shit, it's not even morning. What time is it?"

"Never mind the time. You got any grass here? I wanna get high."

I wrapped a blanket around my shoulders and stood up. Gray dawn was just seeping over the hills in Berkeley. I stretched out and walked over to the hotplate. "Forget the grass. I'll make some coffee."

"I don't want no coffee, I want some weed. I took a little hit a while ago and I like to follow it up with some weed. Where's your stash?"

"I don't have a stash. Man, sit down! I'll make some coffee."

"She-it!" Milton paced back and forth. He stood next to the hotplate. "I want you t' go see Crow right away, I gotta have that bread!"

"Nobody's up at this hour, so you might as well cool it. I'm sure as hell not going to wake Crow up at six in the morning and try to hit him up for some bread. Use your brains, damnit!"

Milton watched while I brewed the coffee. I set the cups on the table and he sat down. He sat hunched over, shaking his head.

"That fucking Burkhardt. I shoulda never got mixed up with that faggoty bastard! All my vibes told me t' stay away from that whole set-up."

"What happened, anyway?"

I knew what happened. The same thing that always happens. Milton lifted his eyes and looked at me. He shrugged his shoulders.

"I was deliverin' some shit. Burkhardt let me in an' then said he didn't want it, said t' get it out of the house. I said what the fuck, man, you told me t' bring it. What I didn't know was the man was due there any minute and Burkhardt was havin' a last minute change of heart. I just happened to glance out the front window and see them. There were three cars full of heat. I took one look and dropped my stash and ran. That cocksucker! If I ever see him again, I'm gonna kill him!"

I sighed. The same old shit. I drank my coffee and dressed. Milton got up from the table and began pacing the loft. Every few minutes he paused at one of the windows and stared out. His paranoia vibes hung over the loft.

"Damnit, Milton, stop stalking around!" I said. "That pacing around isn't going to do you a damn bit of good."

Milton sat down. I put on my coat. "I'm going to see Crow. Stay here until I get back."

"I ain't goin' no place. You just come back with that bread."

31 I walked up Pacific Avenue to Jones Street and turned right for Russian Hill. The streets were deserted. On top of the Broadway tunnel I turned around just in time to see the sun lifting up from behind the East Bay hills. The Bay Bridge gleamed in the light. I walked up Jones Street to the park where Frankie and I had sat, where she had told me about her early life. I wondered what she would do if Milton really split. Follow him probably, right down to the junkie cellar.

I sat down in the park for a few minutes. I wanted to watch the sunrise. I also wanted to give Crow a chance to wake up. The sun rose above the hills, spreading soft mauve colors around the bay, deep blue on the lower slopes, misty gray toward the top. Flashes of copper and gold gleamed off the buildings where the sun hit them. I remembered the time Frankie and I had sat here together in the early morning chill while the sun climbed slowly. It was then that I had felt closest to Frankie, closer even than the few times we had slept together. Her body seemed to fit into mine. There were no images of Milton in my mind, nothing but the sun slowly rising above the hills and the closeness of Frankie's body.

I sat on the bench for half an hour. It seemed to me I was always on missions of this sort. Half the beach lived in an aura of incompetence, unpaid rent, no place to stay, no money, food, nothing. The more I thought about it, the more pissed off I got. It seemed I was the crying towel for North Beach, the soft touch; everybody laid their laments on my back as if I were a banker ready to give out emotional loans on the spur of the moment. Even the idea of going to Crow, knocking on his door at this hour of the morning and wheedling a loan out of him, bugged the shit out of me. It bugged me because I had to ask for it and it bugged me because I knew Crow wouldn't be happy lending it. Who the fuck was Milton anyway, imposing on my friends this way?

I rang for a long time on Crow's door. Finally the door-opening buzzer answered and I pushed into the foyer and started up the stairs. When I arrived at Crow's apartment, he was standing in the doorway. "Kid!" he said. He turned around and walked back into his pad.

I followed Crow down the hallway to the kitchen. He lit a fire on the stove and set his coffeepot on the burner. I sat down at the table. Crow looked at me. "Jesus," he said. "What's happening? You been out walking all night?"

I told Crow about Milton. While I spoke, he got up and fixed the coffee. He poured two cups, shaking his head.

"I can't understand your friends, they seem to live in a world of streetcorners and alleys. Why the fuck don't they get things together? Why don't your friends get out of this drift and give things a chance to grow?"

He sipped his coffee and looked at me. "Don't your friends know that you've got to do something with your tummy and something with your dork and anybody who says they're not going to do anything with either is full of amalgamated bullshit! And if you're going to do something with them, you've got to get out of that fucking back alley bag! Man, that's a dead-end street! That's why your friends sell their babies and shoot dope. It's all bullshit!"

Crow didn't have to tell me this. I knew even better than he. I thought of Little Gus and felt like crying.

"Why should you rescue Milton?" Crow asked. "What the fuck has that bastard done for you in the last few months but suck you down into his scene like every other two-bit junkie on the set?"

"I do owe him the bread."

"Why?"

"Because I agreed to sell dope for him."

"Well, fuck you then."

Crow stood up and poured himself another cup of

coffee. "All you bigtime dope dealers are always around on the set flashing bread, but when it comes time for your own problems you don't have any. Why don't you wise up?"

Crow stirred his coffee furiously. His upper lip was beaded with sweat.

"Milton's also my friend," I said. "If you don't help your friends when they need it, who do you help?"

"Fuck help!" Crow laughed bitterly. "Do you really want to help Milton? Then don't give him the sixty bucks! Let him go out and solve his own problems. That's what's wrong with half the assholes on the Beach, they've been helped too much. Shit, half of them don't even know how to wipe their goddamn asses. Are you going to wipe their asses for them? Get wise, Kid, and get off this jive trip you're on."

"You're probably right, but Milton's got a lot of problems we don't have, because he's black."

"Oh, Jeesus." Crow laughed. "You're really locked into that black shit, aren't you? Well, I got problems because I'm white. I don't got no rhythm, so what do you say to that? Listen, Kid"—Crow bent his nose down to mine—"do you want to know what Milton is? Milton's a walking phallus, he's a black pioneer who's moved onto the set so he can fuck white chicks and peddle a little dope, and as soon as he's fucked them and strung them out, he's going to be moving on, you watch him."

I stood up. I knew the loan was useless. In a sense I was glad that Crow had made it so easy. I didn't even have to ask for the money. Crow had been on the set for a long time, but he understood very little. He seemed to have no feeling for the people on the Beach.

I moved toward the door. Crow said nothing. I remember Frankie had said not long after I'd introduced her to Crow, "He misses so much, doesn't he?" I hadn't understood what Frankie had meant at the time, I didn't know if I understood right now what she meant, but it did seem to me that Crow missed a lot.

When I got back to Roach Alley, Milton was gone. So was my typewriter and the buckskin jacket JoJay had given me. To anyone else the buckskin jacket Milton had taken was almost valueless. The most Milton could hope to get out of it would be twenty dollars. To me, however, it was my most precious possession.

My loft was a mess. Five silver dollars I had been saving in a jar beside my bed were gone. My clothes and books were scattered about the floor. The journal Scott had left me and that I had been keeping notes in was upside down on my bed, a few pages carelessly ripped out. Half a dozen pages concerning Frankie were missing. *The Journal of Anxiety's Child.* I held a ripped-out page between my fingers. The words seemed foreign to my eyes, unfamiliar, as if they had been written by a stranger. I fitted the torn-out pages back in the journal and set it on the table beside my bed. I thought of Scott, who had given me the journal, and of Milton, who had desecrated it. I tried to imagine a common bond between the three of us, and the only tie I could think of was our loneliness. I looked around my loft and felt sick.

It surprised me that Milton had done this, yet now that it had happened I was even more puzzled that it hadn't happened sooner. The junkie has a virus in his bloodstream that infects everything he touches. He has a deep cave in his soul, there is no light, and nothing he can throw in will fill it—wives, friends, lovers, parents, typewriters—nothing. Junk is a blanket the junkie pulls over his head that keeps him warm in winter and cool in summer, that shields him from the sun and protects him from the rain; it is a premature coffin lined with satiny reminders of broken friendships and marriages, lost children and parents, abandoned lovers and forgotten dreams and promises. I didn't feel angry at what Milton had done, I felt helpless.

I grabbed my coat and stumbled down the stairs, across Roach Alley, and headed for the Beach. I had no idea where I was going. I knew only that I had to get out of my loft. I wanted to see somebody, a friend. Maybe Bob Seider or Shoeshine Devine would be in Washington Square. I hurried up Pacific Avenue to Columbus and headed for the square. When I arrived, though, no one was there—a few Italians sitting on a bench, a young Chinese mother playing with her child. The sound of churchbells rang out over the square.

Suddenly I knew that I wanted to see Frankie. I realized that I had been heading toward her place all along. I needed to talk to her and ask her what was happening. I wanted her to tell me what was wrong.

When I reached Milton's pad, I climbed the three flights of stairs and tapped lightly on the door. "Milton?" Frankie said softly.

"It's me, Frankie."

"Who is it?"

"The Kid. Open the door."

Frankie opened the door a few inches and peered out across the safety chain. She looked disheveled, her hair was uncombed, and the shirt she was wearing, one of Milton's, was wrinkled and dirty. Her face was a mixture of anxiety and relief. A weird aroma emerged from the apartment. "Where's Milton? I'm expecting Milton. What do you want?"

"Frankie, I'd like to talk to you. Open the door."

"I'm sick. Where's Milton? I've been waiting for him all night."

"Milton's been over at my place. I want to talk to you, Frankie. What's wrong?"

Frankie unlocked the safety chain and turned back into the room. I followed her inside, closing the door softly. She walked to the back bedroom and flopped down on a mattress, pulling a blanket over her. She was shivering and sweat glistened on her forehead. The smell of stale vomit and catshit permeated the apartment. I switched on a light and knelt down. Frankie closed her eyes.

"What's wrong? How long has Milton been gone?"

Frankie lowered her blanket and looked at me. Her eyes were glazed, sunken. Her hair hung in swirls over her forehead, clinging in patches of sweat on her cheeks and neck. I reached out my hand and touched her face. Her skin was hot.

"Frankie, you're sick. How long has Milton been gone?"

"Yesterday ... he was going to get some stuff. ... I need ... some stuff."

"Do you need smack? How much smack are you using? Jesus Christ, Frankie, are you that strung out?"

Frankie pulled the covers up over her head and sobbed quietly. I looked at her hands holding the blanket. The knuckles were bone sharp. Her skin looked translucent, like the head of a drum.

"Frankie, Milton spent the night at my loft. Did he tell you he was going to come back here? Answer me!"

"He went out to get some stuff. . . . He said he'd be right back. . . . He was going over to the Fillmore."

I stood up. My head was reeling from the smell in the apartment. In the kitchen two gas rings on the stove were burning. I turned them off and opened the window. Frankie sat up on her mattress. "Don't turn those off. I'm cold."

"Damnit, Frankie, this pad is going to kill you. You've got to get some air."

I opened another window in the bedroom and then knelt back down beside her. She looked at me. I couldn't believe the change in her appearance.

"Milton said he was going to be right back. Where is he?" Frankie snuffed as she talked, rubbing her nose with her fingers.

"Listen, Frankie, Milton's in trouble. He almost got busted last night. He spent the night at my loft. Has anyone knocked on your door while you've been lying here?"

She held the blanket up to her face and stared at me, swaying her head from side to side. "Is Milton in jail?"

I put my hand on her shoulder. "He's not in jail. Look, he almost got busted last night when he went over to the Fillmore. He got out of it, though, and he's all right. He was afraid to come back here because he thought the police were following him. Has anyone tried to get in the apartment?"

Frankie shook her head. I felt relieved. If the police hadn't come, then maybe Milton wasn't as hot as he thought he was. Frankie moaned softly. I brushed her hair out of her face.

"Listen, Frankie, I'm going to run over to Dr. Wenner's office. You need some help."

"No! I don't want to see him!" Frankie sat up. "I want to see Milton, he was supposed to get some stuff."

"Milton's not here. He's gone, do you understand me? Milton's hiding from the police."

"Where is he? I want to see him. I've got to get a shot."

Frankie clutched at my leg as I stood up. I pried her hand off and knelt back down. "Goddamnit, Frankie, you're really sick! I've got to get a doctor. I can't let you lay here like this."

"I don't want a doctor! I just need a little hit. I'll be all right. Just go find Milton."

"Fuck Milton! I'm not going to run after that asshole so he can shoot you full of more shit! I'm going to go get Dr. Wenner."

"No, don't!" Frankie clutched my sleeve. "I don't want to see Dr. Wenner, he's . . ." Her fingers cut into my arm.

"What's wrong with Dr. Wenner? You've seen him before. He knows you're using, doesn't he?"

"No he doesn't! I've been seeing him because I'm pregnant. I don't want to see him."

I stared at her. "Pregnant? How long have you been pregnant? Does Milton know you're pregnant?"

She nodded, let go my sleeve, and slumped over. Her thin shoulders heaved under her robe.

"How long have you been pregnant? Jesus, Frankie, why didn't you tell me?"

"A few months . . . three. I was going to get an abortion . . . Milton wanted me to get an abortion."

"Was Dr. Wenner going to help you get an abortion? Was that why you were seeing him?"

"No! He doesn't know anything about it. He was giving me medicine. I was sick . . . morning sickness. I was throwing up all the time."

"And Milton was shooting you full of smack? Do you realize what that stuff does to you? Do you realize what would happen to your baby?"

"I wasn't going to have a baby! I was going to have an abortion! Milton knows a man—"

"Milton knows a man! Probably the same man he

scores his shit from! Listen, Frankie, do you really want an abortion, or is this Milton's idea?"

"It was Milton's— No, it was mine! I wanted an abortion. We both wanted one!"

I stood up. "Listen, Frankie, Milton's not concerned with you or anyone. He's concerned only about himself. He ransacked my loft this morning and took all my stuff. He's not going to come back here. He's hot and he's desperate. He's going to burn everyone he can so he can get away, do you understand that?"

Frankie held her face in her hands and swayed back and forth, moaning. I felt panic choking my throat. I wanted out. I knelt back down beside her and shook her shoulder. She kept moaning and swaying, bumping her head repeatedly against the wall.

"Jesus, Frankie, stop it! Look, I'm going to get you a doctor. You can't stay here in all this shit with that baby in your womb. I'm going to go get Dr. Wenner and bring him back here. He'll get you into a hospital where they'll give you what you need."

"No! No! I don't want to go to the hospital! I want to find Milton! I'll be okay as soon as you find Milton. He'll take care of me. All I need is a little hit."

"Goddamnit! Can't you see that you won't be okay? That smack isn't going to leave you alone. It's in your blood. It's in your baby's blood! Do you understand that? Milton's not going to help you. He's not here. He's run away, he's gone!"

Frankie lifted her face from her hands and looked at me. Tears were streaming down her face. I wanted to curse Milton for running out on her, but cursing Milton wasn't going to help Frankie. She was sick, desperately sick. I pulled the blanket up around her shoulders and tried to make her lie down. She struggled against me.

"You know where Milton is, don't you, Kid? Go find him, tell him I need some stuff. He'll help me."

"Listen, Frankie, Milton's not ..." I stopped. I brushed the hair out of her face. She struggled to smile. I smiled back at her. "Listen, baby, Milton's in trouble and he can't help you right now. He's gone over to Mill Valley to hide out. I'll go get Dr. Wenner and then I'll look for Milton. Everything's going to be all right."

"Has Milton gone to Mill Valley? Has he gone to Jere's? Jere's a good friend of Milton's."

"Yes, I think he went to see Jere. He said he was going to lay low for a few days, and when everything's cool he'll be coming back—or I can take you over there."

"Take me over there now, Kid. I want to go now!" Frankie struggled up from her mattress.

"You can't go over there now; you need a doctor. You can see Milton later."

Frankie sat still. I pushed her gently down on the mattress. She sank slowly under the pressure of my hand.

"Everything's going to be all right, baby. I'll get Dr. Wenner and then I'll go find Milton."

She lay quiet on the mattress, staring straight up at the ceiling. She was shivering, so I pulled the blanket up over her shoulders and tucked it in. Her eyes were blank. I stood up and moved quietly toward the door. "I'll be back in a little while, as soon as I see the doctor. He'll give you the medicine you need."

Frankie said nothing. I ran down the three flights of stairs.

Out on the street I felt better. I didn't relish the idea of visiting Dr. Wenner. Every junkie on the set congregated in his waiting room. I had no choice, though. Dr. Wenner knew Frankie and I knew he'd help her—with no questions asked. It amazed me to think that she'd been visiting him with her pregnancy and he didn't know about her habit. I was sure he did know; he was no fool. He was peculiar, though. I could conceive of him treating Frankie for her morning sickness and not mentioning her use of heroin at all, except in an oblique manner. Dr. Wenner treated the whole drug scene with a matter-of-factness that to many people bordered on indifference. He wasn't indifferent, though; he was simply realistic. He knew that all he could hope to do with his talent and skill was simply to supply the aid, medicine, and sometimes the sustenance that the various addicts needed.

The waiting room was full of people. I nodded to Tambourine, the black conga drummer who hung out in Aquatic Park, who was sitting in the corner. The receptionist looked up when I entered. "I'm sorry," she said, "Dr. Wenner's not here right now. May I help you?"

It hadn't occurred to me that the doctor wouldn't be in his office. I stared at the receptionist. She smiled. I leaned my hands on the edge of her desk. "Listen, it's an emergency. There's a pregnant girl who is very ill."

"Dr. Wenner's on board ship right now. He'll be back within an hour. Would you like to wait?"

I knew it was useless. Dr. Wenner was the official doctor for the Scandinavian Shipping Lines and was notorious for extending his ship visits out all afternoon. He loved to sit on board ship and talk with the sailors. Patients back in his office had to wait.

"I can call Dr. Baker, Dr. Wenner's emergency backup. Would you like me to call him?" The receptionist was all smiles. She had two gold teeth.

"No, I'll come back later. Thanks."

I rushed out of the building. On the sidewalk I debated going back to Frankie's place or running down to the Coffee Gallery to find D'Artagnan Pig. I could use his car to take Frankie to Mill Valley. I couldn't afford to get another doctor. The minute they saw Frankie, they'd probably call the police. I ran toward the Beach. I didn't know what to do. I knew it was useless looking for D'Artagnan Pig before early evening; he never got up before then. I ran back toward Frankie's place. At least I could stay with her until Dr. Wenner returned to his office.

When I reached Frankie's pad, I didn't want to climb the three flights of stairs. I wanted to continue on down to Aquatic Park and bury my feet in the sand. I wanted to forget all the hassles and hangups, the dirty little shit-end details of Milton's and Frankie's affair. I felt helpless and bitter, helpless because everything I did seemed ineffectual, bitter because of Milton. It pissed me that he had run out on Frankie, leaving her sick and pregnant in a filthy pad. When I thought of him, my fists clenched. I kicked the stairs as I climbed them.

When I reached the apartment, the door was open. I had closed it when I left. I pushed the door open all the way and looked inside. Frankie was gone.

She couldn't have been gone more than half an hour, forty-five minutes at the most. I walked down the hall to the window that opened on the roof and stepped out. Frankie wasn't there.

Back inside I sat down at the kitchen table. Frankie's sewing machine sat on one end of the table. Pieces of cloth were strewn about the machine, parts of a shirt Frankie was making for Milton. An overwhelming sadness came over me. It seemed strange sitting in the deserted kitchen. I looked at the peeling paint, bright orange, a color Frankie loved. I remembered when Frankie had painted the kitchen, Milton and I had laughed and drunk beer and teased her. I felt like crying. The unfinished shirt lying on the table seemed like the remnants of a stranger, a memento left after a friend has gone. I knew Frankie had gone to find Milton. I knew also that when she found him he'd give her the heroin she needed. Maybe my fantasy was just as big as hers, maybe I dwelled inside illusions just as she did, neither of us ever seeing the reality that loomed so huge around us.

I turned off the lights, closed the door, and walked downstairs. Outside, the piercing clear cries of the children running home from school filled the air. I walked slowly as the children ran past me on their way home, books and papers fluttering in the breeze. Above the hills of Marin I saw the huge weighty clouds billowing in, full and redolent in their swift charge over the Gate.

32   The next morning someone knocked at my door. I knew it was Milton. I put on my Levi's and walked slowly downstairs. I thought of what I was going to say to him, all the things I'd been holding inside of me because of Frankie. I was through holding things back. I was going to tell him exactly what I thought. I opened the door and saw Goodnews Gary. I looked at him. "Frankie jumped off the bridge last night," he said.

"What?"

"Frankie. She jumped off the bridge. It's in this morning's paper."

As Goodnews Gary was blurting out the details, I shut the door and walked upstairs. I sat down on my bed. A strange feeling lodged itself in my chest. The feeling was intangible, huge, like a four-masted sailing ship beating its wings against my lungs. I felt like I was suffocating, my lungs were expanding into vast bladderlike sails that were attempting to beat their way up my throat and out my mouth. I stood up. I stood in the middle of the floor for a long time gulping down the fluttering movement in my chest. I hadn't cleaned my loft; the things Milton had scattered about were still lying on the floor, books and shirts and papers. I picked up one of my books. *Pelle the Conqueror.* I started picking up the books from the floor, arranging them back on the shelf. I hung up all my clothes and then I got a broom and swept the floor. As I worked, the fluttering in my chest softened. I moved what furniture I had over against the walls and then filled a bucket with soapy water and scrubbed down the whole floor. I opened the windows so the floor would dry, then I dusted all the shelves, cleaned my hotplate and scoured my sink. I moved my bed away from the white brick wall to a new spot under the windows. The sunlight streaming through the open windows fell across my bed. The paintings McCracken and Arthur and Bowen had given me I moved, hanging them in new places. Each painting took on a different dimension in its new spot. The fresh air from the produce market swept in the open windows, erasing all the old smells, the stale smoke and sweat and dirty blanket smells, the cooked food and old socks, all the smells that accumulate in a place where someone has been locked away for a long time.

When I finished, I undressed and took a shower, staying under the water for a long time, cleaning myself with soap, letting the hot water boil over my body until I could stand it no longer, then quickly turning on the cold. My skin felt vibrant under the biting chill of the water. After half an hour I stepped out of the shower and rubbed myself down with a rough towel, pulling it back and forth across my skin until my whole body stung. After drying I stood in the loft nude. I felt lighter, weightless, like a miner who has been working underground in the pits for years and years, chopping away at the seams of coal, and who has emerged into a world of clean blankets and fresh water and sunlight at last. I walked around the loft feeling the wooden floor under my feet, leaned against the white bricks, letting the coolness of the wall seep into my skin. In the rear of the loft, among the discarded machinery, I rubbed my hands on the cold metal.

After an hour or so I put on a clean shirt and a fresh pair of Levi's. I liked the way the Levi's buttoned up tight and fit snug around my waist, the way the shirt felt crisp and soft at the same time. My body felt completely natural underneath the clothes. After dressing I walked downstairs. Roach Alley was the same, yet it had a different feel to it, as if I'd walked into it for the first time and just now had seen how the wood on the old building opposite shimmered in the bright sunlight, moving and rippling under its patina of age like the sandy bottom of a shallow creek sometimes appears to move under its sheet of crystal clear water.

I walked down to Spadelee's. The bell on the door rang as I entered the tiny grocery store. Spadelee shuffled out from his back room, nodding slowly. I nodded to him, surveyed his shelves, noting each bottle, observing the colors, the way the light struck them, concentrating on each mote of dust that hung suspended in the shaft of sunlight that struck through the dusty windows and imbedded itself in the linoleum floor. I took a jug of Valley of the Moon port off the shelf and handed it to Spadelee. He started to wipe the jug off with his rag, but I took it out of his hands, paid for it, and carried it out of the store. The jug felt good in my hands, clean, the bottle perfect, containing itself in every respect like a work of art. Back in my loft I got a clean glass from the shelf above my hotplate and poured it full of the rich, sweet wine. I pulled a chair over next to the open windows and sat down, the jug beside me.

There's something about a clean room, a clean shirt and a fresh pair of pants, a jug of sweet port and a clean glass. There is a sense of benediction in the ritual, like when you take the glass in your hand and lift the port up to your lips you are partaking of a sacrament, a minute part of the totality of what things are.

I sat in front of the open windows for a long time sipping port, watching the colors and shadows on the buildings outside move and change. Twice somebody knocked on my door but I didn't answer. It was soon too dark to see. Still I sat, the darkness itself becoming an object that I watched with keen intensity, like an observer on a bluff watches a column of men and their accompanying cloud of dust moving for a long time across a distant plain. I sat in my chair by the windows long after the produce market came alive with the whirring energy and activity of the reefer and bobtail trucks thundering past outside. Several times Little Joe called, "Kid, hey, Kid," under my window, but his voice sounded muted, far away. All the sounds from the street were muted, sounding to me like a symphony one is familiar with and can hear odd portions of through the walls of a neighbor's room. When Pippen started practicing sometime after midnight, I undressed and lay down on my bed. The loft took on a curious aspect, familiar, yet strangely foreign. Quiet, almost not breathing, it seemed to me that I was being lifted up, that I was a traveler borne along over a great desert, that I was alone on an incredibly broad expanse of white shimmering sand that stretched away on all sides as far as the eye could see. I was lying nude on my bed and the light from outside reflected off the white bricks onto my body. When I lifted my head to see if I could discern any boundaries to the space I was treveling in, I saw that all of my internal organs were made out of hammered gold. The flesh and bone and blood had disappeared off my abdomen and upper chest and I could see all of my internal organs—heart, lungs, intestines—and they were all made out of soft, malleable hammered gold.

I stayed in my loft for three days. Each day a dozen or so people knocked on my door. On the second night Little Joe stood outside in Roach Alley for half an hour hollering up to my window. I didn't answer. On the third day I got out of bed. I wanted to find Milton. I wanted to look at him. I wanted to crush his face underneath my fists.

I walked around the Embarcadero to avoid the Beach. If Milton wasn't in his pad, I'd go to Mill Valley. It felt strange being out of my loft. Even though a light fog drifted through the streets, the sunlight seemed too bright. When I reached Milton's place, I looked up at his windows. They looked blank, bare panes reflecting back the light. As I climbed the stairs, I thought of all the people on the Beach: Hube the Cube and Francesca; Joanie and Ed; Frankie herself and Debbie O'Brien; Crow and Little Joe and Keith and Groovy; Artie Ritchers and Betty; Bowen and Arthur and McCracken; Dr. Wenner and Dr. Frick Frack; Crazy Alex and Dick Moore, the champion hopper; Red Fred and Carol Joseph; Patrick Cassidy and Zeke; David and Tina; Kell Robertson and Lawrence Smith and Bad Talking Charlie; Dick Partee and Pony and Padraic Seamus O'Sullivan; D'Artagnan Pig and Sammy; Glen and Julius Karpen and Frank Deffrey; Abby and Doorknob and Carl Eisenger; Bob Seider and Richard Bloomer and his dead brother, Frank; Lesley Albert and Alan Dienstag; Pierre and

Lois and their kids; Jimmy Carter, Jack Carraige and
Adolph the Harkener; Indian Joe, Dean Lipton, Ruth
Lopez and Ray; Linda Lovely, Phil McQuire and Phil
McKenna; Trout Fishing in America Shorty and Ron
Rice and Walter Chappell; JoJay, Jose, Joselito and
Trinidad Archelito; Cornsilk and Shoeshine Devine;
Bernie Uroniwitz and Pete Spears; Clementi and Charlie
Mews and Neal Cassady; Allen Ginsberg and Al Sub-
lette and Jack Kerouac; Barney Google and Mark
Green and Alex Geluardi; Peter LeBlanc and Merge
Kelly and Laury Porter; Laury Seagle and Shig and John
and Tom Reed; Don Graham and Fred Roscoe and his
wife, Nancy; Bob and Richard McBride; Dennis and
Janey and Henri Lenoir; Mel Brown and Moham-
med; Bob Brannaman, Moscoso and Deedee; Motor-
cycle Bill and Pippen and Price Dunn; Nick Gravenites
and Linda; Mad Marie, Jay Hoppe, and Walt Donnely;
Dante Cosatino and Joe Spagna; Stan Fullerton and
Dick Kiggens; Hank Brooks and Bob Kaufman; Serena
and Ilene K; Wally Sands and Larry Devers; Shorty
Salvatori and Ferlinghetti, and how many hundreds of
others? Each step was a name—a dozen names! And
each name was part of the litany that ran through my
head. When I reached Milton's door, I paused. I knew
he was inside, I could feel it. Suddenly the door opened.
Milton stared out at me. The abruptness of the door
opening caught me off balance. I reached for the handle. I could see the thought of closing it flash across
Milton's face. I looked at him. "What are you doin'
here?" he said slowly.

I was shaking so hard I could barely control myself.
Milton turned around and walked into the apartment. I
followed him. He stood beside the kitchen table staring
at me, his eyes sullen and raw-looking. For a long moment we stood thus, facing one another. I wanted to
touch something, anything. I clenched and unclenched
my fists, then slowly, as if it were in slow motion, I
doubled up my fist and swung against his face. He saw
the blow coming and ducked away, causing my fist to
slide off the edge of his brow. Almost in a daze, I
swung sideways and grabbed his shoulder, pounding on

his face with my fists. He flung me aside and struck me, his fist landing on my face with no feeling whatever. It was as if I were watching a silent movie in which I was the participant, every move was before me but I could neither hear nor feel anything. I twisted out of Milton's grasp and pounded his face. He blocked my fists and grabbed me and we tumbled to the floor. I twisted around and kicked him, pummeling my foot into his side as he scrambled away. He grabbed my foot and twisted it, forcing me on my side. From that position he leaped on me, grabbing my hair with his hands. He pounded my head on the floor as I struggled desperately to get up. "You motherfucker!" he cried, slamming my head down on the floor.

I struggled under him, pounding at his face. Milton held his face sideways and continued beating my head on the floor, yelling as he did so. Suddenly we both stopped, our blood and sweat mingling as we separated. I panted hoarsely and fell against the kitchen wall. Milton slumped against the opposite wall and shook his head. He was crying. "You motherfucker!" he said. "You crazy motherfucker!"

I sat against the wall for a long time, tears and blood streaming down my face. I was numb with fatigue. While Milton shook his head, I pulled myself to my feet and stumbled toward the door. Milton wiped his eyes, his tears glistened on his swelling cheek. "Maan, I was lookin' for her when she jumped. I was comin' back . . ."

I staggered out of the apartment and down the steps and leaned against the railing, trying to press the buzzing out of my ears. Everything was over. It was foggy and the mist hung low in the streets. I stumbled down to Columbus Avenue and leaned against a building. I was exhausted. Milton had kicked the shit out of me. I heard the distant ding of a cable car bell and the sound of the cables whirring under the street. I'll catch a cable car home. Ding dong dolly on the jolly jaunting car. I thought of the fight. Nothing. It was all over. When the cable car clanged past on its way up Columbus Avenue, I stumbled after it. As I swung aboard, I thought of Henry Miller. What did he say? He could say it for me: "Ladies and gentlemen, don't believe a word of it, it was all a hoax. Let me tell you in a few words the story of my tragedy. I can do it in twenty pages."

San Francisco
Big Sur
1969–1972

ABOUT THE AUTHOR

JERRY KAMSTRA was born in a mining camp in a shack buried under thirty-five feet of snow. His father, a Dutch immigrant, made his living as a hard-rock miner. His mother was the daughter of a fruit tramp, Nettie Cody, a distant relative of Buffalo Bill Cody. By the time he was fourteen, Jerry had broken his arm eight times and had read every book in the Colton Public Library. Since then, he has worked as an abalone and salmon fisherman, construction worker, trucker and marijuana smuggler. He is the author of *Weed: Adventures of a Dope Smuggler*, his story of the marijuana industry, and *The Frisco Kid*. Jerry Kamstra moved to San Francisco in 1957 and has lived there ever since.